Haft sighed again, but wasted no time in picking up his crossbow. He loaded a bolt into it as he ran forward. The archers who had stayed behind when the Bloody Axes and Guards ran to fight blade to blade followed in a wide line. Several of the Skraglanders dashed back to pick up bows, returning to rain arrows on the backs of the retreating Jokapcul.

Flames were spreading rapidly on the pyre, whipping through the ventilation channels built into it. Burning wood shifted on the southeast corner of the structure, dislodging the Phoenix egg balanced there. The fiery bird cawed out of its shell and unfurled its wings, sparking new flames, and incinerating the three Jokapcul in the van of a group assembling there to race around its far side and envelop their attackers from the side. The rest of the soldiers in that group screamed and fell back, their fighting spirit broken. Jokapcul swordsmen and lancers ran from the minefield, their only thought to escape from the arrows raining onto them from behind. The Jokapcul archers now had clear targets to shoot at, and their arrows began to strike home. Four of his men were down before Haft called a withdrawal....

By David Sherman

The Night Fighters
KNIVES IN THE NIGHT
MAIN FORCE ASSAULT
OUT OF THE FIRE
A ROCK AND A HARD PLACE
A NGHU NIGHT FALLS
CHARLIE DON'T LIVE HERE ANYMORE

Demontech
ONSLAUGHT

THERE I WAS: THE WAR OF CORPORAL
    HENRY J. MORRIS, USMC

THE SQUAD

RALLY POINT

BOOK II OF
DEMONTECH

DAVID SHERMAN

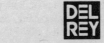

BALLANTINE BOOKS • NEW YORK

A Del Rey® Book
Published by The Ballantine Publishing Group
Copyright © 2003 by David Sherman

All rights reserved under International and Pan-American Copyright Conventions. Published in the United States by The Ballantine Publishing Group, a division of Random House, Inc., New York, and simultaneously in Canada by Random House of Canada Limited, Toronto.

Del Rey is a registered trademark and the Del Rey colophon is a trademark of Random House, Inc.

www.delreydigital.com

ISBN 0-345-44375-6

Manufactured in the United States of America

First Edition: February 2003

10 9 8 7 6 5 4 3 2 1

For
Mary Helen.
You know why, Toots

RALLY POINT
BOOK II OF
DEMONTECH

PROLOGUE

The Dark Prince stood alone in the topmost room of the highest tower in the keep of Prince Aepling, high above Zobra City. He was dressed—shirt, trousers, boots, cape, belts, and scabbard—all in black. It wasn't the ebony of midnight or the shiny black of obsidian. His was the blinding, all-absorbing black of the bottom of a mine. With gloves and a mask, the Dark Prince could have vanished in a shadow.

The room had little in the way of furnishings or decoration: a small table with ewer and basin; a small chest with a broken hasp; a chamber pot tucked under a narrow cot. A small tapestry was folded alongside each window, ready to draw over the openings against the elements. The room had been used as prison or as a lookout post from the time of the tower's building and had no need of better furnishings. The Dark Prince was not a lookout though he stood, hands clasped behind his back, looking out the eastern window; nor was he a prisoner. He was, rather, a conqueror. Before his gaze, the southern coast of the Principality of Zobra stretched southwest past the great harbor then, beyond the horizon, southeast. As he watched, a man rose through the unrailed hatch in the center of the floor. He wore bronze-dyed leather armor studded with steel rectangles. He carried a helmet of the same materials tucked under his arm. Two swords—one long, the other short—hung from opposite sides of his belt.

"You called for me, Lord Lackland," the man said on gaining the room's floor.

The Dark Prince did not deign to turn his head. Had he looked at the Kamazai Commanding of the Jokapcul forces, he might have drawn sword and killed him for using that hated sobriquet. Unfortunately, killing him would not do; he needed the barbarian to control the armies that were building his empire. He could be dealt with later. Instead, the Dark Prince continued to gaze out the east-facing tower window.

"The coast turns soon?" he asked.

"It does, Lord." The Kamazai joined him at the window, just far enough behind his left shoulder to demonstrate his subordinate position. "A day's sail farther and the coast bends to the south and back to the east in the beginning of the Princedons."

"Are we secure here?" The Dark Prince dropped his gaze from the horizon to the sprawling streets of Zobra City below.

"Yes, Lord."

"Our flank?"

"All of southern Nunimar from the western jungle to Zobra is ours for several days' march inland. We now hold Skragland as far as Oskul, and have taken that city."

The Dark Prince turned his head. The Kingdom of Zobra was South of Skragland, the Princedons were to the east. "What of north of Princedon Gulf?"

"North of Princedon Gulf lies the Low Desert," the Kamazai said dryly, as though a geography lesson was beneath him. "North of that is the High Desert. There are no kingdoms, principalities, or duchies north of the gulf until the Easterlies. The deserts are nearly trackless and almost devoid of water. We have naught to concern ourselves from north of Princedon Gulf."

"There are no armies there?" The Dark Prince's voice was soft, unnaturally so.

The Kamazai Commanding snorted. "Bandit bands only."

"How many? How large?"

"If all of them joined together they would form less than half a legion. The largest of them is said to number not more than a hundred, including camp followers."

The Dark Prince paced across the tower room and looked out the west window. He stepped back from the window and crossed the barren room to its north-facing window. "What of beyond southern Skragland?" he asked.

"Total chaos." The Kamazai Commanding shrugged. "Deserters fleeing. Panicked refugees headed into winter lands and the wilds beyond, where they will starve if the denizens of the Night Forest don't devour them first. It is rumored that panicked Skraglanders overthrew their king and killed him for failing to stop us." The ghost of a smile creased his face.

"No one resists us?"

"Only a few bandits. Mostly, though, the bandits prey on the refugees and sack villages."

"None of them attempt to resist our forces which move north?"

"Only one belligerent band has been reported." The Kamazai chuckled. "It is rumored that band is led by two Frangerian sea soldiers." He chuckled again. "The sea soldiers the Frangerians call 'Marines.'"

"Frangerian Marines? Where did they come from?"

The Kamazai Commanding shrugged. "No one knows." A ragtag band of fewer than a hundred, including camp followers, and led by two very junior Frangerian sea soldiers—clearly the Kamazai Commanding felt they were of no consequence, nothing for him to concern himself with.

"'Said to number,' 'it is rumored,' 'no one knows.'" The Dark Prince turned fiercely on the Kamazai Commanding. "*I* wish to know!"

"Lord, a small band led by two common soldiers—nay, less than common soldiers. They are sea soldiers! They know nothing of fighting on land. They pose no threat save to the other bandit bands and to what few herders and hunters eke out their miserable lives in the Eastern Waste."

"The last rumor I heard of Frangerian sea soldiers was that a small band of them wiped out an entire troop of your soldiers. Do you not pay attention to the world? Since their 'Lord Gunny' arrived and began calling them 'Marines,' the Frangerian sea soldiers have become far more potent fighters than anyone has ever seen."

The Kamazai Commanding kept his face expressionless as

he looked at the barbarian who held nominal command over him and his armies. He gave fleeting thought to the pleasure he would feel when the High Shoton finally gave him leave to impale the half bastard fourth son of Good King Honritu of Matilda. He would make a fine ceremony of the impaling, and Lackland's death would be long in coming.

"The world has never seen armies to match mine, Lord," he said in a voice that betrayed none of his thoughts. "As for that lost troop, the reports further say a few Frangerians accompanied a force of the giant nomads of the steppes, and the nomads had powerful magicians with them. The nomads had wandered astray and were headed north, back to the wasted land they call home. The Frangerians, no matter their number, are no threat."

"The Frangerians would dispute the point with you."

The Kamazai shrugged. "Their opinion," he said scornfully. "It doesn't matter how fierce they are as individuals. Those guardians of ships are few in number. There have never been armies as great as mine. If they attempt to fight us openly, I will crush them."

In his mind's eye, the Dark Prince pictured the armies commanded by the insufferably arrogant Kamazai. Indeed, the armies were huge. Hundreds of thousands of soldiers. The Frangerian sea soldiers numbered only a few tens of thousands. Yes, the armies of Jokapcul could defeat the Frangerians, piecemeal or *en masse*, but at how great a price?

"I wish to know about that band rumored to the north. Is it the nomads heading home? Or is it a force led by Frangerian Marines, a possible threat? Have a magician send bees to spy on them."

The Kamazai Commanding dipped his head; it was not nearly as deep a bow as he would have given to a subshoton of his own nation. "It shall be as you command, Lord."

Before he could turn, the Dark Prince added, "And have your armies secure all of Skragland to the Dwarven Mountains."

Once more, the Kamazai Commanding kept his face expressionless. Skragland was already secured as far as its capital city, Oskul. Nothing lay between Oskul and the Dwarven

Mountains but farmland. Securing that land so early in the campaign was unnecessary. But—

"As you wish, Lord." Without seeming to hasten, the Kamazai Commanding left the tower room before Lord Lackland could order any more unnecessary diversions of his forces.

"Wazzu wanns," the demon demanded in response to the magician's summons. The bald, naked demon was small, hardly taller than the length of a big man's hand. Its heavy muscles were gnarly and its arms seemed too long for its body. It hunkered down into a deep squat on the alchemist's table but not too close to the magician, who sat on a stool reading a parchment scroll spread across the table.

The magician pursed his lips and stared over steepled fingers at the demon. At length he unsteepled his hands and pointed a long, thin finger at the demon.

"I require the services of bees," the magician intoned.

"Bzz?" the demon asked, cocking its head curiously. *"Oo whattin 'oneyz?"*

"Silence, dolt!" the magician thundered, slapping a palm on the tabletop. "I don't want honey, I want spies!"

"Zpiez!" the demon exclaimed, brightening. *"I gittum oo. Naw zwetz."* It bounced up from its squat and scampered away.

The magician watched the demon until it disappeared through a crack in the wall, then turned his head toward the imbaluris that sat on a perch in a corner. "Fools," he snorted, shaking his head. "They give me only fools to work with, and then they wonder why I don't make better magic." He shook his head again and looked back at the parchment. It instructed him to send bees to find some petty band of worthless refugee bandits. "Just because I'm young," he muttered, "they think I know nothing. Just because they think I know nothing, they give me fools to work with. *Pfagh!* Give me good demons to work with, and I'll show them how much I can do. Instead, they give me a petty chore that could be accomplished by any junior mage." Still muttering, he reopened the magical tome he'd been studying before the petty order arrived. Maybe if he read the passage a few more times, he'd figure out the meaning of the phrase "CS gas" and how to conjure a demon that had that attribute. As he read he absently swatted at flies with an oxtail whisk.

After a period of time at the end of which the magician had still failed to ferret out the essence of "CS gas," the droning of bees intruded into his consciousness and he looked up, bleary-eyed. The demon had returned with a smallish cloud of bees.

"Bzz!" the demon exclaimed. *"I bringum bzz."*

"Yes, you did," the magician agreed. He flicked dismissive fingers at the demon, who skittered away to crouch atop a precariously piled stack of tomes near the perched imbaluris.

"Northeast of here and north of Dartsmutt at the source of Princedon Gulf," the magician said to the cloud of bees, "you will find the Eastern Waste. You will enter the waste and fly five days north. From there you will commence a search. You will . . . What?"

He leaned close to the cloud of bees to better hear what they said. The individual bees in the cloud hovered, swayed side to side, flitted up and down or to and fro, then curlicued around one another. Every random-looking movement modulated their buzzing, and the modulations had meaning. The young magician had spent three half-days a week for two long years learning to interpret the bees' buzzing. He listened for a moment, then his eyes popped wide and he sat erect, staring at them in disbelief.

"What do you mean you won't go? Too late in the season? No flowers in bloom! I'm not sending you to harvest nectar or build a hive, I'm sending you to spy!"

Greater movement rippled through the cloud of bees and the volume and pitch of their droning rose.

The magician's face turned red, then purple as he listened to the buzzing. "I am the magician here!" he shouted. "You must do as I say!" He suddenly swung his oxtail whisk diagonally through the cloud. Struck bees spun uncontrollably away and the buzzing of the two halves of the cloud rose to a shrill peak as the bees reformed to retaliate then darted forward. The magician shrieked. He flailed at them with the whisk, but there were too many. He scrambled backward off his stool and stumbled, falling heavily to the floor. He tried to cover his face with one arm while striking with the whisk.

The demon and the imbaluris scrabbled in their corner, each trying to hide behind the other. They needn't have; the bees spent their energy and selves on the magician, with no mind for the demons.

The garrison commander looked at the dead magician curled on the floor. A few bees still moved feebly on the corpse, their lives ebbing.

"Why did you assign this to him?" he asked the ashen-faced troop commander.

"The other magicians were busy. Simple job; I thought he could handle it."

The garrison commander shook his head. "Bees are never simple. They don't require great magic to command, but they do require patience and respect. This one," he toed the corpse, "had yet to learn either." He looked at the lesser officer. "Now, thanks to your error, the mission is delayed and I have lost a tome reader. You are fortunate this mission is of little importance, I would have you kill yourself if it was important. Your transgression is slight enough that you need cut off only an ear. Your *right* ear." He turned and left the room. Behind him, the troop commander silently drew the shorter of his swords. . . .

A cloud of bees, summoned and charged by a magician who knew patience and respect, settled onto the sunny warmth of a flat rock. As soon as they were sufficiently rested and warmed, their first mission would be to find nectar to fuel themselves. Then they would seek shelter against the night's chill. If they starved or froze, what they found or did not find would not matter; they wouldn't live to report it.

I

THIS WAY AND THAT

CHAPTER
ONE

Winter was come to the land east of the Rieka Flod, the great river that drained the vast area south from the Dwarven Mountains to where it entered the sea at Zobra City. Farther to the east, the ground that slowly rose to the plateau of the High Desert was too deep with snow to permit travel; the ground between the river and the slopes was blanketed with snow kept shallow by the constant, scouring, wind. The goats that were herded there in the summer were long gone south or west, along with the other grazing animals that could survive on the coarse leaves and twigs and sour fruits of the trees that bowed before the wind. The predators that hunted the goats and grazers and, sometimes goatherds, were likewise taking sunnier climes. Even flocks of late-migrating birds avoided that land once the snows began.

Few people other than the seasonal goatherds lived there, and those were as coarse as their land—and as unyielding. Year-round residents hoarded food for the winter and hid well what sparse wealth they had. They hid themselves as well, for unwary travelers who failed to bring enough food to last their entire journey across the harsh land were sometimes driven mad by hunger and turned to eating their fellows to sustain themselves. Travelers often found eating a stranger somehow less reprehensible than eating their own. Winter life in "the Eastern Waste," as it was called by the Skraglanders to the west, was almost impossible. The nomads who dwelled in the sere deserts farther to the east considered the land an inhospitable jungle.

11

A band of refugees fleeing northeastward before the advancing Jokapcul armies was discovering the harsh realities of the Eastern Waste as they huddled around small fires in the lee of the rude windbreaks they'd erected to shield themselves from blowing snow during the night. They'd planned to work their way to where the High Desert came up against the southeastern edge of the Dwarven Mountains, then thread a perilous route between the mountains and the desert as far as Elfwood Between the Rivers, and thence tiptoe between the top of the High Desert and the bottom of Elfwood Between the Rivers all the way to the Easterlies. Once in the Easterlies they should face an easy trek to Handor's Bay and shipping across the Inner Ocean to the continent of Arpalonia, and its free kingdoms and principalities. Now they faced the need to abandon that plan; the fires were for warmth as the refugees had eaten the last of their food that morning and the game they'd hoped to catch during the trek north had evidently already migrated to more clement climes. Even the wolf hadn't caught so much as a shrew since they'd entered the Eastern Waste. Had it not been for the snow they melted in pots in the fire, even water would have been in as short supply.

"We have to go west in the morning," said the taller of the two men who led the refugees. He was called Spinner, for the way he used the quarterstaff he carried.

The shorter of the two leaders glumly nodded. He'd thought in the beginning they should try the southerly route, but had yielded to everyone else's argument. Having agreed, he was committed, and he hated having to go back under any circumstances. Even though turning west wasn't back the way they'd come, it was still the opposite direction from where they wanted to go. They called him Haft, for he seemed to become one with the mighty battle-axe that was his primary weapon.

"Not your fault," rumbled the giant. Alone in the band he looked comfortable in the cold, with his cloak made from the hide of a huge, white bear. He had argued in favor of crossing the Eastern Waste during winter. On the Northern Steppes he

called home, game could be found even in the deepest depths
of winter, when the sun appeared over the southern horizon
for only long enough each day to assure the True People it
still existed. He'd been certain game would be relatively plentiful in the Eastern Waste, where the sun was up for so many
hours each winter day, and the stunted trees grew in relative
profusion. In all his years on the Northern Steppes and the
time spent wandering the land south of them, he'd never seen
a place so barren of animate life. The giant had adopted the
name Silent, for the vow he'd taken to not speak about his
land and people while wandering the south lands.

The woman with the golden hair and eyes of gold, peeked
out through the gray silk cloak in which she was nearly invisible in the early night. She thought that if they went west they
might reach Oskul, the capital of Skragland. In Oskul they
might find Mudjwohl. But she said nothing. She was Alyline,
also called "the Golden Girl" for the color of her skin, eyes,
and hair. Her favored dress was also golden.

"How far do you think it is?" Spinner asked.

The lean man with the longbow said, "We won't get there
tomorrow, maybe the morning after." His name was Fletcher,
but he made bows as well as arrows, and was a veteran of the
Bostian army.

At another fire a baby cried for breast. A small child at another fire whined for food nobody had.

Haft flinched. "Who'd have thought?" he said softly.

A Skraglander refugee muttered. After first arguing the opposite, he'd finally agreed with the steppe nomad that they
could safely traverse the Eastern Waste in winter. He should
have known better. He was Takacs, a Skragland army Borderer, the sole man of his company to survive battles against
the Jokapcul.

"We could eat the horses," someone said.

Haft brightened at the suggestion; he didn't like horses.
The giant, who was said to have been born on horseback,
glowered at the one who'd spoken out.

"Only as a last resort," said Spinner. "We can travel farther
and faster on them than on foot."

"As long as we can feed them," someone else murmured. Fodder for the horses was nearly gone as well, and under the blanket of snow grazing was almost as nonexistent as game.

They were up before dawn and ready to move by the time the reluctant sun rose. They followed their shortening shadows westward.

A day and a half's march into the wind brought the band of refugees to the valley of the Aramlas, a tributary of the Rieka Flod. The Aramlas Valley's trees did not bow to the morning sun, but rather stood straight and proud. Snow dusted the branches of the trees, but the ground beneath them was mostly bare and dry. As soon as they began their descent into the valley, the refugees saw deer, and hunters ran ahead. By the time the refugees had reached the valley floor, the hunters were ready for them, roasting haunches of venison over fires much bigger than those they'd had in the waste.

Somewhat to the south, or perhaps east of south, unseasonable bees were constructing a hive and packing its cells with nectar.

Hunger was sated. Women set about erecting shelters less rude than those they'd used on the Eastern Waste. Men jerked venison over slow fires. Children squealed in play. They were out of the wind and blowing snow. Spinner and Haft put out sentries, then sat to rest and plan.

"We've come far," Spinner said as he looked over the rough camp and the people who depended on them.

"But we're less than halfway there," Haft said with a grimace. They were Marines from Frangeria, an archipelago nation off the south coast of the eastern continent, Arpalonia. All seagoing nations had sea soldiers, but only a Frangerian sea soldier went by the name "Marine." Spinner and Haft had been in the freeport of New Bally, on the southwestern coast of Nunimar, the western continent, when it was invaded and captured by the Jokapcul during a daring night amphibious operation. As far as they knew, they were the only foreigners to escape from the captured city.

"That's not what I mean. Look at those people. We started off alone, now we've got all of them."

"Yes?" Haft looked at the people. There were the Golden Girl; Fletcher and his wife Zweepee, and Doli, slaves they'd freed in a remote part of Skragland; Xundoe, a Zobran army mage whom they'd rescued; Silent, the giant nomad of the Northern Steppes, who they'd first met at a border post between Bostia and Skragland. Along the way they'd collected enough trained soldiers to make a reinforced platoon. There were Royal Lancers, Prince's Swords, and Border Warders from defeated Zobra; Guards and Borderers from the still-fighting Skragland army, along with two squads of Bloody Axes. Since Zobra had been completely conquered, those soldiers were refugees. The Skraglanders were technically deserters because part of their country remained free and remnants of its army still fought. There were a handful of sea soldiers of various nations who'd somehow managed to escape from Zobra City when the Jokapcul overran it. Some of the soldiers had family with them. A few townsmen and farmers, along with their families, accompanied them for what small protection the soldiers offered.

The Bloody Axes were a special case; when they'd seen the Rampant Eagle on the half-moon blade of Haft's axe, they immediately swore allegiance to him, and they addressed him as "Sir Haft." The axe had been his grandfather's. He didn't know what war his grandfather had carried it in, but the eagle raised eyebrows among veteran soldiers nearly everywhere he went. Some day he was going to have to find out what it meant.

"All these people expect us to lead them to safety," Spinner said. "Why us? We're just a couple of pea ons." Spinner had never understood the term "pea on" that the Frangerian Marines used to describe their junior men. Maybe they used it because peas were small, but the "on" didn't make any sense. No matter, the term was one of the least of the many changes Lord Gunny had instituted when he rebuilt the Frangerian sea soldiers into what he called "Marines."

Haft shrugged, he wasn't impressed by the people who depended on him and Spinner. "So we're pea ons, so what? We're Marines and they aren't. If they want to travel with us, it's only right that we're in charge." Self-confidence to the point of arrogance was another of the changes Lord Gunny had wrought in his Marines.

Spinner shook his head. Like Haft, he had a great deal of self-confidence; sometimes he thought Haft had too much. "We aren't doing a very good job of leading them."

"How many of them would be dead by now if they weren't with us?" Haft didn't think many, or maybe any, of these refugees would survive very long on their own.

It was Spinner's turn to shrug, Haft was probably right. Of course, some of the soldiers might have turned to banditry. "We can't cross the Eastern Waste, we learned that the hard way. Not unless we carry enough food to make it all the way. We'd need several wagons to carry enough food, and we don't have any. So where do we go now?"

Haft's face briefly turned sour, he hadn't wanted to turn away from the Eastern Waste. "The Princedons. I said that's where we should have gone when we found Zobra City blocked."

"But we figured if Zobra City was taken, the Jokapcul were probably already in the Princedons."

Haft cocked an eyebrow at him; it was Spinner who'd thought that. But he let it slide; the two of them were in this together. "If we thought that then, it's more likely now."

"We haven't heard any rumors that the Jokapcul are in the Princedons."

Haft snorted. "We've been moving north too fast for rumors to catch up." That was true enough, the only people they'd encountered during their northward journey were small units of Jokapcul, or refugees who had left the south earlier. The Jokapcul they'd met were dead; some of the refugees had joined the Marines. He looked to the north. That way lay the Dwarven Mountains. He didn't have any real knowledge of what was there, nobody seemed to. Travelers' tales said whoever went into the mountains never came out. If they went north, they'd have to travel the entire length of the boundary between the mountains and the Eastern Waste. There was no food in the Waste, would there be any at the foot of the mountains? In the winter? Could they collect enough between here and there to make it through to the boundary between the High Desert and Elfwood Between the Rivers? He was willing to risk it—except for one thing: the winter. The farther north they went, the colder it got. He was from Ewsarcan, which was even farther north, though it seldom got as cold as he'd just experienced in the Eastern Waste. One reason he'd left home was to get away from the cold; he certainly didn't want to go someplace colder. He turned his gaze to the south. Were the Jokapcul moving deeper into Skragland?

Spinner was thinking along similar lines. "If the Jokapcul are still moving into Skragland," he said, "they probably haven't taken the Princedons yet."

"So let's head for the Princedons and find out."

"But if they're moving north and we're going south, we'll run into them." Spinner looked at the people again. Their work was mostly done and the adults were resting while the children played. "Then again, there are few enough of us we can probably evade the Jokapcul if they are moving north."

Haft looked at the soldiers and camp followers. There were about two score fighters, including the two of them, and almost that many women and children. Of the fighters, they, Silent, Fletcher, and Xundoe were the only ones who had won every time they fought the Jokapcul. Some of the others had fought and won since joining with them, but they'd lost severely before. He wouldn't want to fight the Jokapcul with the soldiers who knew more about losing to them than winning against them. Maybe with the Kondive and Easterly sea soldiers, they might be good enough—they'd managed to get out of Zobra City when it was captured, which was something few other men-at-arms had accomplished anywhere.

"We can go north and risk starvation and freezing, or we can go south and risk running into the Jokapcul."

"Those are our choices." Spinner sighed as he looked at the woman who left off whatever she'd been doing and came striding toward them.

Haft heard the sigh, saw the woman, and shook his head. Alyline, the Golden Girl. She was trouble, but Spinner was so blinded by her beauty he couldn't see that. Not that Haft would have been unwilling to give her a tumble himself, but . . . No, that woman was trouble; a man should keep his distance if he didn't want to risk losing important body parts.

Spinner rose to his feet to greet Alyline; he was unaware of the silly grin he wore. Haft remained seated. He looked relaxed, but was ready to move instantly in any direction if she pulled the gold hilt dagger she wore against her hip. She wore the gray silk cloak over her shoulders, but the day was warm enough that it hung open, revealing the patchwork garments she wore under it. They were patterned on her traditional golden garb, that of a Djerwolh dancer from the mountains of Arpalonia—a short vest that didn't quite close between her breasts and pantaloons that hugged her hips but ballooned out over her legs.

"We will rest here for another day, then head south," Alyline said without bothering to greet the two Marines.

"That's right, we're going south," Spinner agreed. "We move out at dawn."

"I said we rest for a day," she snapped back.

"But we can't, every day we wait the Jokapcul get closer."

"The children are tired. They have to rest. One of the women has an injured foot. We stay here for a day."

"They can ride, we have enough horses."

Alyline shook her head. Her golden hair swung out like a sun-washed cloud above her shoulders—though Haft might have sourly described it as an avalanche of yellow snow.

"You're not listening to me," she said sharply. "We stay here for a day. Tired and injured people need to rest."

Haft surreptitiously increased his distance from her.

"But—"

"No buts!" Her voice suddenly softened and she stepped

close to him, raised one hand to finger the merman clasp that secured his cloak at the throat. "You like me don't you, Spinner?" She gazed up into his eyes.

There was nothing subtle about the way Haft scooted farther away.

"You know I do," Spinner whispered huskily.

"Then we are going to rest a day."

"But . . ."

Her fingers wrapped around the merman clasp and yanked down hard. "I said we're going to rest and that's that!" she snarled. Her fingers flipped free of the clasp and she jabbed them into the base of his throat hard enough for the nails to leave marks. "One day!" She spun about and strode away.

"But—But—" Spinner turned to Haft, confusion and pain on his face. "What did I say wrong? Why is she mad at me?"

Haft turned away from him without a word; he looked like he wanted to spit in disgust.

The next day they rested.

Midwinter's day passed, but the deadliest part of winter didn't descend on them as harshly as it would have had they continued north. Instead, the days grew milder as they lengthened. Days and weeks passed during the southward trek, but they saw no troops of the invader. They saw signs of Jokapcul passage, though—burnt-out farms and wrecked, depopulated villages. Except to forage for food and usable goods that might have been left behind by the conquerors, they never stopped to investigate the farms and villages; no one needed to see mutilated corpses to know the ferocity of the foe, least of all Spinner, Haft, and the others of the original group, who'd encountered numerous sites of Jokapcul victory. The farther south they went, the more game they found, and ripe fruits and other edible vegetation also became available. They took the few bees that buzzed about them as a sign of a rapidly approaching spring.

The Eastern Waste gradually drifted eastward and they followed its drift. The closer they were to it, they thought, the less likely they were to encounter Jokapcul. They weren't afraid of bandits; bandits would shy away from twoscore fighting men. They did find refugees, though.

CHAPTER
TWO

They found a small caravan camped alongside a stream that dribbled wanly though a clearing where trees began to shrink from healthy forest to the stunted growth of the Eastern Waste. The dozen people or so gathered around the cook fire were startled when the group of armed and mounted men suddenly appeared at the edge of their clearing. Three or four children ran and hid. Some of the adults stared fearfully at the strangers, others cast anxious glances toward the ten horses they had tethered on a drag line. A couple of the six armed men were about to draw their swords, but held back when a woman in late middle age waved a hand to stop them. She stood and advanced halfway to the edge of the clearing to greet the newcomers.

"Everybody hold in place," Spinner said. "Don't draw your weapons." He dismounted and handed his reins to Haft. "I'll go and parley." He glanced around, then added, "Do you think it's a good idea to put out some security?"

Haft eyed the armed men around the fire for a moment and briefly tattooed his fingers on the haft of his axe before deciding they were no threat. He snorted. "Already doing it." He handed the reins of his and Spinner's horses to the rider next to him and dismounted. In a moment he was leading a quartet of Skragland Borderers away to place them where they could observe the approaches to the clearing.

Spinner unbuckled his sword belt and hung it on his saddle's cantle. He held his quarterstaff like a walking staff and stepped toward the woman in the clearing.

"Wait a minute, Spinner," Alyline called to him. "Doli,

21

come with us." She joined him and spoke before he could object. "There are all these armed men, these people are afraid. If women come to talk to them they'll see us as less of a threat."

"But . . ."

"Do you know what language these people speak? Neither do I. Doli speaks more languages than either of us. She doubles our chances of finding one we have in common."

Haft stifled a sigh. Alyline was right about languages. Still, some of those men looked ready to strike fast and run faster and he didn't like exposing the women to that danger. He turned to call for Silent to join them, but the Golden Girl guessed his intent.

"Just the three of us, we don't do anything threatening. Let's go." Alyline strode to the woman who stood alone waiting for them. Spinner caught up with her in two long strides but Doli had to scamper to catch them.

"Just remember, I'm in charge," Spinner said.

"Of course you are," Alyline said dryly.

Doli saw what Alyline had in mind and walked at her side opposite Spinner so the Golden Girl was in the center of their short line.

Alyline threw the front of her cloak over her shoulders to demonstrate that she wasn't carrying a sword. When they reached the woman she stopped directly in front of her. Placing her hands together with the fingers in front of her chin, she bowed.

"Lady," she said in heavily accented Skraglandish, "we are refugees from the Jokapcul invasion. We seek a port of refuge and wish harm to no one."

"There are many of you, and many armed men," the woman replied warily. Her Skraglandish was also accented but with the sounds of a different language.

Doli listened carefully and mentally played with the sounds. She worked some saliva to wet her throat, then spoke in Bostian. "Lady, there are bandits and Jokapcul about. We need the men and the arms for defense against them."

The woman looked at her in surprise and answered in the

same language. "How do you come to speak my language? I can't place your accent, but Bostian is not your native tongue."

"I used to work in an inn that had visitors from many nations. I had to speak many languages in order to properly serve the guests. Some of the guests were from Bostia."

"I did not expect to encounter someone who speaks my tongue so far to the east," the woman said. She placed her hands together and bowed to Doli as Alyline had to her. "I am Nightbird," she said.

Doli introduced her companions and told them what Nightbird had just said. Spinner spoke enough Bostian that he had been able to follow the exchange but Alyline had no Bostian. Soon the conversation got more complex and they both needed Doli's translation.

Nightbird was a robust woman with lines at the corners of her eyes and mouth and a streak of white in her otherwise black hair. Most village women of her age were well on their way to becoming crones, but she retained the firmness and litheness of a younger woman. She was a healing witch from a village in southeastern Bostia, which had fled ahead of the Jokapcul invasion. She, the women and children, and three of the armed men, were all that were left from her village. Two of the other men were Zobran farmers who joined with them after their farms had been burnt and their families killed. Fortunately both were veterans, one from the Skragland army, the other Zobran, and knew how to fight.

Spinner looked at the two farmers when Doli translated that. They wore farmer's homespun, but had the attitude of soldiers who didn't want to be where they were. He wondered whether "deserters" would more accurately describe them. He decided it didn't matter as long as they were willing to defend these refugees.

Doli briefly related to Nightbird that Spinner and Haft had escaped from New Bally when it was taken and they were looking for an open port from where they could find a ship back to Frangeria. She was even briefer in telling about how the two Marines had freed her and the other slaves at The

Burnt Man. Her description of their travels across Skragland into Zobra and back in Skragland was sketchy.

While they talked, Nightbird invited the three to join her and the other adults sitting at the cook fire. She continued her narration of the journey of the villagers.

The villagers had made it halfway across Skragland and dipped south into Zobra before they had major trouble. A farmer had given them permission to camp on his land for a few days but a badly disciplined troop of Jokapcul arrived the day before they were going to leave. Enough of them were distracted by raping several women and torturing men and boys they'd caught that half of the villagers were able to escape, though they had to leave their wagons and belongings behind. Back in Skragland they were set upon by bandits who killed several more people before being driven off. Since they'd heard all of coastal Zobra was in Jokapcul hands but the Princedons were still free, the survivors then joined a caravan headed for the Princedons. Then the caravan was set on by another Jokapcul troop. She didn't know if any of her villagers other than the few still with her managed to escape. The day after that attack they were joined by the two veterans, Kozlegeny and Winnan. A week ago they came across another caravan that had been attacked by the Jokapcul. They didn't find any live people, only corpses. Most of the horses hadn't wandered too far and they were able to round up ten. Three wagons were whole or repairable, and there were salvageable goods they consolidated in the three wagons.

And that was how they came to be in the clearing. They hadn't heard of any Jokapcul activity in the Princedons so they were headed there.

Shouts of children in the trees interrupted them. Spinner leaped to his feet and spun in the direction of the shouts, his quarterstaff held ready. Behind him, the men also jumped up and drew their swords, crouched, ready for fight or flight. Then children burst into the clearing, running about, tagging each other, squealing in delight. Wolf romped with the children like a household dog.

The children of the caravan had watched and listened for a

time as Nightbird and the strangers exchanged their stories. Finally, bored by the adult conversation and convinced there was no danger, they slipped out of their hiding places and sneaked into the forest to explore the rest of the strangers. They found the company's children and, after a few moments of uncertainty on both sides, began to play.

Everyone relaxed. If the children became friends so easily, the adults should follow their example.

The company had fresh meat brought down by its hunters, and fruits and vegetables foraged by its women. The caravan had bread, wheat, and sugar. The two groups pooled their foods and feasted that night. Baecker, a villager who actually had been a baker, used some the caravan's wheat and sugar and the company's fruit to bake a few cakes and pies in a makeshift oven. They weren't as good as what he'd made at home, but were nonetheless a major treat for the refugees.

They decided to join forces and set out together in the morning. A few bees curlicued behind them for a time, then turned about and buzzed away.

Haft, with Birdwhistle, Hunter, and Archer, was scouting ahead. Haft wore his double-reversible, four-sided cloak green side out. The other three wore the mottled green camouflage surcoats of Zobran Border Warders. They were on foot so they could move more quietly through the thin forest. The narrowness and ruts of the track forced the wagons to move so slowly that the scouts had no trouble staying ahead of them. Wolf ranged ahead.

The three Zobrans had been poachers before their induction into the Zobran Border Warder elite. Birdwhistle, Hunter, and Archer were men who could move through the forest very stealthily. Each had also shown courage and skill fighting the Jokapcul before their units' defeats. Which was why Haft wanted them to scout with him.

The land was fairly flat. Not so flat it would look like an endless tabletop if the trees were all cut away, but it wasn't cut with ravines or valleys, and few hills humped above it. Its movements were gentle, the rises and dips weren't very close to each other, and the difference between the top of a rise and bottom of the next dip was seldom more than half the height of a man. If the land was cleared and farmed, it would take not much more than a generation of plowing to level it. The trees weren't exactly stunted, their relatively thin foliage made them look more like they were more interested in growing tall than in growing full, like gangly adolescents. They were just close enough to one another that the accumulated mass of trunks, boughs, and leaves kept sight lines short. Bushes grew between the trees, and weeds sprouted where they could find room between the bushes. Game trails tatted the undergrowth into a fine lacework web.

Sound and smell are more important than sight to a man moving stealthily through such a landscape. Haft remembered that when Wolf appeared in front of him and made a show of sniffing the air. Haft sniffed and his nose caught something he didn't like: Jokapcul field rations. He turned his head toward Birdwhistle, a few yards to his left, and tapped the side of his nose. Birdwhistle sniffed, and nodded. Haft pointed to a large tree at the limit of sight, then made hand signals that told Birdwhistle he was going to the other side of the road to alert Archer and Hunter. Birdwhistle nodded again, he'd wait for Haft at the foot of the large tree. In moments, Haft was back with the other two scouts. They came close at Birdwhistle's signal.

"I heard them," Birdwhistle said in the soft voice used by men who move quietly through dangerous territory. "There are at least three. They're trying to be quiet, I heard one hush the other two."

"What language did they use?"

"Jokapcul."

"That's what I thought," Haft said grimly. As quickly as they could move without making noise, he led them through the brush parallel to the rutted track. Wolf left them behind.

The Jokapcul moved quietly as well, but weren't as intent on silence or as skilled as the four scouts tracking them. They were easy to follow. It didn't take long for the scouts to discover there were a good deal more than three Jokapcul on the

roadway. A short distance ahead a narrow track crossed the
rutted road; the Jokapcul must have come from it.

Haft was pleased with his choice of scouts, they moved
through the brush more quietly and faster than the Jokapcul
on the road. They were soon parallel with the trio in front
of them, and heard more ahead of those. They kept going.
A mile farther Wolf was waiting for them; they had reached
a place where there weren't any Jokapcul still ahead. They
hadn't passed any scouts guarding the flanks of the column
on the road.

Haft gave the wolf a suspicious look. He neither liked nor
trusted the animal, but Wolf seemed to have a far greater understanding of human speech than any beast should and, so
far as Haft knew, had never been unfaithful to them. He
forced down the feeling he was being ridiculous and spoke
to Wolf.

"Do they have flankers?"

Wolf shook his shaggy head in an obvious "no."

Haft stared at him, wondering if the wolf really understood
his words and told him the truth. But he and the scouts had
seen no sign of Jokapcul scouts in the trees to the sides of the
road; he decided he had no choice but to accept Wolf's head
shake as verification that the Jokapcul had no flankers out.
They stopped and hunkered down to count the enemy soldiers as they passed by. There was a score plus three of them.

As soon as they were past, Haft tapped Hunter's shoulder.
"Go back and tell Spinner. Come back with men."

Hunter nodded, rose to a crouch, and melted into the forest,
back the way they'd come.

"Stay here and wait for them," he told Birdwhistle. "Come
with me," to Archer.

Half an hour later the Jokapcul found a small clearing at
the side of the road and stopped. Haft smelled the smoke
from their fire. He sent Archer back to guide the fighters.

He placed his crossbow at the foot of a tree, and lowered
himself to the ground. Moving slowly and carefully, he crawled
to a place where he could observe the Jokapcul without being seen himself. They were small men, saffron skinned with

almond eyes. They wore leather leggings and jerkins, and leather sleeves covered their arms. Metal rectangles studded their jerkins. All of them had removed their helmets, also leather studded with metal rectangles, and some had loosened the laces on the sides of their jerkins to let fresh air get inside and cool their bodies. A pair of leather gloves studded with metal rosettes lay near each man, scabbarded swords lay near to hand. Two officers relaxed, helmets and upper armor off, on campstools. Four men were working at two cook fires, two at each, preparing food. Haft counted, twenty-three. These Jokapcul must be very sure there was no danger in this land—they didn't have any security out! He watched for a while longer, then slithered slowly, silently, backward and retrieved his crossbow. His three scouts were waiting for him.

"Spinner wants you," Birdwhistle said softly.

Spinner, Silent, Xundoe, and twenty Skraglander and Zobran soldiers were a hundred yards back. Spinner, Silent, and Xundoe crowded close to Haft when he reached them.

"Tell me," Spinner said.

Haft grinned. "There are twenty-three of them. They're resting in a clearing for a meal break. They have their armor half off and aren't alert at all—I was almost close enough to reach out and touch one of them, and they didn't know I was there."

"It could be a trap."

"If it is, it's a very good one. They have no security out and we didn't detect anyone else in the area. Their officers even have their armor off! You and I can get in close and kill them with our crossbows. You know the Jokapcul, without their officers they don't know what to do."

Spinner didn't say anything; he was looking into the trees in the direction of the Jokapcul.

"Come on, we can do it easily. We have complete surprise. Their officers will be down and we can have swords and axes on them before any of them can drop their dinners and pick up weapons."

"Spinner," Silent spoke up, "Most of our men have never

won a fight against the Jokapcul. We should do this to prove to them that they can beat this enemy."

Xundoe added, "You shoot the officers, and then I crack a phoenix egg on them. They'll panic."

Spinner nodded briskly. "All right, we'll do this. But we have to do it fast, before they finish their meal."

Spinner and Haft spent a few minutes deciding exactly what to do, then gathered their men close and told them the plan. They got in a column and filed quietly to where the Zobran Border Warders waited. Haft told them what he wanted them to do, then he, Spinner, and the three Border Warders melted into the trees. Xundoe followed close behind with Wolf next to him. Silent began positioning the soldiers.

The Jokapcul were nearly through with their meal. The officers, who had been served first, were already finished eating and one was reaching for his armor to put it back on.

Spinner and Haft were close enough to see each other. They exchanged a glance and nodded. They raised their crossbows to their shoulders, aimed, and fired. As the bolts plunged into their chests, the two officers gasped then fell. A couple of the soldiers happened to be looking in their direction at the time and were the only ones who saw them fall. Before either could shout an alarm, broadhead arrows plunged into them. A third Jokapcul soldier also toppled with a broadhead arrow through his neck.

"Now!" Spinner shouted.

Xundoe rushed forward with a phoenix egg in his hand. He twisted the egg's top as he ran then flung it toward the clearing. The egg struck a branch at the edge of the clearing and cracked open before it reached the ground. The phoenix was just beginning to unfold its fiery wings when it landed on its left shoulder. It cawed out in pain as it unfolded the right wing and tried to open the left, as it did so the right wing flapped side to side, igniting everything it touched. The left wing moved more slowly to unfurl. Even so, its heat was enough to start fires in the branches on the side of the clearing. Then with a final *snap!* the wing opened fully and the fiery bird launched itself into the air. It began a slow upward spiral and was soon above the opening in the branches above.

As flames crackled in the branches over Haft's head, he shouted "Charge!" and sped into the clearing with his axe in his hand.

"Charge!" Silent roared, and ran at the head of the twenty soldiers.

They ignored the five charred corpses of Jokapcul who had been struck by the phoenix's wings and raced at those remaining, who were just reaching for their weapons.

It was too one-sided to be called a battle. All of the Jokapcul were dead in moments. Only four members of the company had wounds, none of them serious.

CHAPTER
THREE

His hands clasped over his face, Xundoe the mage sat under a charred tree. Horrified eyes stared from between his fingers. He'd almost made a terrible mistake—if that egg had bounced backward when it hit that branch, instead of deflecting down . . .

He didn't want to think of the consequences, but was powerless to stem his thoughts. The phoenix would have emerged from its egg trapped among the trees. It wouldn't have struck many of the Jokapcul. Instead its wings would have incinerated him! And Spinner and Haft as well, and probably some of the others. The fiery bird's wings would have set the forest ablaze to clear a skyward path for itself. The entire company would have been in jeopardy! The thought that most of the Jokapcul would have survived and fallen on the rest of the company made him feel even worse. He closed his eyes and his fingers over them and keened thinly.

Yards away from where Xundoe sat in anguish over what might have been, the victorious soldiers searched the dead men for valuables, but came up with little of use—they didn't even want the strange food the Jokapcul ate. The officers had parchments in leather pouches carried on their belts, but no one in the company knew how to decipher the strange hieroglyphs of Jokapcul writing. They stripped the bodies of their weapons, but left their armor—none wanted to wear the armor of the conquerors. Haft led the axe men as they gathered the armor then chopped it up. The understrength platoon had no demon weapons.

By the time they finished searching and stripping the

bodies, the rest of the company had moved up and joined them in the clearing. Nightbird tended the wounded. Fletcher organized and supervised the men who hadn't been involved in the fight in removing the bodies and digging graves to bury them in. Alyline set some of the women to work covering over the bloodstains and removing the charred remains of bodies. Doli helped Zweepee lead the other women and older children in readying their own cook fires and meals. Everyone ignored the bees that investigated the foodstuffs and bodily fluids in the clearing and then buzzed away.

As soon as the fight was over Silent and Wolf had taken off to check the back trail—the platoon might have been the van of a larger force moving toward the head of Princedon Gulf. Spinner and Haft put out security, two soldiers a hundred yards up the trail in each direction, four pairs an equal distance into the trees away from the road. The soldiers on watch all felt confident—for the first time since the Jokapcul invasion began, they'd all been on the winning side of a battle.

When everything else was under control, Spinner and Haft went to deal with the mage's misery.

"What happened?" Spinner asked. The two of them squatted in front of Xundoe.

"I almost killed us all!" the mage wailed.

"Almost doesn't count in combat," Haft said sternly. "You either do it or you don't."

"He's right," Spinner said. "You didn't kill us. But something went wrong with the phoenix egg. Why did it break open before it hit the ground?"

Xundoe's head sunk down between his knees. "Because I threw it and it hit a branch. It cracked when it hit the branch." His shoulders shook with sobs.

Spinner patted the mage's shoulder. "Stop crying. None of us got hurt. Why did it hit the branch?"

Xundoe raised his head and looked at Spinner, his face was drawn into deep lines, his eyes were red lined, his nose ran. "I don't know! I saw a big gap between the trees, I could see all the way into the clearing. I ran up and threw the phoenix egg.

It wasn't supposed to hit a branch!" His voice keened again
and more tears flowed. He hid his face once more.

Haft put his hand on Xundoe's head and pushed back to lift
his face. "Were you still running when you threw it?"

"Y-Yes."

Haft let go and nodded. "That's what happened."

Xundoe looked at him, not understanding.

"If you want to throw something while you're running, you
have to practice throwing while you're running."

"But I've thrown phoenix eggs before, you've seen me."

"Yes we did, but you were standing, not running."

Xundoe still didn't understand.

Haft shook his head in exasperation; it was obvious to him,
why didn't the mage see what he was saying?

Spinner explained it. "When you are standing and throwing, or shooting a bow, or swinging a sword, your target is in
the same place you expect at the end of your movement as the
beginning. If you do it while you're running, where the target
is doesn't matter because *you* have moved, are *still* moving.
You have to adjust for that movement or you'll miss. You were
in one place when you began your throw, the phoenix egg had
a trajectory to where you were throwing it. But when you released it, you were in a different place and the trajectory had
to be different. You didn't make the adjustment. That's what
Haft means. It's why archers almost always miss when they
shoot on the run. If you had stopped before you threw, the egg
would have gone where you wanted it to."

The mage looked from Spinner to Haft and back with
dawning understanding. "You mean . . ."

"Stop, plant your feet, and then throw," Haft said. "You
didn't hurt any of us. Now stop worrying about it. Just make
sure you do it right the next time."

"Are you sure?" Xundoe said hopefully. "Really sure it's
all right?"

Spinner shook his head. "It's not all right, you *could* have
done serious damage to us. But you didn't, and you learned a
lesson, you won't make the same mistake again."

"You're right, I won't make the same mistake again." Xundoe grinned broadly, though his face was still drawn.

"Right." Spinner looked back at where food was being prepared. "Now let's go and see if anything's ready to eat yet."

Silent and Wolf returned a couple of hours later. They found no indication of a larger force. They wondered where the Jokapcul had been going. Were they the rear of a larger force moving toward the source of the Princedon Gulf, or somewhere else in the root of the peninsula? That didn't seem likely, the road didn't show much sign of recent traffic. Were they on their way to reinforce an outpost somewhere ahead? That was possible, so they'd have to be alert to danger from the front. Whatever the reason the Jokapcul platoon had been traveling along that road, they didn't worry about it for the rest of that day; time enough for that on the morrow.

By the time Silent and Wolf ate, it was late enough in the day that they decided to bivouac overnight in the clearing. The nearness of the bodies of the Jokapcul they'd killed didn't bother anybody—they were buried, and the buried dead of an enemy weren't a threat. In the morning Haft, as he usually did, led the three former Zobran poachers ahead to scout for danger along the way. Wolf, as *he* normally did, ranged ahead of them.

It was just a walk in the shade for the scouts. Marks on the road showed two or three wagons had passed that way recently, as had some horses and a number of walking people. But none of the traces showed the marks of Jokapcul boots or shoeing. Soldiers often start a long march carrying unessential things. After they walk for long enough they begin to tire and want to lighten their loads, so they discard, bit by bit, anything they don't really need for survival. Haft and his Zobrans found none of the leavings common to an army's march along the sides of the rutted road. On the few occasions when Wolf came close enough to let them see him, he looked unconcerned. So after a few hours Haft let the Zobrans do some hunting, though he didn't allow them time to dress their catch. They left several deer along the road for the company to pick up. The undulation of the land gradually increased, but it didn't become sharp.

In the middle of the afternoon, Birdwhistle was stalking a deer by himself when Wolf came to him. The animal was padding quietly at a fast walk when the Zobran first saw him, slipping from shadow to shadow with frequent pauses to sniff the air to his rear. When he reached Birdwhistle he turned about and growled low in his throat.

"Someone's up ahead?" the man asked. He didn't have the difficulty accepting the wolf that Haft did.

Wolf moved his head up and down, a nod.

"Let's get Haft."

Wolf shook his shoulders and, clamping his jaws on Birdwhistle's sleeve, pulled. Birdwhistle went with him. As soon as he was sure the man wasn't going to turn back, Wolf let go of his sleeve and led the way at a pace that allowed the man to move quietly until they came to a small hill. There, on a game trail that circled the base of the rise, Wolf gripped Birdwhistle's sleeve again and pulled down. Birdwhistle lowered himself to the ground. Wolf bellied down next to him and crawled into the brush that covered the rise. Birdwhistle crawled with him; halfway up he began to hear voices from the other side. They stopped. Birdwhistle listened intently, occasionally making out a word. A faint whiff of fire drifted through the growth. After a few moments he became aware of Wolf watching him. He looked at Wolf and could have sworn the animal was looking at him expectantly, as though asking, "What are you going to do about it?"

Birdwhistle mouthed, "Let's go back," and blinked in surprise when the wolf began working his way backward down the slope. He thought, *Haft's right, that animal understands too much.*

It didn't take long for Wolf's sense of smell to locate Haft.

"What language were they speaking?" Haft asked after Birdwhistle told him what Wolf had guided him to.

Birdwhistle was surprised, it hadn't occurred to him to wonder about the language. "Zobran."

Haft thought they were still in Skragland, or maybe they'd

reached the easternmost edge of the Princedons. He didn't think they were in Zobra. So who might these people speaking Zobran be?

"Men, or men and women?" he asked.

"Men. I didn't hear any women. Or children," Birdwhistle added thoughtfully. Children would be harder to keep quiet. But men keeping quiet near a little-traveled road through an isolated land and speaking the language of a different country could be bandits, though maybe not—bandits sitting in ambush probably wouldn't have a fire going.

"Wait here." Haft crossed the road. He was back in about a quarter hour with Archer and Hunter. Birdwhistle quickly briefed them on what he'd found.

"Hunter," Haft said when Birdwhistle was through, "go back and tell Spinner someone's ahead and we're checking them out."

As soon as Hunter was gone Haft had Birdwhistle lead him and Archer to a place where the foot of the rise was just visible.

"Wait here," he told them. "You, too," he added to Wolf. Wolf made a brief whine, but lay down. Haft looked at him sternly for a moment, then handed his crossbow to Birdwhistle. He crouched and softly trotted to the foot of the rise. He squatted next to the game trail for a few minutes listening and smelling the air. He didn't hear any voices, but did catch the faint smell of fire. Satisfied, he wended his way along the game trail, circling behind the rise away from the road. If an ambush was waiting, the bandits would be facing the road and maybe not watching their rear. When he was a little more than halfway around the rise he heard the wet snort of a horse, followed by soothing words to calm the beast. The voice was light—a woman's, or a boy's. He lowered into a squat and leaned forward to rest his upper body's weight on his hands. He edged forward on hands and feet, with his head held as low as he could and still look ahead. A few yards farther along he saw what might be a gap in the bushes on the right side of the game trail. When he got close, he lowered himself to his belly and crawled.

The break in the bushes was enough for him to see a small clearing from which brush had been removed. Several hobbled horses and a young woman were visible in the clearing. Her back was to him as she tended the horses. Four of them were eating from nosebags. When she turned, her profile told him she wasn't a young woman—not yet—perhaps in another year or two. A horse snorted behind her; she looked back and spoke to it. Haft's Zobran wasn't very good, but it sounded to him like she said, "You've had enough, it's someone else's turn." She held a wet leather bag in her hands and carried it to one of the horses without a nosebag. The horse dipped its head and drank when she held the bag in front of it.

Horses with nosebags and an older girl tending them didn't seem to Haft to portend the threat of an ambush. Still, he wanted to be more certain. As soon as the girl's back was turned, he scooted forward and continued along the track. A few yards farther it branched. He followed the right branch. It passed near a wagon where a woman was nursing a babe and beneath which a few children were napping. Nothing he'd seen was threatening—just a woman, several children, and horses—but Birdwhistle had heard men talking. He reversed direction, found another game trail that roughly paralleled the one he'd followed before back to the front of the rise. How could he find out what, or who, was on the other side?

He made his way back to the game trail where he'd begun his circuit of the rise and lay flat on it. From ground level, he saw the small tunnel under the lower branches of the bushes made by Birdwhistle and Wolf when they'd crawled up the slope. Before he was completely into the tunnel, his axe hung up on a bush. Swearing silently, he twisted so he could reach the buckles of his waist belt and the cross body belt and slipped them off. He felt naked without the axe when he resumed crawling. As he neared the top he heard rattling sounds from ahead.

He caught his breath at the top of the rise. The brush was thin enough to let him see down to the bottom. An armed man sat cross-legged less than thirty feet away. His back was to

Haft and a sheathed sword lay on the ground at his side. Six other armed men sat likewise in a close circle. All seven faced inward. Three of them wore the blue surcoats of the Zobran Royal Lancers. Were they refugees or deserters turned bandit?

The rattling noise came again and one of the men flung his fist up and down, then threw the dice. He softly swore an oath that Haft understood quite well—it was an expression Zobran gamblers used when the dice went against them. The man to his left said something too softly for Haft to make out, which made the others laugh, and picked up the dice to roll in his turn. Haft watched and listened for a moment or two longer, wondering. At least seven armed men were quietly gathered close to a roadside, while their women, children, and horses were hidden away from the road—those were marks of bandits waiting for passing travelers to rob. Yet the armed men seemed to be paying no attention to the road, and he and the scouts hadn't seen any sentries. It didn't make sense.

Haft slid backward until his feet told him he'd reached his axe. He wiggled his way past it, picked it up, and rose to a crouch.

Spinner and Silent were with Archer and Birdwhistle when he got back to the tree. It only took a moment or two to relate what he'd seen—and hadn't seen.

"That's very curious," Spinner said. If they were bandits, where were their lookouts? If they weren't bandits, why were the men gathered quietly by the road with their weapons ready? In either case, why weren't they paying attention to the road?

Throughout the telling, the scouts listened carefully and kept looking from Haft to the rise and back again. Silent was crouched in a squat. He didn't look at Haft or the rise, but cocked his head as though he was listening to something only he could hear. Wolf sat next to the giant, tongue lolling from his open mouth, head cocked, ears perked, looking for all the world like he was aping Silent.

When Haft was through, Silent stood, said, "Wait," tapped

Wolf on the shoulder, and moved toward the road. Wolf huffed a low *ulgh!* and followed.

Spinner and Haft watched them disappear, then Spinner said to the scouts, "Stay here and keep alert." He gestured to Haft and the two of them slipped through the woods back to the main body.

"Did you put out security?" Haft asked partway back.

Spinner shot him a glare. He never needed to be reminded about basic things such as putting out security; Haft sometimes did.

Haft shrugged. "Never hurts to make sure," he said dryly.

The main body was a hundred and fifty yards back. Spinner and Haft quickly filled them in on what Haft had found. They left Fletcher and half of the fighters to protect the women and children, and took the other half forward as far as they thought was safe—they measured safety by how far the noises of the horses would carry. They left them there with orders to be prepared to move immediately.

Silent and Wolf returned shortly after Spinner and Haft rejoined the scouts. They came from the opposite direction from where they'd left.

"There are no sentries anywhere," Silent reported in a low rumble. "Six more men are stationed fifty yards farther up the road. They aren't paying any more attention than these are." He shook his head. "Three of them are even asleep! We found a peddler's wagon and more women and children. The women were at a stream doing laundry. I didn't see the fires, but it smells like they're starting to cook."

Wolf thumped his tail on the ground. Silent briskly rubbed his shoulders.

"There are thirteen men in two groups," Spinner said. "You saw no other men?"

"That's right."

"No sentries, the men you saw are armed but aren't alert?"

"Right again."

"Were any of the women armed?"

Silent shook his head. "Only with knives."

Spinner and Haft turned away from the others and put their heads together to confer. After a moment they turned back.

"Here's what we are going to do."

Silent grinned, the scouts nodded grimly. Wolf wagged his tail.

CHAPTER
FOUR

"Nobody move!" Spinner shouted.

The seven men playing at dice jerked at the command and spun to face it, their hands reached for their weapons but stopped before touching them. Facing them at the top of the rise were a dozen men, half of whom held bows with arrows nocked and drawn, but not aimed. The others held swords. Two of the men glanced at their weapons, but the bowmen's range was so short that their arrows would be in their targets before any of the seven could grab weapons and jump out of the way.

"Who's in charge here?" Spinner demanded in rough Zobran. He shifted his crossbow so it was pointed at the sky.

Three of the men looked uncertainly at one another, the others stared at the bowmen covering them. No one spoke right away.

At the same moment fifty yards farther along the road, Haft shouted, "Don't move!" as he and a dozen horsemen abruptly appeared in a semicircle facing the six armed men at that end of the rough encampment.

"Who's your commander?" Haft asked in harshly spoken Zobran.

He may as well not have asked for all the response he got.

Screams of frightened women and children came from the trees away from the road. A loud, male voice called out, "Be calm, no one's going to hurt you." The screaming continued and the sound of running feet came to the two groups at the roadside.

The thirteen men in the two groups jerked their heads

41

toward the sounds, but none dared move. Outnumbered as they were and without their weapons in their hands, they couldn't fight. But their women and children were being threatened, they had to do something. The tension was palpable.

"Don't do it," Spinner said at his end as one man finally began to inch his hand closer to his bow.

"Move and die," Haft shouted at a man whose eyes flicked to his sword.

Women and children burst upon the two groups and pulled up sharply at the sight of the armed men facing their men. The women and older children stood unsteadily, frightened and not knowing what to do. Small children bawled, then clung to their mothers and buried their faces in their skirts. A woman fell to her knees and cried with her face in her hands.

A man in the first group, one of the three in the blue tunic of a Zobran Royal Lancer, swallowed and held his hands open and wide. He slowly rose to his feet.

"What do you want?" he demanded. "We're poor refugees, we have little more than the clothes on our backs and a little bit of food."

Spinner lowered his crossbow and looked at the man. "What's your name?"

"I'm Guma."

"You're in command?"

Guma looked at the others, they looked away. "As much as anyone," he said as he looked back at Spinner.

"Poor refugees?" he asked. "You are arrayed more like bandits sitting in an ambush."

"If we were bandits sitting in ambush, you wouldn't have been able to sneak up on us like you did."

"So you didn't expect anybody to come along now, that's all," Spinner retorted. "But you were in position if anybody did."

"Defensive position, we don't plan to ambush anybody."

"How do you explain the peddler's wagon. Who did you steal it from?"

"The peddler is part of our party."

Suddenly Silent shouted, *"No!"* from behind the women and children.

An arrow *whiz*zed past Spinner's head.

There was a yelp and inarticulate shouts, then Silent called out, "I've got him."

"Hold!" Spinner shouted. "Be calm! Nobody gets hurt if everybody stays calm."

"That goes for you too!" Silent snarled at a half-grown boy struggling in the crook of his arm. The giant held a bow in his free hand taken from the boy. "This whelp thinks he's ready to be a fighting man," he said, not yelling but loud enough for everyone to hear. "That kind of thinking can get people unnecessarily killed." He looked around and saw a woman with a anguished expression wringing her hands. "Is this one yours?" he demanded.

The woman whimpered as she nodded.

Silent put the boy on his feet and gave him a shove in her direction. "Keep better control of your sprat before he gets himself in trouble he can't get out of."

The woman ran to her son and hugged him tightly then looked at Silent. Silent nodded curtly.

One of the other Royal Lancers tried to take advantage of the distraction and started to grab for his sword. Not everyone was as distracted as he thought—an arrow *thunk*ed into the ground inches from his hand. He froze and looked up, his face white. Five horsemen had drawn arrows pointed at him, the one who had shot was already drawing another shaft.

"The next arrow kills," Spinner announced.

A young woman who had stood silently sobbing near the group of men covered by Spinner and his horsemen suddenly screamed and bolted. Half blinded by her tears, she stumbled through the six men who still sat or lay as they'd been when Haft and his men came upon them.

One of Haft's men, a Kondive Islands sea soldier, suddenly shouted, "Wanita!" He broke ranks and galloped after the woman. As soon as he was close enough he bounded out of his saddle and grabbed her. His momentum carried both of them to the ground.

"Wanita!" he exclaimed, and held her face in his hands. He kissed her. She struggled to break away, but he held her close and cried the name again and again.

Suddenly she stopped struggling and looked into his face. She gasped. "Pisau! Is it really you, Pisau?" she said in a language only one of the others understood. She rubbed a wrist at her eyes to push away the tears.

He kissed more of her tears away. "It's me, Wanita," he said in the same language, his voice almost unable to get through his constricted throat.

"Pisau!" she cried and threw her arms around his neck. "I thought you were dead!"

"And I you, my love!"

Tension broke as everyone, including Silent, who broke off from searching the camp, gathered around the two where they rocked on the ground with their arms holding them close, murmuring to each other as they kissed.

After an embarrassing moment Spinner cleared his throat. "Do you know this woman, Pisau?" he asked in Frangerian.

The Kondive Islander broke his face away from the woman's and grinned up at the Frangerian Marine. "Know her? She's my *wife*! I searched for her when the Jokapcul took Zobra City. Someone told me he'd seen her killed. I never would have left the city without her if I'd thought she was still alive." He turned back to his wife and repeated what he'd just said in their own language. She giggled and said something. He laughed and spoke in Frangerian. "She says she wasn't killed, but she'll show me the scar later."

"Then these people are really refugees?" Haft asked.

Pisau asked Wanita. She nodded, then struggled out of his grip to stand up. In broken Zobran, she said that some people in Zobra City had taken her in and hid and cared for her after a Jokapcul soldier stabbed her.

The Jokapcul thought they had locked the city down tight but unlike the free port of New Bally, which the invaders had taken in a matter of hours, Zobra City had been subject to invasion many times during its history, and people knew how to retain communications with the countryside, and routes out of the city unnoticed by their captors. For weeks, people and uncaptured soldiers slipped out of the city and made for what they hoped were rendezvous points where they could get organized and begin resistance to the conquerors.

When Wanita's wound had healed well enough, her saviors—who were among the people she was traveling with—had taken her on their own exodus. But the Jokapcul were more successful in beating down all resistance in the countryside than they had been in the capital city, and the rendezvous points were worthless. This group, eight Royal Lancers and five other men, three of whom were former Zobran soldiers, along with several wives and children banded together and headed east in hope of meeting more Zobrans en route to the head of Princedon Gulf. Until their capture they hadn't met any other refugees, though they'd often had to avoid Jokapcul units marching northward.

Silent took himself away to bring the rest of the company forward while Spinner and Haft told their story to the refugees. Then the two bands agreed to join forces. They sealed the agreement with a communal dinner to which both parties contributed. The new people were surprised by the way Alyline, Doli, and Zweepee took charge of preparations. Baecker again constructed a temporary oven and they had cakes and pies, which were a particular delight to the refugees from Zobra City. Nobody begrudged a wandering bee the crumbs it dined on.

While the dinner was being prepared, the half-grown boy who shot the arrow at Spinner approached him.

"If the giant hadn't startled me by yelling, I would have hit you," the boy said belligerently. "You know that, don't you?"

Spinner looked down at him. The fuzz on the boy's cheeks and upper lip told him the boy was of age to learn the ways of men. One of the ways of men was learning how to use weapons and fight.

"I believe you," he said. "Did you learn something today?" The boy looked at him curiously, not knowing what he meant. "Did you learn that it's a bad idea to shoot arrows at people who outnumber you and aren't shooting at you?"

"If you hadn't been refugees like us, if you were the bandits we thought you were, it wouldn't have mattered that you outnumbered us and weren't shooting. You would have killed us anyway. By shooting you when you weren't shooting at us, we could have taken some of you with us. Maybe we could even have scared you off."

"If we were bandits, maybe. But we aren't, so you would have been wrong. We thought you were bandits and you would have proved that to us. We would have killed all of you because you put an arrow into me."

"I'd do the same thing again," the boy said defiantly. He turned and walked away, head high and back erect. Wrong or right, he was the only one to fight back when the armed men cornered them; he was proud of that.

Spinner sighed at the boy's retreating back. The boy was both right and wrong. Being both right and wrong can get people needlessly killed. He hoped the boy learned that lesson before failing to learn it killed him.

Guma, the reluctant leader, had been in the Zobran army for three years. His troop was in the countryside on training maneuvers when the Jokapcul invaded. They found out about the invasion when they were attacked by two troops of Jokapcul light cavalry. The fight didn't last long—the Jokapcul had magicians with them, the Zobrans didn't. As far as he knew, he and the seven other Royal Lancers in this group were the only survivors from the troop.

"Our captain was killed by a phoenix. I was close to him when it happened, the phoenix's wing just missed me. It was the most horrible thing I'd ever seen. They had demon spitters as well. It wasn't much of a battle, mostly it was a slaughter. More than half of us were dead or down with wounds before they even closed to sword and lance range."

"How did you survive?" Spinner asked.

Guma shrugged. "We ran. Some of us ran before they reached us." He looked away from the two Frangerians. "Those who didn't run soon enough died."

Haft opened his mouth to say something, but a sharp

glance from Spinner stopped him. Haft grimaced; he had little use for soldiers who ran from a fight, but he kept his peace.

"Ealdor's family," he named another lancer, "was visiting their home village," Guma continued, "which wasn't far away. We went there and got them. A few of the villagers joined us, but most didn't believe the Jokapcul would murder civilians and destroy the town." He went silent for a moment, looking west. "I hope I'm wrong," he said softly, "but I'm afraid they're all dead now. Dead or slaves." He shook himself, then continued his story in a stronger voice. "A little east of there, we came upon Mangere, the peddler, and he joined us for protection."

Haft snorted. "Mangere, the peddler with a full wagon. And you told us you only had the clothes on your backs and a little bit of food."

Guma smiled. "Little enough for this many people trying to survive."

"It's more than we had for more people."

"But you have officers who know how to lead. We didn't even have a sergeant."

"Officers!" Haft hooted.

"That's enough," Spinner said sharply. He thought they were better off if the Zobrans believed he and Haft were officers until they proved themselves. Haft gave him a crooked grin, but didn't say more. "Please continue," Spinner told Guma.

"We passed not far from the farm Sulh grew up on," said another lancer, "so we gathered his family as well."

There was more. Two of the other Royal Lancers also gathered family, and other refugees joined them for what protection could be afforded by eight leaderless soldiers. There were a few unwed or widowed women in the group, but not as many as there were men without wives.

"That Kondivan of yours—Pisau?—made several men unhappy when he turned out to be Wanita's husband. We understood that she didn't want anything to do with a man, not so soon after what happened in Zobra City. But when she was ready . . ." He shook his head ruefully.

"Fortunes of war," Spinner said with sympathy. He understood waiting—he was waiting for Alyline.

Just then the Golden Girl walked up to them, backed up by Doli and Zweepee. She thrust a sheet of paper at Spinner, who jumped to his feet like a puppy eager to please.

"I don't imagine you've done this yet for the men," she said.

"What?" Spinner looked at her quizzically, then at the paper. It held a list of names, many with numbers or other annotations next to them. He handed it to Haft and looked at the women. "What is it?"

Haft glanced at the paper and smacked himself on the head. "She's way ahead of us, Spinner."

"What do you mean?"

"This is a roster of the women and children. It gives the ages of the children and shows which children belong to which women." He cocked an eyebrow seeking confirmation. Zweepee smiled and nodded at him. "And, unless I miss my mark, it tells which women are with their husbands and what special skills they have," he added smugly. "Am I right?" He grinned.

"You're not always the fool you normally seem," Alyline acknowledged in a tone friendlier than the words.

Haft's grin snapped to a scowl.

"We don't really need a roster," Spinner said. Haft and I know the soldiers and other men who have been with us, and we'll get to know Guma and the others soon enough."

"Spinner," Alyline said, "you may know their names, but do you know what skills they have beyond fighting and hunting? We need a roster. I'll make it if I must, but I think the men will be more cooperative about giving information if you make the roster."

"But . . ."

"Make a roster. Note which men have their wives and children with them and what skills they have."

"We aren't a little group anymore," Zweepee broke in. "We have almost a hundred and fifty people now. We need to know these things."

"But . . ."

"We've begun an inventory of goods," Doli said, "but some

of the people are reluctant to tell us everything they have. They need our *commander* to make the request official. You're the only one who can do that, Spinner."

The tip of Haft's tongue poked between his lips as looked at Spinner. *Commander?* It was a shame that as moon-eyed Doli was over Spinner, she didn't seem to like him, Haft, at all—and Alyline had no more use for him than she did Spinner. If either of them liked him even a *little* bit, he could probably get her and Zweepee to say *he* was the commander! *He* wouldn't be acting so thick headed about it if the women were calling *him* the commander! He glanced at Guma. The lancer seemed confused and uncomfortable; maybe he was beginning to understand that neither of the Frangerian Marines was an officer. *Hmpf!* As if either was wearing officer's rank insignia. Why—

"We don't have time to make an inventory," Spinner said. "We're pulling out first thing in the morning."

"No we aren't," Alyline said. "We need another wagon. Do we have a wainwright? Carpenters? A wheelwright? Now get that roster made so we know what crafts we have. And hope we have the skills to make a wagon; we'll move faster if we have an extra wagon to carry the small children." She spun on her heel and marched back to the middle of the camp. Doli and Zweepee went after her.

"Well, *commander*," Haft said with amusement, "shall we get started on that roster?"

As it happened, not only were there men with backgrounds as a wainwright, a wheelwright, and two carpenters, they also had a hooper, a cartwright, a brewer, a chandler, a coldren, a cooper, a farrier, a lorimer, three masons, a mulliner, a saddler, two sawyers, a tanner, and a former apprentice baker, as well as men trained in several other crafts. Alyline was particularly interested in the tucker and the dyer, and spent some time with them detailing her clothing requirements. They were so dazzled by her beauty and what she wanted that they swore to come up with the garments she wanted, and properly dyed.

It took three days to build the extra wagon—the sawyers

didn't have the right saws to cut proper boards, the hooper lacked the iron strapping with which to clad the wheels, and all of the men involved in making the wagon were out of practice in their crafts. But it was finally ready and the wagon rolled, filled with young children who shouted in glee at riding in the ungainly thing.

For the first time in the months ago since they'd first turned northeast, away from Zobra City's burning harbor, Spinner and Haft had more recent information about Jokapcul movement along the coast. As of two months after capturing capital city, the Jokapcul hadn't begun moving east into the Princedons. That information was now more than a month old, but during that month and more, both parties had watched so many Jokapcul units moving through Zobra and north into Skragland that it seemed unlikely that the invaders had yet begun to move east. Even if the Jokapcul had entered the westernmost of the small principalities on the long peninsula, the company could likely bypass enemy units easily enough and make its way to a port that was still free. They would head for the ocean coast of the Princedons.

CHAPTER
FIVE

"Which way?" Haft asked. He let his horse turn to face away from the hot wind blowing from the north, but held the reins so it didn't begin to move south.

"I don't know," Spinner murmured. The wind that whipped around them tore the words from his mouth and cast them away almost before Haft could hear them. His horse wanted to face south as well.

The road they'd followed into the root of the Princedons meandered into the southern fringe of the Eastern Waste, where it merged with the southwestern corner of the Low Desert. For two days the lack of trees or other high growth had allowed long sight lines and they hadn't bothered to put out scouts. They were in an arid land covered with tough grasses and spotted with low-lying shrubs. Here and there stunted, twisted, trees endured a hard life. Spinner looked slowly side to side, along the paths of the two trails that forked from where they stood. The left fork continued east and a little bit north, leading into a rising land that turned sere so abruptly a sharp brown line marked the place of change. The grass of the arid land almost completely disappeared and the shrubs were smaller and far fewer. There were no trees to the east. That fork led to the head of Princedon Gulf. The right fork descended a very gentle slope. In that direction the land gradually turned from arid to healthy-but-dry to lush. The outlying trees of a great forest stood an hour's easy ride distant.

Haft curled his hands around his eyes and looked east along the road into the sere land. The sun was almost directly overhead and heat radiated from the rocky surface. The air shimmered above it. Tiny specks drifted high in the sky; carrion eaters on watch for the carcass of anything foolish enough to wander into that outcropping of the Low Desert.

"It fades out," he said.

"What?" Spinner asked. He also looked through curled hands into the Low Desert.

"The road. It only goes a short way into the desert, then it fades to nothing."

Spinner grunted.

"Now down there," Haft pointed with his chin toward the distant mountains that seemed to float above the forest, "we'll find water and food. And maybe a ship home."

Spinner grunted. "If the Jokapcul haven't moved east." They'd met only a few more refugees since encountering the group guarded by the Royal Lancers, and those had no recent knowledge. Still, those people had been accepted into the company. But without newer information, they had to wonder whether the Jokapcul might have resumed their eastward advance. If they had, the next place they would be was the Princedon Peninsula. If they had moved into the Princedons, they controlled the ports on the southern coast for as far east as they had gone. Spinner and Haft had made port in the Princedons a few times and they knew none of its principalities was strong enough to offer more than token resistance to the invaders. The gulf coast was more likely to be free. But Princedon Gulf was shallow toward its western end, and had little in the way of ocean shipping, its harbors mostly held shallow-draft fishing craft.

Spinner looked toward the forest. Something gray was loping in their direction.

"Wolf's coming back," he said.

Haft grimaced. He doubted he'd ever trust the overly intelligent wolf that had attached himself to their company somewhere in upper Zobra. At least he *thought* they'd made it into Zobra when the wolf first joined them; they hadn't been traveling on roads clogged with refugees and the border was unmarked.

Two sets of hooves clopped behind them, one set those of a horse, the other sounded too loud to be merely a horse. The hooves came to a stop and they turned to see who was with Silent, the rider of the thing that sounded too big to be a horse.

"We need provisioning," Fletcher said.

Haft turned to him and nodded, feeling vindicated.

"I'm hungry enough to eat one of these puny ponies," Silent grumbled. His mount looked far too large to be a horse, though horse it was.

"Yes," Spinner said so softly the wind tore the word away before the others heard it. Food had been hard to come by since the road led them to the merge of the Eastern Waste with the Low Desert; they were on strict rationing.

Another set of hooves clopped up, angry sounding in their haste, and didn't stop until they were between Spinner and Haft; Fletcher had to dance his horse aside to avoid a collision with the newcomer.

"Why do we stop here?" demanded Alyline, the Golden Girl, though she hadn't been gold for some time. Her short vest, open between her breasts but laced to keep the sides from flying away, was silk, its mauve dye was running. The pantaloons that covered her legs were a garish orange flannel. A maroon girdle was tied below her bare waist. She wasn't at all happy with the tucker and dyer who had promised her new garments and so far had delivered only those, which she didn't think an improvement over the patchwork garments she'd stitched together herself from scraps of cloth.

Haft tried to ignore the Golden Girl. Spinner glanced at her with the pained eyes of an unjustly scorned suitor, but didn't answer. Instead, he looked again toward the approaching wolf.

Wolf saw the five people looking at him, stopped, and stood with his flank toward them. He raised one forepaw and awkwardly pointed toward the forest. His tongue lolled and he nodded. He looked at the four unmoving people and cocked his head expectantly. When they still didn't move, he looked away for a moment, as though thinking. Abruptly, he went on the alert for a second, then pounced. He worried his head back and forth between his outstretched paws, as though dispatching a careless rabbit. Finished with his make-believe kill, he bounded back to his feet and spun around a couple of times, finishing with his hindquarters toward them and his head looking back over his shoulder. His meaning was clear:

Get a move on, people, there's food this way.

"What are you waiting for?" Alyline demanded. "We have a lot of people who are hungry and thirsty. They need food and water." She flicked her stallion's reins and heeled his flanks. The horse began cantering toward the waiting wolf.

Spinner looked after her unhappily, then turned his horse onto the right fork and followed at a walk. He removed his cloak and turned it so the leafy green side showed rather than the sandy brown and tan he'd shown during the trek these past several days.

"This is the rally point," he said. "Pass the word to everybody. Fletcher," he said when he didn't see Haft—where had he gone to?—and added, "Send scouts ahead."

"Right." Fletcher turned his horse about. Spinner hadn't seen Haft because he had already gone back to the main body of the band to gather his normal trio of scouts. Haft had already turned his cloak green side out.

"Wait for me!" Xundoe cried after Spinner. The Zobran army mage who was the sole survivor of his guard company when Spinner and Haft found him, urged his pony into a trot. A donkey laden with two mage chests followed the tether that ran from its bridle to the pony's saddle.

Haft grinned as he called out the names of his men. "Archer, Hunter, Birdwhistle, let's go. We need to check out the forest." He pointed. The three eagerly joined him; they preferred being out front to riding with the main body. They happily donned mottled-green surcoats once more.

"Mister Fletcher, the troops are yours," Haft said when Fletcher arrived. He clumsily heeled his mare and led his scouts in a cross-country canter toward the forest.

Fletcher watched the four until they were far enough away that they couldn't possibly hear what he said. "Kocsokoz, Kovasch, Meszaros, ride with me. The rest of you follow Spinner." His trio were Skraglander army veterans; he preferred Skraglanders to any of the Zobrans. Unlike Zobra, Skragland hadn't been completely defeated—yet. To Fletcher, that meant the morale and self-confidence of his Skragland Borderers were probably higher, and their lust for vengeance lower. He was more confident they would fight smart when a fight came—and a fight was likely in the Princedons. Fletcher and his trio set out at a trot behind Haft and his three. The Skraglanders untied their fur cloaks from their bindings on the back of their saddles and hung them over their shoulders as they trotted. They wouldn't be as hard to spot under the trees as the Zobrans, but the shaggy cloaks and the horns on their helmets might make a foe mistake them for animals for an instant—and an instant might be all they needed at the beginning of a fight.

Except for two who dropped out to act as rear security, the other fighters took the road; they'd soon enough catch up with the leaders. Nobody noticed the solitary bee that circled above them.

At the start of the forest proper, Haft and his trio of scouts turned toward the road the rest of the company traveled on and followed it into the forest. They leaned forward on their horses, peered deeply into the shadows to the sides of the road, looked sharply to the front, listened intently to the forest sounds, sniffed the smells of vegetation and wandering animals. The road was a mere rutted track on which grew enough grass and wild flowers to tell them it had seen spare use for some time. A hundred yards into the trees they dismounted then tethered their mounts for the company to pick up. Haft signed Archer and Hunter to go into the forest on the right side of the road, he and Birdwhistle went into it on the left. One man in each pair kept visual contact with the road; the other went deeper into the forest but maintained contact with the road watcher. They advanced silently. Wolf watched to see how the men arrayed themselves, then ranged ahead of them.

Air wafted softly under the trees as relief from the heat of the sun, and quickly evaporated the sheen of sweat that had covered their bodies. The scouts were alive to the sounds and sights of the forest: Birds sang and squirrels chittered as they darted and skittered about their business in the trees. Woodpeckers *rat-a-tatt*ed. Insects buzzed and flitted about; salt-eaters and bloodsuckers inspected the exposed skin of the scouts and supped on the more succulent bits. A lone bee bumbled about in seeming vain search for nectar. Up ahead a pack of feral dogs bayed in pursuit of its dinner, a deer cried out its death. Soon after, they heard canine yelps—followed by a wolf's victorious howl.

Tree trunks, many thicker than the width of a man's body, climbed heavenward, only the youngest had branches low enough for a tall man to reach without standing on his horse's back. Branches flared out into terraces high above, forming multiple canopies that blocked direct sunlight from reaching the ground; little undergrowth managed to survive in the dimness of that part of the forest. Strangle vines looped about many trees, their aerial roots drooped heavily from high branches. Here and there where age, a storm, or strangle vines had felled a tree, sunlight broke through and inspired saplings to grow in manic competition with their siblings and rivals of other species. There also, small lizards basked on exposed rocks or on the fallen trees themselves. A few lookout trees shot high and pierced the canopy; nubbins of old, dead branches a man could use to climb spiraled their way up the mighty trunks from near their bases.

The forest's multiple canopies were not so thick that they prevented rainfall from dribbling down in a constant drizzle; so the ground was soft and moist, but not so wet as to squish underfoot. All around, fallen leaves and twigs spotted the ground and quietly rotted away, returning their stored nutrients to the soil.

Even though the light was merely dim, and no treetop dwellers scattered slops at him, the forest reminded Haft uncomfortably of the short stretch he and Spinner had traversed leading to the border between Bostia and Skragland. There, as they reentered the light at the border, a giant cat of the forest had attacked them and nearly won.

Bare patches of dirt bore the tracks of deer and other grazers, occasionally there were signs of boar. Ground dwellers scampered through what undergrowth there was, *squee*-ed out their alarms and flashed white-tailed alerts. Haft went suddenly cold when he saw the pug of a hunting cat. He dropped to a knee to examine it. It was half the size of the paws of the gray tabur he and Spinner had fought and killed. He thought the cat more likely to flee a man than try to eat one. Still, when he stood and continued to move through the trees, he was more wary. He checked that his axe was loose in its belt loop; his fingers caressed the trigger of his crossbow. Man-eaters or not, cats were frightening, deadly, beasts and he had no desire to encounter another.

In places, the spacing of the trees allowed the scouts to see as far as a hundred yards though the dimness of the light made objects at that distance hard to make out. After a time, Haft dimly made out Wolf in the distance, where it was bolting down a meal. The beast looked directly at him as he approached and seemed to laugh. Then, finished, Wolf ran forward before Haft reached him.

Haft stopped to examine the scene. There were many paw marks of dogs around the half-eaten carcass of a yearling deer. Wolf had interrupted the pack in its meal and sent it to flight. With the bigger predator gone, the feral dogs were edging closer, to retake their stolen catch. Haft was suddenly aware of their growls. He casually walked away. Dogs might attack a man who displayed fear; they were less likely to attack one who displayed an air of confidence.

The ground rolled in gentle swells and troughs, it angled slowly, imperceptibly, downward toward the distant sea. Streams and rills cut every which way through the land; the mountains that formed the spine of the Princedon Peninsula and divided the flow of water north and south were some distance ahead. In flat places and broad hollows, water from heavy rains pooled in season.

Haft couldn't see the position of the sun under the trees and had to guess at the passage of time. When he was sure enough time had passed for the sun to be halfway from zenith to dusk, he began to look for a suitable flood clearing, one with a stream of fast-running water and large enough to bivouac the entire company. When he found one he sent his three scouts to make sure the lack of human sign truly meant no one was near, and went to wait by the side of the road, where he was surprised when Fletcher joined him from the direction of the bivouac.

"Where's everybody else?" Haft asked.

"Kocsokoz, Kovasch, and Meszaros are with your men scouting the area." Fletcher grinned. "We followed you. Eight pairs of eyes are better than four."

Haft looked away, muttering to himself. *He* thought four pairs of eyes were enough—and he was head scout; nobody should be scouting without him knowing about it. He turned back to Fletcher.

"And just what do you think would have happened if we realized we were being followed? How many of you would we have killed before we realized who you were?"

Fletcher shook his head. "None. You would have waited until we were close enough to recognize before you fired."

Haft looked away, muttering again; Fletcher was right. Otherwise their arrows might miss. He'd rather get quick kills with arrows than go into the uncertainty of a close fight with men of whose fighting abilities he wasn't fully confident. Still, he was upset that other scouts had trailed them without him knowing.

"That's a good place for a camp," Fletcher said. "I don't think anybody in the company could have found a better one."

Haft grunted in reply, but the compliment pleased him.

They didn't have to wait long until the rest of the company came into view; already they heard the clop-clop of horses, and the creaking and rumbling of wagons following the horses.

CHAPTER
SIX

Four horsemen came first: Spinner led, Alyline rode at his side. Silent and Xundoe were close behind. They reined up next to Haft and Fletcher.

"All's quiet?" Spinner asked.

"Only birds and bears and lots of deer," Haft said. He decided not to mention the pug of cat or the feral dog pack, they weren't food and they didn't present a danger to the company. He looked to the side. "There's a glade right over there big enough for a bivouac. Complete with running water. The rest of the scouts," he shot a glance at Fletcher, "are making sure we're alone."

"Where's Wolf?"

Haft shrugged.

"Well, if there was danger nearby Wolf would have alerted you." Spinner looked into the trees where Haft had looked. "Can our wagons get through there?"

"If they go slowly," Fletcher said. "There's enough room between the trees."

"Then lead on."

Fletcher turned and led the way into the trees. Haft stayed by the road to make sure everybody followed. First came a squad of Skraglander Guards on foot, looking very fierce and unmilitary in their homespun, furs, and horned helmets. Next came the rest of the Zobran Border Warders, mounted, in their forest-blending uniforms, followed closely by a squad each of Zobran Royal Lancers and Prince's Swords in their differing blues, and a squad of Zobran Light Horse in yellow. The wagons carrying the small children and the company's goods trailed the Zobrans. Pisau and another Kondive sea soldier, along with a quartet of sea soldiers from the Easterlies—all soft-footed men—provided guard on the wagons. Other soldiers, mostly Skragland Guards and Borderers, walked in the forest as flank security for them. After the wagons came a motley of armed men, again mostly competent Skraglanders, and a few Bostians who managed to flee their country before it was completely overrun. The group included men who in the past had served in a number of armies and men who had never served under arms, but had become willing to do so. Bringing up the rear, Sergeant Phard led the two squads of Skraglander Bloody Axes in fur cloaks that bore the distinctive maroon stripes of their unit.

Soon enough, the company was in the bivouac. The animals and birds that called the glade home vacated in the face of the human invasion. Salt-licking and bloodsucking insects stayed, as did a few buzzing bees. The horses were cooled and watered, curried, put on tether lines, and fed. The women and children set about hearthing cook fires and gathering what few edibles were available in the clearing and the forest fringe. When the scouts came in to report that they'd found no sign of anybody in the area they brought carcasses with them, three deer and a wild boar. Everyone cheered at sight of the game. That night they would eat better than they had in more than a week. Women happily abandoned the small hearths they'd made in favor of the larger hearth pits the men dug to roast the game.

Spinner and Haft set out watch posts and sent Fletcher with several men downstream from the camp to dig privy trenches under the trees. Most of the soldiers had at first objected to the nonsense, their word, of digging latrines downstream away from camp. They didn't care what *Lord Gunny Says*, the legendary *Handbook for Sea Soldiers* of the Frangerian Marines, had to say about field sanitation. To the knowledge of most soldiers, books were written by people who hadn't done any of the things claimed in them. As time passed though, they couldn't deny that there was less illness in the company than among any similar number of soldiers with whom they'd ever traveled in the past. Some of them grudgingly admitted there might be something to what *Lord Gunny Says* had to say about making camp in the field.

The camp followers, mostly women and children, had grown to outnumber the men. Another peddler, too old and feeble to be of use as a soldier, had recently joined the company. He and the peddler who had been with the group guarded by the Royal Lancers were quite willing to trade some of the goods in their laden carts for food and protection—and the occasional copper or silver coin. Most of the people who joined them since the group guarded by the Royal Lancers were individual families: grandparents with their grandchildren, mothers with their many offspring and few husbands. Four unmarried women with their own brightly painted wagon had attached themselves to the company during the previous week. There were still more men without wives than women without husbands in the company, and the four women were glad to provide various wifely services to unwed soldiers in exchange for the protection the company provided. The wives were divided in their reaction to those four women—half were offended, half were glad their presence kept the unmarried soldiers from bothering them.

In short, the company was increasingly self-sufficient, at least for the time. Eventually, they'd need to find a village or town where they could replenish the few items that they couldn't make or repair themselves. They weren't at that point yet—not quite.

It wasn't long before the scent of roasting meat wafted through the campsite, while edible leaves, florets, and mushrooms simmered in pots, and tubers wrapped in wet leaves roasted in coals. The sun was down by the time the feast was ready to eat.

Pairs of older children were dispatched to the listening posts, one child with a brand to light the way, the other with a trencher piled with hot food for the soldiers on duty. Wolf rejoined the company as they began to feast and made his way from one group of diners to another, gleefully gobbling the chunks of meat they tossed to him.

At length everyone's hunger was sated; there was no rationing on this night. Fletcher and the Zobran Border Warders then set about jerking the remaining meat to carry with them on the morrow. Zweepee and Doli saw to the equitable division of the remaining food among all of the people. Then members of the company sat about the dying embers and told stories, or talked of what else they might find in the forest. When time came, Spinner and Haft sent soldiers to relieve those on watch. The fires burned down to little more than embers and the camp began to settle for the night, people drifting off to whatever bedding they had.

Spinner and Haft, and their original group of Alyline, Doli, Fletcher, Zweepee, Silent, and Xundoe—and Wolf—were the last still up, sitting at ease in the warm glow of a fire's embers.

"We've come far," Zweepee said from her comfortable place, tucked under her husband's protective arm.

"We have farther to go," Haft said.

"Maybe so, but now we're not just a few frightened, fleeing refugees; now we're with all these people."

"People who slow us down," Alyline said a bit sourly.

"People who we have responsibility for," Spinner said gently.

"It's nice to have all these people with us," Doli said. "All those *men*." Her eyes flashed at Spinner in hope that he would take the hint. He ignored her, she stuck her tongue out at him.

"They're on their own once we find a port," Haft said. He glanced at Doli from the corner of his eye. "Unless they want to board ship and go to Frangeria with us." She ignored him, but he hadn't expected any more positive response from her than she ever got from Spinner.

Zweepee shook her head and Fletcher gently squeezed her to warn her against saying anything. She smiled up at him and kept her peace.

Wolf tucked his face under his paws as though he didn't understand why those four kept this farce going. It seemed simple enough: They were two and two, why couldn't they simply sort it out and pair off?

"Do you think we'll find a port?" Fletcher asked.

"Oh, we'll find ports aplenty in the Princedons," Spinner said. "The question is, will any of them still be open and free."

"Certainly on the gulf side," Haft said, not that he was having second thoughts about heading toward the ocean side of the Princedon Peninsula.

"Maybe. But deep-sea ships are more likely to be on the ocean side."

Silent, for once, lived up to his name and said nothing. He had traveled farther on land than any of the others, and had even farther to travel before he finally returned to his home on the Northern Steppes. Especially if, as he thought he would, he boarded a great ship to cross the Inner Sea with Spinner and Haft. He'd heard the continent on the other side of the ocean was even larger than Nunimar, which was the only continent he'd seen. A bigger place was indeed a marvelous thing for a wandering nomad to see.

"It grows late, and we must be on the move in the morning," Fletcher said, removing his arm from Zweepee. He stood and helped her to her feet. They said their good-nights and moved away.

A soft snore told them Xundoe was already asleep. Silent stood, stretched, made sure that Spinner and Haft knew where his bedroll was in case they needed to wake him during the night, and went off. The others sat quietly for a time. Spinner kept looking hopefully at Alyline, who ignored him, Doli made eyes at Spinner, but he ignored them. Haft wondered *what's wrong with me?* Then Alyline rose and made to leave.

"I made a shelter big enough for two," Spinner said to her in quiet invitation. His lean-to, not far off, did look big enough for two—if they lay very close together.

"Mine is sufficient," she said tiredly and turned away. He stood watching sadly as she strode into the darkness toward the small lean-to she'd erected for herself.

Doli, sidled up to Spinner and stood watching the Golden Girl crawl into her small shelter. She stood just close enough for the side of her breast to touch his arm. "I have a proper tent now," she whispered. "You can lie in it with privacy." Unlike Alyline, she was anxious to show her appreciation for her rescue. Her heartbeat speeded.

Spinner grunted. "I had best sleep in the open so I can move fast if we are attacked in the night," he said in a gruff voice. He turned away without even glancing at Doli and stomped into the darkness.

Haft, as he often was at this hour, was very nearby. "Tent for two, my lean-to will hold two," he said loud enough for Doli to hear. "It's all the same to me." He looked toward a sudden sound of twigs and branches breaking and being kicked and saw her demolishing Spinner's lean-to. "Tent, lean-to, in the open, I don't care. Do you need an extra blanket, Doli?"

Doli shot him a piercing glance and sniffed. She flounced alone to her tent.

Haft stood up alone and shook his head. "Women," he said to himself. Doli wasn't at all willing to express her gratitude to him the way she was with Spinner, and he couldn't imagine why not. After all, he was equally responsible for her freedom. And, unlike Spinner, he expressed interest in accepting her gratitude. He looked to where Spinner had disappeared into the night and said softly, "I don't understand women at all, and Spinner understands them even less than I do." He shook his head again and headed alone to the smooth patch of ground that would serve for his sleeping place. Along the way he passed the tent Zweepee had erected for herself and Fletcher. She crouched just inside the open flap, watching silently.

Fletcher's voice floated to him from inside the tent, "Don't try to understand it, boy, just go with the flow."

Haft shivered, wrapped his cloak more tightly about himself, and hurried on.

Spinner stood at the edge of the glade, hands clenched at his side, his teeth grinding. What was *wrong* with that woman? She had changed so radically since that first night, her last night as a slave. *That* night, she had been so tender in his arms, so willing to accept him. He wouldn't take her as a slave, instead he promised he would free her—and he *did*! But ever since, she'd acted as though he was another master—one who she *wouldn't* serve. Anybody would think he'd stolen her from one durance vile to another. And that first night he hadn't even taken her, seductive and desirous though she'd been. So pliant that first night. And so, so—hateful—ever since. *Aaah!* He couldn't understand.

A large pebble lay near his foot; he swung a foot back to kick it, then stopped himself. The pebble might hit something and make too much noise if he kicked it, the camp would rouse to defend against a danger that wasn't there and he'd look the fool for having woken everyone. But he couldn't sleep, not with the Golden Girl so near. So near and so unwilling. But he had to do *something* since he couldn't sleep. He looked about and saw where he was. He took a few steps to a deer track that led from the glade and followed it into the forest, careful to make enough noise to alert the sentry he approached.

"Can't sleep?" asked the sentry, one of the veterans who'd joined the company, after they went through the recognition procedure.

"No." It was a strain, but Spinner said the word without grumbling. "You go get some sleep. I'll take your watch."

The sentry looked at him but couldn't make out Spinner's expression in the dark under the trees. "All right," he said, and told Spinner who his relief was.

Once he was alone, Spinner sat leaning against a tree trunk. He was motionless for several minutes except for his eyes that roved, studying the shadows to his front, memorizing their shapes and locations so if any changed or if new shapes or shadows appeared he would know. The night sounds slowly returned to normal after the sentry left, and Spinner set himself to knowing them as well—the sounds might change at the approach of an intruder. He had looked and listened so intently that he scrambled to his feet, quarterstaff ready, when he had no warning by sight or sound before a warm body bumped against his hip.

"Ulgh," Wolf said softly. He lay stretched out next to where Spinner had sat.

Spinner took a couple of deep breaths to calm his suddenly jangled nerves, then sat back down. He put his hand on Wolf's coarsely furred side and rubbed briskly. Wolf made a happy noise deep in his chest.

"Don't sneak up on me like that, Wolf. You gave me quite a start."

"Ulgh," Wolf replied in a curiously apologetic note.

Spinner shook his head; sometimes Wolf sounded entirely too much as though he were actually talking instead of making wolf noises.

He settled back comfortably against the tree and let his mind wander—Wolf wouldn't let anybody sneak up on them. What was wrong with that—

No!

He couldn't allow himself to think about the Golden Girl anymore tonight. Thinking about her was why he couldn't sleep. Thinking about her now would only madden him more. He wrenched his mind away from Alyline. Thoughts of the company leaped in to take her place.

He and Haft were very junior Frangerian Marines, all they were doing was trying to find a way back to Frangeria. How on earth had they become the commanders of a company of refugees that included isolated soldiers of many armies? Why were *they* in command? To be sure, there were no officers among the refugees, but there were several sergeants and corporals among the soldiers and other refugees who were veterans of various armies—even sea soldiers from two other countries. For that matter, more than half of the junior men among the soldiers and veterans had more experience than he and Haft. Why were *they* in command? The sergeants and corporals, *everyone,* readily accepted them as being in charge. *Why?*

The Frangerian Marines were reputed to have the best training of any military in the entire world. Still, everyone—their drill instructors in boot camp, their trainers in both infantry school and sea school, even Sergeant Rammer, their detachment commander on the *Sea Horse*—had drilled into them that all training did was prepare them for the real learning and knowledge that came only with experience. So why had so many more experienced soldiers accepted *them*, two very inexperienced Marines, as the commanders?

How could they lead? They didn't have the knowledge that only came with experience—their experience was too limited for them to automatically know what to do in too many situations. Too often they had to refer to *Lord Gunny Says*. Spinner was glad that he had thought to take his copy when he and Haft went back to the *Sea Horse* to salvage whatever equipment they could from under the noses of the conquering Jokapcul who held the ship.

So far the company had been lucky. Lucky was the only word Spinner could use to characterize the fact that they hadn't encountered any Jokapcul in more than a fortnight, that they hadn't run into even a full company since that fateful day when he and Haft and the six companions they'd had then first fought the invaders somewhere in Zobra.

But that luck couldn't hold. Most of the fighting men of the company as it was now constituted knew they could defeat small Jokapcul units; they'd done it. What would happen when they ran into a whole troop of Jokapcul light cavalry? What would happen when they had to fight Jokapcul who had demon spitters or other magical weapons?

The longer he thought about it the more his mind tied itself in knots, thinking about the *why* of command proved no more fruitful than thinking about the *what happened* of Alyline. He was more than glad when his relief came and broke his mental knot. Wolf stayed on post while Spinner returned to the campsite. He was so exhausted by then that he thought he would fall asleep instantly when he lay down.

"You were gone long enough." Alyline's voice swept away his sleepiness. Straining to see her, he turned, picked her out deep in the shadows.

"Alyline?" His voice cracked and he began to move toward her.

"Sit right there," she commanded, low but sharp.

He sat, staring at the blacker hump that was her in the shadows.

"We need to talk," she said so low voiced he barely heard her.

"Yes," he managed to say, and stopped because he was certain his voice would crack loudly if he tried to say more.

"You wonder what is wrong, why I won't have you."

He nodded, silently cursed himself when he realized she probably couldn't see the movement in the dark, croaked out, "Yes."

"I will tell you." He held his breath during the long pause while she decided how to start. "Spinner, I am a Djerwohl dancer. You don't understand what that means, do you? *Pfagh!* You lowlanders, you are so ignorant of your countrymen who live in the mountains." She was quiet for a time again.

"I will tell you what it means, Spinner. It means I dance. But it's more than that. Dancing is my *life*. I am nothing, I am nobody, if I do not dance. I cannot dance now."

"Yesyoucan!" He ran his words together for fear he couldn't say them otherwise.

"No I can't. You see, a Djerwohl dancer can only dance to one man's music. She and her sothar player are bonded when they begin their training. Any other player, no matter how skilled or talented, never sounds right. There are always differences between the music of your own sothar player and another. You cannot dance properly to someone else's music; it's impossible. The rhythms are different, the timing is subtly off.

"When you sent Mudjwohl away, you took my dancing."

"Who? Wha—?"

"Mudjwohl. Remember? My musician at The Burnt Man Inn. You sent him to Oskul City with the other freed slaves. You kept me without him. Do you remember how angry I was then? How I said you were kidnapping me?"

"I freed you from slavery!"

"Yes, you did. I was captured into slavery. I was forced to dance for rude men, crude men, men who could not truly appreciate my art. And the slavemaster sold my body to anyone who could meet his price. A man who bought my body for a night could do anything he wanted to me so long as he broke no bones, left no marks.

"It was a horrible life. But at least I could dance. When you sent Mudjwohl to Oskul with the others, you took my musician from me. I can no longer dance. You took my life from me. Do you wonder that I hate you?"

"But—"

"Spinner, I can never give myself to you. You freed me from slavery, for which I am grateful. But every time I see you, I remember how you took my dancing from me. How you took my life."

"Alyline, I never intended to cause you any harm. I would kill myself rather than harm you."

"You have a knife, you have a sword. Don't let me stop you." She rose and returned to her own shelter.

In the morning Spinner set the glade as the rally point, the place the company would regroup if it got separated, or where people would go to be found if they got lost. The glade wasn't a good rally point, as it wasn't a landmark that was easily seen from a distance, but in that part of the forest there weren't any landmarks that could be seen from a distance.

The company broke camp with the quickness of long practice and set out in the same order as the day before. Haft again took Archer, Hunter, and Birdwhistle ahead as scouts. Fletcher trailed them with Kocsokoz, Kovasch, and Meszaros. Only this time, Haft and his trio knew they were being backed up.

Wolf loped ahead. Nobody paid any attention to the bees that lazily looped through the air along with them.

THE PRINCEDONS

A Brief Investigation of the Curious Political Structure of That Agglomeration of SemiAutonomous Principalities Known Collectively as "The Princedons"

by Scholar Munch Mu'sk
Professor of Far Western Studies
University of the Great Rift
(excerpted from *The Proceedings of the Association of Anthropological Scholars of Obscure Cultures*, Vol. 58, No. 5)

Look for a moment at a map of Nunimar, the western continent. Rotate it so that north, rather than the more common east, is at the top. Now imagine, as many do on first seeing a map of Nunimar in this orientation, that it is a crude drawing of the head of a sperm whale. The long peninsula that runs west to east along its right bottom and resembles the slightly gaping jaw of that whale is the Princedon Peninsula.

In all the centuries of known history, indeed in all the millennia for which records of any sort exist, the Princedons have never been united into one nation state. Instead, the Princedons have always been city states of varying strength and duration, some having great control over the surrounding lands, some having control of virtually nothing beyond their own walls; which walls often were—and are sometimes still— low and weak. From time to time, one such city state might have strength enough that it could bring one or more neighboring city states under its control for a time, albeit that time is always brief, never extending much beyond the lifetime of the "prince" who subjugated the neighbor.

I put the title prince inside quotes in the previous sentence as, while that is the title most commonly used for the regents of the Princedon city states, various among their number have used the titles duke or earl, a few have declared themselves kings, and one (with ambitions generally thought of by scholars as extraordinarily grandiose) even called himself emperor.

The city states of the Princedons are almost all coastal. Those on the southern coast are in frequent contact with the rest of the two continents via the trading and military, mostly Frangerian, ships that ply the oceans and make port in them. For their livelihood those on the northern shore rely more heavily on fishing in the Princedon Gulf and have slightly less contact with the larger world.

Inland, matters are somewhat more problematic. The Princedon Mountains are a formidable range that forms the spine of the peninsula and, if we may indulge in understatement, restricts easy north-south movement. The multiplicity of towns and villages that fills the land between the coasts and the mountains claims allegiance, generally, to one or another of the city states, but such allegiance is normally quite fluid, and one town's patron city this year might next year be its archenemy. The fluidity of city-town and town-city loyalty is abetted by the historic failure of the city states to establish military garrisons in the hinterlands of their holdings.

That fluidity combined with the lack of military garrisons has, over the centuries, allowed the founding and growth of a number of fully independent settlements, some grand enough to be called towns. Although most such settlements rely on agriculture (farming, husbandry, or both) for their sustenance and even prosperity, some turn, by design or happenstance, to brigandry. Those brigand settlements send out heavily armed bands of men to prey upon travelers in the interior of the peninsula and even to attack and pillage other, more law-abiding towns and villages.

Due to the fact of the brigandish depredations on the highways and byways, those who must travel from place to place in the Princedons' interior most frequently do so in large, heavily armed troops. Hence, each settlement, be it village or town, has within its confines an inn far larger than one might reasonably expect in a village or town of its size.

Owing to the lack of garrisoning by the coastal city states, even the most peaceful and law-abiding settlements of the interior find it necessary to maintain armed forces of a size inconsistent with their own sizes; that is to say, small armies independent of the city states. The richness of the land allows the profligate expense of maintaining these small armies. The land is fertile for the growth and harvest of bountiful crops and for the husbandry of domestic food animals. Similarly, the forests that grow large between the settlements abound in flowering, leafy, and tuberous foodstuffs. Additionally, game animals are frequently plentiful in various locations. In addition to which, those settlements closest to the mountains ofttimes have access to the mineral wealth provided by mining.

Fortunately (or otherwise, as the case may be and ofttimes is) almost all of the "soldiers" of these independent settlements are part-time soldiers who normally make their livelihoods as farmers, husbandmen, tradesmen, craftsmen, or otherwise. Naturally, that means most are not the match of the well-trained and effective soldiers maintained by the city states of the Princedons or, indeed, any other proper state in the known world. The great majority of the defensive forces, however, do possess a cadre of experienced soldiers who have training and experience in the army of one or another of the Princedon city states or, with surprising frequency, a proper nation state from elsewhere in the known world. These cadres most generally consist of one or two officers and anywhere from one sergeant to three or four sergeants, though a few have no more than one properly trained and experienced sergeant as their cadre.

[Note, please, that the author wishes to imply no offense to sergeants in that last statement. Any more than the most cursory study of military matters and the history of warfare is sufficient to convince all but the most aristocratic that the fighting ability of any armed force relies more on its sergeants than on its officers. Whilst officers make strategy, draw plans, and provide for the arming, uniforming, supplying, and provisioning of armies, it is the sergeants who do the training and enforce discipline, without both of which no army can win any battle. (Note: The Jokapcul appear to be the sole exception to this rule. In the Jokapcul army, sergeants appear to be simply relayers of officers' orders.)]

There is, however, an ameliorating factor in the disunity of the Princedons. To wit, language. The city state of Penston, on the seaside of the root of the peninsula, some hundred miles east of Zobra City, speaks a dialect of Zobran. As one travels eastward from there, the language deviates more and more from its Zobran root until by the time one reaches Harfort, at the easternmost tip of the peninsula, the local tongue is hardly recognizable as being related to Zobran. The matter worsens along the gulf coast. As the natal Zobran influence of the local tongues lessens, the tongues are increasingly affected by the guttural language of the little-known denizens of the Low Desert to the north of the gulf, until at Dartsmutt, at the gulf-side root of the peninsula, the local tongue is almost a dialect of the little-known language of the Low Desert. (Some scholars, however, argue that the tongue spoken by the Low Desert nomads is, in fact, a dialect of the tongue spoken in Dartsmutt.) Inland, close to the spinal mountains, the local tongues follow a similar pattern, though they are frequently little related to their geographically nearest coastal neighbors. The local tongues drift as they move from coast to spine, so that in the middle they are mixes of the tongues spoken at the extremes. Thusly, communication between city states is difficult at best, and often problematic.

In these days, any paper on Nunimar requires a note on the practice of magic. The magics practiced in the interior of the Princedons are most commonly those practiced by healing witches and other healing practitioners. Magicians who control demon weapons, such as are said to be used by the nation states of southern Nunimar west of the Princedons, and to greater effect by the ravening Jokapcul from the Far West, are largely unknown in the Princedons, or if not unknown, in the main are unused; similarly, guardian demons are in minimal use, if used at all. Healing demons such as aralez and land trows are the only demons known to be in use.

In conclusion, the Princedons are an agglomeration of loosely affiliated but potentially wealthy city states that need merely to become affiliated less loosely and to clear out their native brigands in order to join the first rank of the known world's nation states.

—Correspondence; Not for Publication—
From the Editor
The Proceedings of the Association of
Anthropological Scholars of Obscure Cultures

Scholar Mu'sk,

It aggrieves me to see yet another paper from you written in a style so totally inappropriate for publication in a learned journal such as *The Proceedings*. As I have on innumerable occasions in the past when you have submitted such inappropriately worded papers, I struggled with the jury to get this paper past the peer review process to acceptance. You are, when all is taken into proper consideration, a preeminent scholar in Far Western Studies, and held in general high esteem. In selecting this paper for publication, however, I had to go considerably beyond what is considered proper editorial influence. So far beyond, that my position as editor of this scholarly journal has been threatened.

I am required, albeit reluctantly and with less than full enthusiasm, to inform you that should you submit another paper written in anything other than a proper scholarly style, I shall be compelled to return it to you forthwith without submitting it to peer review.

Munch, kindly forgive the tone of the preceding paragraphs. Our friendship and mutual respect have entirely too long a history for me to speak, or write I should say, to you with such disrespect. But I am under a great deal of pressure to raise the tone of *The Proceedings* to the highest levels of scholarship. To that end, I *cannot* accept another paper from you written in the popular style you have recently adopted in many of your papers; to do so could well cost me my position as editor.

In friendship,
Klules

II
THE TOWN

CHAPTER
SEVEN

They progressed only a few miles from the bivouac before the character of the land and the life it nourished began to change. From an imperceptible downward slope, the ground began to ripple easily upward toward the spine of the peninsula, and a rocky substrate broke the surface in places. The canopy trees thinned out to competition from shorter trees whose major branches sprouted lower on their trunks, whose boles split and split again until the leaves formed a bloomlike ball. Direct sunlight reached the ground, allowing an undergrowth of bushes, weeds, and flowers. Animate life changed along with the landscape. Butterflies displaced many of the salt-lickers and bloodsuckers under the canopy. There were more bees than before. Tracks of wild goat mixed in with those of deer. Rabbits scampered from the approaching men, foxes peered at them from behind screens of grass. Ground birds hunkered under brambles. Somewhere an elk bugled and was answered.

Following the changing lay of the land, the road wound about more than before, went around rather than over the higher or steeper groundswells. In places the roadway had been cut into a rise rather than climb over its top. On the approach to one such cut, Haft began hearing the muted clops of walking horses, the tree dulled jangle of tackle. The sounds echoed in the trees, making it difficult to tell their direction. He whistled to get Birdwhistle's attention, then angled toward the road. When he reached it he listened. The sounds came from the front, ahead of them. He signaled Birdwhistle, then darted across the road where he found Archer coming his way. Unlike Spinner, Haft had no questions or qualms about his right to command.

"Horsemen," Archer said. "They came across our front and turned onto the road."

"How many? Who are they? Jokapcul?"

Archer shook his head. "We weren't close enough to see. It sounded like a squad. They didn't talk, so we heard no language."

Haft thought for a moment. They needed to know the identity of those people; they also needed to remain unseen until they found out. "Could you tell how fast are they going?"

"A slow walk."

"All right. Maintain contact, but keep your distance. Don't let them see you. Send Hunter back to tell Fletcher to close up with us."

Archer nodded. "Right." He turned into the forest to find Hunter.

Haft dashed back across the road and looked for Birdwhistle. He saw him not far away and headed for him, then spun toward a shadow that darted through the trees ahead of him. He whistled to alert Birdwhistle, and lowered himself to a knee with his crossbow at his shoulder, sighting along it toward where he saw the fleeting shadow.

A shape leaped out of the shadows and bounded toward him, it twisted in time to evade the quarrel he fired at it and was on him, grinning jaws clamped on his right sleeve, before he could draw his axe. It was Wolf.

Haft jerked his sleeve from the animal's mouth and glared at him as he rearmed his crossbow. "One of these days, Wolf," he snarled, "you're going to do that but I'll be faster. That'll end your games."

He half expected Wolf to snort and vigorously shake his head as he usually did when Haft made such remarks, but the wolf didn't. Instead, he looked at Haft expectantly.

Haft looked toward Birdwhistle. The scout was watching them intently and angling closer. He signaled him and Birdwhistle came straight over.

"A squad crossed Archer and Hunter's front," he said when

the Zobran reached him. "They weren't close enough to see who they were. I sent Hunter back to bring Fletcher and his men up. Now I want to find out who those people are." He looked in the direction from which Wolf had come and saw the ground rise in a nubbin of hill. "They're beyond that rise somewhere."

When he said that, Wolf grabbed his left sleeve and pulled hard enough that Haft had a choice of going with him or being pulled off his feet.

"Whoa, what are you doing?" he growled.

"*Ulgh,*" Wolf growled deep in his throat, and jerked Haft's sleeve again.

"I think he wants to show you something," Birdwhistle said softly.

"Nonsense!" Haft snapped. "Let go," he ordered Wolf. The wolf let go, but kept looking at him expectantly.

"I had a dog acted like that once. Let's see what he wants. Maybe he saw them and wants to show us."

"*Ulgh,*" Wolf said, and bobbed his head up and down.

Grumbling quietly, Haft let Wolf lead him. Wolf kept his head and shoulders low. Without conscious thought, Haft followed his example. They ran at an angle away from the road, around the rising ground. The sound of the horses dimmed almost to inaudibility.

A streambed with a mere trickle of water in its bottom cut through the forest floor and meandered toward the farther end of the high ground. It was deep enough for them to stand slightly crouched and not be seen. Wolf led them into it and followed the watercourse for a short distance, closer to the rise, before he stopped and looked at Haft. They could again hear the clopping and jangling of the horses. The wolf bellied down and began to climb the bank. Haft started to stretch fully erect to look over the top of the bank, but Wolf grabbed his sleeve and pulled him back down.

Haft looked at him oddly for a couple of seconds, then said softly, "All right, I'll do it your way."

Wolf immediately let go.

Crouched below the lip of the streambed, Haft leaned onto

it and slithered up its side until he could peer over the top. He dropped right back down.

"Bandits," he whispered to Birdwhistle. The armed men he saw lying in watch over the road in his quick look probably weren't soldiers; they weren't dressed uniformly, nor did they carry the same arms. More carefully than before, he looked over the bank again. A dozen or more men lay on the slope of the rise where they couldn't be seen from the road. They weren't lying relaxed; they were alert and armed with a variety of short bows and swords, positioned to jump to their feet and rain arrows down onto the road from their higher vantage. The horses on the road were closer now, nearing the ambush's killing zone. He twisted to his right at another sound and brought his crossbow to bear. He let go of the trigger just in time to avoid shooting the Skragland Borderer named Kovasch. Meszaros was right behind him.

Haft resisted the impulse to snap at them for sneaking up on him. "Bandits," he said softly.

Kovasch nodded. He and Meszaros stayed hunched below the top of the bank and waited for instructions.

Haft rose back up. What should they do? He didn't know who the horsemen were. If they were Jokapcul, he should leave the ambush alone and let the bandits kill the enemy. But what if they weren't? They hadn't seen any sign of Jokapcul in several days; there was an excellent chance the company was still ahead of the invaders—especially inland on the peninsula. It was more likely the horsemen were refugees, in which case they should help them. But how? Four men and a wolf. What could they do against the dozen ambushers he could see? Worse, how many more bandits were there that he couldn't see? The best he could hope for if he simply called out a warning was the bandits would run and all of them would get away. Even that best wasn't very good—the bandits would all be free to attack them or other travelers another time. Yet the odds were too great for him and his few men and the wolf to attack directly.

He heard the horses almost directly to his front now and saw the bandits ready themselves, the ambush was about to be sprung. He had to do something. A passage from *Lord Gunny Says* came to his mind; *When you are in doubt as to the best course of action, choose one and follow it decisively. Inactivity when action is required is the worst enemy of the warrior. Any action, taken decisively, is better than no action.*

He made a decision and dropped back down.

"There's at least a dozen of them," he said. "There might be more I can't see. We need to even the odds right away." He took inventory of his men's weapons as he talked. Birdwhistle and Meszaros carried short bows, only Kovasch had the more powerful, more accurate longbow. It didn't matter, they were close enough the short bows could hardly miss. "Wolf, go that way," he pointed along the streambed. "When you reach the far side of the ambush, attack the man at that end." He felt stupid giving the wolf instructions, but sometimes—usually, though he didn't like to admit it—the beast seemed to understand.

Wolf gave Haft a look that, had he been a man, Haft would have interpreted it as, "Are you crazy? And what are *you* going to be doing while I run the suicide mission?"

"We," he addressed the men, "will wait for Wolf to attack. The instant he does, we shoot the four men on the right side of their line. With any luck, the rest of them will be so distracted by Wolf's attack, they won't notice right away and we can charge and hit them from the rear."

Wolf nodded, seeming satisfied that he wasn't being sacrificed, and sprinted up the streambed.

Haft kept giving instructions as he watched Wolf head for his part of the attack. "Kovasch, you've got the best bow. Put a couple more arrows into them while the rest of us charge. Questions?"

The three looked at him grimly; they understood the need for this desperate action.

"Let's get up and get ready. See where you are in our line. Meszaros, you're on our right side, take the man farthest to the right. Everybody else follow suit. Got it?"

They nodded. Haft slithered back to the bank top. He looked to his sides before drawing his axe and laying it on the ground where he could grab it as soon as he fired; he ignored the bee that briefly crawled on his cheek before buzzing off. The three scouts were readying their bows. Kovasch laid out three extra arrows. Haft aimed his crossbow and waited for Wolf's assault. Before Wolf reached the end of the ambush line, the people riding on the road fully entered the killing zone. Someone shouted a command and the ambushers rose to their knees and fired arrows. Shouts came from the road, commands and screams.

Without hesitating, Haft fired. He had his axe in his hand and was on his feet racing forward before the quarrel hit its target. Birdwhistle and Meszaros were with him. He heard screaming from the distance, Wolf's attack on the other end of the line. An arrow from Kovasch's bow *zing*ed past, rapidly followed by two more. Then they were on the ambushers.

Haft swung his axe in a mighty overhead arc and buried its half-moon blade in the back of a man who was looking toward the commotion to his left. He saw Birdwhistle race past and thrust with his sword to skewer the next man in line. Meszaros was right behind him and chopped through the neck of the next. Haft dashed toward the next ambusher. That man heard the footsteps coming toward him and turned to look, but it was too late, Haft was already on him and his swinging axe clove its way deep from the bandit's shoulder into his chest before the bandit could reach his feet—but not before he cried out a warning. Other ambushers looked back and shouted surprise and anger at the attacking quartet. They leaped up to counterattack.

Suddenly, uniformed men rushed up the slope from the road, swords in hand. The newcomers saw Birdwhistle's uniform and recognized it instantly—its fur and helmet were very similar to their own. They attacked the men Birdwhistle and his three companions were fighting.

Haft was distantly aware that the screams and shouts from the far end of the ambush had lessened. He wondered fleetingly how many men they were attacking; if it was only the dozen or so he'd seen the fight should be over already with the reinforcements they suddenly had. But it wasn't, there were still too many bandits. Three charging bandits, one armed with a pike, came at him.

Haft swerved to the side, avoiding the thrust of the pike and moved inside the arc of its swing. He swung his axe, chopping into the side of the pikeman. On his backstroke he sunk the spike on the back of the half-moon blade into the shoulder of one of the other attackers, knocking him down screaming. He wanted to look to see how his men were doing, but didn't have time—each of the two bandits he'd downed was immediately replaced by two more. He backpedaled rapidly to keep them from surrounding him. One of them used his sword to block a swing of the axe, but the blow shattered the blade. The bandit dropped the useless hilt and picked up the pike. He steadied himself and felt the balance of the long weapon, then lunged forward and thrust its point at Haft. Haft barely had time to see the strike coming. He reached out and hooked one of the others with the corner of his axe blade and yanked him into the path of the oncoming pike. The pike's long, steel point went all the way through the bandit's body. The mortally wounded man screamed three times— when the axe point hooked him; when the pike's head burst through the front of his body; when Haft twisted the axe to turn him and throw his body to the ground. The pike tore out of its wielder's hands, its shaft slammed into the legs of another man and knocked him off his feet.

For the moment, Haft only faced two men armed and on their feet. He roared a battle cry and leaped toward one, swinging his axe in a diagonal arc. The mighty blade severed the bandit's arm and thunked into his side—he toppled, dying. Before Haft could turn to the other, the man who'd been knocked down by the pike shaft was back on his feet and charging in with his sword arm cocked for a swing; the disarmed bandit had a fresh sword in his hand and was shouting instructions to the other two. The charging bandit skidded to a halt before he got close enough for Haft to strike at him. The one who shouted orders moved slowly, methodically, toward Haft, the other two just as methodically moved to the sides to come at him from different directions.

Haft backed up to keep them from reaching his sides but his heel caught on a root and he staggered, windmilling to regain his balance. The center bandit cried out in glee and rushed in to drive his sword into him, but the weight of the axe at the end of Haft's right arm twirled him back and to his right, the sword merely grazing his abdomen. The bandit to Haft's right rushed in at almost the same instant, but Haft's swinging axe smacked into the point of his extended sword and deflected the blow. Knocked farther off balance, Haft fell heavily. Now the third bandit rushed in, sword high above his head, ready to swing down.

Before he began to swing his sword forward and down, an arrow thudded into his chest. His mouth opened to scream, but all that came out was a gout of blood. He dropped the sword and clutched at the shaft protruding from his chest, staggered forward until he tripped over Haft and fell flat on his face. His body shielded Haft from sword blows from the other two. Then a second bandit fell with an arrow through his neck, and the other was fleeing.

Fletcher and the other three scouts had arrived. Spinner, Silent, and Xundoe were right behind them. All except the mage fired arrows after the fleeing bandits and knocked down several of them—but the panicked bandits were running so fast that Spinner had time to get off only one bolt from his crossbow before they disappeared through the trees.

"After them!" Haft shouted. He sprinted into the trees where the bandits had vanished. The other dismounted scouts and the men the bandits had ambushed raced with him. The two mounted warriors and the mage galloped through their ragged line.

Though the bandits were out of sight, their voices were clearly audible. So were the jangle and the creak of tackle as they clambered onto concealed horses, the thud of hooves as they sped away. Silent broke into a small clearing where bandits were still mounting their horses. His war cry boomed and echoed off the trees as he crashed into the bandits, swinging his sword. Several went down immediately then Xundoe screamed "Back!" at the steppe nomad. Bouncing on his pony, the mage fumbled a phoenix egg from a sack carried over the crown of his saddle. Silent saw what he was doing and kneed his horse into a leap to the side. The maneuver bowled over several bandits and horses.

With one hand the mage pulled on his pony's reins. The pony skittered to a stop, almost throwing the mage over its shoulder. Xundoe retained enough balance to turn his movement into a clean dismount, looked to see where the most bandits were, planted his feet, twisted the top of the phoenix egg, and threw it.

The egg struck the ground under a horse leaping away from the fray and cracked open. The phoenix burst forth and unfurled its flaming wings. Men and horses screamed as the fiery bird's wings and the heat of its flames beat into them.

Spinner quickly shouted "Hold!" when he saw Xundoe throw the phoenix egg. He jerked on his reins and twisted around to see that his order was being obeyed. Not even Haft or Silent looked anxious to pursue the bandits through the fire and ash left by the phoenix as it rose through the trees.

"Is everyone all right?" Spinner called. "Where's Wolf?"

He heard Haft and Fletcher checking their men. A throaty *Ulgh* from the side told him Wolf was well.

"Who are you?" he asked one of the men in the uniform of the Skragland Blood Swords.

CHAPTER
EIGHT

"I am Captain Dumant of the Skragland Blood Swords," said one. He was a big man, even by Skraglander measure. His shirt and breeches, though of the same design and cut, were of far finer woven cloth than other Skragland soldiers Spinner and Haft had met. His fur cape, like those of his men, was dyed a deep red. The chain that secured it around his neck was silver, as was a medallion on his chest. He carried a bastard sword, too big for most men to comfortably use one-handed, not quite big enough to be a two hand sword; he was big enough to wield it one-handed. "Who are you?" He quickly glanced at the men who had broken the ambush. "Skragland Borderers, Zobran Royal Lancers and Border Warders, and, and—Frangerian Sea Soldiers?"

"We prefer to be called 'Marines,' " Haft said.

"Call us 'armed refugees,' " Spinner said before Captain Dumant could react to Haft. "They call me Spinner. Haft," he nodded toward his friend, "and I are trying to find an open port and a ship back to Frangeria."

"All these soldiers," Dumant mused. "Where are your officers?" Dumant looked about.

"We are the commanders," Haft said.

Dumant looked at him curiously. He'd never met any Frangerian sea soldiers, not even before they began calling themselves "Marines," but he had seen color engravings. These two Frangerians had silver mermen on their cloaks rather than the gold worn by the officers, and their jerkins didn't have the gilt rank insignia so evident in the engravings.

"We don't actually have any officers," Spinner put in quickly. "These—"

"Then I'm in command here," Dumant cut him off. "Put people to caring for the wounded. Gather the dead in one place. I want a roll of everyo—"

"Excuse me, Captain," Spinner interrupted him before Haft could speak again, "the dead and wounded are already being taken care of. And, with all due respect, the Skragland army is not in our chain of command. We," he indicated himself and Haft, "are not under your command. As I said, Haft and I are making our way back to our own command."

Dumant, much taller than Spinner, used his greater height to overwhelm them. Or he tried to. "I recognize your uniform," he said. "I've seen engravings of Frangerian sea soldiers. Your uniforms and insignia indicate that you're junior enlisted men. You say you have no officers. I am a captain. That puts me in command, I don't want to hear you arguing that point. You say you are trying to make your way back to your own command. How do I know you aren't craven deserters who have turned to banditry? As senior officer present, I am in command, and you are under my command. Take care I don't have cause to discipline you for insubordination."

"Now listen here," Haft said heatedly, but Fletcher cut him off.

"Sir, with all due respect, we are not in your army, Captain," Fletcher spoke calmly but firmly. "Nor are any of us deserters. These two," he nodded toward the two Frangerians, "are survivors of the Jokapcul capture of New Bally, and they truly are seeking a way back to their own command. These people you see all around here, including the soldiers, some of whom are sergeants in their own armies, have chosen to accompany these Marines to a place where they might find safety. Perhaps you can claim command of the Skragland soldiers among us, but I don't think you can assume command of the Zobrans or other soldiers. You most certainly cannot simply assume command of me and the other veterans who are no longer members of any army. Please disabuse yourself of the notion that all of us are under your command."

Dumant sputtered, then snapped, "You are under arrest!" He turned to his men. "Take the arms of these three." The seven Blood Swords who had gathered around him moved hesitantly to obey, checked when they saw Zobrans and other men, armed but without uniforms, gather close to the two Marines and put their hands on their weapons.

"That's not a good idea, Captain," Silent said. He had quietly come up behind the Skragland officer during the conversation and now placed a huge hand on his shoulder. As big as Dumant was, he was almost dwarfed by the steppe giant. The big hand pressed down hard enough on Dumant's shoulder that his knees almost buckled. "You see, it's like this. You're a Skragger. You fought the Jokaps and you lost. If you'd won, you wouldn't be here in the Princedons with only one squad. Them there two Frangerian Marines? First thing they did was they were the only ones to escape from a city taken by the Jokap invasion. Next, they single-handedly took on and killed a squad of Jokap light cavalry. If that wasn't enough, all by themselves, they freed a whole lot of slaves held by a Jokap slavemaster. Then, with me and a couple other folks, they fought and killed a whole Jokap troop. They've fought Jokaps other times, too, and they've beaten them every time they fought. That's why these other folks joined up with them—they win. On top of that, they've got themselves a war wizard—you saw the phoenix egg. Now what do you have to compare with that? You've got seven soldiers who fought the Jokaps and lost, that's what. That little bitty one?" He pointed at Haft, who glared back—Haft might be slightly less than average height, but he wasn't "little bitty." "He's the one who led three other men in the counterattack that broke up the bandit ambush that would have killed you and all of your men. Think about that, then tell me who you think should be in command here."

Dumant thought about it, but not for long. There were at least two dozen men arrayed against his seven, and the two dozen looked very professional, all of them carried their weapons like men who knew how to use them. And no man's hand should weigh as heavily on his shoulder as the giant nomad's did.

"All right, go your way," Dumant said with little grace. "You Skraglanders," he looked at Kocsokoz and the other Borderers. "You're wearing the uniform, that means you are still in the Skragland army. Form up with my Blood Swords. We will leave this rabble. Are there any others? You there!" Some yards away he saw Sergeant Phard of the Skragland Bloody Axes coming toward them. "Report!"

"Sir!" Pfard came to attention in front of the Blood Sword officer. "Sergeant Phard, Bloody Axes."

"Are there any more of you?"

"I have two squads, Captain."

"Two squads? Good. Are you the ranking Skragland sergeant?"

"Yessir."

"Fine, you're my second in command. Assemble your squads over there with my Blood Swords and these Borderers. You're back in the Skragland army." Dumant smiled. With the addition of the Borderers and two squads of Bloody Axes, he would put a quick end to the insubordination here. He didn't notice the bemused expressions the Borderers turned on him.

"Sir, under normal circumstance I would be honored to do so," Pfard said calmly.

"What? I don't care what the circumstances are. Do it. That's an order, Sergeant."

"Begging the captain's pardon, but Sir Haft bears the Rampant Eagle on his axe. I and my Bloody Axes have sworn allegiance to him."

Dumant gaped at him. "Sergeant, do you know what you are doing?" he asked in a low, threatening voice.

"Yessir. The Bloody Axes have always followed the Rampant Eagle."

"The Rampant Eagle is a myth, Sergeant!" Dumant screamed, his spittle sprayed Phard's face. "Now do as you are ordered, or you'll hang for mutiny!"

The sergeant's face darkened, though his voice remained

calm. "Sir, the Rampant Eagle has led the Bloody Axes to the salvation of Skragland in the past. It will do so again. We follow it."

Before Dumant could speak, Silent leaned on his shoulder again.

"You aren't in Skragland now, Captain," the heavy-handed giant said. "And none of the Skraglanders in this company are Blood Swords. If they were, then you'd have an argument that they belonged under your command, but there aren't any." He looked around at the Skraglanders, all of whom were now close and observing. "Do any of you want to go with this man?"

The Skraglanders looked at one another—except for the Bloody Axes, who had already lined up in formation behind Haft. Almost as if obeying an order, the rest of the Skraglanders fell into formation with Sergeant Phard's men.

Haft stood erect, looking firm, concealing his thoughts. There it was again, the eagle on the half-moon blade of his axe. Whatever it meant, he wasn't about to let anyone realize that he didn't know.

Phard looked at Haft and the men behind him, then back to Dumant. "Sir, it looks to me like all the Skraglanders here except your Blood Swords have joined the Bloody Axes."

Dumant looked at him, stunned by their blatant mutiny. His face turned so red it was almost purple, his hands clenched and unclenched, and his whole body seemed to vibrate. He took two or three deep breaths to get himself back under control.

"That's mutiny," he snarled at Phard. "I'll remember you and these other mutineers. You will answer for it when this war is over." He spun on his heel and signaled his squad to follow. The seven Blood Swords looked nervously at the other Skraglanders, then turned and followed their commander.

"What about your wounded?" Spinner called after them.

The Blood Swords stopped. One of them said something to Dumant. The officer spun on him. He and the one who had spoken exchanged heated words, not quite loud enough to be understood by anyone more than several yards from their group, then the one who questioned the captain turned his back on the officer and headed back to the Frangerians and their comrades. The other Blood Swords looked at each other, glanced at their captain, then followed the first.

"I'm Corporal Maetog, sir," the one who had spoken to Dumant said as he stepped up to Spinner and Haft and saluted. "I will see to our casualties." He saw the others join him. "And we'll be glad to join your company if you'll have us." He looked to Sergeant Phard. "We'll join the Bloody Axes if the sergeant thinks we're good enough."

"We're glad to have you aboard, Corporal Maetog," Spinner said. He turned to the Bloody Axes. "Sergeant Phard. Front and center."

"Gladly, sir," Sergeant Phard said and marched briskly to face him and Haft. He wasn't as big as the departed Captain Dumant, but was still big, even for a Skraglander.

"Corporal Maetog, this is Sergeant Phard," Spinner said in broken Skraglandish. "He's the ranking Skraglander in this company. For now, put yourself and your squad under his command."

The two Skraglanders looked each other over and each recognized in the other a worthy leader of fighting men.

"Welcome, Corporal. I'm glad to have you and your men with us," Phard said.

"I believe we'll prove ourselves worthy, Sergeant."

"Over here, I'll introduce you to the rest of the men." Phard led the Blood Swords to where the Skraglanders waited to welcome them.

Spinner watched them go, then turned to Fletcher with a look that asked why us?

Fletcher understood the look and shook his head. "Because no one else is willing to accept the responsibility?"

"Twenty?" Alyline screamed in Haft's face. "You attacked twenty men with only four of you and the wolf?"

Haft mumbled something.

"What did you say?" Alyline clenched her fists at her sides and leaned forward threateningly.

"I said 'I thought there were only twelve,' " Haft said a little louder.

"Only twelve?" she shrilled into his face.

"There were at least forty," Spinner said. Haft and Alyline started, neither had noticed him come up.

Alyline spun back at Haft. "Forty?" she shrieked. "Forty? You attacked forty bandits with only three scouts and Wolf?"

Haft had enough. He might be somewhat shorter than average, but he was still a bit taller than the Golden Girl. He jammed his face close to hers and rose onto his toes to increase his height advantage. "What should I have done?" he shouted. "Should I have left them unmolested to kill those Skraglanders and then ambush you?"

Alyline rose to her toes to counter Haft's movement. She began on him again, but her scream cut to a shocked squawk as her feet totally lifted off the ground and she was twirled about—Spinner had wrapped his arms around her from behind and turned away from Haft. He set her down facing away from Haft.

Then he made a mistake—he opened his arms and let her go.

The Golden Girl spun on him with her mouth opened indignantly. She swung her arm with the force of her spin and slapped Spinner's face so hard the blow rocked him and its report was heard by all the nearby soldiers.

"You touched me!" she shrilled. "How dare you touch me! When I was a slave, any man who could meet the slave-master's price could touch me. Now no one, not even you, may touch me without my leave! I don't give you leave." She swung at him again, but Spinner grabbed her wrist before her hand reached his stinging face—he was certain his cheek was already red and would soon turn livid.

"Haft did the right thing," he said softly, the only way he could speak to her. "He had to attack the bandits, he had no time to wait for us."

"But he and the scouts might have been killed!"

Haft cocked an eyebrow. "I didn't know you cared about

what happened to me," he said, careful to keep his voice low enough she wouldn't hear.

"And you could have been killed if he hadn't." Spinner looked at her sternly. Or tried to, anyway.

"But . . ."

"Enough of this nonsense," Zweepee said. She deliberately brushed by close enough to bump Alyline. "We need to attend to the wounded."

"Wounded?" The Golden Girl looked beyond Spinner to Haft and saw the bloodstain on the front of his shirt. Her eyes darted to the others who had attacked the bandit ambush. Hunter, Birdwhistle, Kovasch, and Meszaros were also bleeding.

"See!" she shrilled, but stopped berating Spinner and Haft. She caught up with Zweepee. "Give me some bandages," she said gruffly. She took the bandages Zweepee shoved at her and turned to tend Birdwhistle's wounded arm.

"Lie down," Zweepee told Haft.

"It's nothing," Haft protested, holding a hand over the gash in his belly. "Bandage someone else first."

Just that fast, Fletcher was standing over him. "When my wife tells you to lay down so she can tend your wound, you lay down," he rumbled in a much deeper voice than he normally used.

Haft looked up at him—Fletcher was taller than Spinner, who was taller than Haft. "You know, you're lucky I'm wounded. If I wasn't already bleeding, I'd break you across my knee for talking to me like that."

Fletcher laughed. "Lay down and let Zweepee take care of your wound."

Haft looked down when his sleeve was tugged. "Not you, too," he growled. Wolf looked up at him around the sleeve he gripped in his mouth and growled back at him. He tugged again.

Zweepee, a tiny woman, reached her hands up to Haft's shoulders and pressed. "Lie down like a good boy and let me take care of your wound," she said in the kind of voice a mother uses when tending a young child's boo-boo.

Haft rolled his eyes, but lay down on the ground. Several bees buzzed about the wounded, as though examining the wounds to see if they held nectar.

Fortunately, most of the wounds were minor though two Blood Swords were dead and space had to be made on a wagon for two others injured too badly to walk. It wasn't long before the company was on the move once more. The same quartets as before scouted ahead. Captain Dumant of the Blood Swords was nowhere to be seen, unlike his seven men who were clearly happy to be added to the company.

Some time later, Haft became aware of voices coming from the road.

"Why are we stopping?" he heard Alyline demand, her voice was almost shrill.

"Because we're moving faster than the scouts and we caught up with them," Spinner replied softly, his voice straining for patience. "The scouts have to stay ahead of us if they're to do any good."

"*Pfagh,* they aren't doing any good now. Look at Wolf."

Wolf yipped, and jumped in stiff-legged play in the middle of the road some twenty yards ahead of them.

"See? He's already scouted ahead, he says it's safe." She trotted forward and leaned low in the saddle to scratch Wolf behind his ears. Wolf whined in pleasure.

Spinner muttered something Haft couldn't make out from his position off the road, then called out, "Scouts in."

Haft swore softly. It wasn't that he mistrusted Wolf, it was more that he didn't fully trust the animal. How could a wolf truly know what presented a threat to a human party? Besides, he couldn't forget that wolves are dangerous animals.

He spun to level his crossbow at the sound of a branch snapping in an unexpected direction, swore again when he saw Kovasch and Meszaros walking toward him through the forest.

"You've got to stop sneaking up on me," he snapped. "Or one of these days I'll shoot before I know who you are."

"We trust your quickness of sight," Kovasch said with a barely contained smile.

"As much noise as you're making, anybody in a mile would know you're coming, then I'd have to save you."

The former poachers exchanged glances, Meszaros offended, Kovasch amused. They'd gotten awfully close to Haft before the Frangerian Marine had heard them.

"Mount up," Spinner told the scouts when they all reached the road. He turned his head slightly so they couldn't see the lingering imprint of Alyline's hand on his cheek. "We'll go faster if everybody's riding."

"Someone can still come in on our flanks. The rest of those bandits are out there somewhere," Haft replied as he hesitantly mounted the docile mare that had been his since weeks before when they left the border between Bostia and Skragland. He heeled his horse and pulled on her reins then trotted off the road. Birdwhistle followed at his signal. Meszaros and Kovasch joined them when Fletcher nodded at him. Fletcher himself led Kocsokoz, Hunter, and Archer off the right side of the road.

"Ulgh!" Wolf whined, shaking his head. He looked indignantly up at Spinner, as though in complaint that nobody wanted to believe him. *"Ulgh,"* he said more firmly and began loping down the road, head held unnaturally high. He looked for all the world like he was showing them the road was so safe they could simply walk along it without even bothering to watch where they were stepping.

Spinner shook his head at the wolf. Before leading the column on, he called to the two quartets of scouts, "Find food!"

Two miles along, the main party caught up with Wolf where he lounged in the middle of the road, watching over a pile of rabbits and a brace of pheasants. On one side of the road, Fletcher lay back against a boar that Archer and Kocsokoz had helped him bring down. On the other side of the road Haft, Kovasch, and Birdwhistle were gutting and skinning a stag, two does, and a fawn they'd killed.

"We eat well tonight!" Alyline exclaimed. She spun her

stallion about and cantered back to the camp followers to organize them in setting up firepits over which to roast their plenty.

"Not until we find a bivouac for the night," Spinner called after her.

Haft sidled his mare up to Spinner. "May as well bivouac here," he grumbled. "You know that women never listens to you." He spat to the side. "Damn woman never listens to anyone."

Spinner shot Haft a pained glance. He really didn't want to be reminded of how little attention the Golden Girl paid him. As coldly as she treated him, nobody would ever guess he was the one who had rescued her from a most horrible slavery. He really hadn't understood how important her dancing was to her—and how essential her own sothar player was to the dance.

CHAPTER
NINE

Yellow shafts of sunlight spiked through breaks in the tree cover as the middle of the following day found the company only four miles beyond the night's bivouac. Birds sang and darted from place to place in the canopy. Insects buzzed and flitted about, some drinking fluids from the passersby. Bees trailed them. Basking lizards froze in position and held their ground in imagined invisibility.

Scouts were sent out the same as on the days before, but the only danger they found was the danger they presented to the forest's animals. The scouts bagged three dozen quail, an elk, and five deer. Not to mention the rabbits and squirrels Wolf added to the harvest when he wasn't ranging ahead or far to the flanks. Movement was slowed enough by the hunting that many of the women and children foraged along the way, joking, laughing, and singing as they went. Fletcher began calculating how soon he should call a stop to the hunting; it wouldn't do to continue to take so many animals; they wouldn't have time to dry all the meat before it started going bad. Nor should they take so many that the animals would learn to flee at first sign of men.

Spinner was also concerned about the slow pace. The time needed to preserve the meat didn't occur to him, though he did wonder at how easy the hunting was—it was as if these animals didn't know about hunters and weren't afraid of man. His concern was the need to find a town or village. Zweepee had told him the band was almost out of thread and needles, and other supplies they couldn't easily make themselves were running low. Except for those few items the company already had in good supply, the peddlers had already sold all of their most useful goods to members of the band. The slower their travel, the longer it would take to find a town, and the more things they'd run out of. For the first time, Spinner understood the emphasis *Lord Gunny Says* put on logistics, a topic to which he'd never before paid any attention.

Haft's thought processes were much more direct and immediate. Game's ready to be caught? Catch it and eat it. Is this a road? Roads lead to villages and towns; don't worry about it; we'll reach one sooner or later. In the meantime it's a fine day, game is plentiful, there's just enough breeze to blow off the light sweat raised by the exertion of walking, the insects aren't too bothersome and there isn't a bandit or Jokapcul to be found. So just relax. Stay watchful in case bandits or Jokapcul do appear, but otherwise relax and enjoy the day.

That was the situation when Wolf came galloping back along the road, his tongue hanging out with sweat flying off it.

"Whoa!" Spinner pulled on his gelding's reins and signaled a halt. Behind him, tackle creaked and wagons groaned as the column shuddered to a stop. Voices called out asking what was happening, why did they stop.

Wolf didn't slow his charge until he was nearly on the lead riders. Then he leaped and twisted about, but was so close and going so fast his momentum carried him as far as the hind legs of Spinner's mount. The gelding shied as Wolf landed rump first, skidded backward a few feet, then tumbled over and rolled. He quickly jumped out of the roll and landed on his feet. He bounded forward to Spinner's side and stood with his forepaws on the gelding's withers, which made the horse prance nervously aside. Wolf dropped to all fours and panted heavily for a moment, head up to look at Spinner. A small puddle grew beneath his lolling tongue.

"Catch your breath, Wolf," Spinner said, "then tell me what you found." It was a fine day and he was feeling good, even if he was concerned about the band's logistics.

Alyline leaned to look over the gelding's shoulder at Wolf. Wolf looked up at her for a second, turned his head away, then sat with a faint whine.

"That's how a proper dog is supposed to behave," she told him with a crisp nod.

Wolf replied with a sharp *Ulgh!* and bounced back onto all fours.

"I think he doesn't like being called a dog," Spinner said. "He's a wolf, and proud of it."

The Golden Girl sniffed. "Dogs are descended from wolves, and I think there's more than one dog in this wolf's lineage."

Wolf looked at Spinner as though exclaiming, *The nerve of her!*

Spinner shrugged. He couldn't tell Alyline anything without getting an argument.

Wolf had his breath back. *"Ulgh!"* he barked, and grabbed Spinner's trouser leg where it bloused before tucking into his boot. He gave it a tug as he stepped along the road, then let go and barked *"Ulgh!"* once more.

"What do you have?" Spinner asked as he heeled the gelding to walk with the wolf.

"Ulgh! Ulgh!"

"You have to speak more clearly than that if I'm to understand you."

"ULGH!" Wolf grabbed Spinner's trouser again and worried it almost out of the boot.

"All right, all right," Spinner laughed as he jerked his trouser leg out of Wolf's mouth. "I'm sorry if I made fun of you. Show me what you found."

Wolf looked at him suspiciously, waiting for another joke at his expense. When Spinner didn't offer one, he began trotting along the road.

Spinner twisted in his saddle and waved *forward* at the people and wagons behind. He tapped the gelding's sides to get it to keep pace with Wolf. Alyline cantered ahead of them.

Silent had returned a moment earlier from one of his frequent solo scouting forays. He moved his horse into the Golden Girl's place on Spinner's right.

"Mighty fine looking little bitty woman," he rumbled as he watched Alyline diminish into the shadows and distance—

she was "little bitty" only in comparison to his hugeness. "Too bad she's going to get herself into some serious trouble one of these days."

Spinner grunted. "I think any trouble she gets herself into will find itself in even more trouble before she's through with it."

Silent barked out a laugh so loud and sharp it startled the nearby horses and turned all heads in his direction. Then he turned serious.

"You've seen your share of trouble, my friend, and she's seen worse. But, I'll tell you, together you haven't seen anywhere near the worst people have to offer." He didn't have to lean to look over the gelding's back at Wolf. "What'd you find up ahead, Wolf, a town?"

"Ulgh!" Wolf said excitedly and wagged his tail.

"See?" he said to Spinner. "Wolves are easy to talk to. All you have to do is ask leading questions."

Soon the *thock*ing of wood chopping echoed distantly through the forest. The thocking ebbed and stopped by the time the lead riders reached a clearing so large they could hardly see across it. Alyline was sitting her stallion, waiting for them, peering into the town, almost a mile distant, that centered the cleared area. To the north, mountains jutted above the forest, beginning their progress as the spine of the peninsula.

"Where are the people?" she murmured with an unsettled edge in her voice.

The place didn't look deserted, it showed no sign of having been ravaged by invaders or bandits, but not a soul was in sight.

Haft and Fletcher joined Spinner, Alyline, and Silent to look over the town and decide what to do.

"Now what?" Spinner asked, almost to himself.

"Don't ask me," Silent said. "You and Haft are in command here."

"We need to find out where the people are," Haft said. "Find who's in charge and," he looked back at the column of wagons emptying into the cleared area, "see if we can get some help for our wounded."

Spinner nodded, Haft was right. "Haft, Silent," Spinner said, "put out security, get the rest of the soldiers into defensive positions around the wagons. Haft, join me when you're satisfied with the disposition. The foot of those mountains," he nodded to the north, "is our rally point."

Haft nodded. He didn't see anything wrong here, even if no people were in sight. But then, The Burnt Man Inn had looked fine to him as well, and he'd been very wrong about it. He looked at the mountains that rose to the north; finally, a rally point that could be seen from all around. He went to assemble the soldiers and made sure everyone knew where they were to meet and reassemble if they got scattered or lost.

"Fletcher," Spinner continued, "circle the wagons in that area," he pointed to a nearby copse, "and make sure all the women and children are inside the circle. Then stay in command while we go ahead."

Fletcher nodded. "Right." He turned and went back to move the camp followers into place.

"You go to the wagons with the other women," Spinner said to the Golden Girl.

She sniffed and didn't move.

Spinner looked away from her and his gaze fell on Wolf. "You stay here, boy. Help Fletcher and Silent."

Wolf whined, the whine quickly shifted to a low growl. Spinner wasn't sure if the wolf was disappointed or relieved at being left as security for the wagons and women.

After some further discussion, they decided to bring Xundoe the mage with them. The five set off into the town.

If "town" was too grand a word, it wasn't too grand by much, for the place was too large to be a village. A straight road led into the center of the town. At first the road passed between fields; grain on one side, vegetables on the other. To the south of the town were orchards of fruit trees; to the north, water fowl splashed and swam in ponds. Beyond the fields, clumps of small houses, mostly of thatch and wattle, sprouted helter-skelter, seemingly plunked down wherever whim decreed, with large swaths of open land between, as though they huddled together clan by clan. Tendrils of smoke rose from some of the houses. The thatch on most of the roofs looked to be in need of repair. Few trees stood among the houses, only a few copses stood in the open ground between housing clumps. The houses in those outskirt clumps were smallish and looked not in good repair. Closer to the town center they were larger, with the largest ones closest to the middle. Those largest stood two or even three stories high and sat comfortably spaced on individual lots. All seemed to need fresh paint or other repairs of some sort. Carriages were visible behind some of the larger houses.

The clops of the horses' hooves echoing from the houses emphasized the stillness around them. Beyond the houses were the workshops of metal workers and other craftsmen. Warehouses stood behind the shops and crafts. They passed a stable with a blacksmith's forge behind it. It was eerie to see all those workshops and the forge sitting silent and unattended. Nearer the center of the town the road was lined with shops but their displays seemed sparser than they should. Nobody was shopping or selling.

Spinner and Haft rode side by side into the town with Silent and the Golden Girl close behind. None of them had weapons in their hands, but all had their weapons ready to draw at an instant's notice. Xundoe brought up the rear. His fingers nervously tapped the spell pouch laid across his saddle and he hoped he wouldn't need to use the small demon spitter and two phoenix eggs he brought, and that they'd be enough if he did.

"They're all inside, watching us," Alyline said softly.

"I wonder what they are afraid of," Spinner said, almost as softly.

Haft looked around the settlement. No watch towers or breastworks, no defenses of any sort. "If I lived in a place like this and I saw fourscore armed men approaching, I think I'd be afraid, too," he said.

Silent kept his peace.

Xundoe thought long before speaking. "The land here is rich, the crops are growing lushly, but the town looks poor. I wonder why?"

At length they entered the town center, a largish square ringed by a road paved with gravel that was dampened with oil to keep down the dust. To their left was what looked like the hall of a prosperous town. A surprisingly large inn that stood opposite the hall reminded Spinner of The Burnt Man; he didn't know what use so remote a town had for so large an inn. They would have thought the institutional-looking building on one side was a barracks, if the town had been large enough to need so big a garrison. The fourth side held a mansion and two smaller but no less grand houses. A canopied stage, perhaps a bandstand, graced the side of the square before the town hall. The inn had its own corral and stable, which were visible around its side. Other roads as straight as the one they'd ridden entered the square from the north, east, and south. To the east, the edge of the forest was much closer than on the west. They turned toward the town hall and saw the first people.

The hall, constructed of massive granite blocks, was the largest building in the town. Spinner thought it must hold an auditorium as well as offices and meeting rooms. Three rows of windows testified to its height. Lamplight showed through cracks in some of the shutters that closed all the windows. A bell was visible in the cupola of a tower that stuck up ten feet or more higher on the roof. A flight of seven or eight broad stairs spanned the building's front, each step was less wide than the one below until the topmost step was half the width of the building, and emptied onto a deep porch. A roof some twelve feet high, supported by four ornate pillars overhung the porch. A legend was emblazoned across the front of the porch roof.

"Does anybody recognize that language?" Spinner asked as the group slowly approached.

"It's Zobran," Xundoe immediately replied.

"What does it say?" Spinner asked impatiently.

"Oh." It just says, 'Eikby Town Hall.' "

A rank of a dozen soldiers stood on the lip of the porch. They held halberds, long handled axes with fearsome spikes that protruded more than a foot beyond the axe heads, at their sides. The uppermost tips of the halberds nearly reached the porch roof. Two steps below them stood another rank of soldiers, these held swords with their points resting on the step before their feet. The soldiers were dressed oddly—at least to Spinner and Haft, who had never before seen such uniforms. They seemed to be of one piece, or at least the shirts and pants were of the same material and pattern. They bore red and white vertical stripes with scalloped edges. The arms and legs of the garments were ballooned and cinched tightly at elbow and knee. The chests were also ballooned, or perhaps they were stretched over cuirasses underneath. Each soldier wore a helmet that was flared on the bottom and topped by a crest that ran from front to back.

The two Frangerian Marines exchanged a quick glance. As sharp as the soldiers' uniforms were, their postures left something to be desired for ceremonial troops, and their ranks were ragged enough that any Marine sergeant would have happily chewed them out with enthusiastic invective. Despite their obvious nervousness, all of the soldiers ogled the Golden Girl.

A man probably not in uniform stood in the middle of the rank of swordsmen. He wore a brilliant blue cassock of simple cut, cinched at the waist by a broad leather belt. A chain of gilt medallions hung around his neck almost to his waist. An oversized, floppy hat sporting a large, blue feather topped his head.

"That's the lord mayor," Xundoe volunteered.

"I figured as much," Spinner muttered. Then louder, "Thank you." It was usually a good idea to keep a magician happy, seldom advisable to make one feel unappreciated or misused.

They pulled up on line in front of the steps, facing the mayor: Two Frangerian Marines in uniform, their four-sided reversible cloaks blue side out, cocked and loaded crossbows secured by a hook that protruded from their saddles' cantles;

the giant nomad of the steppes, clad in white and brown bear-
skins, a sword so outrageously long and broad it looked able
to cleave three men at a stroke rested loose in its scabbard on
his back; the Golden Girl in a patchwork imitation of her
dancing costume, but wearing a veil of gold thread and beads
and a girdle of gold coins, her hand almost touching the gold
hilt of the dagger in the gold scabbard that angled across her
belly just below her waist; a magician in robes so cluttered
with cabalistic and runic symbols only the naive wouldn't
know he probably wasn't very experienced; he struggled to
control the nervous twitching of his fingers as he tried to decide whether to use a phoenix egg or demon spitter first if
they had to fight.

Spinner assayed a shallow bow. "Lord Mayor," he said in
his best Zobran, which was better suited to portside taverns
and brothels than to a meeting with a town mayor. "We are
peaceful travelers who wish to reprovision in your town. We
have both skills and coin to pay for goods and services." His
Zobran was good enough for that much, but haggling, well—
if the mayor had been a tavern owner, Spinner could manage
to bargain with him, otherwise he'd have to trust Xundoe or
one of the Zobran soldiers with negotiations.

The mayor was startled by the polite greeting given in
badly accented—what *was* that accent?—Zobran by the dangerous looking young stranger.

"Peaceful travelers are always welcome in Eikby," the
mayor replied formally. His Zobran was about as closely related to the tongue spoken in Zobra City as was Spinner's harbor Zobran. Still, they were intelligible to one another—so
long as they spoke slowly and clearly.

The mayor was very aware of the edginess of the town
guardsmen around him—and equally well understood it.

Could he believe the young soldier's claim that they were
peaceful travelers? He cleared his throat.

"Sirs, and Lady," he tipped his head to the Golden Girl, "as
I say, peaceful travelers are always welcome in Eikby. But,"
he swallowed and cleared his throat again, "you come with
so many armed men. There have been new bands of bandits

in the area of late." There, he'd gotten out his main concern, the reason he'd ordered everyone to hide, and the guard to assemble.

Spinner knew his Zobran wasn't up to what he had to say now; he signaled Xundoe to move to his side to translate and switched to Frangerian.

"Lord Mayor, we are aware of bandits. We met a large band of them yesterday." He wondered about the mayor saying "new" bands.

"How many were there?" the mayor asked.

"About forty."

The mayor flinched and wondered which bandits they were.

"We killed several of them and the rest fled. We have more wounded than our healing witch can easily handle. Do you have healers who we can hire to help her?"

The mayor glanced quickly at their weapons and remembered how many armed men his scouts had said were in their band. Yes, he could believe that many men, if they were all like these, could kill several bandits and make the others flee. And how many wounded did they have?

"We have healing witches and a healing magician. Perhaps they will be willing to assist your healing witch." He refrained from asking how many dead these people had lost.

"As to why we are here in the numbers we are, am I correct in assuming that you know of the Jokapcul invasion of Nunimar?"

The mayor swallowed to wet his suddenly dry throat and nodded; he didn't trust his voice. No matter the bandits, all he'd heard of the Jokapcul made the bandits seem like friendly, helpful, neighbors.

"I am a Frangerian Marine, what you might know as a sea soldier. They call me Spinner. My fellow Marine, Haft, and I were the only people to escape when the Jokapcul captured New Bally. We have been traveling ever since, seeking an open port where we could sign on with a ship that would take us back to Frangeria. Along the way we have encountered and fought Jokapcul. Our companions also seek safety from the invaders. That's why we have all banded together, to find safety in numbers.

"We don't come to harm anyone—unless they are Jokapcul. Them, we will kill."

Spinner listened to Xundoe finish translating, then listened some more. When the mage was through he asked him, "What did you say?"

Xundoe started and looked at him wide-eyed. "What? What—I translated most faithfully what you said."

"Yes, but there, at the end, it sounded like you added something. What was it?"

"Oh, what I added." He giggled almost like a nervous girl. "I told him we have some Zobran Border Warders in our party. If he doesn't believe you, he can ask them." He twisted his shoulders. "If we had the Border Warders with us now, he might be more welcoming to us."

Spinner nodded. "Very good, mage. I wish I'd thought of that myself, we could have brought one or two of them along." His face turned hard. "And frightened these poor people even more by having an even larger group of armed strangers standing in front of them."

He turned back to the mayor. "Sir, we left our party encamped on the outskirts of town to demonstrate our peaceful intent." To Xundoe, "Translate that—and don't make me ask if you add anything."

The mayor considered for a moment, then said, "I wish to see your Zobran Border Warders. I have met some of them."

"He's a trusting soul," Haft muttered.

"With bandits like those we met yesterday in the area, he's got a right to be suspicious of armed men," Silent said.

Spinner tried to ignore them. "Gladly, Lord Mayor. Tell me when and where you would like to meet them."

"Right here. As soon as you can fetch them."

Spinner looked at Xundoe. "Do you have an imbaluris (a messenger demon) with you?"

The mage shook his head. "You need a magician at each end to use an imbaluris. I'm the only magician we have, so I left the imbaluris in the big spell chest."

While Spinner thought about whether he should send one of their number back for the Zobrans or all go, Silent suddenly stood on his stirrups and twisted around to look back toward the place they'd left the rest of the band. They all turned, but an inn and other buildings blocked their view.

"How do I get up there?" Haft demanded and pointed at the bell tower. "Never mind." He jumped off his horse and raced up the stairs, through the ranks of guardsmen without waiting for an answer. The guards hastened out of his way. One pikeman was a half step too slow; Haft grabbed his arm and shoved him through the entrance to the town hall ahead of himself.

"Show me how to go up!" Haft demanded in harbor Zobran—it came out as, "Show me top!"

The pikeman saw he wasn't being immediately threatened, Haft didn't have his hand on his axe, and said, "This way." He pointed to a grand staircase.

Haft pushed him ahead and repeated, "Show me."

The pikeman sped to the stairs and began to race up them. The point of his halberd hit the ceiling and he staggered, almost falling backward. With an apologetic look at Haft, he lay the long axe-spear on the stairs and ran up the stairs. At the top he turned left. A few paces along the corridor another stairway went up; the pikeman pointed to it. The stairway turned back on itself and again so it seemed to go all the way up. Haft took the steps two at a time and didn't notice whether or not the pikeman followed. He was panting by the time he reached the top of the bell tower and looked out of the cupola. He looked over the buildings and through the intervening copses to the place they'd left the rest of the band.

Haft waved away a bothersome bee, then curled his hands in front of his eyes. "The camp's under attack!" he shouted down.

"By more of these?" Spinner asked, pointing at the guardsmen.

"No. Looks like bandits."

"Get down here, we've got to go to them." Spinner looked at the mayor to tell him their encampment was under attack.

The mayor looked doubtful, but another voice called down from the bell tower. It was the pikeman who'd shown Haft the way to the tower.

"What's he saying?" Spinner asked Xundoe.

"He says bandits are attacking our camp." The mage was so excited he almost tripped over his words.

"Tell the mayor we have to get back to our people."

Haft's voice called out, "Silent, catch me!" He'd climbed down the face of the building and sat dangling his legs over the edge of the portico.

The steppe giant heeled his mount and guided the huge horse with his knees up the stairs to just below Haft. Guardsmen scattered out of his way. He stood in his stirrups and reached a hand up. Haft leaned forward, grasped the hand in both of his and slid off the roof. Silent lowered him to the steps, let go, and grinned.

"That was faster than the stairs inside," Haft shouted an explanation as he ran to his mare and bounded into the saddle. The five spun their horses and galloped off.

While Silent was getting Haft down, the mayor was shouting orders. A swordman ran into the hall, the other guardsmen ran off the stairs and formed into marching ranks. Moments after the others had left, a dozen mounted swordsmen were speeding after them in a file of twos. The swords- and pikemen, in files of their own, began trotting along behind. The mayor followed in a coach.

CHAPTER
TEN

They heard the din of close combat before they got close enough to see any details. The fighting was in the open, closer to the campsite than to the forest's edge. The sounds of metal clanging on metal and metal chunking into wood, shouts of battling men and screams of wounded, sounded out of a roiling cloud of dust from the scuffling, stamping feet and hooves that tore up the ground under the melee. The combatants didn't notice the charging reinforcements until Silent let out a bellowing war cry. By then they were less than fifty yards away and closing fast. Spinner and Haft each fired a bolt into the attackers, then slung their crossbows and drew their close-combat weapons.

"Break!" Fletcher cried out when he saw them coming. "Fall back!"

The defenders disengaged as best they could and back-pedaled from the attackers, many of whom were turning to meet the flanking charge. Some of the defenders, freed from their struggle with the main mass of the attacking bandits, charged into a lesser melee inside the half-finished campsite to repel the bandits who were ransacking stores and chasing the women and children.

The five horses crashed into the bandits and sent many of them spinning to the ground. Silent leaned over to swing his mighty sword, the blade connected again and again, and each time it did the bandit he hit was flung away, head or limb flying in a different direction. Haft swung his axe, and its great half-moon blade caused nearly as much damage to the bandits as Silent's sword. Spinner tucked his quarterstaff under his arm like a lance and used it as a spear to crack heads, crush throats, and bowl over bandits who couldn't scramble out of his way fast enough. Alyline tucked her stallion's shoulder next to the gelding's left flank and slashed her dagger left-handed, opening a long, deep, gash on the face and arm of a bandit who leaped to drag her down. Xundoe was a magician, not a cavalryman—he screamed in fear as he tried to keep his pony tucked close behind the others.

Thirty yards beyond the bandits, Spinner shouted a command and the five pulled up to face about. Most of the scattered bandits were trying to organize to charge them, some were stringing short bows, but all were distracted by arrows flying at them from within the camp and by the soldiers under Fletcher's command who harried their flank with swords and pikes.

"Your demon spitter!" Spinner shouted to Xundoe as he fed a quarrel into his crossbow.

The mage rummaged in his spell bag, pulled it out, but before he could aim and command the tiny demon that inhabited it to spit, the demon popped out of the handle.

"Veedmee!" the demon commanded in a high-pitched voice that sounded far too big to come from something so small.

"What?" Xundoe squawked, he'd fed the demon just that morning, it shouldn't need feeding again so soon! But he knew too well how temperamental demons could be and was rummaging in the spell bag for demon food even as he squawked.

"Veedmee!" the demon repeated, and looked hungrily at the web of the hand Xundoe had wrapped around the demon spitter's handle.

"It's coming, it's coming!" Xundoe fumbled the box of demon food open and popped out a pellet. "Here!" He shoved the pellet at the demon, who yanked it out of his fingers and popped back inside the handle of the demon spitter. The mage immediately raised the weapon and pointed it at a bandit who had an arrow nocked and was aiming at them. He tripped the signal, and the demon spat like the crack of a tree bough snapping. Blood spurted from the bowman's chest and he crumpled to the ground with an expression of stunned disbelief on his face. Xundoe pointed the demon spitter at another bandit, another tree bough cracked, and that bandit fell dying.

Spinner and Haft were already firing their second bolts. Arrows flew from the camp into the bandits, and soldiers hacked at them from the side. A halloo sounded, and they looked to see Eikby's mounted guardsmen charging. Those bandits who were able to break away screamed and ran to where a few of their mates held their horses just inside the edge of the forest.

"After them!" Spinner bellowed. He shot another bolt, then took a second to hang his crossbow onto the cantle hook before heeling the gelding forward. Haft and Silent were already halfway to the fleeing bandits. The Eikby mounted guardsmen paused to look back at the mayor, who was following in his carriage. They reined in at a signal from him.

Haft swore at his mare when she pulled to the side just shy of colliding with the bandit he wanted her to gallop over. Instead of being trampled under her flashing hooves, the bandit was sent tumbling by a kick from Haft as he sped past. Then horse and rider were in the midst of the fleeing bandits. Haft swung his axe into the back of one bandit and the man fell forward with his spine split. In another couple of strides, the mare was among the lead bandits. Far more comfortable fighting on his feet, Haft yanked viciously on the reins, leaped from the saddle, and spun about to attack the mass of bandits. Some parted in front of him, too afraid to stop and fight. One was so intent on reaching the forest he was slow to recognize the Frangerian Marine in front of them as a foe and was chopped down as soon as he was in reach of Haft's axe. He died so suddenly that neither surprise nor pain had time to register on his face.

Silent had learned to fight mounted almost from the moment he could first keep his balance on horseback. His huge horse had also been trained to combat—it slammed into the bandits, kicked at them with its hooves, trampled fallen bodies. Silent roared battle cries as he swung his sword, each swing sent out gushes and sprays of blood from the bandits he struck.

The defenders, led by Fletcher, crashed into the bandits just as they reached their horses and were leaping into their saddles. Some bandit horses were knocked over, screaming in fear at the assault. The company's defenders hacked at the bandits, sometimes hitting them, sometimes chopping into their horses, sometimes missing altogether.

"Hold!" Spinner shouted when the bandits who managed to mount sped into the forest. "Let them go."

Silent twisted his great mount around and glared at Spinner.

"What do you mean, 'hold'?" Haft demanded. "We can catch the rest of them."

"You can't," Spinner said, and looked at Haft's feet, which were firmly planted on the ground.

"Where's my horse?" Haft shouted, turning around looking. The mare was some yards beyond the body and blood littered area, calmly chomping on grass.

"They aren't coming back," Spinner said loudly enough for all to hear. "And we will needlessly lose people if we go in the forest after them."

He noticed the mounted guardsmen sitting their horses much closer to the campsite—he didn't see any blood on their weapons.

Puffing heavily and stumbling a bit, the running files of swords- and pikemen arrived and formed a protective square around the mayor's carriage.

It was time to assess the butcher's bill.

More than thirty bodies lay on the ground. Groans and whimpers came from some of them. A badly wounded bandit, doing his best to crawl to the false security of the forest, trailed a lengthening rope of intestine.

"Leave him," Haft growled at a dismounted Eikby cavalry-man who stalked toward the crawling bandit. "He'll die soon enough." When the cavalryman looked like he was going to ignore the order, Haft stepped in front of him and swung his dangling axe in a way that was only superficially casual. "You weren't in the fight, you don't have the right."

The cavalryman looked into Haft's eyes and knew he was outmatched. He turned pale, swallowed, and bowed himself away, mumbling apologies.

The crawling bandit almost made it to the shade of the trees before he expired.

Now that the ground was no longer being tramped by fighting men and horses, Nightbird and Zweepee ran forward to see to the wounded. The mayor paled at sight of the dead, dying, and wounded, then got hold of himself and sent three horsemen racing back to summon the town's healers to the battlefield. He bent over one of the bandits, went even paler. He swallowed and tugged at the collar of his cassock.

Spinner, Haft, and Xundoe walked together, examining the battle scene and looking for men still alive—people still alive. Several of the casualties were women and children, evidently cut down in the beginning of the attack. One woman obviously died where she crouched over her children in a vain attempt to save their lives from the combatants. Two little ones lay half-covered by her corpse, one stared skyward from sightless eyes parted by a sword-cleft, the other crushed by a falling bandit.

Xundoe dropped to his knees beside a stripling boy of ten years. The boy cried silently with one hand clamped as tightly as he could over the stump of the other. A bloody knife lay nearby where he'd dropped it when a sword took the hand that still gripped it. The mage quickly took a length of cord and tied off the stump.

"Do you hurt anywhere else?" he asked when the tourniquet was in place.

The boy made a sound the mage couldn't understand, but his head shake was clear.

"Over here," Xundoe called out.

A soldier ran over and gently picked up the boy to carry him to the place the still living were being gathered for what healing they could have. Alyline and Doli, along with other women, gave Nightbird and Zweepee what help they could.

Most of them could apply bandages to wounds. Those who couldn't, gathered cloth for bandages, hot water for cleaning injuries, needles and thread for closing cuts.

"How could this have happened?" Spinner asked, pained.

Haft glowered. "They must have caught the listening posts sleeping."

"How many did you put out?"

"Three," Fletcher answered.

Spinner looked into the forest. "Let's look for them."

"Right," Haft growled. He strode toward the trees. Three bees followed.

Fletcher didn't share the anger the other two held for the sentries.

Spinner signaled to Silent, who gathered six Bloody Axes and led them at a trot to catch up. The ten men trod quietly through the forest, alert for bandits who might be waiting in ambush. Birds barely paused in their songs, lizards alerted but didn't abandon their basking. A hare bounded to ground at their approach, another grazing with it didn't even notice them until they were past.

"I put the first one over here," Fletcher said as they neared a low mound alongside the road, about seventy-five yards in from Eikby's clearing.

They found the soldier, a Zobran deserter, lying behind the mound, seeming to look around its side. The soldier wasn't watching for danger, though. With an arrow through one eye, he'd never look for anything again. His pierced eye was open, he hadn't been asleep when the bandits came on him. Fifty yards north of him they found the second lookout, a woodsman from upper Zobra. Someone had slipped very quietly behind him and silenced him forever with a garotte. The third, a Skraglander hunter, was sixty yards farther from the road. He had evidently stood up to relieve himself when three arrows struck him simultaneously.

"Whoever these bandits are," Silent murmured, "they move well."

"Too well," Spinner said softly. An arrow through the eye from an unseen attacker, a man who could slip so quietly through the forest to come unnoticed upon a woodsman, archers who could simultaneously hit a man as soon as he stood—these were not ordinary soldiers, much less the common run of forest bandits.

Haft looked deeper into the forest. "But not good enough," he muttered. He was firmly convinced that no fighters in the world were as good as Frangerian Marines.

Silent looked a question at him, but Haft didn't elaborate.

"Let's go back," Spinner said. He assigned Silent to take the six axemen and bring in the bodies of the dead lookouts. If the company was going to be here for any length of time—if they did anything but leave immediately—they needed to come up with a better defense than the hasty perimeter they set when they arrived.

While they were gone the rest of the soldiers, under command of Sergeant Phard of the Skragland Bloody Axes, gathered the dead. They reverently lay the band's dead in a neat row near the copse where they'd been setting camp when the bandits attacked, and carelessly threw the dead bandits into a heap closer to the forest.

The first of the town's healers arrived as the last of the bodies were being carried away. Nightbird spoke briefly with him, and set him to work on a woman with a deep wound in her back. Shortly, two more healers arrived—a magician with a spell chest, and a healing witch with a sack of herbs and poultices. The mayor conferred with them, then sent them to Nightbird.

The mayor approached Spinner and Haft. He looked them in the eye when he spoke, though his knees trembled.

"Young sirs," he said with more strength than he felt, "I owe you an apology." Xundoe translated his words. "I feared you were bandits come to raid Eikby. This," he swung a hand to encompass the battlefield, "proves you are what you said." He cast a worried look into the forest.

"Maybe next time strang—" Haft began sharply, but Spinner clamped a hand on his forearm and spoke over him.

"Lord Mayor, with bandits like these about, your fear was understandable. We hold no blame for you."

"You are most kind, young sir," the mayor said and bowed deeply after Xundoe's translation. When he straightened he looked at the pile of bandit corpses. "These bandits have been marauding the countryside since long before the rumors of war first came to us. Travelers have not been safe on the roads unless they were in strongly armed parties. Even those, the bandits would attack and cause death and injury before fleeing. We have taken in refugees from villages the bandits have raided." He shuddered. "The refugees have told us tales of murder, rapine, and destruction." He turned plaintive eyes on Spinner. "They have stolen away women for their unspeakable purposes."

Spinner and Haft glanced at each other when the mayor said the bandits had attacked heavily armed parties.

"As we told you before, we met some of them yesterday," Spinner said.

"We killed many of them yesterday," Haft added. He glared at the pile of corpses. "I guess we didn't kill enough of them."

The mayor nervously fingered the collar of his cassock. "Did they follow you here?"

"Maybe," Spinner acknowledged. It was certainly possible that the bandits had spent a day gathering more of their mates and come after the company for revenge. He nodded. "It's very possible they came to get vengeance on us after yesterday. I can't think of another reason they would have attacked us when they could have waited and attacked the town after we left." He nodded toward the pile of bodies. "It cost them more than a dozen dead. We can't tell how many of them may have fled with wounds."

"At the cost of how many losses of yours?"

Spinner shook his head, he didn't know yet. He looked around for Fletcher and saw him coming toward them.

"What are our casualties?" he asked as soon as Fletcher was close enough.

Fletcher spat angrily. "Too many." He sighed and spoke with less anger. "Thirteen dead, seven of them soldiers. And the bastards killed two women and four children." He glared at the forest.

"How many wounded?"

"Too many." He looked down and shook his head. "Two or three of the wounded may yet die." He paused to heave a deep breath. "About twenty are down with wounds. Some are minor, some will be a long time healing." His voice broke and they allowed him a moment to recompose himself. "Most of the wounded are women and children."

"Zweepee?" Spinner asked, he hadn't yet had time to look in the camp, to see who was whole, who was hurt—who was dead.

"Zweepee's all right," Fletcher said. "So is Doli."

Spinner knew the Golden Girl was also uninjured. The anger and tension that had been slowly building in him eased; it was somehow important to him that the quartet of slaves he and Haft had freed was still whole and safe—or as safe as they could be, in a land subject to the ravages of bandits. He wondered once more how the other slaves had fared that he and Haft freed when they destroyed The Burnt Man. They had armed them and sent them toward Oskul, the Skragland capital. Rumors of Jokapcul advances made him fear they had not fared well.

He shook those thoughts off. "Tell us what happened here."

"I was inspecting the ranks when they came at us," Fletcher explained. "The men were relaxed, I think they were relying on the listening posts to give warning. I was relying on the listening posts. They were nearly on us by the time anyone shouted. They killed the women and children before any of us could strike back."

"How many of them were there?" Half asked.

Fletcher shook his head. "I was too busy fighting to count, there were more of them than of us, though. Maybe eighty of them."

Haft snorted. "They were good when they got the listening posts, but they aren't good close up."

"How do you figure?" Spinner asked.

"They had surprise and outnumbered our men, yet we killed more than a dozen of them and we only lost thirteen, including women and children, that's what I mean. *Hrmmpf.* Given those odds in our favor, I'd expect an easy victory with fewer casualties on our side."

"They weren't ready for our counterattack," Spinner reminded him.

"That wasn't it," Fletcher said. "The bandits who weren't engaged with our soldiers broke from the fight and attacked the camp itself. Some of them managed to carry off booty before you arrived."

Startled, Spinner looked at him. "What about people? Did they carry off any women or children?"

"No, none. Zweepee already told me all women and children are accounted for."

Relieved on that score, Spinner turned to the mayor to ask his opinion of what the bandits might do next, but the mayor had slipped away unnoticed while Fletcher gave his report.

"That's odd," Spinner murmured.

"I don't trust him," Haft said. He glared about for the mayor, his hand twisted around the top of his axe where it hung on his belt.

They walked into the camp to see how the wounded were being cared for. Nightbird had managed to set up an efficient field hospital in a hastily erected pavilion where the wounded were being tended. Women and a few soldiers bandaged and splinted the less severely injured, and did what they could to stop the bleeding and ease the pain of those who had to wait for better treatment. Nightbird and Eikby's healing witch mixed their herbs and applied mixes and poultices to injuries. The town's healer went about setting and splinting broken bones so they would knit straight and strong. They were diligent in their attempts to avoid interfering with each other, and not offer further pain or hurt to the wounded. Xundoe alone didn't grimace and flinch away from the healing magician, who had set his various demons to work on wounds that demanded their attention.

"Aralez," Xundoe whispered, awed. "You have aralez—three of them!"

"I do," the healing magician affirmed. He watched his demons carefully. Shaped like miniature dogs, the three small aralez scampered from wound to wound, lapping at the injuries. The healing magician moved them along from one wounded man to another as soon as his wounds perceptibly changed from raw, ragged, red to deep pink under the ministering tongues of the little demons. He kept a closer watch on his fourth demon.

"What's that one?" Xundoe asked of the gray demon that the healing magician watched closely. "I've never seen its like." It was the shape of a man but less than half a man's height. It went from casualty to casualty, lifting and peering under bandages. In one place and another without cause Xundoe could detect, it probed into a wound with a hand and drew out something that glowed an insubstantial green. It vanished when the demon threw it off its hand with a flick of its wrist.

"It's a land trow," the healing mage answered.

"A land trow!" Xundoe wove his arms in patterns he hoped would protect the people under the pavilion.

"It's all right," the healing magician assured him. "The trow likes me. It's safe to use in healing as long as I keep it away from young mothers and infants."

Xundoe looked at him in disbelief. "I've never heard good of trows," he said, but low enough the demon couldn't hear. He hoped the trow couldn't hear, anyway.

The healing magician shrugged. "Demons have their own motives," he said. "When one wants to help me, I don't question why."

Xundoe watched suspiciously for several minutes as the trow went from pallet to pallet, probing at wounds, horned fingers drawing out glowing green things.

"Do we have any prisoners?" Haft asked as they neared the pavilion.

"Two. Over there." Fletcher pointed at two men lying on bare ground at the outer edge of the pavilion. They turned to them.

The head of one of the bandits was swathed in bloody bandages, only his nostrils and most of his mouth weren't covered. His hands were bound. The other was missing an arm from the elbow and had a leg crudely splinted. Spinner saw that the soldiers engaged in completing the pavilion's canvas covering and making pallets were less careful about where they trod around the two bandits. Five older children were guarding the prisoners. Three of the children were boys one or two years too young to become soldiers, the other two were girls of about the same age. The boys looked serious, as though they wanted to prove themselves worthy of the trust placed in them. Haft grimaced at the expressions on the girls' faces; they reminded him of how Alyline, Doli, and Zweepee had looked after questioning a Jokapcul prisoner taken during the battle in Zobra. The prisoner had died horribly under their questioning.

"We'll question them shortly. First, let's see to our own people." Spinner led the way under the pavilion roof. He and Haft spoke briefly to each of the wounded and assured them they'd done well and would soon be on the mend. The most painful for them to see was the boy who'd fought and lost a hand. They were suspicious of the demons controlled by the healing magician, but they saw how eagerly Xundoe followed him about, so they kept their distance. Then it was time to question the prisoners.

"Where's Silent?" Haft asked as they moved carefully among the wounded to the injured bandits.

"I don't know," Spinner answered as he looked around. "I don't think I've seen him since we got back from checking the listening posts."

"I didn't see him come back with us, either," Fletcher said.

"Did the others who went with us come back?"

They looked around and saw the six Bloody Axes who had gone into the forest with them. They had returned safely with the bodies of the three lookouts.

"Where's Wolf?" He was nowhere to be seen either. They wondered where the steppe giant and the wolf had gone, but felt no need to worry about their safety, particularly not if they were together.

Four soldiers moved the prisoners away from the company's wounded and the rest of the camp. The soldiers weren't gentle about it, neither did the two Frangerian Marines want them to be.

"Now, we're going to have a friendly little talk," Spinner said after he settled himself comfortably on a camp stool next to them, "and you're going to tell us everything we want to know."

Haft grinned wickedly at the two from his camp stool and said, "You look like smart men who want to live, so I know you're going to tell us what we want to know because you know it's the right thing to do, not just because we make you tell us."

The bandit with his head bandaged spat in the direction of their voices but, lying supine as he was, wasn't able to put enough force behind it and the saliva landed on his own leg. The one-armed bandit tried to scowl, but was in too much discomfort and pain to look dangerous.

"Maybe they don't speak Frangerian?" Spinner said, looking at Haft.

"Inlanders? You're probably right." Haft repeated what Spinner said in Zobran but got no response.

"What's this?" Spinner yanked on the belt of the one-armed bandit. His hand came away with a Skragland army badge. "Are you a Skraglander?" he asked in that language. "Or did you steal this from someone you murdered?"

The bandit's only reply was another scowl, but a flicker in his eyes made it clear he understood the question.

Neither Marine spoke more than a few words of Skraglandish. Haft looked around for someone who spoke it. The nearest person was Doli, who hovered nearby.

"Doli," Haft called. "Can you help us, please?"

"What?" Doli asked as she joined them.

"We need a translator," Spinner said. He wanted to glower at Haft, but couldn't with Doli right there looking lovingly into his face. He wished his friend had called someone else to translate for them.

Doli gave the prisoners a sweet smile. "Tell me what you want to know. I'll get Zweepee and Alyline. We'll question them the way we did that Jokapcul soldier. They'll tell us everything we want to know."

Haft leaned away from her; he didn't want to subject another prisoner to that kind of questioning. Not until they'd tried gentler methods.

Spinner swallowed; he didn't either. "Ah, I don't think that will be necessary, Doli. These two look like reasonable men, I'm sure they're willing to talk without that kind of, ah, 'feminine persuasion.' "

Doli gave him an exaggerated look of disappointment. "But, Spinner, you know how much information we can get from a man." She smiled sweetly.

"We want them alive and whole afterward," Haft snarled.

They spoke in Frangerian, the language they had most in common, so they were surprised when the head-swaddled bandit spoke.

"What you want know?" His bad Frangerian was intelligible even through his fear. The one-armed bandit swore at him in Skraglandish, and he swore back. The other quieted, but looked furious.

Haft was convinced that if he could see the bandit's face he'd see a terrified expression. Spinner wondered how the fellow knew what happened to prisoners when they were turned over to the women. Had he seen a soldier after an enemy's women had their way with him? Did the bandits give prisoners to their women after a battle? None of that mattered, they wanted information from him: Why had the bandits attacked? How many of them were there? Where was their base? What did they know about Jokapcul positions and movements on the Princedon Peninsula? Doli's Skraglandish helped with the questions and answers the two Marines' Skraglandish couldn't manage. They suspected that in her translations she embellished what they said so they carried greater threat.

As it turned out, their surmise had been right, the bandits didn't allow anyone to get away with hurting them; they'd come to kill all the people who had broken up their ambush.

Since the company beat off the first attack, they would gather more bandits and come back again as soon as they gathered a large enough force. The prisoners weren't sure, but they thought that altogether there were three or four hundred bandits in that part of the Princedons. Most of them could be assembled for a joint action. They didn't have just one base, there were six or eight bands, each with its own base. They couldn't tell where the other bases were, just their own. They could find their way to a couple of others, but only from their own base, not from here. The directions they gave to their base sounded incomplete and possibly led along well-guarded roads and trails, but the Marines didn't press the issue. If the bandits were gathering force to attack again, they needed to prepare defenses, not send out a retaliatory force. As for the Jokapcul, all the bandits could say for sure, or perhaps all they would say, was they recently took a small part of the southern coast of the peninsula. Perhaps the invaders had taken more than that—rumors of their strength and location abounded, with each rumor more fantastic than the previous one.

When the questioning was done—they didn't think the bandits had held back much except for the location of their base—they had soldiers take them into the hospital pavilion for treatment. By then the healers were through with the most essential care of their own casualties and were able to tend to the wounded bandits. "Gently," Spinner admonished when the soldiers started by picking up the prisoners roughly. They gathered Fletcher and Xundoe to begin planning a defense against the anticipated attack. The mayor showed up with the Commander of the Eikby Guard, who had just arrived with more guardsmen. Doli hovered nearby, as usual. Alyline joined the group without invitation.

"Where's Silent?" Fletcher wanted to know.

No one knew where he and Wolf were. Nor did anyone notice the cloud of bees that formed, headed south, and coalesced into a birdlike formation and speeded up as it vanished over the tops of the forest trees.

CHAPTER
ELEVEN

Captain Stonearm, commander of the Eikby Guard, and a squad of guardsmen had been investigating a reported disturbance in the forest on the far side of the town when the company arrived. Even though he and his troops came back as soon as a runner brought word of the strangers, they hadn't gotten back to the east edge of the cleared area until the fight was ending. The plume of tail feathers from a bird of paradise arching high on the crest of his helmet and a silver sash embroidered with gold thread crossing his chest served as the commander's insignia of rank. A collection of badges and ribbons, none from any of the city states of the Princedons, on the chest of his red and white striped tunic testified to his experience and valor under arms. But under his finery, his grizzled beard, scarred scowl, rock hard forearms, roughened hands, and spear-for-a-spine posture said unmistakably what he had been before taking command of the Eikby Guard—a sergeant.

Stonearm ran his scowl up one side of Spinner and Haft and down the other, a looking over that never failed to make an ordinary soldier pale and go weak in the knees.

The two just looked back at him.

"Frangerian sea soldiers, eh?" Stonearm said in passable Frangerian. "You used to be pretty good."

"Most people think we're better than ever, Captain," Spinner said levelly.

Leaning suddenly toward the Eikby Guard commander, Haft said with a growl, "We prefer to be called 'Marines.' "

Stonearm looked pointedly at the single chevron-over-paired-crossbows on their sleeves. He'd seen that insignia before, and knew it indicated some sort of junior enlisted man a couple of ranks below sergeant. "*You* are in command of that ragtag band?" he asked sarcastically.

A sergeant of another military, even if he was a captain, could only be allowed to get away with so much. Spinner planted his fists on his hips and stuck his face inches from Stonearm's.

"That 'ragtag band' beat off a larger force of bandits that had your guardsmen so frightened they stood back and watched rather than join in the fight."

"Your band only won because you and that giant crashed through the bandits. And they didn't run until my horsemen got there."

"The way I saw it," Haft snarled, "they were already running when your horsemen finally showed up."

They glared at each other for a tense moment, then Captain Stonearm burst into laughter and clapped a powerful hand on each of their shoulders. "Now that you're called Marines, you Frangerians are even *more* arrogant than before! Calm down, I was just testing you. Anybody can put on a uniform. If you didn't react like you did, I would have suspected you weren't what you say you are." He grinned and held out a hand to shake. "I was a sergeant in the Easterlies Household Guard myself, before I decided to retire someplace where it was warm all the time.

"Now, tell us about your meeting with the bandits," Stonearm changed the subject.

They told the story without embellishment and briefly answered all questions the captain and the mayor asked.

When they were through, Stonearm said, "Those are the Rockhold Band, our local bandits, all right. But what happened to that Blood Swords captain after he left you?"

"We don't know. I wanted to ask you if he was here," Spinner replied.

"No, I haven't seen or heard of him. Lord Mayor, have you?"

The mayor shook his head, he'd neither seen nor heard of the Skragland officer before this.

"Now, do you have a copy of that famous *Lord Gunny Says* with you, and does it say anything about what to do in a situation like this?" Stonearm changed the subject again.

Captain Stonearm and the mayor had no doubts, they were certain the bandits would come back—and in larger numbers. When they came back, both said, the bandits would not only attack the outlander party that had fought and beaten them twice already, they would attack the town itself. Beyond that they were in complete disagreement. Stonearm wanted to prepare to defend the town; the mayor insisted that if the outlanders left right away, the bandits would leave the town alone when they came.

"That is a bad idea," Stonearm growled. "The way they'll see it, we harbored these people. If they aren't here for the bandits to fight, they'll attack us instead. More, I think it's about time we put paid to them."

"Captain!" the mayor snapped. "I am Lord Mayor here. I have lived in this area all my life. I have dealt with these bandits the entire time I have been Lord Mayor. You are a newcomer. I know how the bandits think and what they will do. You know nothing. You," he turned to Spinner and Haft, "must leave immediately."

"Marines never run from a fight," Haft said harshly.

"With all due respect to your position and experience, Lord Mayor," Spinner said more calmly, "I suspect Captain Stonearm is right. We've done the bandits severe hurt—not just once, but twice. They'll want vengeance. And I think Captain Stonearm is right when he says if we aren't here when they show up they'll take their revenge on you. Besides," he glanced toward the pavilion where the wounded were being treated, "we have wounded who can't be safely moved yet."

"I tell you the bandits *won't* attack us if you aren't here!" the mayor shouted, wide-eyed. "They wouldn't harm themselves so. *I* am Lord Mayor, *I* give the orders. Captain Stonearm, you will escort these people out of town and send them on their way." A wicked grin slashed across his face. "Send them to the south."

Haft started to draw his axe, but Spinner stopped him with a hand on his arm.

"Are you ready to fight *us* before you're attacked by the bandits?" Spinner asked coldly.

Stonearm turned his back on the mayor and looked over the landscape. "We better start preparing defenses," he said.

"Captain, you are dismissed!" the mayor shrilled. He spun toward a nearby squad of swordsmen. "Arrest him!" The swordsmen looked uncertainly at one another and their commander.

Stonearm studied the mayor for a long moment, then said, "Lord Mayor, when I contracted to command the Eikby Guard, it was not with the expectation that I would run away the first time danger threatened. Nor did I expect to be in league with bandits." He turned to the squad of swordsmen, who still had not made a move toward him and calmly addressed their sergeant. "Assemble the guard in company formation. We need to start getting ready."

The sergeant looked from Stonearm to the mayor and back, thought matters over, and concluded that he liked his commander and his commander's ideas better than he did the mayor and his. He looked at his men; they looked like they were ready to do anything he told them to. Eikby had been too poor for too long because of the bandits.

"Immediately, Captain," the sergeant said, and sent all but two of his men running to the other squads to assemble them. He looked pointedly at the mayor, ready to arrest him if ordered to do so.

The mayor paled. "This is insubordination," he croaked. "Worse, it is mutiny. I will see you hanged for it. All of you!" He twisted about and stalked rigidly to his waiting carriage.

"What is that all about?" Spinner asked when the mayor was gone.

"Later. We have to start on the defenses."

According to *The Manual for Sea Soldiers*, the only totally untenable defensive position was one the defenders refused to defend. Eikby's defenders seemed willing—at least their commander and some of the guardsmen were—but it certainly seemed that the mayor didn't *want* the town to be defended. What the townspeople thought was anybody's guess at first.

The land created problems for defenders. To begin with, it was nearly perfectly flat—the only high ground was garden compost piles, and all the low ground was underwater in ponds, streams, and a few irrigation ditches. There wasn't a single guardhouse unless they counted the barracks on the town square, neither was there a watch tower other than the bell tower on the town hall. The outermost houses were too widely scattered to join together as defensive works, and too flimsy to use even if they'd been closer together. There weren't any fences.

"We need fences that will break up charges," Spinner said.

"And channel the attackers into killing zones," Haft added.

Captain Stonearm pulled a map of Eikby from a pouch on his belt and, kneeling, spread it on the ground. "Here, here, and here are good places for fences," he said as he drew lines with a blunt finger. "Not only will fences there be good at channeling attackers, they won't be disruptive to farming because they follow the borders of different fields." While he talked he indicated more places to build fences. "I need a stylus," he muttered. Then to the leader of the horse squad, "Fetch Plotniko and Stupnikow to me."

The horse sergeant saluted and said, "Immediately, Captain." He mounted up and cantered toward the town.

"Here are a stylus and ink, Captain." Doli moved into the circle next to Spinner, close enough that their arms brushed. She offered the writing implements to Stonearm. In a few strokes, he marked where he wanted fences.

While they waited for Plotniko and Stupnikow, Eikby's master carpenter and master builder, Spinner and Haft introduced Fletcher to Stonearm. Then they set their men in the best defensive positions they could in the open ground. They also sent out several strong security patrols to the west and north. By the time they were done, Plotniko and Stupnikow arrived. There was still no sign of Silent and Wolf.

Plotniko and Stupnikow examined the map carefully.

"This is a lot of fencing, it will take ten days or more for the carpenters to construct these fences," Plotniko said.

"I don't think we have ten days," Captain Stonearm said somberly. "We need more than just the carpenters and wood cutters building the fences. The farmers will have to help, and the husbandmen, too."

"We can do it if we put everybody on the fences," Stupnikow agreed. "But if we do, who will weed the fields and tend the flocks?"

Stonearm snorted. "If we don't build the fences in time, we won't need to worry about weeding the fields or tending the flocks."

Stupnikow looked at the guard captain somberly. "You're right. I will line up work crews now."

"Will they come when you tell them why?" Stonearm asked.

"They will come," Plotniko said. "This is rich land, the people are tired of being poor. Now, I'll assemble the carpenters and woodsmen to get started on the stakes." He followed Stupnikow back into the town.

"Now tell us about the mayor," Spinner said when the masters were gone. "And why does the town seem so poor in such a rich land?"

Stonearm sighed. "He's afraid, and with good reason. The mayor and my predecessor had an arrangement with the Rockhold Band. They paid the bandits a 'tax'—a tribute—of food and supplies, including the entire production of two arrowsmiths. That's why the town is poor, its wealth goes to the bandits. In return the bandits promised not to raid Eikby—so long as the town didn't build any defenses."

"Then why did he think we might be a bandit raiding party when we showed up?" Spinner asked.

Stonearm spat to the side. "The woodsmen who first saw you didn't recognize you so they thought maybe you were a

different band. We heard this morning that the Rockhold
Band lost a fight yesterday. So he thought maybe a new bandit
band was moving in to take over."

"You've got soldiers," Haft said. "Why didn't you go after
the bandits instead of paying tribute?"

Stonearm barked out a short laugh. "You saw my soldiers.
Have you ever seen a sorrier excuse for an army? All they're
good for is parades." He sighed again. "I have to take blame
for that, but I'm only accepting *part* of the blame." He looked
around to make sure nobody could overhear. "I've only been
here for a few months. I'm the only full-time soldier in the
guard. Except for their ceremonial duties, the mayor has only
let me have the guardsmen one day a month for training.
'They have their occupations and families to look after,' he
says when I tell him I need time to train them. 'We don't need
a real army,' he says." He spat again. "I've tried and tried to
get him to see the fallacy in his thinking. All I've accomplished is, I was close to losing this nice, cushy job of mine
even before now." He shook his head. "Some retirement I
picked for myself." He looked around.

"*Your* soldiers, on the other hand, I recognize some of their
uniforms. You've got Zobran Border Wardens and Lancers,
Skraglander Guards and Blood Swords, and sea soldiers of
at least two or three different nations. Those Bloody Axes are
impressive. *Your* men know how to fight, I know that. Even
most of your men who aren't wearing uniforms carry themselves like veterans—like Fletcher here. Plus, you've got a
war magician, and I heard you've got that steppe giant, though
I haven't seen him myself. Still, there aren't enough of you to
defeat the Rockhold Band." He sadly shook his head.

"How many sol—guardsmen do you have?" Spinner asked.

"Four dozen. If I'd been allowed to train them properly, between my four dozen and your—how many do you have, four
score?—we could beat these bandits. But mine are about
worthless without help."

"Are they willing to fight?" Haft asked.

"Willing? They seem to be. But who knows if they can?

They've never had to, and I've had precious little opportunity to train them."

"If the bandits in this area really are joining together to come after us, they'll have to—unless they want to simply surrender. And our men aren't enough to win against three hundred without help."

"I know. And if we don't help you defeat them, when they're finished with you, they'll burn the town because we didn't destroy you ourselves."

Spinner looked over the town's area. It was far too large for even sixscore fighters to defend more than part of it against that large a force, even if it was surrounded by a stout, high palisade with a fighting step on its inside; there was simply too great a perimeter to defend with fewer than five hundred men. And even if they could that would leave all of the crop and grazing land open to the bandits.

"You have woodsmen and hunters," he said. "Do any of them know how to fight?"

"A few probably do, but as individuals, not as part of a unit. Few men from the hinterlands of the Princedons ever go abroad to join foreign armies, so there are hardly any veterans in Eikby. Those bandits will likely be here in less than four days, possibly in only two or three. That *might* be long enough to get those fences up, and build a few barricades, but it's nowhere near enough time to get all the potential fighters organized and even partly trained in unit tactics."

Haft whistled. "Four days? It takes four *months* to give a civilian enough training for him to get to the point where he can *begin* learning how to be a Frangerian Marine."

"We don't need Marines," Spinner told him, "we just need soldiers."

Stonearm chuckled. "Arrogant bastards! I think that's part of why you're so good. You believe you're the best, and so does just about everybody else. That's half the fight."

"It's easy to believe the truth," Haft said.

"How much will the mayor interfere?" Spinner asked, ignoring him.

"He's probably back in town right now, threatening people, trying to coerce everyone into not cooperating with us."

"Do you think he'll succeed?"

"Plotniko and Stupnikow came immediately when I sent for them. They sounded confident when they went to get the people they need for the work." Stonearm shrugged. "We'll know soon enough."

Spinner continued looking around; he couldn't decide how to begin training the guards and anyone else who might be willing to fight. He was afraid they wouldn't have enough time for even the most rudimentary training. "We need something to slow the bandits down, a way to delay their attack by a few days. But what?"

The sounds of people on the move came from the road. They looked toward the town and saw groups of townsmen heading toward them with carts loaded with wood and tools. Plotniko and Stupnikow had been right—the people were willing to defend their town against the bandits, all they needed was someone to tell them what to do. Soon the sounds of sawing, chopping, and hammering rippled through the area.

It was dusk by the time Silent showed up. Wolf was romping at his side.

"I found the bandit camp," the giant said through a grin as soon as he reached Spinner and Haft. He eyed Captain Stonearm, nodded respectfully when they were introduced. Stonearm bowed in return, glanced warily at Wolf. The Golden Girl squeezed in between Silent and Wolf. Wolf licked her hand in greeting, Stonearm looked at her curiously, the others paid her no attention. Doli moved just close enough behind Spinner to hear what they said.

"What did you find out?" Spinner asked.

"It's not really a camp," Silent explained, "it's more like a village; some of the houses have stone walls. There are wells, a smithy, stables. Just about everything you'd expect to find in a forest village." He knelt next to a patch of bare ground and drew a map of the bandit village as he talked. "It's in a small valley, little more than a hollow in the surrounding hills—the hills have steep sides on the valley side. Roads lead in here, here, and here, (north, east, and west). To the south a track too small to be called a road cuts between two hills. There's a two-man watch post here," he drew it in on the west side of the south track, "and another one here." He indicated another to the northeast. "They've got a lone lookout in a tall tree on a low hill over here." He made a mark to the southeast. "I'm not sure about here." He pointed to the northwest. "I didn't get there."

"Ulgh!" Wolf objected.

"*Wolf* went there, but I couldn't quite understand his report." He studied the wolf for a moment as Wolf made movements with a paw on the ground and bobbed his head.

Stonearm stared at Wolf, mouth agape. It looked to him like the animal was trying to communicate something very specific.

"All right, all right," Silent said after a moment. "You're saying there were two lookouts there."

Wolf stopped pawing the dirt and nodded vigorously. He keened in delight when Silent ruffled the fur on his back and scratched behind his ears.

"I don't believe it," Stonearm muttered, looking wide-eyed at the wolf. "I thought that was only a child's tale."

Haft scowled at Wolf; they had important business to discuss, it wasn't right for the beast to take their attention.

"Believe it," Silent rumbled, smiling at Wolf. "But as I was saying." He turned back to his scratched map. "The two hills on the south are thinly wooded, enough trees were cut to give the lookouts a clear enough view of anyone approaching during the day."

"How many bandits are in the village?" Spinner asked.

"It was hard to tell," Silent answered, "but I estimate there were well over a hundred men when I was there. Women, children, and oldsters, maybe two hundred more. I came back this way," he swung his hand in a broad sweep to the northeast of the bandit base, then down to the southeast. "I heard sounds of men and horses heading toward the village, twenty-five or thirty of them. The village is about a four-hour walk on horseback to the northwest from here." He looked at them expectantly.

"So let's say a hundred and fifty of them now," Spinner said softly.

"More than that," Stonearm said. "There were probably more coming from other directions. Some of them will take a few more days to get there. Then they'll likely take a couple of days or so to get themselves ready before they come for us. We might have a week to get ready. Possibly more."

"The fences should be up by then," Spinner noted.

"Some of those guardsmen know a little bit more about fighting than you said," Fletcher added. He'd spent the remainder of the daylight training the guardsmen in swordplay.

Haft's mind was only partly on the discussion, he was more interested in Silent's map. Suddenly he yelped with excitement.

"What's wrong?" Spinner asked.

"Nothing's wrong," Haft said gleefully. "At least not for us."

"What do you mean?"

"Take another look at Silent's map. Think of the scale. Silent, do I have this right? Each of these hills," he tapped the three where Silent had seen lookouts, "is less than fifty yards from the village, is that right?"

"Gods, you're right," Silent murmured. The others looked blank, they hadn't seen what Haft and Silent did.

"You said the sentries have a clear view of the approaches during the day. What about at night?"

The giant grinned. "I came at them right down the trail at night and they didn't see me."

Haft looked at the others excitedly. "They think we're too afraid to do anything to them. Well, we *can* do something to them—and make *them* afraid instead."

Spinner and Stonearm looked again at Silent's map and their faces changed as they saw what Haft had spotted. Once they did, it didn't take Haft long to convince them he was right, especially since Silent enthusiastically backed him. They began making plans. Alyline kept oddly quiet during the planning; nobody expected Doli to say anything, so no one was surprised when she didn't.

They set out before midnight: Spinner, Haft, Captain Stonearm, the eight Zobran Border Warders, four of the Skraglander Blood Swords, a Skraglander poacher, and Xundoe. When Silent had described the land he'd traveled to them, two of Eikby's hunters said they knew safe trails that led near the bandit village. They and Silent served as guides. Four nearly grown boys came along to handle the horses when they stopped. Wolf ranged ahead. Spinner was surprised and Haft relieved when the Golden Girl didn't insist on going along. Fletcher and Sergeant Phard were left in command of the combined defensive forces. Stonearm accepted that, he knew those two had more experience and knowledge than all of his men combined.

A gibbous moon shed enough light through the trees for the party to follow the trails along which the hunters led. The going was easy most of the way and, aside from the occasional *clop* when a horse's hoof landed on something hard, they were quiet enough they didn't disturb the birds and bats that *hoo-ed* and *squee-ed* in the night. Only the night-feasting insects paid them much attention, and they didn't make too much of a nuisance of themselves.

In the small hours of the night, they stopped. Silent estimated they were about three-quarters of a mile from the bandit village. Spinner went with the giant and two of the Zobran Border Warders to scout ahead on foot. Haft objected to being left behind, but Spinner was afraid he might decide to kill any sentries he got close enough to—he didn't know if or when the bandits checked their sentries and didn't want to take the chance that someone would discover dead sentries before the raiders were in position.

It was little more than an hour before dawn by the time they returned. Everyone in the party gathered close to hear their report.

"Wolf met us partway along," Spinner told them. "He'd already checked for new posts, evidently there aren't any that he and Silent hadn't already found on the southern hills during the day. There are two sentries at each of the lookout posts. The trail from the village between the hills is clear. A footpath leads from that trail to each of the listening posts. The sentries didn't seem to be all that alert."

"Careless of them," Haft growled, still unhappy about having been left behind on the scouting expedition.

"Not really," Captain Stonearm told him. "Nobody's ever attacked one of their bases so the bandits have reason to feel secure."

"What else did you find?" Haft asked.

"There's a night watchman inside the village. He's sitting under a lamp." Spinner laughed softly. "The watchman was asleep."

"Could you tell anything about how many people were there?"

Spinner shook his head. "It was too dark to see into the stables, but we saw what looked like a hastily erected corral beyond the buildings. If that's what it was, there are more of them now than when Silent was there during the day."

"So what are we waiting for?" Haft asked.

Spinner looked at the others. All he could see in the deepening dark was silhouettes of men's heads and shoulders, and the spikes of their upright weapons. "Does everybody remember what they're supposed to do?" he asked.

The silhouettes bobbed up and down as the men nodded, voices murmured assent and readiness.

"All right, then," Spinner said.

"Let's do this thing!" Haft ordered with relieved eagerness and rose to stand tall.

Spinner made sure all the horses were on tether lines and the four boys knew how to keep them secure and where to move them when the time came. Then they broke into three groups. Silent led the first group—Spinner and the Skraglanders—away at a trot. A couple of minutes later one of the hunters led the second group—Stonearm and the Zobrans. A couple of minutes after the second group, Haft and Xundoe moved out along with the remaining men led by the other hunter. This time Wolf trailed; he didn't have anything more to do until after things began. The four boys swallowed nervously at being left alone. Then pride at the responsibility they were given took over and their fear drained away. They waited for the signal to come forward with the horses.

The pace was fast at first then slowed as they neared the lookout posts. Seventy-five yards away, the first group stopped. Spinner took two of the Blood Swords toward the post on the left, Haft led the other two to the right.

CHAPTER
TWELVE

Spinner and his Skraglanders didn't head straight at the bandit position, they aimed to its side and circled around to approach from behind. The forest was semitropical so few leaves and twigs lay on the ground to rustle or snap under their passing feet, but thorns stabbed at their flesh and snagged their clothes, and creeping vines groped to trip them. They came to the footpath that led from the trail to the lookout post and readied their weapons. Crouching, they followed the footpath until they were twenty yards from the post and saw its hulking shadow through the thinning trees. They drew their knives and lowered themselves to their bellies. Slowly, probing the ground in front of them with their fingertips for anything that would make a noise, they crawled closer. They breathed through their mouths to reduce any noise they might make themselves, listened intently for sounds from the sentries.

The sentries were quiet but not totally silent. They made small noises as they shifted restlessly—it was that time on their shift that they were tired and wanted relief, but that relief was still some time off. There was a small *clink* as one shifted a piece of equipment. One murmured a few soft words, got a muted chuckle in reply.

When he was eight yards away, on the beaten-down earth of the post, Spinner stopped and signaled the two Blood Swords to move up alongside him. They slithered close. Spinner put his hands under his shoulders and drew one foot under his body, ready to spring forward. To his sides he sensed the

Skraglanders doing the same. He paused, listening and look-ing. Six yards ahead, he saw the shadow of a seated sentry. Just beyond, the other stood looking to his front. Moving ever so slowly, he rose far enough to have his weight on his feet and his hands free. The other two did the same. He touched them lightly and indicated they should both go after the far sentry, he'd get the near one. Then he tapped them and sprinted on his toes.

Spinner slammed into the seated sentry and knocked him off the log with enough force to blast the air out of the man's chest. He was on his man instantly. One hand groped for and clamped onto the nose and mouth of the downed man, the blade in the other flashed then sliced through the sentry's throat. Then Spinner struggled to control the man's bucking and kicking to keep him from making noise. He looked up and saw the others gently lowering the body of the sentry they had killed to the ground.

Spinner looked over the edge of the hilltop, down a slope so steep it was almost a cliff, and saw Rockhold's watchman, quietly nodding under his lamp. A dog barked in the village, but it was a restless bark not an alarm.

"So that's Rockhold," Spinner murmured. He turned to the Skraglanders. "Let's get these bodies out of the way. Go get the others," he told the second. Dawn was edging closer, it was light enough for him to make out the Blood Swords' eyes above the white of their teeth when they grinned at him.

Haft and his Blood Swords took out their listening post just as easily. It was obvious that the Rockhold Band bandits really did feel secure in their stronghold.

In less than ten more minutes the members of the raiding party were all on the hills, ten raiders on each overlooking the bandit village of Rockhold, atop slopes too steep for attackers to swiftly charge up. They waited for the first birds of day to sing the sun into rising.

There was no light to speak of in the hollow, but the dark-ness was gentle enough to allow the raiders on the hilltops to make out the shapes of houses and other buildings when the first birds began to greet the dawn. Seventeen of the men on the two hilltops struck sparks with their flints and lit tiny fires. They touched prepared arrows into the fires and the arrows began to flame just behind their points. They nocked their arrows and shot them into the roofs of the dimly seen buildings in the hollow below. The arrows arched high, trailing fire, before plunging down. Most of them stuck into the thatch roofs and flames began to lick and spread. The seventeen fired another volley of fire arrows, then a third. They nocked normal arrows and waited while fire spread on the roofs of all but the most remote of the houses and buildings.

The night watchman stirred from his slumber, sat straight, and stretched widely before he opened his eyes. He rubbed his eyes in shock, unable at first to believe what he saw. Then he leaped to his feet shouting, *"Fire! Fire!"* and ran from house to house, pounding on the doors and crying the alarm as he went.

The first startled shouts came from inside the houses in almost the same instant the watchman gave his first cry.

Spinner, lying on the southwest hill, couldn't shoot a fire arrow with his crossbow. He lay with a quarrel ready and his crossbow aimed at the door of one of the nearer houses. Despite its accuracy and power, the crossbow didn't have the range to reach even to the middle of the village. He dimly saw a man bolt out of the door and pause, looking back into it. Spinner shot. His quarrel went true and the bandit staggered and fell into someone just coming through the door. The two fell back inside. Spinner looked for another target in range of his weapon while he reloaded.

On the southeast hill, Haft was less patient. He only waited a breath after the watchman's first cry before he shot into the doorway of the nearest structure. Three men piled out, one limping and clutching his thigh, before Haft could reload. The three men didn't stand in front of the door, instead they split up and ran in different directions. Haft carefully followed one, then fired and a second later had the satisfaction of seeing the running bandit stumble and fall when the quarrel hit. He reloaded and picked another target.

Flames quickly engulfed roofs, crackling sparks shot into

the sky and drifted to other roofs, setting them on fire. Flames began to eat their way down the wooden sides of buildings. Women screamed, children cried, men called out fearfully or shouted questions. Horrible screams came out of a burning stable. The growing fires gave enough lumination for the archers to see clearly. They readied and began to shoot as soon as people ran outside the burning structures—they tried to shoot only at men, but couldn't always take the time to identify their targets. Several bandits were quickly down, writhing in pain or lying still in death. So were a few women and a couple of larger children.

Chaos reigned, but only briefly before three of the bandits began bawling orders. One of them started organizing women and children into bucket brigades to douse the fires. He had one bucket line formed and another started before an arrow in the chest put an end to his organizing. Two other bandit leaders saw the direction the arrows came from. One led as many men as he could quickly gather to the temporary corral on the north side of the village. None of the archers could effectively reach that far. The third leader quickly assembled other bandits and led them in a scrambling, climbing charge up the steep side of the southwest hill. Some of them fell to the rain of arrows that came at them from the hilltop, but there were far more of them than there were archers, and the darkness on the hillside made them hard to see.

Xundoe squatted nervously next to Spinner, his hands fretfully twined and retwined around themselves as he watched the charging bandits. "Now, I can reach them *now*," he said with a squeak as he made out the shadow of a climbing bandit.

Spinner laid a restraining hand on the mage's arm as he coldly watched the emerging shadows. He let the leading bandits come closer, waited until the mass of them were where the leaders were when Xundoe said he could reach them, then said, "Stop them now, Xundoe."

The mage snatched up one of the three phoenix eggs he had laid out next to his ankles and twisted its top. He threw it with a straight-armed, overhand lob. The egg sailed out and down the side of the hill. It hit in the middle of the mass of

bandits and burst open. The phoenix reared up with a shriek
and unfurled its long, fiery wings. The bandit it landed in
front of saw it and his eyes popped wide. He started to throw
himself backward to roll down the hill, but he wasn't fast
enough to avoid the flaming bird—he was incinerated before
he had time to scream. The phoenix's flapping wings slapped
bandits as they pumped to lift the bird. The bandits hit by the
wings lit up like torches, screaming and shrieking as they
tumbled down the hill.

The other bandits paused in fearful awe as the phoenix
lifted from the ground and spiraled into the sky, its flames
sharply illuminated them and cast dancing shadows away
from them. Spinner and the archers worked their bows and
struck a dozen of bandits with arrows. When the survivors
realized how many of their mates were already down they
spun about and bolted down the steep slope—some tripped
and tumbled to the bottom with sprained ligaments and broken bones. More arrows followed and several more bandits
fell and skidded for a distance before they lay still. Lightning
flashed and thunder cracked as Xundoe worked his small demon spitter. More bandits fell to it.

The other group of bandits now charged on horseback
from the corral, herding unmounted horses ahead of them as
a shield. They raced through the village, past burning houses
and buildings, trampling women and children who couldn't
get out of their way heading toward the trail between the two
hills on the south side. Stampeding the extra horses would
have been a good idea if they had been attacking a position on
a plain; the stampeding horses would have shielded them.
But the positions they headed for were high above, and the
archers could see down on them, their view unobstructed by
the horses between—and the frightened horses impeded the
bandits, slowing their charge. The archers on the hilltops shot
many bandits, and as many more were thrown and trampled
when their horses were hit before they reached the gentler
slopes between the guardian hills.

Xundoe ran downhill a short distance to get within throwing range of the foot of the hill and threw another phoenix egg

at horsemen who were trying to force their mounts through the mass of frightened animals that crowded the narrow trail. The horsemen were packed tightly so many men and their mounts died or were horribly burned by the phoenix as it unfurled its wings and sought to gain air. The horses beyond the phoenix panicked and fled uncontrollably. Riderless horses scattered into the forest south of the hills, a few ran up them. Others, with riders, galloped madly back into the burning village, trampling panic-stricken people. Most of the horses shed their riders before escaping the burning village.

Everybody on foot in the village was fleeing the rapidly spreading fires, all thoughts of organizing another counterattack or bucket brigade forgotten. It was nearly impossible for an archer to loose an arrow with any certainty it would hit a bandit, and not a woman, a child, or a horse. They shot anyway.

"Pull out!" Spinner shouted. Xundoe and the men with him gathered their weapons and ran down the back side of the hill, angling toward the southbound trail. Spinner raced down the side of the hill and up the other to where the Haft and Silent were with the rest of the party, still shooting arrows into Rockhold.

"Time to go," he panted when he got there. They all jumped up and ran down the hill's back side. With few clear targets remaining, they were ready to leave.

They found the horse boys waiting with their mounts less than a hundred yards back.

"Is anybody hurt?" Spinner asked as they assembled and mounted. A quick roll call showed the raiding party had suffered no injuries. Spinner and Haft told the boys what a good job they'd done and thanked them for it, the soldiers echoed and amplified their praise. The boys beamed all the way back to Eikby. They heard the roar of the burning village for a long time as they cantered away.

The raiders returned to Eikby at midday. New but sturdy looking fences lined the fields in seeming innocence. Head-high posts had been pounded into the earth in angled pairs that crossed each other; longer posts ran from crossed pair to crossed pair and were securely lashed into place. Workers were busily stringing wires the length of the fences along the tops of the upright posts, others were hammering wires onto the posts below where they crossed. Tightly woven gates that blocked the roads entering the town from east, north, and south looked strong enough to withstand a bull.

Captain Stonearm looked critically at the fences as the raiders entered the cleared land from the forest. The wires and horizontal posts weren't so close that it would be difficult for a man on foot to get through them, but they would slow his passage. The fence height and width were great enough that only horses intensively trained to jump were likely to clear them. The layout of the fences was such that charging horsemen would be channeled into narrower and narrower spaces until they reached the easily defended palisades that were going up. The commander of the Eikby guard nodded approval. The town was getting closer to being defensible.

In open ground, closer to the western fence than to the forest, Fletcher and half of the company's men who hadn't gone on the raid were drilling the guard. Already, the guardsmen looked sharper and more confident than they had the day before, but they looked sharper only compared to how they looked the day before. The rest of the able-bodied men of the company were working with the townsmen on the fences. The previous day's campsite was abandoned, the women, children, and wounded were camped inside the fence.

Halloos rose from the guardsmen when they saw the riders, and all training discipline broke as they ran to greet them. Fletcher shook his head, then signaled his trainers that they could join the welcoming party as well and walked behind the guardsmen to the gate on the west road. More shouting came from where the fences were and the people building them waved. In moments, women and children ran to the west gate, shouting and waving.

Spinner stood in his stirrups, but no matter how hard he searched, he couldn't see the Golden Girl among the waving, shouting women who gathered to welcome them back. Haft noticed Spinner's search; he also noted that Doli wasn't among the welcoming women.

When they neared the gate, women forced it open and ran out to greet them. Worry was in the eyes of those whose husbands, sons, or brothers were among the raiders; the worry turned to relief when they saw their men and boys were unharmed. The first guardsmen arrived and shouted questions: "How did it go?" "Did you find them?" "Was there a fight?" Many of the raiders stopped to answer the questions and take in the adulation of the guardsmen. Spinner, Haft, Silent, and Captain Stonearm continued on to the gate. The women and children still coming through danced aside to let them pass, called welcome and thank you, reached out to touch them as they went by. In the near distance, they spied a small cloud of dust approaching, raised by the wheels of the mayor's carriage as it sped toward them. The quartet advanced a little farther and dismounted to await his arrival. Fletcher joined them, along with Plotkinov and Stupnikow. They briefly told each other about the raid and the progress on the town's defenses.

Before any of them could go into detail, the mayor's carriage clattered to a stop a few yards away and he jumped out and came at them furiously. "How many of our innocents have you gotten killed?" he shrilled before he reached them. Not the greeting any of them expected.

"Lord Mayor," Stonearm said with a deep bow. "We have killed no innocents, only bandits. The raid was a success, many of the Rockhold Band bandits are dead or wounded, Rockhold itself is mostly burned to the ground—and we suffered no injuries of our own. It will be some fair time before the Rockhold Band is able to threaten anyone again." He looked again at the fences and gates. "And anyone who sees this may simply decide to go away and leave us alone."

In his fury the mayor ignored Stonearm's statement. "I have sent a message to the prince. He will send his soldiers to put down your coup. Your insurrection will not last!" Spittle sprayed the Guard Captain's face.

"Lord Mayor," Stonearm said calmly, "I have made no

coup, nor led an insurrection. I have done my job as Guard Captain and dealt with a threat to Eikby. You are yet Lord Mayor."

The mayor still ignored what he said. "If the guardsmen weren't all traitors loyal to you, I'd have you in chains! You usurped my authority! You threaten the security of Eikby by leading a band of, of *strangers* into the forest to confront and anger the bandits. Now they will come and attack us! They will rob and rape and murder and destroy us! Captain Stonearm, your name will live forever in infamy for what you have done to Eikby!"

Plotniko and Stupnikow had withdrawn to a discrete distance when the mayor began his harangue, the others had stood in embarrassed silence during it. Finally Haft stepped between Stonearm and the mayor, placed the flat of his hand on the mayor's chest, and pushed. The mayor staggered back. He didn't fall, but the shock of being shoved stopped his harangue. As much as his jaw continued to flap open and closed, no words came out.

Haft stepped in close. "How about if you shut up for a minute and listen!" he bellowed into the mayor's face from only two or three inches away in his best imitation of a drill instructor chewing out an inept recruit. "Look around; everyone who went on the raid is back and whole." The mayor took another step back, Haft stepped forward, maintaining his closeness. "*Listen* to Captain Stonearm's report. *We* didn't suffer any injuries." The mayor stepped back again, tripped on a discarded scrap of wood, and would have fallen if Haft hadn't grabbed his arm to hold him up and close. "*We* killed or wounded too many bandits for us to count." The mayor tried to step back again, but Haft held him close. "We burned down their whole *base*! The *bandits* don't have anyplace to get organized now, and there aren't as many of them left *to* attack us. We *won*! The bandits aren't going to bother Eikby now. *They can't!*"

The mayor's eyes fearfully darted from Haft to Stonearm, to Spinner, and back. He tried to wrest his arm out of Haft's grip. Haft gave a painful squeeze, then let go. The mayor took a tentative step back, Haft let him. He worked his mouth, then spoke.

"Come to the town hall and tell me all about it." It didn't sound like it was what he'd intended to say. He spun about and climbed into his carriage before they could reply.

People and more people, townsfolk and the company's camp followers together, guardsmen and soldiers of the company alike, followed in a parade. People tried to crowd into the mayor's office to hear the report of the raid. Because he thought everyone deserved to hear his report, Captain Stonearm refused the mayor's order to close the door and have his guardsmen keep everyone out. His frustration intermingled with a healthy dollop of fear, the mayor retired the meeting to the auditorium. In moments, the large room was packed to overflowing.

"Quiet, quiet please!" the mayor shouted over the hubbub. He, the two Frangerian Marines, and Captain Stonearm were behind a table on a small stage at one end of the packed room. The other three sat—Spinner and Haft on one side of the mayor looked bemused, Stonearm to the other was expressionless—the mayor stood.

"Quiet, quiet!" The mayor held one hand above his head, pounded a gavel on the table with the other. The excited people ignored him as they shouted greetings to friends on opposite sides of the large room, repeated to each other constantly growing stories of what had happened at the bandit base, laughed for joy at their imagined release from danger at the hands of the bandits.

"Quiet please!" The mayor's voice grew querulous, and he looked helplessly to his sides.

Stonearm nodded and stood, looking out over the crowd. He filled his chest and roared out, *"Quiet!"* in the kind of carrying, penetrating voice that only sergeants ever develop.

Silence filled the auditorium.

The guard commander looked about with the expression drill sergeants reserve for recruits so impertinent as to think they're good enough to be soldiers. Some of the real soldiers in the room hid smiles and chuckles behind their hands, most of the people without military experience sat down and leaned back timorously.

Satisfied that he had everyone's undivided attention, he turned to the mayor and bowed. "Lord Mayor, I believe you have something to say?" He sat and the mayor stood.

"*Hrmpf.* Yes, I do. Thank you, Captain Stonearm." He looked around the room, amazed that the guard commander had been able to accomplish so much with one word when his many words, hand signals, and poundings on the table had failed so abjectly.

"Captain Stonearm and a number of our valorous guardsmen, along with several of these worthy travelers who came among us yesterday—" Spinner elbowed Haft, who had just enough Zobran to understand who the mayor was giving credit to and was about to object—"have just returned from an, ah, *visit* to the bandits of Rockhold. I, and I'm sure you as well, would like to hear from the good captain exactly what happened there." He bowed to Stonearm. "Captain, if you would be so good as to enlighten us."

Stonearm looked past the mayor to Spinner and Haft. His eyes twinkled with amusement. Haft turned his glare on Stonearm, it was he and Spinner who had done most of the planning and led the raid, not Stonearm. Spinner clamped a restraining hand on Haft's arm and nodded for Stonearm to go ahead. Spinner was more interested in the mayor's unexpected change in attitude than he was in who got credit for what. Stonearm was well aware of who was responsible for the raid's success, and he began with that.

"Let us give credit where it is due," Stonearm began. "If it hadn't been for these two bold Frangerian Marines, Spinner and Haft, and their band of brave warriors from many countries, our, ah," he glanced at the mayor, "*visit* to Rockhold never would have happened, much less met with the success that it did.

"It began when these two Marines and four of the Skragland Blood Swords silently took out two bandit lookout posts. We then waited for the first stirring of dawn." He went on to tell the rest of the action in detail, from the time the first fire arrow arched into the village until they withdrew, leaving all in chaos. "The entire action took about ten minutes." He finished the narrative and chuckled. "Less time than it took to tell.

"I estimate that we burned down three-quarters of Rockhold with destruction of an unknown quantity of their goods and weapons, and scattered their horses so far it will take days—even weeks—to recover all of them. There may have been two hundred bandits assembled when we began. When we finished, there were not too many more than one hundred still alive and uninjured." He stopped and looked to the mayor to see if he had any questions or comments.

Before the mayor could speak up a harsh voice rang from the audience, it was Alyline, the Golden Girl.

"Did you kill any women?"

Stonearm hesitated before answering. "Yes, I'm afraid we did. Some arrows meant for bandits went astray and struck women. Some others were trampled by the bandits' stampeding horses. We did our best to avoid hurting women and children, our only interest was in killing the bandits. But anyone inside a battle is liable to be hurt or even killed, regardless of the intentions of the fighters. It is unfortunate that some women were hurt and possibly killed. I regret it. But those things happen."

"What's the matter with her?" Haft whispered harshly to Spinner. "She's seen battles before—she's seen worse than battle. She knows what can happen when the fighting starts!"

Spinner shook his head, he was as surprised as Haft.

Stonearm made to sit but stopped when another angry voice cried out, "What about children?"

Stonearm sighed. He looked at the questioner, but didn't know her, though he'd seen her hovering near Spinner—it was Doli.

"Again," he answered her, "it was as with the women. Some children were injured, some of them may have killed. I, and everyone else in the raiding party, regret that some women and children were casualties. Sometimes that cannot be avoided." He sat before anyone else had a chance to ask questions.

A gloom briefly settled over the auditorium but it didn't last long. If women and children had died in the raid, well, that was too bad, but they were among the bandits and the only way their deaths could have been avoided was to allow the bandits to ravage Eikby. The people knew the bandits didn't hesitate to kill women and children on their raids.

The mayor stood and bowed to both his sides. To the assembly he said, "I thank, we all thank, Captain Stonearm and Masters Spinner and Haft, and all the members of the raiding party for their successful raid. Perhaps because of their efforts, this part of the Princedons will be safer for both towns and travelers in the future." To the men at his sides he added, "If I have any more questions, I will ask you later. Thank you again." Once more he faced front. "This town meeting is now adjourned." He left by a door at the back of the stage, ignoring the questions shouted from the audience.

Stonearm signaled and exited with Spinner and Haft by the same door.

"What's wrong with them?" Haft asked harshly as they left.

Spinner shook his head again. "I don't know," he said weakly.

CHAPTER
THIRTEEN

The company now occupied space within the outermost houses, close inside the fences. Fletcher led the two Frangerian Marines and the other raiders to it when they left the town hall. The first order of business for Spinner and Haft was to see how the men wounded by the bandits were faring. The people who'd stayed behind during the raid and attended the town meeting followed on foot.

"That's what's wrong with them," Spinner said with sudden revelation. "They have our wounded and dead from yesterday on their minds. Some of the bandits had attacked our women and children while the men fought the rest of them. They're upset because of that, they think battle, they think women and children being attacked."

Haft shook his head. "Alyline and Doli knew we were attacking a base before we left, a place that had women and children. They could have spoken up then." He grimaced. "They've both seen battle, they know what happens—and they know we don't make war on women and children."

Spinner shrugged. He was satisfied with his answer. "They'll get over it," he said confidently.

Haft snorted; he wasn't confident of anything where those two women were concerned.

Silent said nothing, he *knew* women's minds worked in ways incomprehensible to men, and the upset of those two had nothing to do with bandit women and children.

None of the wounded had died overnight or that morning. The town's healing magician was satisfied with their progress and had packed up his demons and carried them away. Only the company's own healing witch and two of the older girls were in attendance in the makeshift hospital.

"They're doing as well as can be expected," Nightbird said. "Even better, thanks to Eikby's healers." She hesitated, then added grudgingly, "Even the healing magician and his demons were a help. Only one of the wounded is still in serious danger, and I believe he has a good chance of recovery."

Spinner and Haft went from pallet to pallet speaking briefly with each person who was awake and able to talk. All were happy to see them, and happy about the successful raid. Spinner was in higher spirits when they finished, even Haft felt less grumbly.

"There she is," Spinner said happily and pointed. "Let's go talk to her."

Haft looked and groaned. Alyline and Doli stood with their heads close together in intimate conversation as they darted glances at the two men. Haft thought their glances were distinctly unfriendly. Still, he followed. Even if Spinner was walking openly into an obvious drubbing, he had to go along to rescue his fellow Marine. Even when Spinner was being so stupid that he didn't deserve rescue.

"Alyline, Doli!" Spinner said expansively when he neared them. He stepped close and slipped an arm around each— he felt so good after the night's raid that he was willing to be friendly with Doli even before she brought herself to his attention.

He blinked in surprise when Doli twisted out of his arm to stand with her back to him, and Alyline pushed him away.

"What? Did I say something wrong?"

"You killed women!" Alyline, fists clenched at her sides, spat.

"You killed children!" Doli spun about and jabbed an accusing finger at him.

"No I didn't!"

Haft bowed his head and covered his eyes with a hand; this was about what he thought would happen.

"Oh, you change your story now?" Alyline accused, stepping forward in a threatening manner.

"You said you did!" Doli exclaimed and advanced a step.

"But I never . . ."

"How many women and children are dead from your raid?" Alyline demanded, thrusting her angry face up to his.

"Murderer!" Doli jabbed a stiff finger into his chest.

"But . . ."

"You kill women and children, and expect me to allow you to put your bloody hands on me afterward?" Alyline spat into his face.

Doli elbowed Alyline aside so she could get directly in Spinner's face. "You go out with a mere twenty men to attack a stronghold of more than two hundred bandits, and you expect me to greet you with open arms just because you're lucky enough to live through it?"

Alyline barely glanced at Doli; she instantly turned her attention and ire on Haft. "Is that all you will ever be?" she scolded him. "A fool who forever rushes into situations that should kill you? How many times do you think you can get away with that?" She punctuated her questions with jabs that left fingernail impressions in the top of his chest just below his throat. "Sometimes I think you are learning, that you are becoming less of a fool. Then you turn around and do something like this! Do you *want* to die in hopeless combat?"

"But, But . . ." Haft backpedaled in a vain attempt to get away from her sharp nails.

"You keep raising my hopes and, every time, you do something stupid and dash them!" She jabbed her fist into his chest hard enough to stagger him back a step, then spun about and grabbed Doli's arm. "Let's go away before I get violent with them."

"And you stink!" Doli shouted over her shoulder as Alyline dragged her away.

"Bu-But . . . ," Spinner stammered.

Rubbing his sore chest, Haft grabbed Spinner's arm and turned him about. "Time to go, Spinner. Let's get out of here before they change their minds and come after us again." He dragged his friend away. "Face it, Spinner," Haft growled, "you just made a single-handed frontal assault on a well-defended position. You lost." He shook his head, wondering why Alyline had turned on him the way she had. It was almost as though she cared what happened to him. He thought he'd rather not have her care. "Let's go before our casualties get worse."

When Spinner resisted, Haft grabbed him by the shoulders and turned him around by main force, then pushed him away. He sniffed. "Doli was right, we both need a bath. Let's get one, then go into town." He looked about for the campsite's shower station.

At least the bucket-boys who kept the shower's reservoir tank filled with warm water treated them with proper respect and admiration.

Later, when they were feeling refreshed if no happier, bathed and in clean clothes, they were about to head into Eikby proper when Captain Stonearm intercepted them. He wanted to show them the progress of the fence construction.

"The mayor always objected that putting up fences would take too long," Stonearm observed, "unnecessarily take too much work away from agriculture and other activities." He snorted derisively. "A thousand people have made short work of it."

They certainly had. The frames of all the western and southern fences were up, and the northern fences were beginning to go up. The western fences had wire strung top and bottom. Workers were busy stringing the main wires on the rest of the frames; other teams were stringing vertical strands between the horizontal wires to make crossing the fence more difficult for footmen, and yet other teams were twisting short, pointed lengths of wire into barbs on the wires.

"When all is done, it will take a much larger band than we first expected to get through the fences in large enough force to defeat Eikby," Stonearm said with great satisfaction. "If the Rockhold Band's survivors are foolish enough to come now, we *will* defeat them."

For their part, Spinner and Haft were very impressed with the progress.

Then Stonearm took them to where Fletcher and the Zo-brans and Skraglanders who hadn't gone on the raid were drilling the Eikby guard. When they arrived they found the soldiers using wooden swords to demonstrate how skilled troops with swords could defeat a larger number of less skilled swords- and pikemen. They were demonstrating on two squads of guards—swordsmen and pikemen who used their normal weapons.

"All I can reasonably say," Fletcher calmly told the guards-men, "is you weren't as bad as the last time. This time you lasted almost two minutes—but you still didn't hurt any of the attackers." He shook his head sadly.

"But we restrained our blows, sir!" one of the guardsmen objected. "To avoid badly injuring one of your soldiers." The Skraglanders and Zobrans burst into laughter.

Fletcher instantly jumped in the face of the guardsman who'd spoken up. "These soldiers are professionals!" he roared. "You could lay a blade on them only by sheerest accident!"

The guardsman quailed.

"Now, change defenders," he bellowed, "and this time *try* to hit them. Try hard!" He signaled to the soldiers, who laughingly formed up to attack the guards again.

The other squad of swordsmen and the squad of lancers, dismounted, set their formation in two ranks, swordsmen in front of the lancers who leveled their lances between the swordsmen.

The soldiers conferred among themselves for a moment, then faced the guards and charged in two ranks of their own, the Zobrans in front of the Skraglanders. The Zobrans stopped short of the guards and fenced at the lance points with their wooden swords. Angry at the taunting, Eikby's lancers pushed ahead to get their weapons close enough to break past the Zobran swords, crowding their swordsmen ahead of them as the attackers pulled back. In seconds, their ranks were confused and the Skraglanders in the rear rank shouted then ran around the sides of the deteriorating guard formation and fell upon it from behind. In seconds, all the

Eikby Guards were on the ground or staggering beneath blows from the wooden swords.

"Stop!" Fletcher bellowed, red in the face. "What happened to your discipline? You fell for one of the oldest tricks swordsmen play against spears and pikes! Always remember to maintain your ranks and your discipline, or you will be killed as quickly as you would have been now if these soldiers hadn't been using practice blades!"

Snorting heavily, he turned from the guards and stomped over to Spinner, Haft, and Stonearm. His chest heaved as he brought his breathing back under control. Normal color quickly returned to his face and he grinned at the trio.

"Captain, your men are willing enough, but they don't know the first thing about fighting."

"I'm not surprised," Stonearm said sadly. "It's as I keep saying—I was never allowed to give them proper training." He paused, looking speculatively at Fletcher. "I mean no offense, you're doing a good job, but do you have experience in training troops?"

Fletcher shook his head.

"But you do know fighting. I know fighting *and* training. Together, I think we can quickly teach them the basics, would you agree?"

Fletcher's grin broadened. He, too, recognized the sergeant that Stonearm used to be. "I do indeed."

"Then shall we?" He turned to Spinner and Haft. "May I?"

"Please do."

"All ranks, form on me!" Stonearm called out in a drill sergeant's voice as he strode toward the guards. "Now that you know you *don't* know how to fight, we are going to teach you how *to* fight."

Haft looked at Spinner and saw the sadness on his face. Whether it was because of the guardsmen's fighting ability or the way Alyline and Doli had assaulted him, Haft didn't care. He slapped Spinner's shoulder and said, "Come on, my friend. We don't know any more about how to train fighters than Fletcher does, and we both need a drink. Let's visit that inn. We can get a meal, too. I'm hungry."

Spinner nodded morosely and followed Haft into the center of Eikby.

The Middle of the Forest Inn was the second largest building in Eikby, but not by much. It had to be large to accommodate the large, heavily armed, groups that were all that could traverse the forest with any degree of safety from the bandit bands. Attended cloakrooms stood to each side of the main entrance. A prominent sign barred entry to the corridor that led to the main common room, two smaller commons, and the private dining rooms. Between them, they had just enough written Zobran to translate it:

> ALL WEAPONS
> ARE TO BE
> CHECKED WITH
> THE CLOAKS

Spinner and Haft looked at each other; they'd seen such signs only in the more formal common rooms of expensive inns in large cities, never in a wayside inn—and no matter how big the Middle of the Forest Inn was in Eikby, the whole town was small enough to count as little more than a wayside itself.

Word had come ahead that they were on their way and the innkeeper bustled up to greet them personally. He was a stout man, rather larger through the belly than the chest. He briskly wiped his hands on his apron.

"Welcome, Master Spinner, Master Haft," he said with an innkeeper's unctuous smile and a bow. "The Middle of the Forest Inn is most pleased to serve such distinguished visitors as you. My name is Dommuz, and this is my house." He snapped his fingers and an attendant scurried over to accept their weapons.

Haft reluctantly turned over his axe; Spinner more readily divested himself of his quarterstaff. The attendant stood as though waiting for something more.

"We have several rooms for dining, each for a different

taste," Dommuz continued. "If mightily drinking is your pleasure, we have that. Another room has the most pleasant and pleasing music to serve as dining background. Or if you prefer to hear a skald tell stories, or watch jugglers and acrobats . . ."

"Lead us to the room with the best music, please," Haft said, determined not to let giving up his axe bother him. He stepped toward the corridor.

"Ah, sir?" Dommuz said apologetically. "Your belt knife."

Haft turned back to him. "My what?"

"Your belt knife, Master Haft." The innkeeper shrugged and spread his hands. "The Middle of the Forest Inn allows no weapons of any sort within its public rooms."

"But this isn't a weapon," Haft said, patting the scabbarded knife on his belt.

"Sir, it has a blade, no doubt a sharp one. It can easily be used to wound or, gods forbid, kill a man."

"This madman wants me to give up my knife?" Haft said to Spinner.

"Why such strong insistence?" Spinner asked.

"You understand, sir, that we get many very rough men here, often violent men. So we allow no weapons. It is a town ordnance."

Spinner nodded. "I understand." He took the knife from his belt and handed it over. "Give it over," he told Haft.

Haft gaped at him, then asked the innkeeper, "And with what do we cut our meat, or are we expected to gnaw it like wild beasts?"

With considerable effort the innkeeper puffed up his chest so that it stood almost directly above his belly instead of sloping back sharply from it. "Sirs, our meat is the most tender to be found within several days travel. And we cut it into bite-sized pieces in the kitchen before it is served. Eikby may not be a grand city like world travelers such as yourselves are accustomed to, but neither are we rustics. Our dining rooms offer *forks* for our guests to eat with!"

Grumbling, Haft handed his knife to the attendant.

Spinner laughed. It wasn't much of a laugh, but it was his

first since they'd visited the hospital. He clapped Haft on the shoulder.

"Come, Haft. You heard Master Dommuz, they have *forks*. Even The Burnt Man Inn didn't have forks. Anyway, if trouble comes I'm sure we will have warning enough to get our weapons before we are set upon."

"What if we don't have time?" Haft grumbled, almost to himself.

"Don't tell me you've forgotten your hand-to-hand?"

Haft looked like he wanted to spit in disgust, but the cleanliness of the inn's floor restrained him.

They followed the obviously relieved Master Dommuz along the corridor and into a common room holding not quite twenty tables, each with seating for six or so and sufficient room for the serving maids to maneuver between the tables even when they were all filled. More than half of the tables were occupied, and more than half of those had open seats. Several of the men who had been on the overnight raid were drinking and eating. They shouted and lifted flagons and cups in salute to their commanders. Haft cheerfully shouted and waved back, Spinner waved with less enthusiasm. The innkeeper led them to an open table near the small stage, where a troubadour played a mandolin. A young woman in milkmaid garb stood next to him as they sang a duet.

A serving maid appeared at their table as they were sitting.

"Serve Masters Spinner and Haft our best," Master Dommuz said then bowed himself away.

"Ale, sirs?" she asked as Haft eyed her. She was lovely and blond, smiled prettily and was garbed modestly in a dress that left bare only a smallish triangle at the top of her chest, and whose skirt extended to midcalf. The bodice was snug but not tight, and the skirt was loose but not enough so for a rude hand to flip it up. She looked to Haft to be a year or two younger than he and Spinner.

Spinner, lost in his own thoughts, nodded absently.

"Ale," Haft said.

"Our best," she replied and hurried off. A moment later she

was back and gracefully placed two cold tankards in front of them.

"Would you like some supper, masters?" she asked.

Haft had already looked over the menu posted above the kitchen door. "Do you have any specials today?" he asked and quaffed deeply of his ale.

"Everything we have is special," she said proudly. "It's all posted."

"Well, in that case, I'll have the Middle of the Forest stew. How about you, Spinner?"

Spinner shrugged, he wasn't hungry.

"Make that two," Haft said. "And another of these." He hefted his tankard and drained it.

"An excellent choice, Master Haft," the maid said. "I've had some today and it's exceptional. The Middle of the Forest stew is venison mari—"

"Don't tell me!" Haft raised a hand to stop her. "Please, I'm cosmopolitan enough that I like to be surprised when I order something I've never had before."

She smiled delightedly. "So do I, Master Haft. I'm sure you'll like it." She turned to get their order, turned back when Haft asked how she knew which of them was which, when Dommuz had only given their names without saying who was who. "Oh, everybody knows which of the heroes who slew the bandits in their own lair is which."

"Did you hear that?" Haft whispered to Spinner when she was gone. "She called us 'the heroes who slew the bandits.' "

"Let's hope she didn't speak too soon."

Haft looked at him oddly. "But we did. We went to the bandits lair and we killed them."

"Not all."

"A lot of them."

"Maybe not enough."

Haft shrugged. "Captain Stonearm thinks we did." He turned his attention to the mandolin player and the singer. As cosmopolitan as Haft considered himself to be—and in some ways was—he didn't really have a fine ear for the musical arts. The mandolin and voices sounded nice, but the love song they were crooning at each other wasn't rousing enough to hold his attention. His eyes wandered.

The walls of the room were painted in pastels; lavender behind the small stage, one side wall yellow, the other pink, the wall with openings to the kitchen was pale green and the ceiling a pale blue. Paintings hung on the side walls; forest glades, streams, a lake, and a meadow on one; the other held scenes of happy people eating and drinking in a public room, picnickers frolicking on a grassy sward, boys and girls playing the games of childhood, young lovers hide-and-seeking among trees, a hunter bringing down a stag, mute musicians making frozen music. Nowhere were weapons hung or painted, no scenes or implements of battle. The room was a peaceful place.

Haft wondered whether such a bucolic setting really required the banning of weapons. He drank again of his ale and thought no man, no matter how rough and violent, could want to start a fight in such a pleasant place.

"Here you are, masters," the serving maid said. She had approached unnoticed and quickly moved bowls of stew from the tray she carried to the table, followed by a plate with a loaf of bread.

"Thank you . . . ?" He looked into her eyes and gave her his most charming smile. "I don't know your name."

"Oh! I am Maid Marigold." She curtsied.

"Maid Marigold! So lovely a name for so lovely a lass." Haft took her right hand, free now that the tray was emptied, and lightly touched his lips to its back.

"Oh!" She blushed brightly, took her hand from his not quite quickly enough to truthfully say she'd snatched it away, held it to hide her smiling mouth, and backed away a couple of steps before spinning about and hurrying off.

"I don't think the serving maids do that here," Spinner said dryly.

"Don't do what," Haft asked innocently, "accept compliments?"

Spinner snorted. "Don't act the dummy; you know what I mean."

Then the aromas of the freshly baked bread and the savory stew in front of them caught their attention and reminded them that they hadn't eaten since the night before. They set to ravenously.

Afterward, appetites sated, they contentedly sat back. Only a few crumbs of bread remained, too few for them to bother picking up and eating. Maid Marigold reappeared between them, fresh tankards in her hands.

"Was the Middle of the Forest Stew to your liking, masters?"

"It was every bit as excellent as you said, my lovely," Haft said and patted his belly.

"I didn't even feel hungry before I smelled it," Spinner said with a broad, satisfied smile. "That was the best stew I've had since, since . . . I don't know if I've *ever* before had stew that good."

"Please let me know if you require *anything* else." She deftly removed the bowls and plate, then curtsied and backed away, blushing.

Haft lifted his flagon and drank deeply. He put the tankard down and belched loudly. "If I wasn't suddenly so sleepy," he said, and yawned as if to demonstrate how sleepy he was, "I'd try to find out just what was covered by that 'anything.' "

Spinner laughed, the laugh turned into a great yawn. "I still don't think the serving maids do that here."

A short while later they were nodding. They'd had no sleep the night before or yet this day, and fatigue was catching up with them. Maid Marigold once more popped up between them.

"Masters, you look so tired. Do you have a room above?"

They opened their eyes and looked at each other. Both were so groggy the thought of saddling their horses and riding back to the company's campsite held absolutely no appeal.

"Can we get one?" Haft asked.

"I believe so," Maid Marigold said, smiling at him in a way that would have evoked a strong response had he been fully awake. "Wait for a moment, and please try to stay awake." She touched each lightly on the shoulder as she turned away.

She was back quickly with a male attendant.

"Master Postelmuz will show you to your room."

"Thank you." They slowly, unevenly got to their feet.

"What do we owe?" Haft suddenly remembered.

"Heroes run a tab," Maid Marigold said with lowered eyes.

Haft looked at Spinner and tried to grin, but was too tired to form more than a weak smile. He remembered to fumble a coin from his pouch to leave as a gratuity. He didn't look to see what the coin was, but knew it wasn't a mere copper penny.

On their way out of the common room, Spinner stopped at a table where three of their Zobrans were dining.

"We're taking a room and spending the night," he told them. "No one should worry that we're lost."

A second attendant joined them with their weapons along the way. Their room on the floor above was more spacious than either was accustomed to, but neither was awake enough to appreciate that fact. Nor did they notice their beds were wider than the pallets they had slept on in other inns. They were both fast asleep, each on his own bed, before either removed any more clothing than his boots. Below, unheard by the soundly sleeping men, more people poured into the inn's common rooms for dinner. The sun had not yet set.

CHAPTER FOURTEEN

Some hours later, when they'd slept long enough to ease the worst of their exhaustion, they were jolted awake by a light rapping on the door of their room. The gibbous moon that looked in through the open window cast the room in sharp lights and shadows. They rolled out of their beds and groped silently for their weapons as they listened for a threat. The last inn they stayed in had looked friendly enough, but it held dangers they weren't aware of right away. Eikby was surrounded by danger—they weren't about to take any chances. It took a moment for them to remember where they were and where the attendant had put their weapons. They found them just as the rapping came again.

Spinner called out softly, "Who's there?"

"It's Maid Marigold," a quiet voice came through the door.

"I'll open it," Haft whispered. He gave his axe a test swing as he edged his way to the door. "You get ready to light a lamp if it's safe."

"Right." Spinner didn't bother feeling for a lamp and tinder, if it was safe the serving girl was probably carrying a lamp to see by. If it wasn't safe, he and Haft were better off in the deep shadows. He leveled his crossbow toward the door.

Haft stood in moonlight to the latch side of the door. He signaled he was ready.

Spinner moved a hand into the moonlight and signaled back, he was ready as well.

Haft hefted his axe with his right hand and edged into shadow. He reached for the latch and, with a fast motion, unlatched the door and flung it open.

Soft candlelight spilled through the open door, but no rushing attackers came with it.

"Who's that with you?" Spinner asked from the deepest shadows of the room.

"A friend," Maid Marigold whispered. "May we come in, please?" She looked nervously from side to side along the corridor.

"Quickly," Spinner said.

Maid Marigold darted inside with another young woman on her heels. She closed and latched the door before Haft could reach it.

"Oh!" she exclaimed when they bumped reaching for the door. "I didn't see you there," she said breathlessly.

The two young women stood uncertainly for a long moment just inside the room; Maid Marigold held a candle, her companion bore a sack that looked to be heavily laden. Haft leaned against the door. He wanted to cross his arms over his chest, but couldn't with the axe in his hand. He settled for propping his free hand on his hip and grinning crookedly.

"To what do we owe the pleasure of this unexpected but most welcome visit?"

"Well, we, ah, we . . . ," Maid Marigold said with a sight tremor.

The strike of steel and flint interrupted her and they all looked to Spinner, who was lighting the lamp that stood on a small table between the two beds.

The women gasped when they saw the window's shutters were open. The unnamed companion rushed over and shut them. "We aren't supposed to be in here," she whispered.

Haft's eyes widened and he grinned broadly at Spinner—this could only mean one thing. "And who is your lovely friend?" he asked with as gallant a bow as he could manage with the axe still in his hand.

"Oh! I'm sorry, I forget myself. This is my close friend, Maid Primrose."

Maid Primrose curtsied. "Masters," she murmured.

Haft bowed over her and kissed her hand. "Maid Primrose, my pleasure."

Her eyes widened and her mouth opened in an excited smile.

"A lovely name for a lovely lass. But not too 'prim' I trust."

Maid Marigold turned pink and Maid Primrose lifted a hand to her face to hide a blush and a giggle.

"Please, our manners!" Spinner said quickly to hide his own embarrassment. "Have a seat, please." He stood and indicated the room's two stools, one by the foot of each bed, which he now saw for the first time in the lamp's glow. He wondered what else the room held that he hadn't noticed when they collapsed on the beds.

Maids Marigold and Primrose sat, knees close together, hands clasped on their laps, backs erect, heads high, Maid Marigold at the foot of Haft's bed, Maid Primrose at Spinner's, facing each other. Haft thought they looked quite fetchingly prim. He also thought a man would be hard pressed to choose between them by looks. Both were in the full flush of newly emergent womanhood, each would likely grow more stunning with the coming years. Their coloring was the only significant difference, and he had no great preference one way or the other on that score.

He moved from the door and placed his axe near the head of his bed where he could reach it quickly if he was abed, which he was as soon as he sat down. Spinner also sat back down on his own bed, though where Haft looked ready, he looked distinctly uncomfortable.

"We, ah," Maid Marigold began, hesitated, tried again. "I think you're very nice, the two of you. I mean the way you were when you came in the common room," she said all in a rush. "You had just slain the bandits in their lair, and instead of being rough and crude like so many of the other fighting men who have visited the inn, you were so polite and, and— and *nice*." She darted a glance at Maid Primrose. "And Maid Primrose did so want to meet you, you two heroes, when I told her about meeting you." She paused dramatically. "You are heroes, you know." She looked away and placed a hand against her face. "Oh, I'm afraid I'm babbling." She looked back at Haft and leaned earnestly forward. "But one so seldom meets a true hero."

Haft leaned against the wall at the head of the bed and basked in her praise. "I don't know about you babbling, but poor Maid Primrose has barely had a chance to say a word."

Maid Marigold blushed again.

Haft looked to Spinner. "We didn't bring anything from the common room, did we?"

Spinner looked back blankly, not immediately knowing what Haft was hinting at.

Sitting up, Haft said, "I'm afraid we can't offer you refreshments. Unless," he didn't know the hour, other than it must be late if the serving maids were off duty, "the kitchen is still open and we can get something brought up."

"Oh, no!" Maid Primrose suddenly remembered the sack she still held. "Maid Marigold told me you didn't bring anything and hadn't sent for anything. So I brought these." She opened the sack and placed its contents on the foot of Spinner's bed—two bottles of wine, a loaf of bread, a quarter of cheese, two bunches of grapes, and four wineglasses.

"Ladies!" Haft bounded to his feet and stepped toward them. "I hadn't thought it possible for anyone to be more pleasing company than the two of you already were. You have proven me wrong!" He bent over each of them and kissed their hands.

They smiled at him, openmouthed, in admiration, almost adoration.

He stepped to the sideboard and deftly removed the ewer and basin from its top, replaced them with the wine, bread, cheese, grapes, and glasses. He twisted the partly drawn corks from the bottles, then patted his side where his knife would have been if he had put it back on his belt before lying down to sleep, but he hadn't remembered to pick it up when the knocking woke him. He turned to Spinner, said, "Knife," and caught the one Spinner tossed to him. With an almost theatrical flourish, he cut slices from the loaf and chunks from the cheese. As he turned to announce that refreshments were ready, Maid Marigold popped to her feet, reached around him to grab a bunch of grapes, plucked one, and slipped it between his open lips. Surprised by her sudden movement, he still managed to suck the grape in without swallowing it, then catch her fingertips with his lips before she withdrew them. Her eyes went so wide he felt he could dive in and swim in their blueness.

"Oh," she whispered.

He was about to slip his arms around her waist when a faint noise from the beds made him glance that way. Spinner sat with his head bowed and a hand covering his eyes—the faint sound had been a half-swallowed groan. Maid Primrose sat ever so primly on her stool, staring back at him, looking like a wide-eyed, abandoned waif.

Instead of what he had been about to do, Haft took Maid Marigold's hand from his mouth, turned it over, and kissed its palm. He turned back to the sideboard and was pleased that he had enough control to pour wine into the four glasses without shaking. When he turned back, with two glasses in each hand, he kept his mouth closed until he could see he wasn't going to be surprised again.

Maid Marigold stood where she'd been, her eyes still wide enough to swim in, her hand unmoved from where he'd kissed it. Maid Primrose looked just as much the abandoned waif. The only change in the scene was Spinner was now shaking his bowed face behind his hand.

"A glass of wine, anybody?" Haft asked in a jaunty tone.

Maid Marigold blinked, seemed surprised to find her hand where it was, moved it to take a glass from his hand. He smiled at her, leaned forward and brushed his lips against her forehead, then stepped around her before she could react and bowed to Maid Primrose.

"Wine, my lovely?"

Hesitantly, she accepted the glass he held out to her.

Then he strode between the beds, put one glass on the small table, snatched the hand from Spinner's face, and thrust the other glass into it.

"Drink up," he snarled next to Spinner's ear. "Get a grip on yourself, man. Think of why they came here. I want what they are offering."

Spinner pulled his head away, Haft grabbed his hair and yanked his head back. "I want it and you bloody damn well need it!"

"I can't," Spinner said almost in a whimper. "Alyl—"

"Won't give you a tumble. You haven't been with a woman since The Burnt Man Inn. It's driving you crazy."

Spinner shook his head and mumbled, "No!" He didn't mean he wasn't "going crazy," he meant he hadn't "been" with Alyline that night. But he wasn't about to tell Haft all he'd done was hold her.

"Yes it is," Haft hissed. "You're not acting right. Now brace up and treat these lovely women right." He straightened up and turned back to the women, beaming at them. They looked ready to bolt.

"Please excuse us, dear ladies" he said hastily. "At this hour last night we were awaiting the beginning of a fight we didn't know we'd live through. That stresses a man, and he sometimes acts oddly afterward. Spinner still hasn't adjusted to the fact that he survived that fearful night and mighty battle."

"Oh, that poor man," Maid Primrose said and half rose from the stool.

"At times such as this," Haft said, taking full advantage of her reaction, "a woman's touch is the best thing to bring a man fully back to life." He stepped out from between the beds.

Maid Primrose took both the hint and his place at Spinner's side, though where Haft had stood over Spinner and yanked on his hair, she sat against him and brushed a soft hand against his cheek.

Haft took another step to Maid Marigold. Her eyes were no longer so wide, though she still looked uncertain about whether she should be there. He looked at her softly and lifted his glass to her lips. She looked into his eyes for a long moment before she took a sip, then lifted her glass to him. He smiled and took a sip. He leaned forward and kissed her gently on the forehead. She sighed. He lowered his face slightly and kissed her gently on the lips.

She smiled and began to glow.

"We don't have to report back to work until midafternoon," she whispered.

Haft grinned.

The noonday sun shown down on Spinner and Haft as they slowly rode back to camp. Haft felt relaxed and contented. Spinner's body couldn't decide whether to relax or be excited, so it settled on a lolling jitter. A crooked grin adorned his face.

"You know, I don't like to say I told you so . . . ," Haft said with a sigh.

"But you're going to anyway." Spinner's grin straightened out. "You were right, I needed that." He laughed and punched at the sky.

"There's nothing like a lovely lass to make a man feel all's right in the world."

So they were in the highest of spirits when their horses ambled into the campsite. Word of their return spread rapidly and they'd barely reached the corral when Fletcher, Silent, and Captain Stonearm converged on them from different directions. Wolf walked with his head and shoulder brushing the giant's leg. Alyline and Doli were some distance behind the men. The three began talking at the same time.

"Wait a minute, wait a minute!" Spinner held up his hand. "One at a time, please."

"Give us time to get off these beasts," Haft said.

They dismounted and handed the reins over to a waiting boy who took the horses off to unsaddle and brush down.

"Now, what's so urgent?" Spinner asked pleasantly.

The three looked at one another to decide who should speak first.

"You were gone long enough," Fletcher said a bit sourly. "The troops, especially the Eikby Guards, need to see you so they don't think you've abandoned them."

"We sent word where we were," Haft said and stretched with contentment.

"Yes, but we expected you back earlier," Fletcher said. He added dryly, "We would have sent for you, but we thought you wouldn't want to be disturbed."

Spinner flushed and looked away; Haft looked blandly at Fletcher.

"We need to get the guards trained quickly," Stonearm said in ominous tone. "They've made considerable progress since yesterday, but they're a long way from ready for a battle."

"Yes?" Haft didn't understand the urgency. After yesterday's dawn raid, it should be some time before the bandits returned—quite probably enough time to turn the guards into something resembling a proper fighting force. If the bandits ever returned at all. "You say they're making good progress. Keep it up."

Stonearm snorted. "We're pushing the training as hard as we can, as hard as the guardsmen can take and then some. But it won't be enough."

"What do you mean?" Spinner asked.

"New refugees arrived today," Stonearm replied. "Fortunately, we were able to intercept them before they got into Eikby."

Spinner made a gesture to keep him talking.

"They didn't come along the west road, they came from Penston."

"But Penston is to the south!" Haft blurted.

"Gods," Spinner gasped.

"That's right," Fletcher said. "Now we know the Jokapcul are on the peninsula."

Silent finally spoke. "You know what they did every time they invaded another country west of here—they didn't even wait to consolidate before they began moving inland."

Spinner and Haft looked to the south and for the first time noticed that all of the construction teams were working on the southern fences.

"How long will it take to finish those fences?" Spinner asked. "What about trenches?"

"The basic fences will be up by the end of the day," Stone-arm said. "It'll take most of tomorrow to affix enough of the barbs. We need to plan trenches."

"Let me see that map of yours again." The guard captain handed it over. "Are the fences laid out this same way?"

"Yes."

Spinner nodded and lost himself in study of the map.

"Where are the new refugees?" Haft asked. "Tell me what they said, while we're on the way to see them."

"They're over behind the hospital pavilion," Fletcher answered. "We're keeping them out of sight of the town."

"Let's go, Spinner." Haft grabbed Spinner's arm and pulled him along. Spinner took his eyes from the map only to look back to compare something on it with what he could see on the ground. Haft paid no attention to Alyline and Doli who followed them at a discrete distance.

"Put the map away, Spinner," Haft said as they rounded the pavilion and saw the tarpaulin that was stretched tight from the side of a dogcart to two short poles to form a rude shelter for two adults and three young children. Two exhausted dogs lay panting just outside the shelter. Three of the Bloody Axes sat nearby, tossing bones in a game of knuckles while keeping unobtrusive watch over the new refugees.

"Hmmm?" Spinner hadn't really heard Haft, nor had he seen the spread tarpaulin and the people huddled under it.

"Captain Stonearm, take your map, please."

Spinner started as the map was yanked from his hands by the grim guard captain.

"Mind your manners, Spinner, we have company." Haft squatted in front of the shelter and pulled Spinner down with him.

"Welcome," he said in his best harbor Zobran to the nervous man and woman. Their children hid behind them. "They call me Haft, this is Spinner. We seem to be in charge here. You've come from Penston?"

The man scrambled to a kneeling position then bowed low.

"Lord Haft, Lord Spinner! I am so glad to see you."

"Lord? We're—"

Haft gave Spinner's arm a painful squeeze.

"Tell us how you came here. And what is your name?"

"My name is Fleon, Lord," the man said into the ground."

"Sit up and look at us while you talk, you look like you're going to be sick, bent over like that."

Fleon pushed himself up to sit on his heels and looked warily at the two. "Lords, we fled the Jokapcul. They were all along the coast to the east and the west, inland was the only way we could go. We feared bandits, but we feared the Jokapcul more."

"When did you leave Penston—and how many Jokapcul were in the invasion force?"

Fleon and his family had fled two mornings earlier, before dawn, but neither he nor his wife could give any information about the invasion force. It took many questions to get a clear story out of the man and his wife. They had been hearing for months about the westward movement of the Jokapcul and were terrified by the rumors. Two nights before, restlessness had kept Fleon from sleeping soundly. He was up before dawn to relieve a nervous bowel when he looked out a window and saw the shadows of many small craft entering the harbor. There was wave after wave of boats. The first boats tied against ships in the harbor while the rest headed for the wharfs and strands. Armed men, their weapons glinting in the moonlight, poured off them and trotted into the city. Fleon was far enough away that he couldn't make out how big the boats were or how the soldiers were dressed, but he knew they must be Jokapcul. He didn't think to count how many. He hurriedly woke his wife, she bundled the children into the already packed dogcart while he harnessed the two dogs. They left Penston by an unguarded gate and were in the forest out of sight of the city walls before the sun rose. Neither of them had seen any Jokapcul east or west of the city. He'd seen them only from a distance as they disembarked from their boats and ran into the city.

After thanking the man for his information, Spinner and Haft withdrew with the others.

"So, we don't know if Penston was actually invaded or not," Stonearm said. "For all we know he dreamed it."

"I think we do know," Spinner said. "Even though he didn't have any details, his description of the landing was pretty vivid."

Haft agreed. "His description matched the way they invaded New Bally."

"So you think they invaded two days ago?" Fletcher asked.

"His wife didn't look to see the harbor," Haft answered, "but she confirmed how long ago they fled, so yes, I think that's likely."

"How much time do we have?" Stonearm asked.

"It's likely their first troops began moving northward today, perhaps even yesterday," Spinner said. "How many towns and villages are between there and here?"

"Three," Stonearm said. "Two farming villages and a wayside hamlet."

"Then they'll be here in two or three days. Maybe sooner."

"We can't run, can we?" Stonearm asked.

Spinner shook his head. "Not with so many people, no."

Haft had a different idea. "If people start heading north now and the first troop of Jokapcul is small enough for us to destroy, that will give everybody time to move north. Maybe there will be enough shipping along Princedon Gulf to take all of them."

Stonearm looked grimly to the south. "I really thought I was retiring to someplace quiet and safe," he murmured. Then briskly, "We had best get those defenses ready."

"We need to send scouts south to give us warning," Spinner said.

"I'll take care of that," Silent said. He ignored Haft's glare.

Like drovers cutting sheep from a herd, Alyline and Doli separated Spinner and Haft from Fletcher and Captain Stonearm when the four headed to the southern defenses.

"Did you enjoy yourselves last night?" the Golden Girl asked, her voice dripping with scorn.

"While the rest of us were tending the wounded?" Doli added.

"And preparing the defenses?"

"And learning of the new threat from Penston?"

"Well, did you?" Alyline demanded.

"Ah," was all Spinner could say. His face burned scarlet.

"We left word where we were," Haft said with some heat. "Someone should have come and gotten us if we were needed!"

Alyline gave him an *oh, really* look. "What, and interrupt your dalliance?"

"Some things are more important than . . ." Haft's hot words stumbled to a stop and he blushed, unable to say to the women what he and Spinner had done.

"But Alyline . . . ," Spinner's tongue tied and he couldn't fit words to his thoughts.

"What do you care what we do in town?" Haft said. "You don't like him," he said to the Golden Girl, "and neither of you has much use for me. And after we risked our lives to free you from slavery! At least the women in Eikby appreciate what we do for them."

Alyline cocked an eyebrow at him. Shocked, Doli gasped, then slapped him in the face.

Haft rubbed his cheek and worked his jaw side to side.

"But Alyline . . ." Spinner reached for the Golden Girl.

She batted his hands away. "*Pfagh!* You men are all the same. You constantly slaver over me no matter how plain I make it I don't want your attentions. Then the first time we come to a town you bed a trollop! I guess I should expect nothing better of *him*," she flung an angry hand in Haft's direction, "but *you*, you always protest you *love* me. Love! And you do what you did last night!"

Doli pushed her way past Alyline and almost spat in Spinner's face. "You didn't *have* to go into town, you know. You *don't* have to go to someone else!" She turned a glare at Haft, then back at Spinner. "Maybe I'm wrong about you, your behavior can't simply be because of the company you keep."

The two women turned about and marched off.

Wounded, Spinner stared after them for a moment, then turned to Haft. "How does everybody know what we did last night? They came unbidden to us in the middle of the night when everyone was asleep."

Haft shook his head, still rubbing at his stung cheek. "Maybe we were so good they just had to tell everybody? Nah, someone must have been watching us who couldn't keep his mouth shut. But why do those two care?" He wiggled his jaw again.

JOKAPCUL COMMAND

University of the Great Rift

Department of Far Western Studies

The Editors
James Military Review Quarterly

Dear Sirs or Mesdames,

Please pardon any clumsiness on my part in the matter of this submission of the enclosed paper, as the undersigned is fully unfamiliar with the procedures involved in making submissions to what I am told are called "popular" journals, for my papers have heretofore been published exclusively in scholarly journals such as *The Proceedings of the Association of Anthropological Scholars of Obscure Cultures*, which is the very journal in which most of my papers have been published.

Indeed, the enclosed paper, *A Brief Overview of the Command Structure of the Jokapcul Armies Currently Engaged in Conquest of the Nation States and Nation Cities of the Southern Portion of the Continent of Nunimar,* was originally written for that learned journal. However, the current volume's selection jury was weighted in favor of scholars who have had numerous disagreements with the undersigned in the past, and they failed to agree to include this paper in any of this year's numbers. The esteemed editor of *The Proceedings* . . . kindly suggested to me that I should submit it to a more "popular" journal.

Owing to the fact that, when I leave the confines of the university for an occasional foray into the nearby town of College Center, I see more copies of *James Military Review Quarterly* on the periodical shelves of bookstores than of scholarly journals, I hope I am correct in making the assumption that *James Military Review Quarterly* is a "popular" journal. Be assured, before submitting this paper to you, I did take the time to skim through several back issues of your journal and found, to my delight, that not only have you not recently covered the topic of this paper, but the tone of my paper is not too dissimilar to that in which most of the papers in your journal are written.

I have also noted that the papers published in your journal are extensively illustrated. Should you require that I provide illustrations to accompany this paper, I am confident that I can find appropriate wood or steel engravings in the university library.

Thanking you very much,

I am,
Scholar Munch Mu'sk
Professor

From the Desk of the Editor,
James Military Review Quarterly

Mangle,

This guy sounds like your typical clueless academic, but his style isn't too turgid. Besides, having an article by a full prof at a major university'll give this rag a bit of class. Send him a standard contract, minimum rate, he won't know the dif. Make a copy for the art department and tell them to dig up some generic pics to illustrate it.

Chop it down to column length. Oh, and get rid of that gawdawful title, give it a moniker with some pizzazz. I trust your judgement.

Thieph

Jokapcul's Flattened Pyramid

by Scholar Munch Mu'sk

As we all know, the armies of nation states and even city states are sharply pyramidal in their command structure. At the apex is the commander-in-chief, who may be a king, a prince, a duke, or a highly honored general. This CIC is assisted in planning by a staff of varying size depending on the size of the army and micromanagerial style of the CIC in question. Reporting directly to the CIC are the generals or other high-ranking officers who command units of the army. Those generals directly command officers of less lofty station who are in command of subordinate units, who in turn directly command lesser officers, and so forth down to the lowest level of unit commanded by an officer, most commonly a platoon consisting of between twenty and forty of the noncommissioned officers and enlisted men who do most of the actual fighting in which the army engages. Noncommissioned officers, that is to say sergeants and—in some but not all armies—corporals, command units of less than platoon size, which is to say in most instances squads and sections. Senior sergeants assist and advise higher-ranking officers in matters pertaining to the training and welfare of the enlisted men.

As evident from the preceding precis, an army's command pyramid can be quite high. This does not appear to be the case with the Jokapcul army.

The Jokapcul army currently engaged in conquest of all the nation states and city states on the southern portion of the continent of Nunimar is by reputation, and most likely in fact, the largest army ever fielded in all of history, and one would expect that it would have the tallest command pyramid of any army that ever existed. In fact it appears to have the shallowest pyramid of any large army known to history.

The officer corps of the Jokapcul army has only two ranks, to wit, kamazai and something akin to knight (the actual word has no direct translation). The CIC of the Jokapcul army is the strongest, most belligerent, most ruthless of the kamazai and is titled the Kamazai Commanding. Other kamazai report directly to the CIC kamazai. Each of those subordinate kamazai is in command of a corps of knights, many of whom are in command of troops, units of one or two hundred enlisted men and have subordinate knights under them. Which knight is in command of a troop and which are subordinate is sometimes determined among them via trial by combat.

When two or more troops are required to act in concert, the kamazai might appoint a knight other than one of the troop commanders to be in command over them or he might appoint one of the troop commanders to overall command. Sometimes command of the joint troops is determined via trial by combat between or among the commanders of the troops involved. If more than six troops are required to act in concert, a kamazai is generally appointed to command them. Thusly, the size and command structure of units below the level of what most armies call "divisions" and above the size normally known as "companies" is highly fluid, which simultaneously confers upon the Jokapcul army a flexibility and an instability absent from most other armies.

A particular peculiarity of the Jokapcul army is the status and function of the noncommissioned officers. Unlike other armies, Jokapcul sergeants are never placed in command of units smaller than a platoon. Any time a smaller unit is required to function independently of a larger unit, a knight is placed in command of it, even to the extent that an officer might be in command of a single soldier. The sole responsibility of sergeants in the Jokapcul army is to assist the officers by supervising the soldiers in carrying out the commands of the officers. Sergeants may perform duties as servants to kamazai, but never assist or advise them on matters pertaining to the soldiers. Furthermore, sergeants and soldiers are never trained in how to function in the absence of officers giving them commands; they must always have orders from officers to follow. The result of which is, without its officers, a Jokapcul unit of any size is incapable of fighting as a unit but only as individuals.

A final note regarding the command structure of the Jokapcul army is necessary. The preceding description applies only to the army in the field. The army in garrison and on staff has a more conventional structure with kamazai and knights being assigned to a variety of superior and subordinate positions by the commanding kamazai, and determination of superior and subordinate is never decided by trial by combat.

James Military Review Quarterly is pleased to welcome to our pages with this article the highly renowned Scholar Munch Mu'sk, Professor of Far Western Studies at the University of the Great Rift. Scholar Mu'sk has long been recognized as a leading expert in Far Western studies ever since his doctoral thesis, *Sea Raiders on Matilda, Local Brigands in Disguise or Invaders from Beyond the Horizon?*, was published in chapbook form.

III

FURY AND BLOOD

CHAPTER
FIFTEEN

Two hundred yards of open, plowed ground separated the fence from the southern edge of Eikby's cleared area. Because of the orchards, the town itself wasn't visible from where the road left the forest; the fence was obvious.

"Do you have caltrops?" Spinner asked as they examined the open area.

Captain Stonearm shook his head. "I can have a smith make some."

"Good idea," Haft said. "Put more than one blacksmith on them." He didn't look at the guard captain, his eyes were focused on the forest, looking to see how deeply he could see into it.

"Right away, Sir Haft," Stonearm answered sarcastically.

"Would you please, Captain," Spinner said more diplomatically.

Stonearm nodded and signaled for a guard lancer to take a message into town.

They headed back through the gate and calculated bow ranges.

"They'll probably assemble halfway to the fence before they charge," Haft said. "That's in range of our bows. We can take some of them out before they begin their charge."

"It's also in range of *their* bows," Spinner observed. "That means they can shoot our archers before they charge."

Haft thought about it for a moment. "I think you're right. The archers should be back farther and not fire until the Jokapcul begin their charge. We'll be able to cause them casualties before their archers can start shooting at us."

They started laying out trenches and pits forty yards inside the fence.

In another hour a blacksmith and his apprentice were turning out caltrops. They were simple constructions: two pieces of iron rod, each three inches long, bent at a right angle in the middle and crossed together, then heated in the forge and hammered until they welded together. When finished they had four points arranged so that no matter how they were dropped they settled with three points down and one straight up. The rods were cut at an angle to begin with, so there was no need to spend time sharpening the points. They were too small to cause a fatal injury except by accident, but were long enough to be cripplingly painful to a charging horse—or man—that stepped on one.

Then they began planning the evacuation of Eikby—until they were interrupted.

"Stop! Stop!" the mayor screamed as he rode his carriage into the southern defenses. "Everybody, stop working!"

"Who let him out?" Haft snarled, and turned away.

Workers looked up at the shouts, some stopped their labor to watch what was happening. The carriage stopped near the small group of leaders and the mayor jumped out of it, almost stumbling in his haste.

"What is the meaning of this?" he demanded of Captain Stonearm. "What do you think you're doing?" His eyes were wild and spittle flew from his mouth. His cassock was misbuttoned, and his gilt medallion chain of office was askew. He removed his floppy hat to wipe his brow, jammed it back on crooked.

Stonearm bowed. "Lord Mayor, the Jokapcul are in Penston. They will be here soon. We must prepare proper defenses with which to meet them."

"The Jokapcul!" the mayor shrilled. "You expect to fight the *Jokapcul*?"

"We expect to *defeat* the Jokapcul," Haft said in Zobran.

The mayor glared at him. "I don't need foreigners making decisions and causing death and destruction for my town."

The mayor turned back to Stonearm. "Stop all work immediately. Dismantle the defenses. *If* the Jokapcul come, we will do *nothing* to give the impression we are hostile to them. We will welcome them and give them anything they ask for!"

"Lord Mayor," Spinner understood enough of the mayor's words, "the Jokapcul will ask for blood and slaves. Are you willing to let your people die or be turned to slavery without a fight?"

"You are a foreigner here," the mayor snapped. "What we do is not your business." He snorted. "We didn't even have any trouble with the bandits until you arrived!"

"Excuse me, Lord Mayor," Stonearm said firmly. "Before they came, the bandits bled Eikby at will."

"They killed no one, they destroyed no property!"

"At the price of keeping the town and its people poor." Stonearm waved his arm at the landscape. "This is a rich land, this should be a prosperous town. It's not. Instead, all the wealth that by rights belongs to the good folk of Eikby has been handed over to the bandits without complaint. Because you weren't willing to resist."

"They would have killed us!" the mayor screamed. "They would have raped and murdered and taken everything!"

Haft shook off the restraining hand Spinner put on his arm and said harshly, "The Jokapcul are worse than the bandits. They will leave you even less—and they *love* to murder and rape."

Stonearm ignored Haft; he folded his arms across his chest and slowly shook his head. "If the guard was properly trained, the bandits would have been afraid to attack. We could have joined forces with other towns and driven them out."

The mayor stepped back, startled by the captain's further insubordination. His wild eyes steadied and he gave his guard captain a long, hard, look before saying, "I always thought it was a mistake to appoint you to your position. You are dismissed. If you are not gone from Eikby by the time the Jokapcul arrive, I will hand you over to them." He seemed to have forgotten that he'd tried to arrest Stonearm already and failed when the guardsmen refused to raise hand against their commander.

Stonearm returned the mayor's look, then slowly looked around at the men and women of Eikby who had halted their work on the defenses to watch and listen. Their faces showed nothing of their thoughts, but some gripped shovels or picks as though they were weapons, others angrily clenched their fists. Two or three shook their heads.

"I'm tired of bowing down," one woman said just loud enough for her words to carry to the group around the mayor.

Stonearm looked back at the mayor. "I haven't been here long, but in that time I have come to like this town, its people, and its land. I have heard too many tales of how the Jokapcul treat the people they conquer. If I leave as you wish, then I will be abandoning the good people of this town to be enslaved or raped and murdered, and their town burned to the ground. That's what the Jokapcul do."

"He's right," Spinner said.

Haft joined in, "If anything, the horror that will come upon Eikby will be worse than he says."

Fletcher nodded his agreement. "I've seen what they do."

"But we can't resist!" the mayor said.

"We *must* resist," Stonearm said firmly. "And we must evacuate the town, try to move everybody to safety north of here before the Jokapcul arrive."

"No! You will anger the Jokapcul as these strangers have angered the bandits. Captain, leave now, today, or face the consequences!"

Stonearm took a deep breath, and said solemnly, "Lord Mayor, I have never done anything like this before, and it grieves me deeply to do it now. But I must, because this town and its people who I have come to love will suffer greatly if I don't." He turned to two nearby guardsmen who had halted in their work and signaled them to come to him. He turned back to the mayor and said, "Lord Mayor, I hereby place you under arrest on charges of gross dereliction of duty and treason to the people of Eikby."

The mayor gaped at him with shock.

"Take him to his house and mount a watch on him," Stone-arm told the two guardsmen. "He is not to leave his quarters without my express permission."

The two guardsmen looked at their captain, one nervous, the other with a slowly growing grin.

The grinning one slapped his fellow on the arm. "You heard the Captain." To the mayor, "Sir, come with us, please. And kindly do not resist. Except for letting the bandits bleed us, you haven't been all that bad a mayor and I don't want to get rough with you."

Sputtering, the mayor let himself be led back to his carriage and taken away to imprisonment.

When he was gone, Stonearm looked at the others and shrugged. "He should have known better after what happened before." He turned to the laborers, most of whom had already resumed work on the defenses. He waved a hand and the others got busy. Many looked happy at the turn of events, most worked with more will than before.

They didn't want the evacuation to be a panicked flight; if it was to be successful it had to be orderly. That meant people had to leave in groups guarded by armed men—the bandits were still out there. But none of the company's fighters or the Eikby Guard could be spared to escort the evacuees. Was there a place the townspeople could assemble that wouldn't require dividing the forces?

"Up there," Captain Stonearm pointed, "at the foot of the mountains. There's a narrow, steep-sided valley with only one entrance. A few men could hold it against bandits for a long time if they had to."

Spinner and Haft looked where the captain pointed, then grinned at each other.

"We established that as our rally point when we first entered Eikby's clearing," Spinner explained.

"It stands out; we figured people could easily find their way to it if we ran into trouble and got scattered."

Stonearm chuckled. "You picked a great place without realizing it." He looked northward for a moment. "I think we can move half of the people up there in good order over the next two days without cutting into the number of people we have building the defenses. Or stripping the troops we need to defend with if the Jokapcul show up sooner then we expect."

"Captain, this is your town, your people. We'll leave that up to you."

"If you don't need me here just now, I'll get started on it right away."

But the evacuation turned out not to be as easy as the guard captain had thought. Word had spread through the town about the anticipated approach of the Jokapcul. Some people were already in flight to the north—others to the east or the west. Others scoffed at the danger, certain that the defenses under construction and the fighting men who would man them were enough to defend the town.

Silent came back the next afternoon. He expressed admiration for the progress on the defenses, then gave his report.

"I arranged mounted scouts in ten relays between here and Ceaster." This was the next farming village to the south, halfway to Penston. "When the first pair sees the Jokaps, they'll count them and see what they do in Ceaster. Then they'll go fast to the next pair and change horses. They'll change horses with each pair in order that their mounts will still be fresh when they make their final sprint to us. When the second team sees the Jokaps, they'll count them to see if any stayed in Ceaster, then head north, changing horses along the way. And so on. That'll get word to us fast."

Work on the defenses progressed well over the next two days. The evacuation of Eikby's didn't. Too few people were willing simply to pack up what they could take and leave the rest behind. But only the poorest of the villagers were able to take everything; others piled carts and wagons so high that carts fell over or collapsed under the weight. But too many people were convinced that the tales of Jokapcul rapacity were exaggerated and refused to leave or make any preparations at all.

A small cloud of bees buzzed in through a window in a tower room. It wasn't the highest room of the highest tower in Penston; that room was reserved for the exclusive use of the Dark Prince, titular head of the Jokapcul armies that had conquered all of southern Nunimar as far as this westernmost of the Princedon city states. *This* tower room was slightly more than halfway up a tower of middling height—high enough to see above the surrounding houses, but not so high as to give its occupant the impression he was more important than he was.

The room's occupant, a magician of slightly more than middling rank, perched on a stool at an oak board alchemist's table, hunched over one of the magic tomes conjured so many years earlier by the Dark Prince. His eyes had nearly glazed over, the pathways of his mind clotted with useless data, and his thoughts twisted themselves into a Möbius strip as he struggled to understand the workings of the *M249 Light Machine Gun (SAW)*. He was charged with deciphering the drawings that accompanied the largely unintelligible text, to learn which demons properly lived in the object, and its best use as a weapon—if, indeed, it was a weapon.

To be sure, the *M249 Light Machine Gun (SAW)* had vague resemblances to the *M1911A1 .45 Caliber Pistol* and the *AT4 Light Anti-Armor Weapon*, both of which were demon spitters in use by the invasion force. It stood to reason that the *M249 Light Machine Gun (SAW)* also was a demon spitter—it was described and illustrated in the same tome as the two known demon spitters. But the most baffling thing about it was the "(SAW)" in its nomenclature. "Saw" was one of the relatively few words in the tomes to have been deciphered with a reasonable degree of certainty. Peer as he might at the illustrations of the *M249 Light Machine Gun (SAW)*, the magician could discern neither the bladelike structure nor the teeth one expected to find on a saw. Equally baffling to the magician was why a demon spitter would be combined with a carpentry tool. Unless it was a demon-operated carpentry tool that had nothing to do with weaponry. In which case, why was so much space devoted to it in a weapons tome? And why did it bear a familial resemblance to other demon spitters rather than to other carpentry tools?

The magician sorely needed to unglaze his eyes, clear out his mental pathways, and untwist the Möbius strip of his thoughts. He sat straight and winced at the quite audible popping from his spine and shoulders. He really *must*, he told himself again, see a research healing mage to find out if they had yet discovered a demon that could do something for the aching backs of magicians and mages whose charges required that they spend long hours bent over tomes. He twisted and stretched one last time, grimaced once more at the popping as he reached for an amplifying glass, then bent over the tome again. Perhaps examination of the illustrations themselves would do for his thoughts what stretching and twisting failed to do for his back.

The illustrations in the tome never failed to bedazzle him in their felicity of detail. Never before had he seen such, not from the hands of the finest artists and draughtsmen of Jokapcul, or any of the other nations whose paintings, drawings, and tomes he had examined. They had to be engravings or drypoints, but the fingertips he lightly brushed over them felt none of the ridges and burrs left by the press when it squeezed the paper into the ink-filled lines and holes in the printing plate. Neither did the amplifying glass show any ridges or pitting. If they weren't engravings or drypoints, by what magic had these illustrations been printed? They clearly weren't woodcuts or wood engravings; wood was simply incapable of holding the detail of these illustrations. Neither were they lithography; no lithographer's sticks were capable of the fineness of line and detail found here. And the illustrations in color! Both woodcut and lithography required the use of multiple blocks, one for each color. It was inevitable that there be some discrepancy between blocks, it was simply impossible for the registration of lithography stones or wood blocks to be so precise. Moreover, the water used in lithography caused a certain amount of bleeding of colors—bleeding that was not in the least bit evident in these illustrations! And it was simply impossible for hand coloring to be so exact.

The magician's mental Möbius strip took another, unexpected turn and his eyes crossed. The amplifying glass slipped from his fingers and he straightened up with a groan. Gingerly, with a hand clamped on the small of his back, he slid from the stool to his feet and hobbled to the south-facing window. Perhaps if he stuck his head out of the window a waft of sea air would buffet his face and clear his mind and eyes.

That was when the bees, their cloud in the form of a large scavenging bird or smallish dragon, flew in through the north window.

"Gwah?" the magician exclaimed, surprised, when he heard the long-awaited buzzing. He turned away from the south window and saw the cloud of bees, retaining its formation, come to perch on the alchemist's table. The tribulations of understanding the tome forgotten, he cautiously approached the bees, watching the pattern of their dance within the cloud, listening to the changing inflections of their buzzing, peering closely at them for signs of damage.

The cloud was thinner than it had been when he sent it out from Zobra City. The bees within it were thinner as well.

"Poor seekers," the magician crooned. The bees were obviously too tired and hungry to deliver their message. "Poor messengers." His hand brushed soothingly over the cloud, not quite touching the dancing bees. "I will send for sustenance. Is it warm enough for you in here? I can light the brazier if you need." The magician turned his head toward a precariously balanced stack of tomes in a corner of the room and summoned the demon, who warily peeked one eye at the bees from behind a tome.

Hardly taller than the length of a man's hand, the demon pulled itself out far enough to expose chest and shoulders. It tapped itself on the chest and mouthed, *"Ee? Oo wanzz ee?"*

"Yes, you. Right now, right here." The magician firmly

pointed the forefinger of his free hand at the top of the table a foot from the buzzing cloud of bees.

"Oo zurr tha' " the demon squeaked as it darted back behind the tomes.

"I'm sure. Over here. Now." He continued his soothing brushing at the bees.

"Ee?" the demon squeaked. But the magician didn't reply, merely jabbed his pointing finger. The demon sighed with a timbre that belied the squeaking of its words, and clambered to the top of the stack of books, which teetered most threateningly when it bounded from the top of the pile to the end of the table.

The magician tapped the table where he'd been pointing, and the bald, naked demon slunk hesitantly toward the spot indicated, warily eyeing the bees the entire way. Its gnarled muscles bunched and stretched in exaggeration of human muscular movement.

"Nectar. Bring many bowls for our tired and hungry friends."

" 'Annee?" the demon asked, holding up two lumpy fingers.

The magician solemnly shook his head and held up five fingers. "Many."

" 'Annee?" The demon unfolded another finger.

The magician splayed his fingers.

" 'Annee?" The demon held up four fingers but kept his thumb folded.

The magician swatted at it, but the demon hopped back out of the way. It held up all five fingers. *" 'Annee. Ee gittum epp?"*

The magician flashed five fingers twice and nodded. "Get help. Many." He flashed five fingers twice again.

The little demon's face screwed up like it was about to cry. It flashed five fingers twice back at the magician, then hopped off the table and scampered from the room. The magician returned his attention to comforting the tired, hungry, bees.

Sooner than he expected, the door of the tower room slammed open and something at the door gave a menacing grunt.

"Bring it over here, please," the magician said without

looking around. He pointed at the table next to the formation of bees.

Another deep grunt was followed by heavy footsteps that shook the floor and caused the table to shiver. Then the last footstep thudded next to the magician and a tray slammed onto the tabletop where he'd pointed.

The magician gestured and the bees broke formation to feed. He reached out a hand and scratched the troll behind a pointed, tufted ear.

"Thank you," he said. "They needed that."

The troll keened in pleasure and turned his head so the magician could scratch behind his other ear.

The magician groaned as well, but not with pleasure. He stopped scratching the troll's head to suck on his abraded fingertips. He simply *had* to remember to wear a chain mail glove when scratching a troll's head.

At length, sated and rested, the bees resumed their formation. They danced their dance. The individual bees in the cloud hovered, swayed side to side, flitted up and down or to and fro, they curlicued around one another. Every seemingly random movement modulated their buzzing, and the modulations had meaning. The magician listened carefully. He had the bees repeat their message twice to be certain he had it right. Then he thanked them and opened a chest containing an old hive for the bees to live in until more suitable quarters could be found or constructed. Then he ran off to deliver the message.

When the message reached the Kamazai Commanding, after going through several levels of the magician's chain of command, then several levels of the KC's own staff, he considered for a moment, checked his order of battle, and quietly swore.

"Who'd have thought they would come so close to where we were going?" he said to his aide, who wisely said nothing in reply. "I sent that fool knight north just to get him out of the way. He might be able to effectively put siege to that town, but he probably can't defeat its home guard, much less the sole bandit band that has caused us any problem." He looked at his aide, who did his best not to flinch at the look. "I sent no other knights, no other officers with him. The fool is liable to get that entire troop killed if he encounters that bandit band!" The aide swallowed and nodded. The Kamazai Commanding then told his aide which knight to send north with which troops—with a full complement of officers. At greatest speed. With the intent of catching the fool and his mixed troop before they reached that town. Destroy the town first, then hunt down and destroy the bandit band said to be led by two Frangerian Marines.

Destroy, of course, meant pillage or destroy all property and kill all the people.

The southern defenses progressed rapidly enough so they were able to spare people to complete the western defenses and strengthen the weak northern ones. The eastern were the weakest, but they didn't see much reason to defend the eastern approaches to Eikby.

Three blacksmiths turned out hundreds of caltrops, which were scattered in the near part of the open ground between the fence and the forest. Lanes were left open through them so the defenders could safely counterattack if the opportunity arose. The open lanes were marked, but the marks were disguised so they weren't obvious from the forest side. The defenses were constructed to conform to the lay of the land.

"Integrated planning and construction," Captain Stonearm mused. "I like that."

A two-hundred-yard-long, hip-deep, trench was centered on the south road, perpendicular to the funneling fences. Dirt from the trench was used to form a broad berm to its front. More dirt was piled on the berm from a wide knee-deep trench lined with pointed wood stakes that were angled away from the berm. That shallow trench wasn't studded thickly enough with stakes to stop a charging enemy force, but it would slow it down and cause some casualties. A light latticework covering with ground-hugging legumes made the moat invisible. Between the fence and the trench foot-size pits were dug, each with a short, sharp, stake sticking up from its bottom. All were lightly covered with crawling foliage for camouflage. *Lord Gunny Says* called the small foot traps "punji traps" and said they had been very effective in wars where he came from. Everybody believed the claim. Markers, visible only from the trench side, revealed the location of the punji traps. No caltrops were scattered inside the fence. Fourscore men—the Eikby guards' archers, archers from the company, and woodsmen and hunters from the town—were ready to drop their building implements and man the trench when the enemy came into sight. Swords and spears lay with the bows and quivers that stood ready in the trench.

Ten yards behind the archers' trench was a row of chest-deep pits where swords- and pikemen would crouch unseen by the attackers and safe from the Jokapcul demon spitters. When the foe was almost on the archers' trench, these fighters would clamber from the pits and rush forward to join battle with Jokapcul who managed to survive the rain of arrows. When the enemy closed, the archers would retire to the pits where the swords and spears of the attackers couldn't harm them, and fire at the attackers whenever they had a clear target.

That was the main plan. Spinner and Haft—and just about everybody else—knew the plan relied on the Jokapcul to be foolish enough to maintain a frontal assault. *Lord Gunny Says* was quite clear on the fragility of plans.

"No plan, no matter how good," the *Handbook for Sea Soldiers* said emphatically, *"ever survives the first shot."*

With that in mind, they devised a backup plan—but Spinner, Haft, and Fletcher were not at all enthusiastic about what *Lord Gunny Says* referred to as "Plan B," no matter how emphatic the book was about a backup plan.

CHAPTER
SIXTEEN

"The bandits are still licking their wounds," the Eikby hunter named Jakte reported. He was the leader of the group of Eikby hunters and foresters charged with keeping the Rockhold Band under observation in case the bandits got enough reinforcements to mount another attack. "They don't look like they're very anxious to come here again." He had just come in from three days watching the routed bandits and met the command group inside the western defense works.

"How many are there now?" Spinner asked.

"We counted about three score and ten. They don't have horses for everyone. I guess we scattered them too much in the raid." He grinned; he'd been one of the Eikby guides who went on the raid.

"What about women and children?"

"There are well over a hundred, possibly as many as two hundred. We weren't as careful about counting them because we didn't think they are a threat." A bemused expression came over his face. "If there are enough women and children, the bandits will have too much to do taking care of them to attack Eikby in force."

"How far away are they?" Haft asked.

"Most of a day's march. Longer at night."

"So your information is almost a day old?"

Jakte smiled and shook his head. "We have horses posted along the way. I rode fast and got here in less than half the time the bandits would take."

Spinner and Haft both looked at Silent; he had also set relays of horses on the road to Ceaster. Had one copied the other, or did they both simply know more about horse movement than the two Marines?

It didn't matter, they'd both done well.

"So you don't think there's any chance they'll move on us soon?" Haft asked.

Jakte shook his head. "They need many more men. What few reinforcements are coming in are coming slowly. Unless there's a large group coming that we didn't spot. At the rate they're building up, it'll take more than a week for them to raise the strength they need."

"What about the east? Is anybody looking there?" Captain Stonearm asked.

Jakte shook his head.

"Maybe we should have people scouting to the east. Just in case." Spinner looked east, to where the forest came close to the town. The defenses there were almost nonexistent.

Jakte thought for a moment, then said, "There are three men who aren't already to the northwest. I can send them to the east."

"Do it. Then get some rest and a meal and head back out."

"Sounds good. I'll get people out right away."

"What does everybody think?" Spinner asked when the hunter was gone.

"It sounds like we only have to worry about one enemy right now," Haft replied.

"Probably so," Captain Stonearm said.

"If someone attacks from the east we have problems," Silent said quietly.

But they wouldn't have the people to build up the eastern defenses until the south side was finished. Even then, the western and northern defenses were more important.

In the middle of the next morning there was a commotion at the south gate. Readying their weapons as they went, the men of the command group ran toward it. But when they could see the gate, they slowed down and eased back on their weapons—two mounted men in forest garb had just been let through and the gate was closing again. Silent, very large and easy to spot, hallooed and waved at them. The two men waved back and turned their horses toward him. The horses were heavily lathered and breathing hard when they arrived. The riders dismounted and handed their reins over to waiting boys. One of the men was Birdwhistle, the other a local forester.

"They're coming," Birdwhistle reported before anyone asked.

"Are they at Ceaster now?" Spinner asked.

Birdwhistle nodded. "They took their time surrounding it before they attacked. When we left, most of the village was in flames." He grimaced. "They were wantonly killing people—men, women, children." His voice trailed off.

The others exchanged looks.

"How many are there?" Haft asked.

"It's a good-sized company. Mixed weapons, about forty each swordsmen, pikemen, and bowmen, along with a half troop or more of light cavalry."

"Eight or nine score of them," Captain Stonearm said. "We have," he grimly looked around, "not more than half that number who know how to fight—plus my guardsmen."

"Then we'll arm all able-bodied men," Spinner said. "We have extra swords and lances. We can issue them until they run out, and the rest of the able-bodied men can use scythes, hammers, cleavers—anything that can be used as a weapon. After first contact, they can arm themselves from Jokapcul dead."

Stonearm considered that for a moment, then, "I suggest we wait until the Jokapcul are closer before we arm the farmers and tradesmen. If we do that now, they'll have too much time to think and might get frightened enough to run away."

Haft barked out a laugh. "More afraid than the rabbits they already are?" He shook his head, still chuckling.

"They've never been trained, Haft," Stonearm said sternly. "Anybody who hasn't been properly trained and *isn't* afraid of a fight with seasoned troops is not only a fool, he's soon to be a dead fool."

"Even trained soldiers are often afraid in the face of the Jokapcul," Spinner added.

Haft looked at them blankly; *he* wasn't afraid of the Jokapcul, he'd beaten them too many times.

Silent looked away. He didn't understand the talk of fear. Boys of the steppe nomad tribes began training for war as soon as they could hold a toy sword, from so early an age he could hardly remember a time when he hadn't been training or fighting.

They got busy with even more intense drilling of the guard. Fletcher worked closely with Plotniko and Stupnikow in overseeing the workers who were finishing the defenses. Nightbird and the town's healers set up a hospital pavilion behind the defense works. Then they waited for the next pair of scouts.

They came not long before sunset.

"We were surprised how long it took them to reach us," Meszaros reported. "They must have rested after they destroyed Ceaster."

"How fast were they moving?" Spinner asked.

"They were moving briskly enough when we first saw them, but they stopped soon after. Their commander has a heavy limp, he looks like he has a recent wound and can't ride far before the pain becomes too great." Meszaros shook his head. "They set up a small pavilion for him to rest under. We didn't wait to see how long they'd be there."

Kocsokoz and a local forester were the next pair to return, halfway from sunset to midnight. They also reported brisk movement with frequent, lengthy stops. The mixed troop had stopped for the night well before dusk. There were no more reports until the next midmorning, when the Jokapcul company was on the move again. The final pair of scouts was Archer and a local hunter who came in soon after sundown. The Jokapcul had stopped three hours steady march away.

Silent took out two new pairs of scouts to bring word when the Jokapcul started again in the morning, or to give warning in case of a night movement.

The first pair came in two hours after dawn.

"They took their time getting started," Takacs reported. "I think their commander thinks he's invincible."

"What is their order of march?" Spinner asked.

"Swords, pikes, bows. The light cavalry brings up the rear. The commander is behind the swords."

"What about scouts?" Haft asked.

The Eikby forester spoke for the first time. "They have four swords patrolling a hundred meters ahead, two swords and two bows fifty yards out on each flank." He spat to the side. "I've never served in an army—or even a guard—but even I know that's not good enough for a company moving through enemy territory. Not as openly as they're walking along that road."

"What about magicians?" from Xundoe.

"Some of the soldiers carried the big demon spitters, but we didn't see any magicians." Takacs looked at the forester who nodded agreement.

"What was their attitude?"

Takacs barked out a laugh. "Bored. They act like they're on a training march." Then very seriously he added, "But we know how dangerous the Jokapcul can be even on a training march."

"Assemble the troops," Haft suddenly said to Fletcher and Stonearm. "All of them. We can send out an ambush in force and wipe out these Jokapcul while they're on the move."

Stonearm looked at him, surprised.

"Stop!" Spinner snapped before Fletcher could move or Stonearm speak. "If we had a hundred archers and we could catch them in the open, I'd say yes. But we don't outnumber them by enough, and nearly half of our troops are less than half trained."

Silent smiled wryly and shook his massive head. "You're being impetuous, Haft."

"An ambush will work," Haft insisted. "We can begin by hitting them with fifty archers. Then, while they're trying to figure out where the arrows are coming from, we smash into them with forty horse. And we still have more than forty foot to rush in and finish them off!"

"Who will defend Eikby while all our forces are away?" Stonearm demanded with great heat.

"Defend against who? The bandits aren't coming, not now—maybe not ever."

"We don't know that." Silent put a firm hand on Haft's shoulder. "Other bandits could already be on their way."

"But Jakte said the bandits aren't ready. Besides—" Haft began to wave at the defenses being built.

"No buts," Spinner said, stepping in front of Haft. "Four of us say we don't send out an ambush in force. You're the only one who wants to. So we don't."

Haft ducked from under Silent's hand and glared from one to the other of the four who opposed him. "Then what do *you* think we should do when that Jokapcul company arrives?"

"Fight from behind the defenses," Spinner said. He side-stepped to stay in front of Haft. "The caltrops will stop a lot of them before they reach the fences. Then the fences will stop their horsemen for our archers to pick off, and they'll slow down their foot as well. We set archers a bow's range from the fences and shoot at them while they're getting through it. Our horse and foot array behind the archers. We can bring down many of them before they close with us, then our swords- and pikemen come out to fight. The only way their archers can get close enough to shoot at us is to put themselves in range of our archers."

"That's far less risk to us," Stonearm agreed. "It will work. They will suffer so many casualties before they close with us, they'll have to retreat."

Haft turned to him. "Have you ever seen the Jokapcul fight?" he asked coldly. "I have. They don't fight like any other men I've ever seen. When they charge they don't seem to care if they live or die. They *will* close with us. They won't retreat."

Fletcher cleared his throat. "What you say is true, Haft.

But by the time they close there will be few enough remaining that we will be able to defeat them. Remember, I've fought the Jokapcul almost as often as you have, I know as well as you how they fight."

Haft cocked an eyebrow at him, Fletcher hadn't been there when he and Spinner fought a squad of Jokapcul light cavalry—and Spinner already wounded before that fight started! "What about their demon spitters?" Haft demanded, not yet ready to surrender the point. "They can fire from beyond bow range."

"That's why we will be in trenches and pits until the Jokapcul close with us," Spinner said. "The demon spitters won't be able to hurt us in the trenches. Anyway, Xundoe can use his magic to counter them."

Haft turned to Takacs, who had been trying to look invisible so he wouldn't be sent away while the leaders argued about what they would do, and asked. "What kind of demon spitters do these Jokapcul have?"

"They just have the tubes." He held his hands apart to show the length of the tubes, his arms were stretched almost to their full length. "I didn't see any of the small ones like Mage Xundoe has."

Haft gave the others a superior look. "Those demon spitters have greater range than the small ones. Xundoe won't be able to counter them. And they are much more powerful than his, they can break through breastworks."

"Enough!" Spinner shouted. "We don't send out an ambush in force, we defend here. Let's get ready and finish preparing our positions."

Haft studied Spinner for a long moment. "You'll see," he finally said. "You'll see."

Silent took out the squad of Zobran Border Warders to track the Jokapcul closely and send in frequent reports. He stayed out with them.

The reports came in over the course of the morning: The Jokapcul had stopped less than an hour's march from their overnight bivouac and set up the small pavilion for their commander. When he was ready, they broke down the pavilion and resumed marching as briskly as ever. Their order of march was the same as earlier. They stopped again a half hour later. After two more stops, Silent returned and said they should appear at the edge of the southern forest in less than half an hour.

All work ceased and the fighters took their positions, weapons were issued to as many able-bodied men as there were spare weapons. To guard the company's campsite, a small mixed force of Eikby Guards and the Blood Swords was stationed at the western defenses under command of Corporal Maetog. More men were hidden in an orchard close behind the defenses. When they were needed they would come out and take weapons from the wounded and dead. Silent took a squad of horsemen to their position for "Plan B."

Finally, Spinner and Haft took positions standing on top of the archers' berm where, crossbows in their hands, they were fully visible facing the south. With their cloaks blue side out, they were readily recognizable as Frangerian Marines. Fletcher and Captain Stonearm crouched below them.

When the last scouts sprinted out of the forest, the tramp of marching feet and the clop of horses followed them. Then the Jokapcul point scouts appeared at its edge. They walked with a swagger that contrasted sharply with their dun-colored forager caps and uniforms and lack of armor. Two of the four carried swords dangling from their hands, the other two had theirs scabbarded and held bows. None of them bore the bucklers on their left forearms in a manner suggesting they were ready to fight. The quartet advanced a short distance into the open, then stopped and looked about with undisguised arrogance.

"Banty little cocks of the walk, aren't they," Haft sneered. He stood hip cocked, left arm akimbo, crossbow dangling from his right hand.

"As rapidly as they've conquered the southern part of this continent, I think they've earned the right," Spinner replied.

Haft curled his lip.

The van of the Jokapcul column marched into the open, swordsmen clad in the same unarmored dun as the four point-men, save for two who wore purple hats with modest plumes. Their swords were sheathed and bucklers rode easily on their left forearms. The swordsmen advanced to join the pointmen and arrayed into two lines facing the fence. Behind them, led by the commander, came the pikemen. The tall purple plume that jutted from the crest of his cone-shaped, gilt-banded helmet made the commander easy to spot. Archers followed the pikes and lined up behind them. Last came the light cavalry. All but two of the cavalry peeled off in two columns, one to the right and the other to the left, where they formed in double rows at the ends of the lines of swords. Unlike the swordsmen and the archers, the commander and his cavalry were armored; they wore dyed purple-leather armor covered with metal rectangles. Neck flaps studded with smaller metal rectangles hung from the backs of their plumeless helmets and wrapped around to cover their throats. Aprons hung fore and aft from their armored jerkins, and curved shields flared out over their shoulders. Glittery chain mail covered their arms and legs. Studded gauntlets and boots completed their armor. They carried their swords in scabbards on their backs. Each horseman carried a short lance, its butt in a cup on his right stirrup, right hand holding it upright. The commander advanced to a position in the center of the swordsmen. Two horsemen who didn't go to the ends of the formation had small plumes on their helmets. They took positions immediately behind the commander. The sergeants of foot were distinguishable by the small plumes they wore on their purple forager caps. At least four of the swordsmen had the tubes of demon spitters slung over their left shoulders.

"They move like a silent drill team," Haft said, chuckling over the way the Jokapcul had moved into formation without shouted commands.

"Yes," Spinner said softly. "They are well-disciplined troops." He didn't relish the prospect of fighting them.

Without any signal the two Marines could hear or see, one of the lesser-plumed horseman behind the commander moved around him and advanced on the gate. Four swordsmen trotted at his side. None of them stepped on caltrops; they were all on the road, which hadn't been seeded. The envoy reined in several yards short of the gate and looked sneeringly at the fence. Then he spoke loudly in a drill sergeant's voice.

"His Zobran is pretty bad," Stonearm said from his concealed position, "but I can understand him. He's demanding that the mayor come to open the gate and surrender Eikby to the might of the, I'm not sure of this title, High Something or other, and someone he calls 'the Dark Prince.' How do you want me to answer?" The mayor was still under house arrest and they weren't about to release him to answer the Jokapcul.

Haft snorted. "Tell him if he wants the mayor he'll have to break him out of jail."

"Don't," Spinner said before Stonearm could speak up. "I'll answer him." He shifted to Zobran just as bad as the Jokapcul sergeant's, and called out in a voice just as loud, "The free town of Eikby recognizes no superior power and surrenders to no man. Leave or face our righteous wrath."

The sergeant puzzled over Spinner's words for a moment, then glared at him. Spinner didn't need a translation of what he said next, "Surrender now and death for your defiance will be fast."

"Prepare for your own death if you come closer," Spinner shouted back.

"That's the way to tell him!" Haft hooted.

The sergeant understood faster this time. He slapped a gauntleted hand on a mailed thigh, spun his horse about, and cantered back to his commander. The swordsmen raced to keep up.

The sergeant saluted the commander and gave his report, then resumed his position behind him. Once more in response to a command the two Marines neither saw nor heard, five swordsmen ran forward from the second rank, spreading out as they ran. When they halved the distance they unslung demon spitter tubes and dropped to one knee. They balanced the spitters on their right shoulders and sighted along them. *Pthupp*ing noises came from the tubes. An instant later dirt erupted at the base of the fence to the left of the gate and a crossed pair of posts collapsed, sagging a section of the fence. Wires went *sprang* in the gate. Dirt gouted in the open ground between the archers' trench and the fence on the right, more gouted between the trench and the gate.

Haft raised his crossbow, then lowered it—the demon spitters were much too far away for him to reach.

"Fletcher, can you reach them?" Spinner asked

Fletcher stood up and looked. "Maybe," he said. He studied the grassy field to determine the direction and velocity of the wind, then nocked a shaft to the string of his longbow and drew it back. The arrow struck the ground short and slightly to one side of the Jokapcul he aimed at. He tried again. This time his shaft struck the enemy soldier's thigh. The soldier yelled in pain and clutched his thigh, then crawled back toward the line.

"The others are too far," Fletcher said and ducked back down.

While he was engaged in wounding one man, the five demon spitters fired again. One gatepost splintered and another fence support collapsed. More dirt gouted where the demon shots missed and passed between the wires. The rest of the Jokapcul stood their ranks. The four remaining demon spitters kept firing.

"So much for fences," Haft growled.

"They won't take it all down," Spinner said.

Haft snorted. "They don't have to." He watched the demon spitters as they spat again and again, and the swordsmen who carried them fed their demons after each spit.

"Too bad we don't have one of those," Fletcher said, looking over the berm.

"We don't." Spinner shook his head. "If we did, we could destroy their formation, but we don't. Instead, we have to wait for them to move into range of the weapons we do have."

The Jokapcul showed no indication they were ready to advance. The two Marines wondered why the commander didn't send another soldier forward to use the abandoned demon spitter. None of the demon spits reached the trench, though it looked like the soldiers with the weapons tried a few times.

"I didn't know they did that," Haft said after a spell.

"What?" Spinner asked.

Haft pointed. One of the demons had climbed out of its tube and was basking on top of its soldier's hat. The soldier looked to be cajoling the demon, asking it to return to the tube. The demon accepted the food the soldier offered, but refused to return to its tube. "I wonder if Xundoe could explain that to us."

Spinner shook his head. Xundoe was with the small contingent guarding the campsite. Spinner knew demons had to be fed regularly, but he'd never heard of one simply refusing to spit after being offered food.

Moments later another demon stopped spitting, then the last two as well.

The Jokapcul commander drew his sword, looked to both sides, then swept his sword forward. His troop began advancing at a walk toward the fence. Whole sections of fence were down and much of the rest sagged. The gate hung by one leather hinge.

"Archers stand by," Spinner called out. "Stay down until my command."

"Yours nothing," Fletcher said. He stood to look over the berm. "I know a longbow's range better than you do."

Spinner didn't argue the point.

The Jokapcul reached the line where the demons had spat, then broke into a trot.

"Archers, up!" Fletcher commanded. Eighty men stood and nocked arrows to their bowstrings. "Ready!" Fletcher called out, and they drew the shafts to their ears. *"Aim!"* The archers aimed. *"Fire!"*

Eighty arrows arched into the sky and down at the center of the Jokapcul lines. Before they struck, another flight of eighty was in the air. Then another and another. Many shafts fell short or flew over the lines, and the Jokapcul swordsmen raised their bucklers and deflected many of those that found the range. But here and there a man toppled. The commander barked and the orderly trot became a screaming rush that barely maintained the lines. A few footmen stumbled and fell, horses began rearing and kicking, screamed as some of them stepped on caltrops. Riders were thrown, some of them screamed when they landed on caltrops.

When the remaining Jokapcul neared the broken fences Fletcher called out, "Select targets!" The archers stopped volleying their arrows and began picking out individuals to shoot at. More of the swordsmen dropped.

The horsemen heeled their mounts and angled across the front of the advancing footmen toward downed sections of fence. On the left a horse's leg tangled in a coil of broken wire and it tumbled, throwing its rider onto a jagged post stump; the rider screamed once, his limbs flailed, then he lay still. The horse screamed, tried to get up, staggered and fell down, blood coursed from its fetlock where jagged bone cut through its hide. On the right, another horse screamed and reared when a hoof landed squarely on an upturned barb of twisted wire. Its rider struggled to get it under control, but the barb stuck in the quick of its hoof and it stumbled. The rider leaped off and ran toward the trench.

"Swords, advance!" Spinner shouted.

The soldiers in the pits behind the archers clambered out and rushed forward to bound over the trench and stand on the berm in front of it. A hail of arrows came from the Jokapcul archers, who'd stopped at the fence line and drove them back into the trench. The charging Jokapcul were almost to the trench.

"Archers, to the pits!" Spinner shouted, and the archers jumped out of the trench and retreated to the pits the swordsmen had left.

Running swordsmen and galloping horses stepped in the small staked pits and fell, screaming from the agony in their pierced feet or hooves. More of them fell to the arrows of the archers. But most of them still reached the shallow trench before the berm. The thin camouflage covering the shallow trench fooled the leaders of the screaming rush and they fell into it. Some were impaled on the stakes, others fell between them and scrambled back to their feet to wade through and mount the berm. The Jokapcul swordsmen who came behind saw the shallow trench and waded safely through to gain the berm—the horsemen drew up and dismounted to fight as heavy infantry.

The archers, safe for the moment in the pits, shot at the attackers as they came over the berm, and knocked many back or tumbled them wounded and bleeding into the trench. The swordsmen—Zobran, Skraglanders, and guards—swung their blades at the legs of the Jokapcul, trying to cripple them and knock them to the bottom of the trench where they could plunge their weapons down into their chests and bellies. The Skraglander Bloody Axes did the same. Pikemen, Zobran, and guards alike, thrust upward, swung the butts of their lances and halberds, and took a terrible toll. Yet many of the Jokapcul made it uninjured into the trench where the archers didn't dare shoot at them, and fought with a ferocity few of the defenders could match. Some leaped the trench and headed for the pits and the archers they protected. More of them were coming.

CHAPTER
SEVENTEEN

A bellow came from an orchard a short distance to the left side of the trench and a dozen horsemen burst from it. Half of them galloped in a line to the berm and crashed through the Jokapcul on it—Silent was in the lead, his mighty sword swept side to side, chopping deep into Jokapcul flesh, cleaving through the armored plates on the dismounted horsemen. The other six horsemen smashed into the Jokapcul charging the arrow pits and bowled them over. Archers dropped bows in favor of long knives and short swords. Farmers and tradesmen armed with swords and lances, scythes and pitchforks, hoes and hammers, climbed out of the pits to stab and chop Jokapcul soldiers where they lay dazed after the horsemen had knocked them to the ground.

The Jokapcul commander made it all the way into the trench and leaped into it only feet away from Spinner. He grinned when he saw his opponent's quarterstaff—it was too long to be used in the trench except as a blunt spear. He growled something in the gravelly language of his home islands and rushed to dart inside the slight arc of Spinner's weapon. He should have faced the other way when he jumped into the trench—Haft was behind him and wasted no time in bringing the half-moon of his axe down in a powerful overhead swing that caught the commander at the juncture of his neck and shoulder and chopped deep into his chest.

A swordsman saw his commander go down and leaped out of the trench, screaming in terror. In seconds, the remaining Jokapcul were in full flight—sixscore and more Jokapcul had charged through the broken fence to the trench, fewer than half that number fled for the safety of the forest. The defending archers regained their bows and ran back to the trench, leaped across it, and stood on the berm to down the fleeing foe.

Silent roared out another war cry and the horsemen rallied to him. He waited until the fleeing Jokapcul were almost at the fence, and roared again. He led a pursuit across the open, pitted ground between trench and fence. One of his horsemen failed to watch the markers for the punji traps and was thrown violently forward when his horse stepped into one. He hit the ground hard, bounced, and lay still. His horse struggled to stand on its maimed, broken leg and screamed in pain until a swordman rushed forward and ended its agony. A healing witch ran to the rider.

The remaining horsemen bounded over the downed parts of the fence and rode among the fleeing Jokapcul swordsmen, swinging their blades, cutting the running men down like mad farmers scything ripe wheat. Most of them remembered the marked lanes through the caltrops; one who didn't was thrown violently when his horse stepped on an elevated spike and fell. Haft led a score of swordsmen to the field to take possession of any Jokapcul who chose to fall to the ground in surrender rather than die. The Eikby Guards, flush with victory, raced after them.

The Jokapcul archers had fled before the swords and lances of Eikby's defenders and reached the forest edge before their sergeant barked a command to halt and turn. They looked at him uncertainly; he wasn't an officer to be giving them orders. But they launched one volley of arrows at the horsemen, bringing down three of them and four horses screamed from fresh wounds. The remaining Jokapcul swordsmen and cavalry reached the archers and the archers ran into the trees with them.

"To the trees!" Silent bellowed, and heeled his huge horse toward the Jokapcul. Sword swinging, he crashed into the fleeing enemy. The great horse bit out and kicked at the enemy, and suddenly there was a gaping hole in the mass of running enemy soldiers. The other horsemen followed him

into the thick, and hewed the archers and swordsmen like
woodsmen clearing brush. In moments, the archers' sergeant
was dead. The remaining Jokapcul fled faster into the trees.
The guards chased after them.

"Hold!" Spinner shouted from the back of the horse he'd
mounted. "Let them go." Haft, Fletcher, and Captain Stonearm echoed his order, but the guardsmen who had been so reluctant to follow the bandits into the forest just a few days
earlier were wild with bloodlust and none of them stopped. A
few armed farmers followed, yelling and screaming, though
most of the farmers and tradesmen stopped and stood about,
wondering what to do next. Spinner swore, then shouted for
the company's squads to assemble. He wasn't going to madly
pursue the fleeing enemy; his forces must be organized so the
Jokapcul couldn't turn on them.

"Fletcher, take charge of farmers who are still here. See to
our wounded and check the Jokapcul casualties. And get
those demon spitters!"

By the time he finished giving Fletcher his orders, the soldiers were organized in their squads.

"Move fast," Spinner ordered, "Stay in squads. Move out!"
He thrust forward with his quarterstaff and went into the trees
at a trot.

Fletcher immediately began to organize the farmers. They
dealt with the casualties first, litter teams bore the wounded
to the hospital pavilion to be cared for by Nightbird and the
other healers. Other farmers moved the dead into rows, Eikby
Guards in a neat row with the company's slain, Jokapcul in
two haphazard rows. Then they began gleaning the battlefield,
piling up weapons, armor, equipment, and other oddities.

Ahead, Spinner heard the muffled shouts and screams of
men in battle and the clang of weapons. He looked to his
sides and saw other mounted men pacing him.

"Faster!" he shouted, and heeled his horse into a canter.
The other horsemen maintained pace with him. He looked
behind and saw Haft racing with the footmen to keep up. The
din of battle came louder, with more anguished screams than
challenging or victorious shouts in Zobran—the victorious

shouts were far more guttural. His brow furrowed with worry. The Jokapcul must have reorganized and counterattacked the pursuing guards. Could the Eikby Guards hold until he reached them?

"Faster!" He heeled his gelding into a gallop.

In seconds he was startled to see Eikby Guardsmen running toward him in full, terrified, flight—most of them had already dropped their weapons and some were even shedding their armor so they could run faster. Jokapcul were chasing them—not the surviving infantrymen who'd been defeated at the southern barricades, but fresh troops—the cavalry that had headed north at high speed after the messenger bees had reported the company's location.

Xundoe scampered as fast as he could from the west defenses to the south in response to Fletcher's summons. In addition to five demon spitters, the Jokapcul corpses carried numerous items he didn't recognize. Some of those things might be magical tools or weapons but fearing to make a deadly mistake, which could cost lives, neither Fletcher nor the farmers helping were willing to handle them. He needed the mage to identify them and determine what he could use and what could be safely discarded.

"Demon food, wonderful!" Xundoe exclaimed as he lifted a container from next to one of the fallen demon spitters. "Everyone, look!" he shouted. He held the container for everyone to see. "If you find something that looks like this, bring it to me. It's safe to handle; there's no magic in it." A couple of the farmers gleaning the battlefield flinched and others looked away. "Really, it's demon food; there's nothing in it that can hurt you." None of the farmers looked relieved to hear that.

Xundoe hardly noticed as he went back to his search. The first demon spitter he examined had its demon; he fed the demon to keep it from wandering off. He took the tube with him when he ran to the next. Two containers of demon food lay next to the second demon spitter, but its demon was missing.

He collected three more food containers from near the remaining two tubes, both of which had their demons. He fed them as well. Two farmers brought him more demon food while he collected the demon spitters, but most of the farmers merely told him where they found things. Then he went to root through a pile of objects Fletcher had assembled. To his delight, he found four phoenix eggs, badly needed replacements for those he'd used in the attack on Rockhold. And another small demon spitter like the one he already had. Its demon eagerly ate the food Xundoe gave it. Mostly there was food. Where there was so much food, he thought, there must be more demons. He searched more diligently. A nearby, unopened backpack caught his eye when it seemed to move on its own as though an animal was trapped inside. He strode to the pack and squatted to open and look inside it. He fell back onto his rump when he saw the incredible figure the pack held concealed.

"Veedmee," a piteous voice said from inside the pack. A small figure crawled into the light. *"Veedmee,"* she cried again. The figure was very much a she, even though she was no more than a foot tall; she was exceedingly, even excessively, voluptuous. A great mass of hair covered the upper part of her flowing, diaphanous gown.

"A Lalla Mkouma," Xundoe gasped. "I've never seen a Lalla Mkouma before. You *are* a Lalla Mkouma, aren't you?" The Lalla Mkouma were a powerful magic, one most magicians dreamed of but few ever controlled. If he could report to the Zobran army with this Lalla Mkouma, he'd be sure to get a promotion! Except there was no more Zobran army for him to report to.

"Veedmee!" the Lalla Mkouma demanded.

"What? Oh yes, feed you. Oh yes indeedie, feed you. I'll be delighted to feed you," he gabbled, and grabbed the nearest container to fumble its lid off. He plucked a grape-size pellet from the container and held it out to the Lalla Mkouma. The tiny woman-creature squealed then pounced at it. She grabbed Xundoe's fingers in her tiny hands and ravenously nibbled the pellet directly from between them. When it was gone she daintily licked the residue from his fingertips, then smiled brightly at him and merrily chimed, *"Veedmee!"*

Xundoe smiled like a child who had gotten exactly what he wanted for his birthday and held out another of the grape-size pellets.

When she'd finished her second serving, the Lalla Mkouma smiled enchantingly at the mage and trilled, *"Ee likuu, oo nizzum!"* She grasped his forefinger with both hands and tugged very forcefully. *"Komm'ee."* He had no choice but to roll to his feet and follow, bent uncomfortably low.

"Ere," she said, stopping at a mound of captured equipment no one had yet gone through. *"Ere, opup!"* She let go of his finger and patted a pack that leaned against the pile. The pack moved under her hand and muffled squeaks sounded from inside it.

Could it be? If reporting with *one* Lalla Mkouma could get him a promotion, what might he get for reporting with *two*? Xundoe's hands trembled as he reached for the pack and undid its ties. He gasped, his eyes bulged, and he forgot to breathe when not one, but *three* more of the tiny female figures tumbled out, squealing and trilling in joy. *Four* Lalla Mkouma were almost beyond his capacity to believe.

"Lalla Mkouma," the first Lalla Mkouma trilled. *"Lalla Mkouma. Veed'um!"*

Xundoe shook himself. "Feed them, yes indeedie, feed them. Oh, my, feed them. Yes indeedie!" he babbled when he got his breath back. "Feed them indeed." Xundoe fumbled at the lid of a food canister and quickly had it open. He poured three of the pellets into the palm of his hand and extended it to the three Lalla Mkouma.

"Vood!" the three trilled and rushed to his hand. He watched in amazement as they ate. They stuck their faces directly onto the pellets and ate without using their hands—even so they managed to eat with the delicacy of high born ladies at a royal feast. Or how he imagined high born ladies would eat at a royal feast—he'd never been at a royal feast or seen high born ladies dine, or even been closer then a longbow shot from a high born lady. But he could imagine. When they finished

the pellets they licked his palm clean. It tickled. He giggled. Then, remembering how the first one wanted more after he'd fed her, he rolled three more pellets into his palm.

"Naw, naw. Vool," they chimed, and brushed their hands over their bellies like women protesting they were full and needed to watch their figures. That *was* something he'd seen. The first Lalla Mkouma, the one who had eaten a second pellet, put her hands on her cocked hips and flounced her hair. He'd seen women do *that* too. *My* figure's just *fine*, she seemed to say. *My* figure doesn't *need* to be watched.

"What do you have there?" Fletcher asked, coming over to see what was making the high-pitched noises. "By the gods," softly, "what are they?"

"Lalla Mkouma." Xundoe sat mesmerized by the voluptuous creatures as they chimed and trilled at one another and scrambled over the mound of equipment, fondling whatever bauble caught their interest—and there was a great deal for them to be interested in. They gleefully and noisily admired their reflections in the shiny rectangles on the cavalrymen's armor. Then one of them squealed at the sight of her reflection in the even shinier rectangles on the commander's armor. The others skittered to join her and, with a minimum of jostling, each found a rectangle in which she could primp. Their delight was obvious.

"Spinner and Haft had some of them at The Burnt Man!" Fletcher said, but Xundoe was too entranced watching the Lalla Mkouma to hear. Fletcher cautiously backed away—he remembered the Marines' Lalla Mkouma as being benign, but with a temper. They were demons, and he wasn't about to trust demons. He returned to supervising the farmers gathering the battlefield booty.

One of the miniature women spotted something in the equipment pile and grubbed for it. She squealed in delight, pulled it out, and trotted to him with a swaying grace that would have had him in a swoon had she been a full-size woman. She held the object out for him to take and he almost did swoon. It was a burnished metal box with scarlet and yellow flames enameled on it, little more than the length of a man's knuckle and not quite as high. A salamander house! Did it contain a salamander? Had the salamander been fed recently? Trembling, though with fear this time, he pressed the lever that opened the door of the salamander house—if there was a salamander and it hadn't been fed recently, it would clamber out and attack him with hell fire.

A salamander's head popped through its door, crackling and hissing in fury at its incarceration, but struggle as it might, it was too well fed to squeeze through the narrow door. Even though the hand that held the box by its bottom was nowhere closer than a good inch to the fiery demon, Xundoe felt the creature's heat and knew he couldn't hold the door open for long. He let it snap shut, returning the protesting salamander to its prison to await a time when it was needed to start a fire. He dropped the house into a pack along with the phoenix eggs, small demon spitter, and the containers of demon food.

The other Lalla Mkouma saw the first with the salamander house and, squealing, gave off admiring themselves in the makeshift mirrors of the officer's armor. They skipped and spun and danced gaily about the battlefield, trilling at each other, poking into all the piles of equipment, searching the fallen for anything the men had missed. And they found things that they brought to the amazed mage. Two more salamander houses. Another small demon spitter. And food, so much food that Xundoe thought there must be many more demons yet to find—either that or these Jokapcul had expected to be away from fresh supplies for a long time.

Away from supplies for a long time? Xundoe looked hurriedly at the surrounding bodies but didn't see the one he was looking for.

"Has anyone seen a Jokapcul magician?" he called out. Nobody had.

What are they doing with all these demons without a magician? he wondered. Then he stopped wondering about the lack of a magician in favor of wondering over all the demons the Lalla Mkouma brought to him.

The miniature-woman demons found ten more phoenix eggs and a few more demons. It wasn't long at all before he was filling more packs. Xundoe whooped with joy when they brought him two aralez. He wanted to clutch them to his chest, but contented himself with lightly petting the small, doglike healing demons. Now he could do more to help Nightbird heal their injured. He was less enthusiastic when they turned up an imp house. Imps were invaluable as defensive demons but nearly worthless on offensive. But under any circumstances, they were dangerous even to the mage who controlled them. Gingerly, he held the imp house to his ear. He heard a quiet buzz from within; it was filled with imps. He became excited again when the Lalla Mkouma turned up a mezzullas. If he could figure out how to get her to work her magic, the company could have some control over its weather.

There was one demon they didn't bring to him, they took him to it: a hodekin. As tall as a man's hip, the hodekin was too big for the tiny women-creatures to carry. It sat grumpily enclosed in a cage of wire tightly enough meshed to keep its fingers inside. He puzzled over why the Jokapcul had brought along a demon that dug mines and tunnels, but was yanked back from his musing when the Lalla Mkouma brought him another imp house—his skin crawled at sight of it. He quickly recovered when they found the most exciting demon— a yarikh. He had trained with a yarikh in Introductory Wayfinding a couple of years earlier when he was studying for his most recent promotion. With the yarikh, he could infallibly navigate for the company at night. He was pretty sure he could. What was it the instructor had said about the trick of working with yarikhs?

Before he could remember what the Introductory Wayfinding instructor had said, the four Lalla Mkouma emitted piercing shrieks and bolted to him.

"Wh-What? What's w-wrong?" he stammered as they clambered onto his shoulders and wrapped their tiny arms around his neck. One squeezed her face against his jaw and wiggled her shoulders, her diaphanous gown lengthened and spun out to envelop him and her mates. All four Lalla Mkouma and the mage vanished an instant before the first terrified, fleeing Eikby Guardsmen burst from the forest.

*　*　*

Spinner bent low alongside the right side of his gelding's neck and slammed the end of his quarterstaff into the surprised face of a Jokapcul lancer. The enemy soldier flipped backward out of his saddle, blood followed in a sparkling red arch from shattered flesh and bone. Then Spinner was through the first ragged line of enemy cavalry, but had no time to look around and see where Silent and the others were or to assess the situation—another line of horsemen was coming at him, screaming and harshly barking battle cries. He flipped his body to the other side of his horse's neck and the lance point that would have sunk into his chest from the top of his shoulder merely gashed his arm. He swung his staff in a horizontal arc against the back of the lancer who'd just missed killing him, but the blow wasn't hard enough to unseat the cavalryman.

The lancer threw all of his weight into yanking back on his horse's reins, making it stagger as it skidded to a stop, but the horse didn't fall because the lancer leaned sharply to balance the horse's stagger. He twisted hard and the horse heeled around, then he kicked the horse visciously in the flanks and bounded in pursuit of Spinner who, upright, had just crushed the throat of a swordsmen in the third line of Jokapcul cavalry. The Jokapcul lancer screamed a challenge as he kicked his horse into greater speed and leveled his lance at Spinner's back. He screamed once more, briefly, as a blow from a monstrously large sword clove through his side all the way to his saddle.

"On me!" Silent roared as his huge horse leaped over the falling Jokapcul horse and the halves of its rider. More than twice the size of the Jokapcul horses, his mount plunged into them and sent three crashing to the ground and crushed the chest of one fallen rider with a hoof. The mighty horse reared and lashed out at a swordman who tried in vain to wheel out of its way, kicked back and crushed the thigh of another and several ribs of that swordman's horse.

Five Skraglander horsemen, swinging swords, axes, and a war hammer, rallied to Spinner and Silent. The seven lay about with their weapons, and every Jokapcul in range fell bleeding and broken. In seconds, no riders were left opposing them. The din of ferocious battle came from the direction of the clearing.

"Charge!" Spinner yelled, and led the way to the fighting.

"Here they come!" Haft shouted when the line of Jokapcul lancers burst into the cleared land, to run down the fleeing Eikby Guard. The horsemen wore a different color armor than the soldiers they'd already defeated, but he paid that no attention. His side toward a charging lancer, he braced himself and held his axe back over his right shoulder. At the last instant he ducked under the lance point and swung horizontally. The half-moon blade hit the horse low on the shoulder and took its leg right off. The horse screamed as it tumbled to the ground, throwing its rider hard into the trunk of a tree. The *snap* of bone as the lancer hit the tree sunk deep enough into Haft's subconsciousness that he automatically knew that one was no longer a threat. He instantly turned his attention to a Jokapcul who was trying to free his lance from the back of an Eikby swordsman.

In three running steps he was on the lancer, his axe clove the lancer from shoulder to pelvis. Fortunately a half of the lancer's falling body deflected a lance aimed at Haft and the dead lancer's arm smacked the charging horse's legs hard enough to throw it off stride and its rider, off balance from the hit on his lance, struggled to stay on his saddle. Haft swung backhanded and the spike that backed his axe's blade sunk into the lancer's back. The lancer cried out in pain and lost first his balance, then his head when Haft chopped at his neck.

Then the two sea soldiers from the Easterlies were with Haft, and they formed an outward-facing triangle, able to fight in all directions without fear of an attack from the rear. Three more Jokapcul and two of their horses were killed before a lucky thrust got through and took down one of the Easterlies' sea soldiers.

Through it all, Jokapcul officers barked commands, commands echoed by their sergeants. Most of the Jokapcul continued their pursuit into the open, only those who couldn't easily evade the men who resisted them stopped to fight. None of those Jokapcul lived.

The battle in the trees was fierce, but brief. Spinner and the few horsemen with him reached Haft and the other men on foot seconds after the last Jokapcul disappeared into the trees to the north.

"Gods, how many?" Spinner asked as he looked about at the bodies. Most were Jokapcul cavalry, but many—too many—wore the uniforms of Skragland, Zobra, Eikby, or no uniforms at all.

"We can sort them out later," Haft said. "Let's go!" He began trotting north.

"Form up in squads!" Spinner shouted. "Horse, stay with foot!"

They passed scattered bodies on their way to the northern edge of the forest. All were Eikby Guards, nearly all killed from behind. None of the bodies was Jokapcul. They burst into the open and confronted even worse carnage.

CHAPTER
EIGHTEEN

Fletcher tried to stop the flight of the Eikby Guards but they ignored him. In a futile attempt to outrun the Jokapcul, nearly all the guards had dropped their weapons. The farmers gleaning the battlefield didn't know what the guards were running from, but most were infected by their panic and so they joined and ran too—the rest just stood where they were, wondering what was wrong. Fletcher stopped trying to halt the flight when the first Jokapcul charged into the open. He noted the different color of their armor and immediately knew they were a different unit from the one Eikby's defenders had just defeated. There were hundreds of them, and they came in waves that extended beyond the width of the battlefield. He wasted no time or effort wondering where they came from, but drew his sword and resolved to take as many of them with him as he could before they killed him. Five Jokapcul closed ranks and came straight at the lone armed man who stood in their way.

Xundoe gaped at the running guards and the charging Jokapcul. One passed close enough to spear him with his lance but didn't even glance his way, making him blink in surprise before he realized the Lalla Mkouma had made him invisible. He suddenly understood he could fight with little danger to himself. Where he crouched, he was closer to the forest than Fletcher was. He saw five lancers close ranks. Without thinking, he reached into one of his packs and pulled out a phoenix egg. He twisted its top and threw it in front of the charging quintet. The egg burst open and the phoenix arose, unfolding its wings, and incinerated the Jokapcul, who

232

were too close even to realize their danger. He groped in the pack for another egg as he looked around for another gathering of Jokapcul, but the horsemen weren't stopping, they continued their charge toward the nearly unmanned defenses and the town beyond. Some of them flew from the saddle when their horses stepped on caltrops and fell. Xundoe stopped his search for another phoenix egg and drew his small demon spitter. He would make sure the thrown Jokapcul wouldn't rejoin the battle.

A short distance away a lancer speared a farmer as casually as a boy gigs a frog. The sight infuriated Xundoe. He aimed his small demon spitter, the demon spat, and the lancer toppled from his horse as brains and blood spilled from his cracked skull. He looked around, another Jokapcul was heeling his horse after killing a farmer. He aimed, thunder cracked, and a rose bloomed on that Jokapcul's back. The horseman sagged, fell forward, and tumbled to the ground. Then all the Jokapcul except those who had been thrown were beyond the field, heading into the town. Fires began to blossom in the outlying houses. Xundoe ran about searching for downed but live Jokapcul.

Fletcher was the only other man left standing on the battlefield, a dead Jokapcul lay at his feet and a riderless horse casually munched grass a few yards distant. Farmers dead and dying lay about the battlefield. Corpses of guards and farmers were scattered as far as the defensive trench; the mage couldn't see what lay on the ground beyond that.

The company's fighters who had gone into the forest after the Eikby Guards came out from under the trees.

Haft barely took in the carnage of the immediate scene, his attention focused on the Jokapcul horsemen speeding into the town. Without breaking stride, he raised his axe above his head and screamed, "After them!"

From atop his horse, Spinner saw the Jokapcul killing and burning their way into the heart of Eikby more clearly than Haft did. "Hold!" he called out, and heeled his horse ahead of the footmen. Haft kept going and screaming for the others to follow him.

Spinner reined in and turned in front of Haft, blocking him. "Stop!" he shouted.

Haft skidded to a stop. "They're getting away. We have to catch them before they burn down the whole town." He stepped forward and reached out a hand to the gelding's shoulder, to push the horse to face into Eikby. Spinner knocked his arm away with his quarterstaff.

"Listen to you, you're already out of breath. We can't chase after them. They're mounted and moving too fast. Everyone will be too tired to fight when we reach them."

"But—"

"No buts." Spinner looked to the northwest. "We have to see to our own people first."

"But the town . . ."

"We can do more for the town by getting organized first than by wildly chasing after the Jokapcul and getting killed because we're too winded to fight when we reach them."

Haft yelped when he was suddenly lifted from his feet by Silent, who had come up behind and grabbed the back of his cloak.

"Spinner's right," the giant said. "Chasing the Jokapcul is folly. We must get to our people first. Then we fight."

"Look around you," Spinner snapped, "we've been too weakened to charge right into a fight." The company had begun the fight with about a hundred and ten soldiers and other fighting men in the trenches. Of the nearly one hundred who survived the initial assault to follow the Eikby Guards into the forest, fewer than seventy had come out again. None of the four dozen Eikby Guards was present except among the dead that were sprawled across the battlefield.

Haft stopped struggling in Silent's grip when he saw how few of them there were. "You're right," he said reluctantly. Silent put him down. Haft glared over his shoulder at the giant but didn't say anything.

A few farmers who'd somehow survived the charge began to rise and look expectantly at the fighters.

"Where's Xundoe?" Fletcher suddenly asked. "He was going through the Jokapcul equipment looking for magic. Now he's gone."

"Here I am!"

"Where?" Startled, they looked around. The farmers began edging nervously away.

"Right here!" the mage said. "Oh, the Lalla . . ."

An instant later he appeared. No thunder, no lightning, he was simply standing right where his voice had come from. Four diminutive women figures sat on his shoulders, hugging his neck. Silent gasped, the other three stared. The farmers looked about wildly for a place to hide.

Spinner was the first to regain his voice. "Where did you find them?" he blurted.

Haft was less than half a beat behind. "What, do they always come in fours?" He and Spinner had taken four Lalla Mkouma from the slavemaster's men-at-arms at The Burnt Man Inn.

"The Jokapcul had them, I found them in their equipment," Xundoe explained. "And other things. I found a—"

"Never mind right now," Spinner said hastily. "Gather everything you found; we have to get to our people."

"Right. I have all this." He waved a hand at the three packs and the hodekin's cage and shuffled over to them.

"You!" Haft called to four farmers who were sidling away. "Help the mage with those packs."

"Spinner, Haft," Fletcher interjected, pointing toward the town. "Look." A line of Jokapcul cavalry had turned away from the center of Eikby and were heading toward their lightly defended campsite.

"Horsemen, let's go!" Spinner ordered as soon as he saw them. He heeled his gelding and galloped in a circle around the outside of the fence. Three Zobrans who had fought on foot mounted three riderless horses that hadn't wandered off and chased after the others.

"Get these," Haft shouted. He grabbed one of the demon spitters, three of the Blood Swords grabbed the others. "Let's move!" he shouted and put his words to action. The fighters followed.

The farmers Haft ordered to help with the magic items tried to take advantage of the distraction to run to the forest. Xundoe saw them and cried out, "Stop or die by magic!"

One of them looked back and saw the mage pointing his small demon spitter in his direction.

"Don't kill me!" the farmer shrilled and dropped to his knees. The other three heard the cry and looked over their shoulders. They skidded to a stop and dropped to their knees in supplication.

"Get back here and help me as Master Haft told you to." The farmers reluctantly scrambled back. Three of them hefted the packs they were directed to but the fourth stared, appalled, at the hodekin cage.

"Don't drop the packs and don't open them," Xundoe said in what he hoped was a command voice. "And none of the magic will harm you." He herded the farmers as fast as they would move toward the bivouac.

In their haste to reach and defend the campsite, nobody noticed that Nightbird and the other healers who had conscripted the hidden, unarmed farmers and tradesmen for litter bearer duty to move the wounded to the camp hadn't begun to move yet.

Ninety Jokapcul cavalrymen, mixed swords and lances, cantered toward their target. All of the fencing had been laid out to defend against an attack from the forest, not the town. The bivouac was open to the town—open to the enemy. Corporal Maetog saw the Jokapcul coming and ordered everybody to the other side of the fence. They scrambled madly; children, women, the wounded. Maetog had but fifteen fighters, including himself—nine of his own Blood Swords and five Eikby Guards—not enough to hold for long against ninety Jokapcul. But having the fence between them would prevent the approaching horsemen from crashing through at speed. And the tents and wagons would break up their charge, stagger their line so they wouldn't all reach the fence at the same time. Maetog saw horsemen rapidly coming around the fence from the south. The Jokapcul would arrive first, but the camp and the fence might delay them long enough for the help to arrive before the battle was lost.

As soon as enough of the people had crossed the fence, the corporal commanded his Blood Swords and other Skraglanders to "Take bows!" Then said, "Shoot as soon as they're within range." All the Eikby Guards and three Blood Swords took up the bows and nocked arrows. Maetog ran about making sure all the people were safely across the fence, then told the few fighters he had what he wanted them to do when the attackers reached the fence and they could no longer stand there shooting arrows.

A nervous Eikby Guard fired the first arrow when the Jokapcul were still cantering a hundred yards away. It missed, but may as well have been a signal, for at that instant the Jokapcul broke into a gallop. Then other arrows flew. They also missed, but the Jokapcul line lost its sharp dress as swordsmen and lancers dodged the missiles. The first of them tumbled from his horse when they were only fifty yards away. Four more fell before they reached the fence, one when an arrow hit his horse in the face. The first two horsemen who reached the fence tried to jump it but their horses tripped on the high wires and crashed to the ground beyond. One horse landed on its rider's leg. It struggled to rise, but fell back, pinning the Jokapcul. A boy with a knife ran up and slit his throat, then put the horse out of its agony. A dismounted lancer made it through the fence and ran the boy through before a Blood Sword severed his head with a single blow. The other Blood Swords drew their blades and joined the three at the fence, chopping and stabbing at Jokapcul as they clambered through the strands of the fence. The other six backed off and continued aimed fire into the massed Jokapcul. But the Jokapcul fought fiercely, stabbing and slashing as they came through the fence.

"Women!" Alyline screamed. "To the fence!" She brandished her gold handled dagger and sped to the defense.

Other women and the older boys picked up knives and hammers and lengths of wood and followed.

The Golden Girl raced toward a Jokacpul swordman who was hung up in the fence. He grunted as he yanked at the mesh of wires that had hooked onto his armor when he tried to force through without lifting them apart to make space. A wire broke and coiled with a *spang*, and barely missed his face as its pointed end whipped away. He bulled his shoulder against another wire and it gave. Barbs hung in his armor and tried to hold him. Another push and he was almost through. He never made it.

A shriek to rival that of a banshee made the swordman jerk startled eyes up. He gaped at the woman bearing down on him, golden hair flowing behind, a short, patchwork vest didn't quite cover her breasts, patchwork pantaloons rippled with the pumping of her legs, gold coins jangled and glittered on her girdle.

He reacted blindly to the glint of her dagger by thrusting with his sword, but a wire barb snagged his arm and threw off his aim. Then she was on him, pulling the side flap of his helmet, exposing his throat, slashing it. He screamed at the wire of hot pain, then the scream became a gurgle. She let go of his helmet flap and he jerked backward. In vain he slapped his hands to his throat to stanch the bleeding. . . .

Alyline spun toward a woman's scream. A few feet away a woman flailed with a hammer while she grappled with a lancer who had made it halfway through the fence. He was bending her backward, leaning his own weight onto her, buckling her legs.

The Golden Girl's dagger took the lancer across the eyes. He screamed and let go of the woman, his hands slapped over his eyes. The woman staggered briefly then jumped forward and swung the hammer overhead with both hands onto his helmet. She recovered and delivered a crossbody blow that staggered the lancer, dented his helmet. She swung again and the helmet flew off. She beat down on his head with the hammer and his body shuddered, then sagged. She struck him again and the hammer sank into his skull. As Alyline ran to stop another Jokapcul from crossing the fence, the woman was still screaming and pummeling the pulp that had been the lancer's skull. Then another lancer thrust his weapon deep into her side to end her screams.

Zweepee and Doli were preparing food when the Jokapcul began their charge. Zweepee thrust a large butcher knife into Doli's hands and snatched up a heavy cleaver. "Come on!" she commanded in a voice that sounded too big and strong to come from so small a woman. She grabbed Doli's arm with her free hand and dragged the bigger woman along as she ran to the fence.

When they were at the fence, Zweepee let go so she could use both hands to chop at the forearm of a Jokapcul who was spreading strands of wire so another could crawl through. The soldier's chain mail stopped the blade, but a bone snapped inside his arm and he yelped and let go of the wire to dance away holding his injured arm.

Doli squealed as she poked the butcher knife at the face of the man in the fence. He snarled and batted the blade away with his mailed arm. He twisted his body and stepped the rest of the way through the fence. But before he could bring his weapon to bear on the woman who was now backing away screaming, a blow to his back staggered him. Snarling, he turned to see Zweepee beginning another swing. He swung his arm up and back down to intercept the cleaver and knock it away, but Zweepee was off balance and she fell forward—he missed the cleaver and it *thunk*ed into his boot, splitting the hard leather and chopping into his foot. He roared in pain and swung the butt of his lance into Zweepee, flipping her onto her back. He reversed his hold on his lance and stepped forward to plunge it into her body but Doli leaped onto his back, forgetting the large blade she carried. He spun around off balance and crashed into the fence with Doli between him and it. He bounced off the wire—Doli, stunned and hooked by barbs, stayed on it.

Zweepee struggled to her knees and swiped with her cleaver but it slid across the leather instead of breaking through the joint. He bent over and grabbed her by the throat to hold her in place so he could stab his lance into her.

Doli recovered enough to remember the butcher knife. She picked it up and jabbed it up under the rear apron of the lancer's jerkin. He screamed and flinched away, arcing his body away from the blow and wrenching the knife from her grasp. Freed, Zweepee fell away, came back to her knees, and chopped at his foot again. The lancer fell and Zweepee chopped at his neck but the studded leather flaps blocked her blade. Then Doli grabbed the butcher knife and twisted it out, making him scream in pain again. The two women exchanged a quick glance and remembered another time they went to work with blades on a Jokapcul. They were grinning when they went back to work on the lancer.

He screamed again.

The Eikby Guards stood back and fired arrow after arrow into the Jokapcul climbing through the fence, but the attackers' armor deflected most of them. Two of the guards dropped their bows in favor of swords and joined the melee. Corporal Maetog seemed to be everywhere along the fence, chopping, stabbing, slashing at the soldiers clambering through the fence until a thrust to his throat brought him down. There were simply too many Jokapcul for the few fighters and the women and children to keep out. The four remaining bowmen dropped their bows and, swords in hand, charged into a group of Jokapcul who made it through an undefended section of fence.

Five middle-sized boys armed with knives and staves ran up behind a Jokapcul and beat on his back. One tried to hamstring him, but his knife was ineffective against the chain mail that covered the lancer's legs. He spun about, swinging his lance like a sword. Its shaft knocked one boy down, its blade sliced through the belly of another. The other boys ran so the Jokapcul plunged his lance into the chest of the boy he'd knocked down.

The defending soldiers were bigger and stronger than their foes and their swords were better suited to close combat on foot than the lances wielded by many of the attackers, but the

Jokapcul fought with an unnatural ferocity, as though they were possessed by demons—or cared not whether they lived or died. And there were many more of them than there were defenders. They took many with them, but Blood Swords and Eikby Guards alike fell before the fierce attack. Many of the Jokapcul began to rampage among the women and children.

Then more than a dozen horsemen crashed into the mass of Jokapcul, scattering them, many with red-running wounds or broken bones. The Jokapcul quickly recovered and threw themselves screaming at the horsemen, jabbing with their lances, grabbing at their arms and legs, trying to jump on their horses and pull them to the ground. The horses reared and lashed out with their forelegs, bucked and kicked with their hindlegs. Spinner fended off his attackers with his quarter-staff, smashing bones and pulping faces—he wished for a sword but didn't have time to draw his. Silent's huge sword swung in high arcs that carried it from one side of his great mount to the other; it dripped with more red and gore each time it rose. The other swordsmen hacked away at the small men harrying them, breaking lances and drawing blood. But the Jokapcul were like a wolf pack on a stag, and there were too many. An Eikby Guard was gutted by a lance thrust, a Skraglander was dragged off his horse and pinned to the ground by three lances. A hamstrung horse fell, screaming awfully, its rider was stabbed repeatedly before he could pull himself from his downed mount.

Then the footmen, led by Haft, came through the fence and fell on the Jokapcul. Unlike Spinner and the horsemen who had gone around the fence, Haft and the men on foot raced straight across the enclosed area and didn't take much longer to reach the battle.

The fighting was furious but brief. The Jokapcul, surprised one time too many and suffering losses they couldn't sustain, broke and ran back to the fence and through it to their horses. The defenders who could find bows picked them up and fired arrows after them. Xundoe arrived in time to use his small de-mon spitter—five mounted lancers went down to the weapon before the tiny demon in its handle popped out and demanded to be fed.

Beyond the retreating Jokapcul, the heart of Eikby was ablaze, high flickering flames and billowing smoke blotted out the forest beyond. Panicked, screaming people ran in all directions as horsemen galloped about, cutting them down. Other Jokapcul formed up in front of the burning town, facing the campsite and the people beyond it. They began to advance at a trot. Some of them unlimbered the tubes of demon spitters. Two wore magicians robes.

A double column of fresh horsemen appeared at the southern verge of Eikby's land.

THIRD INTERLUDE

DEMONIC WEAPONS

"Infernal Armory;
The Weaponry of the Jokapcul"

by
Munch Musk
(originally published in
Swords and Arrows Monthly
Reprinted with permission)

"The Jokapcul are coming! The Jokapcul are coming!"
For generations that cry was heard only on the coast of
Kingdoms of Matilda and Rumpole on the west of the continent of Nunimar. In those bygone days, it was a sounding of
the alert rather than the cry of terror it is today. Those earlier
coastal raids weren't intended for conquest, the Jokapcul raided
to steal women, food, and sheep. (You can use your own
imagination to figure out why they wanted the sheep.)

Then, within the current generation, Lord Lackland, the in-
famous "Dark Prince" of Matilda, turned renegade and conjured up a vast library of magical tomes for the Jokapcul. The
formerly annoying coastal raiders put those tomes to good
use as they learned how to harness the powers of a variety of
previously unknown demons to make some of the most hor-
rific weapons ever seen.

The Jokapcul then set out to conquer the world. Now when
someone cries out, *"The Jokapcul are coming!"* it's in the nations of southern Nunimar and is a cry of terror, usually followed closely by the thunder of an infernal weapon.

The demonic weapons employed by the Jokapcul can be
divided into two general categories: offensive, and defensive. Here's a brief overview of some of the main weapons in
each of these categories—just bear in mind that almost any
weapon can be used either offensively or defensively.

OFFENSIVE WEAPONS:

1. The most common are Demon Spitters, which come in two sizes. Nobody, other than the Jokapcul themselves, knows the actual names or natures of the demons used in these weapons—until the Jokapcul first employed them in their conquest of Bostia, nobody had ever heard of demons that spit with such explosive results.

The smaller of the Demon Spitters is normally used only by a magician. It is held in one hand and can penetrate any armor worn by a man at a distance of one hundred paces or farther.

The larger Demon Spitter is commonly used by ordinary soldiers who have been specially trained in its use by magicians. It's a tube about 4' long 2.5" in diameter. This one is explosive. Depending on what the demon's spit strikes, when it explodes it can scatter fragments at velocity high enough to penetrate the strongest armor worn by men. A man standing close to it can be shredded into bloody pulp. There are unconfirmed reports that the spit can pulverize rock.

There is another rumor worth noting: Jokapcul magicians are said to be working on harnessing other spitting demons to make weapons midway between the large and the small Spitters and one that is to the big one what the big one is to the small one.

2. Phoenix eggs. This isn't the phoenix of mythology, the beautiful bird that lives for centuries and dies in a glory of fire only to be reborn from the fire's ashes. It's a fist-size jeweled egg that magicians can cause to crack open, releasing a fiery bird the size of an adult Roc. The released phoenix causes incredible fire damage to everything within reach of its wings as it unfolds them and gains flight. No one has ever seen where the released phoenix goes after it takes off.

3. Breathing Dragon. Unfortunately, nobody has ever survived a Breathing Dragon attack to describe it.

DEFENSIVE WEAPONS:

1. The Azren is a man-size demon normally used to guard prisoners, slaves, and other captive populations. It haunts the dreams of those it guards, and mercilessly slaughters any who try to leave its custody.

2. The Green Women guard approaches to Jokapcul installations. They appear at night—in the guise of beautiful maids—to men who think about women (and what fighting man doesn't)? A Green Woman may work alone, or several may appear in the same place at the same time. They attempt to lure soldiers away from their fellows. A soldier who follows one off is never seen alive again though his bones might be found. They are no more than a pleasant diversion to a man smart enough not to get caught alone with one.

3. Gytrash are also used to guard Jokapcul installations, and are far more dangerous. They travel in packs and are much more offensive-minded than are the Green Women. When they come across anyone other than a Jokapcul in their patrol area, they attack with fang and claw and appear to be impervious to all weapons used by the soldiers of the nations of southern Nunimar.

The imp is another defensive weapon, but it's used by many of Nunimar's nations to guard sensitive borders and installations, so no description of it is needed here.

Of course this article also makes no attempt to describe the variety of sprites, dryads, elfs, banshees, and other watchers. None of them are used as weapons, they merely watch and give warning of intruders.

Many other demons are used for weapons by the Jokapcul, but the above are the major ones.

University of the Great Rift

Department of Far Western Studies

The Editor
Swords and Arrows Monthly

Dear Sir,

I am at a lexigraphical loss to describe to you the most powerfully conflicted emotions that beset me when I received by post the three copies of the issue of *Swords and Arrows Monthly* in which was published my paper, "An Overview of a Selection of the Manifold Types of Demonic Weapons Employed by the Jokapcul in Their Current Attempt at Conquest of the World."

The absolute brilliance of the color lithographs used to illustrate my paper was exceeded only by the magnificence of their faithful detail. I stand in awe of the artful skill of your illustrators and printers in rendering these marvelous prints.

Equally, I was astonished to the point of bewilderment by the munificent size of the bank draft that was enclosed with the copies of the issue, it is far more than the honorarium rendered by *James Military Review Quarterly* when that journal published a paper of mine.

However, I must strenuously object to the changes that were made in my paper.

Firstly, whilst I understand that the titling convention in "popular" journals is different from that held proper in scholarly journals, I must take issue with the title with which you replaced mine. There is nothing "infernal" about the demonic weapons employed by the Jokapcul, and I made no inference anywhere in my paper to suggest that they are "infernal."

Secondly, I am appalled by the changes made to the text of my paper. I readily see that the paper as published follows with a reasonable amount of felicity the content of the paper as I wrote it, but I could scarce find a complete sentence of my own construction! I am almost speechless that you omitted the reference to my earlier papers on the subject of Lord Lackland and his association with the Jokapcul, which papers appeared in *The Proceedings of the Association of Anthropological Scholars of Obscure Cultures*. Your readers will be hard pressed to find the necessary documentation to illustrate that association.

Thirdly, I was initially outraged by the egregious omission of my honorific and the misspelling of my patronymic. In final analysis, however, and in regard to the manner in which you or someone in your employ so thoroughly rewrote my paper in a manner which I find unacceptable, I am relieved that should anyone of my acquaintance or any of my scholarly peers come across this issue of *Swords and Arrows Monthly*, it is entirely possible that they might not recognize the "authorship" of this paper as attributable to me.

I cannot say this too strongly: I will *not* submit another paper for consideration for publication in your journal without assurances that it will not be so bowdlerized.

> Respectfully yours,
> Scholar Munch Mu'sk,
> Professor

IV

HIT AND RUN

CHAPTER
NINETEEN

The ground climbed steadily north of Eikby, growing more and more rugged until it became, unmistakably, the flank of mountains. The going was difficult for people on foot and hazardous for horses—wagons couldn't negotiate it at all. Both the slope and its ruggedness were hidden from view from the south by the forest tops, which made the land appear to rise smoothly and gently. It was impossible to distinguish where the mountain ridge that seemed from Eikby to climb so cleanly from the land actually began. The first members of the company to reach the place where the rise was clearly the flank of the mountains, three Zobran Border Warders, scouted for the defensible position that Captain Stonearm had told them about, a valley with space enough for all and a source of fresh water. They found some two hundred Eikby townspeople, nearly all women and children, already there when they arrived. They searched the valley from its narrow mouth to its narrower end and confirmed that it had no other entrances. More important, it was free of both bandits and Jokapcul. The Border Warders left to scout about for refugees trying to find their way there. The first of the company's people they found were being herded by Wolf. They put the three women and four children in the new campsite and had the five men join in the search for others.

Haft and Silent reached the rally point before Spinner did. They reorganized the searchers, who had grown in number, and set out a line of pickets to guide people to the valley. They sent the Zobran Border Warders and Skraglander Borderers along with those of Eikby's hunters who had arrived out to patrol in front of and beyond the ends of the picket line to search for groups and individuals. Wolf ranged farther and found several people who otherwise would have completely missed both the pickets and the patrols. The patrols were pulled in and the pickets relieved at sunset.

"They didn't even stop to fight us," Haft said in bewilderment. "They were just interested in burning the town. They didn't seem to care about us."

He and Spinner sat around a shielded fire with Fletcher, Silent, and Alyline discussing ways to find the rest of their people. Doli was just outside the circle, sitting close enough to Spinner's back that her knee brushed him every time she moved—evidently she had forgiven him his recent indiscretion. Or perhaps she was afraid and wasn't going to let what she saw as his infidelity force her out of his protective circle. Xundoe was among the many still missing.

Silent hawked and spat into the fire, his saliva sizzled into steam. "That's the Jokaps for you," he rumbled. "They probably had orders to destroy the town."

"But why?" Spinner asked in a weak voice. "It makes no sense for soldiers to bypass fighting men in favor of cutting down civilians and putting the town to torch."

Silent shrugged his massive shoulders. "Maybe someone reported armed men in the town and they were after them. Maybe they wanted to make an example, to terrify other outlying towns into surrendering. Maybe they thought if they attacked the town we'd lose discipline and would be easier to defeat." He shook his head. "They don't think like real people. They don't even think like you people, and you people think mighty strange on your own account."

"They did it because they like to kill and destroy," Alyline said angrily. "They could kill more people if they attacked the town first, then attacked us." She looked around the fire and said harshly, "You remember, they attacked our campsite next. We were mostly women and children in the camp. They must have thought we'd be easy to slaughter." She stared into the fire for a moment, then said less harshly, "But we weren't easy to slaughter."

"They're still out there, you know," Silent said into the quiet after the Golden Girl spoke. "They're looking for us and they're going after our people who are trying to reach the rally point."

Spinner looked up at the valley's sides. "When I saw the mountains rising above the forest I thought their foot would be easy to find."

"That's because you don't know mountains," Haft said ruefully. "I should have thought of it myself at the time and come up with a better rally point for us." He shook his head. "But I didn't."

"Don't blame yourself, either of you," Fletcher said. "We'd never had to use a rally point. Anyway, this is still the best one in sight from Eikby. Now, Silent's right, they're still out there looking for us. So what do we do?"

"Find them and kill them first," Haft answered. He was always ready with a direct solution.

"There're too many of them," Spinner said. "First we have to find the rest of our people and lead them to this valley."

"And what do we do when the Jokapcul find this valley and trap us in it?" Alyline asked scornfully.

"This valley's easy to defend," Silent said. "We've got water, and there aren't enough of them to starve us out."

"That would be true if we had food," Fletcher said, "but food is in short supply."

"Right before we withdrew we saw two more troops arrive," Spinner said. "How many more have joined them since?"

"None." Silent looked at him. "I wasn't only looking for our people when I went south. I was also looking to see if more of them came. They didn't."

"We killed one full troop's worth of them," Haft said. "Maybe more. We can beat them."

"How many of us did they kill or capture?" Alyline asked. No one answered. So far no more than fifty of their people had found their way to the valley. Fifty of their own people, plus they weren't sure how many Eikbyers who had made their way to the hidden valley over the previous couple of days, or stumbled onto them during their flight from the Jokapcul.

"Nobody knows what happened to Captain Stonearm?" Spinner asked after a long moment's silence.

Nobody replied at first, no one remembered seeing the guard captain since early in the battle with the mixed troop of Jokapcul.

"He must have been killed while we were too busy fighting to notice," Fletcher finally offered. No one said anything.

Wolf slipped into the circle and squeezed between Spinner and Silent. He stretched out and lay with his jaw resting on his paws. He whined.

"Couldn't find anybody else, boy?" Silent asked, ruffling the fur on Wolf's shoulders.

Wolf whined again and rolled his head side to side, an obvious "no."

"Is anyone still out there?"

Wolf bunched his shoulders, a shrug.

"We'll look again in the morning."

"Ulgh." Wolf closed his eyes, and soon his paws began twitching as he chased rabbits in his sleep.

Soon after, the others also drifted off.

It took a long time for sleep to overtake Spinner. Had he done the right thing when he ordered everybody to scatter and find their way to the rally point? Should he have ordered a better organized withdrawal, one where they would have come here together? Maybe not. Even Haft had been ready to run. Silent, who never showed fear of the Jokapcul, preferred to be on his own to get away.

How many of the people who depended on him and Haft for leadership and protection had been killed? How many were still out there, looking for sanctuary? *Was* this valley sanctuary? They had almost no food, and they'd had to leave nearly all of their other property and supplies in the camp. How long could they hold out when the Jokapcul found this valley? Could they find the rest of their people and head north before the Jokapcul found the valley? Did they have any chance of evading the Jokapcul when they pulled out?

He'd resolved none of his questions before exhaustion finally pulled him under.

Haft had no trouble falling asleep. He *knew* their only chance to survive was to go out and kill the Jokapcul before the Jokapcul found and killed them. He had no illusion that it would be *easy*, but neither did he doubt it could be done. Since the Jokapcul outnumbered them so badly the remains of the company would have to catch them in small groups. If the enemy was conducting a serious search for them, he would have to break into small groups to cover enough ground, so it would be possible to catch the Jokapcul in the necessary small groups. Tomorrow was soon enough to begin looking for them. Yes, Haft had no trouble falling asleep. There was nothing they could do before morning anyway, and they were safe enough that night.

The pickets were relieved in the morning and fresh patrols sent out. Silent and Wolf ranged independently in search of wandering survivors and Eikby refugees—and scouting for Jokapcul movement and reinforcements. Beginning in mid-morning, more members of the scattered company dribbled in, along with a few more Eikby survivors.

Spinner went up the valley, which didn't extend very far before its rising bottom narrowed to little more than a crack in walls twice the height of a man. He found a place where he could easily climb to the top of the wall. There he climbed a tree that allowed him to look over the forest into the distant Eikby clearing. He was too far away to make out anything more than a black smudge where the town had been, a few tendrils of smoke that still rose from it, and tiny, moving, specks that were probably Jokapcul. There must have been something he could have done differently to prevent the Jokapcul destruction of the town. But what? He had no idea, and *Lord Gunny Says* gave no clues.

Haft patrolled for a time, then found a lookout tree to climb. He was only half as far from Eikby as Spinner was and, even though he couldn't make out details, was able to see more.

A troop of mounted Jokapcul paraded about in maneuvers while people tended the fields and flocks under the watchful eyes of mounted soldiers. He saw others lugging bodies to heap in a growing pile. Some people were building a wooden structure. He estimated that less than a full troop of Jokapcul was watching the laborers. He looked at the forest west of the town, and between the town and his lookout tree. If his guess was right, two full troops—probably more—of Jokapcul horsemen were in those trees searching for stragglers. But the canopy was too dense for him to see through.

When the sun was halfway down the western sky he descended from the tree and began a looping route back to the valley. When he arrived he had five people with him, four members of the company who were wandering lost, and a woman from Eikby who had lain down to die because she was lost and thought she would never find the valley. By then Xundoe was in the valley along with the four farmers who had carried the packs and the hodekin's cage for him; they'd been found and led in by one of the patrols. The farmers who the day before had been so reluctant to carry the magic-filled packs were now very glad they had because they thought the mage would have left them behind to fend for themselves if they'd been without their burdens.

The number of survivors who made it to the small valley steadily declined over the next three days until Spinner and Haft reluctantly decided no more were coming. Fletcher and Zweepee made rosters of those present from the company and Jakte, the Eikby hunter, made one for the townspeople. The rosters weren't encouraging. Hardly more than half the people of the company had made it to the valley. Some four hundred of Eikby's residents were present, but Captain Stonearm, the mayor, the master builder, and carpenter were not among them.

All but two of the Skragland Blood Swords were dead or missing; Spinner and Haft refused to give up hope that some might have survived. Two of the sea soldiers, a Kondiver and one from the Easterlies, were killed and half of the Skraglander Guards and three of the Zobran Royal Lancers hadn't made it either. Only three of the Skragland Borderers had lived through the battle. Most of the Border Warders were in transit or thought to be on their way. As were the Zobran Light Horse. A third of the Skraglander Bloody Axes were gone. Fewer than half of the veterans of other armies survived. The only squad that made it through intact was the Prince's Swords of Zobra. In sum, nearly half of the fighting men were dead or missing.

Nightbird and three of the four comfort women had made it to the valley, but close on half of the company's other women were still missing and more than half of the company's children.

Six Eikby Guardsmen, four pikemen and two swordsmen, were there, along with a hundred farmers, merchants, and tradesmen. Close to two hundred townswomen had made it, some with their children, including suckling babes. Most of the townswomen had brought their children in the expectation the men would join them later. Only half of those husbands had. A few children had come in without parents.

Spinner was deeply depressed. He'd never before been on the losing side of a battle. He didn't know how to cope with such a loss. He saw no chance that what was left of the company could find any kind of safety in the Princedons—at least not on the ocean side of the peninsula. They had to go in a different direction. But where—and how? Almost half of the camp followers who had depended on the soldiers and other fighting men to protect them were gone. And those who were missing represented many of the trades and crafts the company needed to sustain itself. Most of their goods, nearly all of their horses, and all of their wagons, were gone. How would—how could—they survive?

He had never asked to be leader of that company, he'd never wanted leadership and its burdens—he didn't feel competent to be in charge of so many people, responsible for their safety and well-being. He'd been right, a pea on like him shouldn't be in command; he wasn't competent. Some mistake he'd made must have cost the lives of so many of the people who depended on him. The simple fact that he had no idea what that mistake was proved him unfit to command.

He and Haft should strike out on their own. And take Alyline with them; the two of them could protect her well enough. If Silent wanted to come he was welcome. Maybe the giant steppe nomad should have been the commander from the beginning. Or Fletcher. Fletcher was intelligent and very knowledgable. Yes, Fletcher should have been in command. And Zweepee, his wife, was always ready to take matters in hand and organize the women and children in an emergency. Even now she was seeing to it that the orphaned children in the valley were being cared for, that the women who had lost their husbands weren't abandoned. But they—Silent, Fletcher, and Zweepee—were the strongest voices saying he and Haft should be in charge.

Yes, he and Haft should drift away with the Golden Girl and leave Silent, Fletcher, and Zweepee to lead the remnant of the company to safety. He wouldn't let himself think of it as deserting the people who'd depended on him and Haft; they would be better off without the two of them in charge and making mistakes that cost people their lives. Yes, he'd put it to Haft and Alyline the first chance he got. No, not to Alyline. She was too contrary; she'd resist his idea, no matter how good it was, simply because it was his. He'd tell Haft and together they would *take* Alyline and slip out of the valley and head north.

"Look at you!" A loud, harsh voice speaking broken Zobran snapped Spinner's head up. Haft was standing in the open, clumps of defeated people scattered around him.

"Look at you!" Haft shouted again. He turned slowly around as he talked, his mighty axe held ready in his hand. "Sitting there like scattered sheep huddling from a wolf. Anyone would think you were beaten and just waiting for the deathblow. You look like you're thinking, 'We can't do anything, the Jokapcul are too strong.' You Eikbyers think you can't go home because you don't have a home to go to. The Skraglanders, Zobrans, and others who came here with me and Spinner think we can't go north because we don't have the supplies and wagons we need to move this many people into the waste.

"Is that it? 'We can't do this,' 'we can't do that,' so you've given up?

"Well, *I* haven't given up!" he roared. "Nobody attacks people I'm protecting and kills them and destroys their property and then makes *me* run. *Nobody!*" He flung out his arm, pointing his axe in the direction of Eikby. "I'm going back there. And when I'm finished, the Jokapcul will have paid for what they did to you and to that town.

"Who's going with me?"

No one answered, most looked away from him. It was a long time before a farmer spoke up.

"We *think* they beat us? That's because they *did* beat us! Look around you." He stood and swept his arm to encompass the valley. "How many people were in Eikby a few days ago? Including you? How many are here now? How many have they already killed? How many are enslaved? If we go back, they'll kill or enslave the rest of us!"

Haft stared coldly at the farmer until he'd finished saying his piece. Then he said in a low voice that cut through the crowd, "Nobody's asking you to go if you'd rather run like a clip-winged duck runs from a farmer's wife with a butcher knife." The farmer flinched but didn't back down. Haft continued in a louder voice, "So we lost one little battle. So? It was just one battle, not the entire war. Haven't you ever heard of Corregidor or Wake Island?" He stopped, blinking. "No, I guess you haven't. But that doesn't matter. The point is, the first battle doesn't make the war. What that battle means is, they think they've got us whipped. They think they can ride us down anytime they want.

"They're wrong."

"There are hundreds of Jokapcul down there and we have fewer than a hundred fighting men," someone else objected. "Or do you expect women and children to do battle with them? How can we make them pay for what they did? They'd only finish killing the rest of us."

Haft turned toward him and lowered his axe to stand with

his legs apart and fists on his hips; he leaned forward aggressively. "I don't want the women and children to go," he snarled. "I don't even want all the men to go. But he," he stuck an arm out and pointed, "has the means for a few of us to go and make the Jokapcul pay dearly."

People turned and looked where he pointed—at Xundoe the mage. They gaped at the tiny, voluptuous woman draped in a diaphanous gown who perched on his shoulder.

"You know he has phoenix eggs. Some of you have seen what the phoenix eggs can do in a fight. You know he has demon spitters, and most of you have seen what a demon spitter can do. He now has another weapon." He signaled the mage.

The people watched as Xundoe raised a hand to the figure on his shoulder, and gasped with fear as he vanished.

"You saw him, you know where he's at," Haft shouted. "Attack him. Throw stones, shoot arrows, charge and swing your swords at him. Go, he's the enemy!"

The people gaped at Haft, stared at where the mage had disappeared. One, bolder than the others, walked hesitantly to where Xundoe had vanished and groped about. He stood and looked around in amazement as great as when the mage vanished.

"He's not there!"

"That's because I'm here," Xundoe said, and he reappeared at Haft's side.

"Invisibility isn't the only new weapon the magician has to help us win. Now, who's coming with me?" Haft turned in a circle, looking at everyone. He finished by looking directly at Spinner.

Spinner was aghast. Had Haft gone mad? Even if he had enough Lalla Mkouma for all the fighting men they had, there were still four hundred Jokapcul light cavalry, maybe more, where Eikby had been. The odds against them were horrendous. They had a few demon spitters captured from Jokapcul, but how many did those troops of horsemen have? And what other demonic weapons did their magicians control?

"With the Lalla Mkouma and the other magics our mage now has, a very few brave men can cause enough damage to the Jokapcul that the survivors will know they can't win. They might even flee." Haft continued to look at Spinner as he spoke, a very clear challenge.

Spinner thought attacking the Jokapcul with any fewer than two hundred fighters and magicians heavily armed with demon weapons—which they didn't have—was foolhardy to an extent far beyond simple folly. But he was a brave young man—and a Frangerian Marine. He had a reputation to uphold, even if it meant his death. He stood and walked to Haft's side.

"Who comes with us?" he asked.

There was hesitation, but in the end most of the remaining soldiers volunteered, so did several other men. There were only four Lalla Mkouma and four working demon spitters, so not all of them could come. In the end, they settled on Silent and four of the Skragland Bloody Axes.

"If we fail, you must take command and get these people to safety," Spinner told Fletcher in telling him he couldn't go with them. "No one else in the company is as able for that mission as you are."

"He's right," Zweepee said. "You must stay here."

"Eight against four hundred," Spinner muttered when it was settled. "It's madness. Pure madness."

Haft grinned at him; Spinner thought he saw mania in the grin.

"Did you sleep through the history lectures in boot camp? Did you miss the story of the Marines on the legation wall, or the story of Howard's Hill?"

Spinner shook his head. "Those stories aren't history, they're myth," he said. "Or if they are real history, they're the history of different Marines on a different world." In the first, a handful of well-armed Marines held out for nearly two months against thousands of ill-armed and poorly led attackers. In the latter, an isolated platoon beat off hundreds of attackers in an overnight battle. "Anyway, those were defensive actions," he added. "We're going on the offense."

"Only until we get them to counterattack." Haft grinned

wickedly. "Then *we* go on the defense and the Jokapcul will be in *real* trouble."

They sent hunters and foresters out to watch for Jokapcul patrols and hunter-killer platoons while the men going on the raid made their preparations. The hunters and foresters reported that the Jokapcul weren't looking in force, most of them were at Eikby driving the enslaved people in caring for the fields and flocks and the construction of a strange new building. They also found and brought in more survivors.

Alyline and Doli confronted Spinner when the eight raiders took a break from their planning. Haft was with Spinner, but the women intended to ignore him.

"You have to be a hero, don't you?" Alyline accused.

"Don't do it, Spinner," Doli spoke at the same time. "You'll just get yourself killed.

The two women's voices almost drowned each other out. Still, Spinner heard both.

"I'm not a hero, and I have to do it," he answered, looking at them earnestly.

"There aren't any heroes," Haft said. "They all died proving their heroism."

Alyline and Doli ignored him and looked at each other to decide which would speak next. Doli deferred.

"These people depend on you," the Golden Girl said, "though the gods know I don't understand why. If you go out there and get yourself killed, what's going to happen to them?"

"He's no more a hero than I am," Haft said. "He isn't going to get killed—and neither am I. I mean, if anybody wants to know." Which the women apparently didn't.

"Think of me, Spinner. I'll do anything you want, you know that," Doli interrupted whatever Spinner might have been about to say. "But I won't be able to do anything for you if you go out there tonight and get yourself killed."

Alyline also spoke before he could say another word. "Even if everyone went, there are too many Jokapcul and they're too strong; we can't defeat them."

"I don't want to lose you, Spinner. If you die, that would be as bad for me as going back into slavery."

"Please, Spinner. For the sake of the people who depend on you."

"Please, Spinner, don't go."

"You can't defeat them."

"They'll kill you, and everyone with you."

Haft cleared his throat loudly and stood up, stretching himself to his greatest height, which was barely taller than either of the women.

"We aren't going to get killed," he said firmly.

"That's exactly why I'm not talking to you about this idiocy," Alyline snapped, unable to continue ignoring him. "You honestly believe you can do the impossible. But it's simply suicide for the eight of you to go up against all those Jokapcul." But she looked like she was pleading with him.

Doli turned on Haft. "You're going to get Spinner killed if you go out there!"

"I'm gratified that you're so concerned for *my* survival, Doli," Haft said dryly, then growled at the Golden Girl, "I may not be the most intelligent person ever, but I'm not stupid. And we aren't going to commit suicide tonight—any Jokapcul foolish enough to fight us will be the ones committing suicide.

"You see, we don't have to defeat them tonight. All we have to do is hurt them. And we are going to hurt them very severely."

Alyline sagged, she knew she couldn't get them to change their minds. She and Doli walked away. Doli's shoulders shook with her sobs.

"The merely difficult we do immediately," Spinner murmured. "The impossible may take a little longer. At least, that's what Lord Gunny said."

"If Lord Gunny said it, it must be true," Haft replied with a grim smile.

CHAPTER
TWENTY

The eight men left the valley after an early dinner and reached the edge of the forest west of Eikby's clearing shortly after the sun set but before the moon rose. It wasn't the best of nights for an attack on an enemy position, an even worse night for an attack on a position where the defenders so decisively outnumbered the attackers—when the moon rose it would be full. But the attackers counted on the two clear advantages they had over the defenders—total surprise and the Lalla Mkouma.

The first part of the attack was devoted to Xundoe's preparations. The mage picked up a pack filled with various implements and demons, put a well-fed Lalla Mkouma on his shoulder, took a deep breath to steady himself, murmured something to the miniature woman figure on his shoulder, and vanished.

When Haft first made his proposal, Xundoe had readily agreed. Now, with the campfires of the Jokapcul army only a few hundred yards away and the guttural laughter of the soldiers drifting to his ears, he wasn't so sure of the idea's brilliance. He thought he was a fool for not instantly recognizing all the manifold problems with the plan. Somewhere closer than the fires and laughter, he heard the soft nicker of a horse and imagined Jokapcul light cavalry prowling about in search of him. He shivered and stood in place, listening carefully, but no other sound of search or pursuit came to him. He continued with trepidation.

When he stumbled on a divot he recognized the place

266

where their first, brief campsite had been a few days earlier, the area where the final fight had taken place just before they scattered in flight from the massive cavalry charge. His breath speeded up, and the already dark night seemed to grow darker. He walked slower, more deliberately, with a hand extended before him, waving it slowly up and down. When his questing hand found a strand of wire, he stopped. He took a moment to bring his breath back under control, and tried to relax. After a couple of moments he looked to the eastern horizon and swallowed nervously; the moon was rising. Well, he should be safe with the Lalla Mkouma making him invisible. And he needed the light to be able to do his work. Now when he looked side to side he could see the crossed posts of the fence. There, twenty yards to his right front, was the gate. He headed toward it.

The gate had been ripped from its hinges and its pieces lay scattered about. He had to step carefully to avoid tangling his feet in coils of broken wire or trodding on barbs. He put the pack down at the corner of the open gate, careful that it didn't touch the gatepost. Squatting, he opened it and began withdrawing items which he carefully laid out in a specific order.

When everything was ready, the first thing he did was the job he most feared: he took one of the imp houses and carried it thirty yards to his left where he affixed it to the crossing point of a pair of fence posts. Under the best of circumstances, imp-warding a fence was a delicate job, and these weren't the best of circumstances. As bright as the full moon's light was, it was far dimmer than the full daylight under which a magician would normally mount an imp house on a fence. The houses were designed to be mounted on a single, vertical fence post, not at the juncture of a pair of crossed posts. It was essential that the magician mounting the imp house avoid touching the strands of the fence while he attached the leads to them from the house—essential because the leads came through the house's door and he had to unlock and open the door to get to the leads. But the worst circumstance was, this was the first time Xundoe had ever imp-warded a fence. He dried his sweaty hands on his robe and began. His concentration was so focused that his fingers were as steady as they could be.

Finished at last, he stepped back and heaved a great sigh of relief. His relief didn't last long; he had to mount the second imp house on the fence on the other side of the gate. He managed that with just as little problem.

"The army really should have promoted me," Xundoe breathed to himself. "I'm a much more accomplished magician than a mere mage."

Then he was back at his pack contemplating his next job. Just then the next job scared him more than imp-warding the fence had. He knew the theory of imp-warding a fence but he'd never read about or been trained in what he was about to do. When Haft described it to him, it sounded very straightforward and simple. But now that it was time to actually *do* it, he was anything but certain it was in the least bit possible. If it wasn't, he was about to commit suicide, which was something he absolutely did *not* want to do.

He gathered three of the six phoenix eggs he'd removed from the pack, a handful of three-foot-long dowels, and a trio of cones he'd constructed after dinner, and carried them into the field beyond the fence. Somehow, he had to rig the eggs so that anyone passing within a couple of yards of one would cause it to crack open and release its phoenix.

Before Haft's proposal, he'd never heard any hint of a magician doing such a thing. He knew about deadfalls and spring-operated traps, but those were purely mechanical devices that didn't use the magic of demons. The closest magical entrapment he knew of to—what was the term Haft used?—*booby-trap?* a phoenix egg was an imp house, and that was quite different. How do you set an egg to crack when someone passes nearby when you have to twist its top before it will crack?

Haft's solution was so simple it was obvious. But if it was so obvious, why hadn't anybody ever thought of it before? Surely if anyone had ever done it and it worked, he would have heard about it. If it worked it would have been taught in Elementary Fire Demons. Wouldn't it?

He went through the gate at a sharp angle to the right and stopped about ten yards from the fence. On his hands and knees, he balanced the cone point-down on the ground. He then laid out a trio of dowels around it and attached one end of each to notches in the top of the cone. The cone was now held erect by the dowels. He reached for a phoenix egg and a shiver ran all the way to his fingertips when he twisted the top of the phoenix egg and he drew back to wipe away the sweat running down his face and compose himself. Trembling everywhere except for his fingers, he gingerly balanced the phoenix egg in the top of the cone. When he withdrew his hands, the egg and cone wobbled slightly, then settled into balance. Gently, not daring to breathe, he gathered the other cones, dowels, and phoenix eggs, and eased back until he was far enough away that if the egg fell he'd be out of range of the phoenix's opening wings.

Now if a foot or hoof landed nearby hard enough to dislodge one of the dowels, the phoenix egg would fall and crack open on the ground. That was the theory, anyway.

Fifteen yards farther along the fence and a little farther out, he set another egg in place. The third went fifteen yards farther but a little closer to the fence. When it was in place, he went weak-kneed to the fence and followed it to the gate, where he gathered the remaining phoenix eggs and materials. He not only repeated the process to the left of the gate, he lived to tell the tale. Or at least report to Haft that he had done it; he felt so shaken he couldn't swear he was still alive.

Xundoe had one more job, the most frightening thing he had to do that night. He needed help to begin it. He still had no idea why the Jokapcul brought a hodekin with them, but *he* had certainly found a use for a digging demon. He and Haft wore heavy leather gloves when they opened the hodekin's cage and lifted it out. The Marine struggled to control the demon while the mage fitted a harness to it. When the harness was tightened around its chest and Haft set the demon on the ground the hodekin stopped biting and clawing at their hands and began to dig. Fortunately, Xundoe had attached a stout leash to the harness before Haft released the demon, and a sharp yank on the leash brought the hodekin to heel. As long as Xundoe kept moving, the hodekin walked calmly with its head next to his hip. The instant he stopped, it jumped one way or another before hunkering down to dig. What was most frightening about this job was he had no way to know in which direction the hodekin would jump when he stopped. They would be working near the phoenix eggs he planted. If the hodekin's jumping or digging disturbed one of the dowels, a phoenix egg would fall and crack open, releasing the fiery bird. If it jumped in the other direction, it might hit the fence and summon the imps.

There was no help for it. Xundoe walked the demon through the gate and along the fence, keeping himself between the hodekin and the phoenix eggs. Every few yards he stopped. The instant he did the demon began digging. He only gave it a few seconds, the hodekin's broad hands dug faster than a spade. If he didn't stop it before it had dug a hole it could duck into, he wouldn't be able to make it stop until *it* was ready to stop; instead, it could drag him along as it dug deeper and farther into the earth. Anyway, he didn't want pits that could swallow a man, just little holes maybe a foot deep and as much in diameter—just big enough to trip a running horse— or man—and break its leg.

Well beyond the southernmost phoenix egg, Xundoe turned away from the fence. Again the hodekin dug small holes as he zigzagged in the direction of the Jokapcul campfires. At a safe distance beyond the phoenix eggs, he turned left and went in wide zigzags to well beyond the northernmost egg on the far side of the gate before turning back and digging holes closer to the fence.

The night was more than half gone by then and Xundoe was drenched with sweat. But the fence on both sides of the gate was imp-warded, a half dozen phoenix eggs lay in wait to be cracked open, and a forty-yard-wide swath of ground on the other side of the fence was pitted with holes big enough to trip a galloping horse and break its leg. Now all they had to do was goad the Jokapcul into attacking them.

"You're sure the lane is clear along the road?" Spinner asked.

"The road is clear passage," Xundoe replied. "That's the only way to go safely between here and fifty or more yards beyond the fence."

"Then I better go," Haft said. The raid was his idea; he believed it was up to him to take the most dangerous part of it. Of course, Xundoe would have disagreed with him on that score. Xundoe believed *he* had the *most* dangerous part of the raid, Haft merely had the *second* most dangerous part.

Haft fed the demon in one of the demon spitters and gave a food pellet to a Lalla Mkouma who was simply *delighted* to climb on his shoulder and spin her diaphanous robe to turn him invisible.

Demon spitter in hand, Haft padded quietly along the road toward the Jokapcul campfires. He wasn't concerned about being seen by sentries, still, he walked as quietly as he could.

Halfway from the fence to the nearest fires Haft stopped and lowered himself to one knee. He tapped on the door on the side of the demon spitter. It popped open and the demon poked out its head and peered at him suspiciously, as though making sure of who he was.

"Wazzu whanns, gud'ghie?" the tiny demon demanded.

Haft remembered his first meeting with the demon and had to smile. The tiny demon had crawled over his head and shoulders, sniffing at his hair, behind his ears, up his nose, around his mouth. When it went to smell his armpit it froze, looking down at his axe.

"Zhow mee," it had said, pointing a gnarly arm and hand at the axe where it hung on his belt.

Haft looked questioningly at Xundoe, but the mage said he should do as the demon asked. He withdrew his axe from the loop that held it and lifted it to where the demon could examine it. The demon climbed down his arm and settled on his wrist inches from the axe. It reached out a lumpy hand and traced the rampant eagle engraved on the half-moon blade, then settled back on its haunches and stared at the eagle for a long moment. It gave a satisfied nod, clambered back up Haft's arm, and settled on his shoulder.

"Oo gud'ghie," the demon said. *"Likuu. Ee fi'gt zhame-zhame."*

Haft blinked, startled. There it was again, his axe! What was it about his axe that caught the attention of so many men?—and demons, it seemed.

Xundoe had gaped at the demon. When he saw Haft's perplexed look, he mouthed, *Later.* But "later" hadn't come yet, Haft still didn't know what that had been about. Now wasn't the time to wonder about it, he and the demon had a job to do.

"Do you see the fire over there?" Haft asked low-voiced.

The demon, inside the Lalla Mkouma's cloak of invisibility, could see Haft. It laid his head against his pointing arm and looked along it. *"Yss. Zho? Whatch abou'em?"*

"Can you spit that far?" He hadn't had the opportunity to fire the demon spitter when Xundoe admitted he didn't know their range; Haft hoped the demon would tell him the truth.

"Zpitz var'n whanns."

That didn't answer Haft's question. He tried a different approach. "Do you want to spit that far?"

The tiny demon studied the distance to the fire. It craned up and down, side to side, trying to gauge the range without all the visual cues it would have during the day.

"Dry id," it finally said, and popped back inside. The little door shut with a *snick*.

Haft shook his head. *Try it.* The demon didn't know if it could reach that far. He thought about it for a moment, then stood and advanced another twenty yards before kneeling again. Laughing voices drifted to his ears from the Jokapcul camp. He balanced the tube on his shoulder and sighted along it. When Xundoe introduced him to the demon spitter he had been vague about how to aim it. Haft remembered the Jokapcul who had these demon spitters had elevated their muzzles when they fired. He tried to imagine how high he'd have to aim a longbow to reach the fire and held the tube about as high. He wrapped his hands firmly around the hand-grips that protruded from the bottom of the tube and squeezed the lever that told the demon to spit.

Nothing happened for a second, then a loud *pthup* sounded from the tube and it bucked on his shoulder. Again, nothing happened for a second, then the fire he'd aimed at exploded, scattering embers and flaming brands in all directions. Shouts and screams came clear from the camp.

The demon flung its door open and popped its head back out, vigorously rubbing its mouth with the back of its wrist. *"Naw zo 'igh,"* it said. *"Awmoz mizzd."* It disappeared back into the tube.

Encouraged, Haft aimed at a different fire—but didn't elevate the front of the tube as high. This time, the demon spat almost as soon as he squeezed the signaling lever. He didn't wait to see what happened, but aimed at another fire and squeezed again. Two more fires erupted, one after the other. A tent was ablaze, set afire by a brand from the first fire.

Pthup! went the tube. The door popped open and the demon wiped the back of a gnarly hand across its mouth. *"Veed-mee!"* it demanded.

Haft didn't argue, he got the canister of demon food and pulled out a pellet for the demon.

The demon gobbled it down, wiped its mouth, burped more loudly than anything so small should be able to, grunted, *"Thass gud."* It cocked an eye at Haft and added, *"Aimz betta, too,"* before it withdrew back into its tube.

By then more tents were burning and the entire Jokapcul camp was in an uproar. The shouts were louder and more guttural, voices of command rang out above them. He also heard a booming crack, like the sound made by Xundoe's small demon spitter. By the lights from the burning tents and undisturbed fires, Haft saw bucket brigades forming to put out the tent fires. Elsewhere, soldiers were mounting horses and forming ranks.

He aimed, squeezed, and the demon spitter spat at one cavalry formation. Horses screamed and reared, throwing their riders. A couple of horses fell and didn't rise again. Another small demon spitter *crack*ed in the Jokapcul camp. The magician must have been firing wildly, not sure of where he was. He aimed at a knot of milling Jokapcul and felt a jolt of the grimness that in combat passes for cheer as half of the horses in the knot were knocked off their hooves. The air next to his ear *crack*ed—either a magician had gotten off a lucky shot, or one had figured out where he was. He got off another spit into a fresh formation of horsemen that had started to move in his direction. He started to aim into their midst for another shot, but the demon opened its door and cried out, *"Veed-mee!"* most piteously. As he fed it, the formation broke into a canter toward him before he could level the demon spitter and take aim.

Instead of aiming and spitting again, he sprinted back toward the fence gate. Behind him came the thundering hooves of the approaching light cavalry. They were gaining on him, and horsemen shouted back and forth. He risked a glance back and gasped in shock—the horsemen were closing rapidly, and their line was too wide for him to dodge to one side or the other. They lashed to their sides with swords as they came, as though they were seeking invisible targets to slash. He put on an extra burst of speed. Ahead and getting closer, he made out the fence in the moonlight, but the horsemen would be on him before he reached the gate.

The pounding of the horses' hooves began to shake the road beneath his feet and he worried that the drumming of their hooves would dislodge the phoenix eggs. He glanced back again. A horse was bearing directly down on him, it would reach him in seconds. But neither the rider nor the horse saw him inside the Lalla Mkouma's concealing vortex. He dove to the left and the horsemen thundered harmlessly by. But a second line of cavalry was right behind the first and he had to roll back to his right to avoid being run down. No more lines of horsemen followed. Haft stopped and watched the cavalry approach the fence.

Suddenly, a horse screamed and flipped forward, catapulting its rider over its head. In seconds, four more horses were tripped up by the pits. Then someone knocked a phoenix egg over and the fiery bird stretched its hellish wings. Horses screamed and leaped away, crashing into each other. Jokapcul riders tumbled from their terrified mounts and were trampled. Two *pthup*s, muffled by distance, sounded, followed by explosions in the midst of the Jokapcul. One of the eruptions cracked another phoenix egg and the newborn bird reared up, incinerating everything within the span of its wings before it spiraled skyward. A horseman fell with an arrow protruding from his throat. Sharp *crack*s sounded within the mass of Jokapcul.

More and more of the horses screamed in panic, they bucked and kicked to dislodge their struggling riders. Hodekin pits brought more horses down with broken legs. A third phoenix egg cracked and the phoenix added its hellfire to the mix. The distant *pthup*ing came again and again, and there were more eruptions within the ranks of the Jokapcul. Above it all, Haft heard the sharper *crack*ing of small demon spitters wielded by Jokapcul magicians. There was another, louder *crack*, followed by a line of green light that arced into the sky from near the gate. At the apex of its arch, the line of light burst into a ball of brilliant fire that illuminated and slowly floated toward the ground. A *crack* sounded from it a second after the line burst into the ball. There was a sudden rattle of *crack*s from the Jokapcul magicians, but Haft couldn't see through the mass of milling men and horses to know if they could actually see who they were shooting at.

The Jokapcul officers were trying to funnel their men through the broken gate. There! Haft spotted a magician. He grinned harshly, balanced the demon spitter on his shoulder again, and aimed. The weapon spat into the mass of cavalry crowding the gate. More men and horses were thrown away by the violence of the explosion when the demon's spit struck. He quickly fired twice more, then bolted to the side before the demon could pop its door open and demand to be fed again. He was just in time; two squads of horsemen descended on the place from where he fired. The distant demon spitters spat again for the first time since the fireball opened above them, and two eruptions near the gate tumbled wounded horses and men.

He fed the demon again, then aimed the weapon and it spat into the Jokapcul who were looking for him where he had just been. Before the survivors could recover, he was on the move again, away from the fence. Fifty yards farther from the fence, he turned and sprinted to the other side of the road. As he ran, another Phoenix egg burst open and there were more explosions from the demon spitters wielded by the men with Spinner.

Then the Jokapcul jostling to get through the fence bumped the gateposts, and a sudden, shrill sizzling announced the emergence of the imps from their houses. The night filled with the screams of more men and horses as the imps grasped them and began feeding. An officer barked out in a voice of command and the horsemen broke, galloping back toward their camp. The Jokapcul magicians answered with their own *crack*s, but not with the same concentration they had when the fireball burst above the edge of the forest. A half dozen of them fell to two large demon spitter *pthup*s, and one to Xundoe's smaller one. Only one regained his feet and stumbled along the road after his troop. The retreating Jokapcul ran head-on into another troop heading toward the one-sided battle. The troops milled about in confusion for a moment, but Haft didn't see the encounter—by the time they met he was already sprinting for the gate.

"We were afraid they'd found you," Spinner said just inside the trees beyond the fence.

"Find me?" Haft grinned. "Never! Not when I've got one of these lovelies." He stroked the thigh of the giggling Lalla Mkouma who preened on his shoulder.

"We beat them!" Xundoe said in hushed excitement.

"No, we didn't beat them," Spinner said.

Haft clapped the mage on the shoulder and added, "But we certainly hurt them. Much thanks to you."

"We better go," Silent said, looking toward the Jokapcul camp. "They're coming again."

The others looked. A thick, dark line was heading toward them along the road.

"They're hurt, but they aren't beaten," Spinner said. "Let's go."

"Let's give them a farewell present," Haft said, and balanced his demon spitter on his shoulder again.

Spinner shook his head, but shouldered his demon spitter as well. So did Balta, the Bloody Axe who had the third.

"One at a time," Spinner said. "Me first. On my command, Balta. Haft last."

Haft and Balta told him they understood.

Spinner aimed his demon spitter along the road and waited until the dark line resolved itself into a column three horsemen wide. When the van of the Jokapcul column was less than fifty yards from the gate he squeezed the signaling lever. The demon spat and the first two ranks of Jokapcul were flung to the ground like they'd hit a wire stretched across the road.

"Balta!" Spinner barked, and the Skraglander's weapon spat into the Jokapcul who were manically trying to avoid trampling on or tripping over their fallen companions. Five more crashed to the ground. Injured horses screamed, other horses screamed in fear.

"Haft!" Haft's weapon spat and the eight men ran into the forest. Behind them more horses, forced off the road into the area Xundoe had prepared, screamed when their legs broke in hodekin holes. Another phoenix egg cracked open, men and horses screamed as the newborn bird unfurled its wings.

CHAPTER
TWENTY-ONE

It took a few minutes for the officers to regroup their squads when they realized no more destruction was coming their way, but the Jokapcul finally poured through the gate and spread out to search for their attackers. Some squads went north or south to search the open, moonlit fields, but most went into the forest where they thrashed about in the dark, their only illumination the few shafts of moonlight that pierced the foliage.

A squad of seven threaded its way between a thicket and a wide boled tree. When the last man reached the tree, the end of a quarterstaff arrowed out of nowhere into the space between the neckflaps of his helmet, crushing his throat. He tumbled backward and was caught by a strong arm that lowered him quietly to the ground. The strong arm's mate then thrust downward with a mighty sword and shattered his heart—the Jokapcul died before the drumming of his heels could attract attention. The horseman next up in line was silenced by the huge sword that nearly severed his head. A crossbow bolt slammed through the metal-plated leather armor of the next man forward and blew through his spine. He thudded to the ground. The sound spun the others around, weapons raised. No one opposed them and, search as they might, they couldn't find anyone in the deep shadows they'd just passed—though someone in the shadows found them. In moments the entire squad was dead.

Fifty yards to the south, a horseman probing into the shadows with his lance was momentarily surprised when a half-moon axe blade swung out of thin air. The blade clove into his chest, ending his surprise and his life. Five yards to his left, another lancer probing shadows didn't even see the sword that thrust into the thin armor under his arm. The six remaining members of that squad were unwittingly saved when they galloped toward the four briefly surviving members of the squad to their north who were yelling in their panicked search for unseen killers.

Throughout the forest, Jokapcul horsemen who'd lost their officers at the approach to the fence sped toward the yelling. Several were intercepted by axe or sword wielded by invisible men.

Elsewhere, the few remaining officers kept their men under control and continued the search. They never found their quarry, but sometimes the quarry found them. The invisible hunted found the hunters, and when they did one officer died for every three soldiers whose blood nurtured the earth. Finally, the invisible men broke off their attacks and withdrew. By then the Jokapcul, their panic growing, had begun to lash out at every shadow.

Farther to the north, under cover of the confusion caused by the unseen attackers, four men sped away: Xundoe—carrying two demon spitters—and three Bloody Axes, two of whom bore a caged hodekin between them.

By the time the few remaining officers withdrew and rallied their men in the open before the forest, eleven of the fifteen officers and forty of the 190 soldiers of the second force to approach the gate were dead or dying. Many others would recover from their wounds, though not all would be whole enough to fight again.

"I did it!" Xundoe squealed. "I did something no other Zobra army magician ever did before!"

"You did it!" Haft said loudly then staggered the mage with a clap to his back.

"I had confidence in you, Xundoe," Spinner said. He could hardly believe all eight of them had made it back to the valley.

"Spinner!" Doli shrieked, and raced to throw herself into his arms. She gripped the sides of his head and smothered his face with kisses. "You're alive!"

"Yes, I'm alive." His voice was muffled by her mouth and hair. He grasped her wrists and tried to pull her off, but she tangled her fingers in his hair and clung more tightly.

Haft and Silent looked at each other and shook their heads.

The Golden Girl approached with more dignity than Doli had. She spared Spinner and Doli a dismissive glance and planted herself in front of Haft and Silent. Others eagerly began to gather about.

"Are you going to tell us what happened," Alyline asked softly, "or are you just going to watch her slaver all over him?"

Haft turned his face aside, glad it was still night and she couldn't see the red he felt spreading over his face. "Ah, yes, tell you. Well, we set out to hurt them and we did."

Alyline cocked her head, the mocking expression on her face not quite discernable in the moonlight. "That's it? You hurt them? There's nothing more to tell?"

Haft sighed. He darted a glance at Spinner, still trying vainly to free himself from Doli's close attentions. "All right. Get everybody together and we'll tell you." He looked directly at Spinner and Doli. "Maybe by the time everyone is gathered, she'll release her prisoner so he can help us tell about the raid."

Alyline nodded sharply. "Go over there." She pointed at the place he stood earlier that afternoon when he challenged the people to defy their despair.

"Yes, mistress," Haft said to her back as she went off to gather the people. He looked up at Silent. "What do you think, should we try to rescue him?"

The giant slowly shook his head. "There are a few very important truths a man must know if he wants to survive in this world. One of them is never stand between a woman and the man she wants, even if he doesn't want her."

Haft shook his head. "I don't know what's wrong with that

man; the only thing wrong with Doli is her dislike for me. Let's go." He signaled Xundoe and the four Bloody Axes and led the way to the place Alyline had assigned to them.

It was still before dawn, but everyone was up and gathered in front of Haft and the other six raiders. Few looked at them—most looked through the shadows at Spinner, who was still locked in place by Doli. Someone tittered. Doli looked manically about, saw everyone looking, and looked like she desperately wanted to be somewhere else.

Spinner took advantage of her distraction to walk briskly to Haft's side. Haft leered at him and Spinner shook his head in embarrassment.

"All right," Haft said loudly, turning to the crowd. "We're back from the raid—all of us, as you can see, and uninjured. The Jokapcul can't say the same." Wild cheering stopped him and he smiled in openmouthed pleasure.

"Are guards posted?" Spinner asked as soon as the cheering dropped off enough for him to be heard.

"You left me in command," Fletcher answered. "You know there are."

"Thank you, Fletcher." Spinner looked to his side, at Xundoe, and continued, "We owe our success to our mage and the demons he controls. He used imps, phoenix eggs, and the hodekin to set traps for the Jokapcul when Haft lured them into attacking us. We have Xundoe to thank for the Lalla Mkouma that allowed Haft to make a foray to the edge of the Jokapcul camp without being seen, and allowed four of us to close on them when they searched for us in the forest." Then he described the night's work in greater detail. Xundoe told some of how he booby-trapped and mined the fence and the area just beyond it. Haft reported in lurid and slightly exaggerated detail what he did on the Jokapcul side of the fence. Balta, the Bloody Axe who had stayed with them, Lalla Mkouma on his shoulder, gave an account of the one-sided fight in the forest. The other Bloody Axes also contributed to the telling. Alyline, Doli, Zweepee, and Nightbird translated for those who didn't speak the languages the stories were told in.

When they were finished a man called out, "Did you hurt them badly enough to make them go away? We still have people held by them."

Spinner and Haft quickly looked at each other, uncertain how to reply. Silent spoke up before either of them could.

"The only way to hurt the Jokapcul that badly is to kill all of them. Or at least kill all of their officers. We did neither. But I think we *did* hurt them badly enough that they are now afraid of us."

"So how do we rescue the rest of our people from them?" a woman asked.

No one had a ready answer.

It was past noon when Spinner and Haft woke. Doli was kneeling by Spinner's side, where she'd spent the hours of his sleep. He groaned and rolled away from her, insisting his sleep had been too poor for him to want to see anybody yet, but she fussed over him and insisted on feeding him. He allowed her to fetch a meal for him. When she was gone he turned a pained expression at Haft and groaned out, "Why does she pester me? Can't she tell I don't want her?"

Haft grinned, his sleep had been sound and he was feeling much more refreshed. "She wants you for the same reason Alyline doesn't. You freed her from slavery."

Spinner groggily shook his head. "That makes no sense."

"Sure it does. Doli looks at you and remembers you freed her from slavery. She's grateful. Alyline looks at you and remembers that you freed *her* from slavery. That brings back all the bad memories." He shrugged. "It's obvious."

"Then why do they dislike you?"

"Ah, that's different! Alyline dislikes me for the same reason she dislikes you. Doli dislikes me because before I knew she was a slave, I treated her like a common tavern wench." He turned his gaze to the wall of the valley beyond which lay the ruins of Eikby. "Not all women who work in taverns and inns are as friendly as Maid Marigold and Maid Primrose," he added wistfully.

Spinner snorted. "You didn't treat Maid Marigold like a common tavern wench, that's why she liked you."

Haft didn't answer right away. He was lost in thought, still looking beyond the valley wall. When he did, he spoke softly. "I wonder if they're still alive."

Doli returned just then and insisted on feeding him with her own hands.

"What about me?" Haft asked when he noticed. "Don't I get breakfast?"

Doli ignored him. Spinner tried to say something, but Doli shoved a spoon into his mouth.

"Well, maybe there's some food around here someplace for one of last night's heroes," Haft said as he stood. "Some people!" he said with a grin and a shake of his head as he walked away. A couple of minutes later someone handed him a bowl of stew and a hunk of bread and he settled under a tree to eat it. When he was through eating he went in search of the Golden Girl.

"Did you have fun last night?" she asked with a sneer when he told her he wanted to talk about the Jokapcul in the remains of Eikby.

He answered more politely than she expected. " 'Fun' isn't a good word here. In combat you're trying to kill people who are trying to kill you. That doesn't qualify as 'fun.' But am I glad we did it? Am I satisfied? We all came back whole. They didn't." He nodded. "Yes, I'm glad and I'm satisfied. But it wasn't fun."

"So you're not looking for an audience to gloat in front of?"

He shook his head. "I'm thinking about the people who didn't get away in time, the ones who are captive."

She cocked her head. "And what are you thinking?"

"A few weeks ago you were talking to a dyer and a tucker in Nightbird's company about making a costume like your dancing clothing. You didn't like the first outfit they came up with. Did they ever get it right?"

Her face went cold. "What does that have to do with the captive people?"

"I'm thinking of a diversion."

"What *kind* of diversion?"

Haft knew he was on dangerous ground. "Whatever else we can say about the Jokapcul, they are men. All men react the same way when they see a beautiful, graceful woman. As long as I can look at you from a safe distance, you're the most beautiful, most graceful woman I've ever seen and I love looking at you." She opened her mouth, probably to make some scalding reply, but he hurried on. "If they can see you in your gold clothing, you can distract them enough for us to attack them and free the captives."

"You're not standing at a safe distance now." Her hand lashed out at his face. He saw it coming but didn't try to deflect or block the slap. She pulled her blow and merely caressed his cheek. "Spinner wouldn't ask me to do that."

"Spinner loves you."

"And you don't."

"I'm not fool enough to love a woman to whom I bring bad memories."

She flinched then gathered herself and looked at him speculatively. "You've changed. You wouldn't have said that when you and Spinner saved us from The Burnt Man Inn."

He shrugged, but not enough to disturb her hand where it still lay against his cheek—her touch surprised him, and it felt strangely good. "I was still just a pea on then. Now people depend on me the way they depend on Spinner. There are a lot of things I say now that I wouldn't have said then."

"But you'll still do insane things that should get you killed."

He grinned crookedly. "If I'm good enough, those things won't kill me—and if they don't kill me, they aren't insane."

She searched his eyes for a long moment, then said, "I will think about your proposal." She lowered her hand and took a step back.

"Thank you." He bowed and turned away.

"Haft." He looked back at her voice. "I'm not saying yes, but even if I do I won't dance. You know that."

He looked at her blankly for a moment, then remembered. "Right. Your musician."

She nodded. "Mudjwohl. A Djerwohl dancer and her sothar player are joined as soon as their training begins. She cannot dance without his music. Did you know that?"

He shook his head.

"I told Spinner."

"Spinner doesn't tell me everything that passes between the two of you."

She shrugged. "I told him my dancing is my life. When you sent Mudjwohl off to Oskul with the others the night you kidnapped me, you ended my dancing."

Haft grimaced. "We didn't kidnap you, we rescued you. I'm sorry we didn't know about Mudjwohl."

"You have an excuse, but Spinner is Apianghian, the same as me. He should have known. *Pfagh!* Lowlanders, they are so *ignorant* of the people of the mountains." She spun around and stalked off.

Half an hour later Haft, his favorite Zobran Border Warders and two Zobran Light Horse, slipped out of the valley on horseback. Most of them were armed with close-combat weapons, only Birdwhistle carried his longbow. Haft carried a short sword in place of his axe—he wanted to evade the Jokapcul, not engage them, so they did not take the demon weapons that Xundoe had offered. If they were heavily armed, the temptation to attack a target of opportunity might be too great. Their route went around the toe of the mountains then headed east through the forest north of Eikby. After an hour they began encountering oddly tame ducks and geese with clipped wings, all honking unhappily as they wandered under the trees.

"The Jokapcul must not be tending the flocks," Haft observed.

"Must be they dislike fowl," Birdwhistle replied dryly. He licked his lips, *he* liked fowl.

Haft chuckled. "Maybe we can collect a few on our way back."

Archer and Hunter licked their lips as well, they also liked fowl.

If Eikby's food birds had wandered here, Haft judged they must be almost directly north of the town. Soon after they encountered the first stray birds he angled toward the south. A short while later they stopped and dismounted. Haft left the two Light Horsemen to hold the horses and led the Border Warders south on foot—if they had to come back in a hurry, he didn't want to have to waste any time removing hobbles or unhitching horses.

They examined their surroundings carefully as they moved south through the forest. The Jokapcul weren't known for their sentries' ability to hide, but they sometimes used watch demons. The three Zobrans were keen-eyed, their ability to spot anything even slightly out of place in the forest honed by years of successful poaching before they accepted the prince's pardon and joined the Border Warders. Haft wasn't certain he could spot a watch-sprite's telltale red eye before the demon spotted him, but he had full confidence in the Border Warders' ability to do so.

They were closer to the northeast corner of Eikby's clearing than they had realized, it only took a few minutes for them to reach the forest edge. Haft put Archer and Hunter in a position from which they could observe the distant activity in the clearing, then he and Birdwhistle backed into the trees and continued in a circle to the east side. He thought that since every contact the Jokapcul had with the company was to the south and west of the town, they'd be less alert to the east.

To the north, west, and south of Eikby, the forest was neatly cut back and the land between it and the town proper devoted to fields, orchards, and fowl herding. Haft knew the forest came closer to the town on the east side, but he was surprised to discover just how close. The forest didn't have a distinct edge and the nearest burnt-out buildings were less than fifty yards away.

The Jokapcul had mounted a six-man guard post on the

east road just inside the trees. It was a poor post; a sheet of
green canvas was strung over a crown bar between trees to
provide rudimentary shelter from rain. The trunk of a felled
tree served as a bench. There was not even a hearth for the
guards to cook on.

Haft lightly tapped his fingertips on the hilt of his short
sword when he saw the guard post. The soldiers didn't look
very alert. If he wanted he thought he and his Border Warders
could overrun them all in seconds.

Haft smiled grimly—this was *exactly* why they were so
lightly armed. An attack on this guard post, even if it was
completely successful, would alert the Jokapcul to watch
their east flank more closely, and that would defeat the pur-
pose of this reconnaissance. They scouted farther and found
no other guards on this side of the clearing.

"If the guard post wasn't there we could probably walk
straight down the road into Eikby," Haft whispered.

Birdwhistle gave him a startled look. "The town's not there
anymore," he whispered back.

"You know what I mean, the ruins." Haft peered intently
into the ashes, charred timbers, and broken foundation stones
that were all that remained of the town. Except for a few soldiers guarding prisoners who seemed to be searching through
the ruins for anything usable, he couldn't see any Jokapcul in
the town. The tents of the Jokapcul camp were clustered close
to the southwest corner of the town. A large pavilion with
rolled-up sides was to the southwest of the camp. They were
too far away for positive identification, but Haft thought
he recognized one of the people moving around under the
pavilion roof as Eikby's healing magician—he was surprised
at the idea of the Jokapcul treating their wounded. Then he
thought they might have trouble getting reinforcements quickly
and might need to heal those they had. Closer to where he and
Birdwhistle watched was a large fenced area with unidentifi-
able objects lying flat on the ground. It was difficult to make
out the activity east of the ruins, but they knew from earlier
observations that some kind of construction was going on

there. Far to the west they saw mounted Jokapcul patrols entering and leaving the forest.

"Probably looking for us in all the wrong places," Haft observed.

Here and there the soldiers were drilling under the close supervision of their officers and sergeants.

The two watched for an hour, then moved and watched from the new location for a second hour. During that time the guard post was relieved. The new group of soldiers joked among themselves and with those they replaced, the ones being relieved sounded like they were complaining that their relief was late. Haft and Birdwhistle were about to leave when they saw new activity at the fenced area so they waited to see what it was.

Women and children were herded into the enclosure. Most of them went directly to the unidentified things on the ground, identifying them as bedding.

"The fiends make them sleep in the open!" Haft growled. His hands twisted as though they held his axe.

They weren't close enough to hear, but they saw an officer lead a squad through the gate into the enclosure. The officer held something in his hand, it appeared to be a sheet of paper that he read from. A couple of the women reluctantly stood. The soldiers grabbed them and shoved them outside the entrance into the waiting arms of other soldiers. They then moved among the rest of the women and grabbed a few, forcing them out. Faint wails and cries came to Haft. The soldiers secured the gate and hustled the women they'd taken to the cluster of tents.

"What are they doing with them?" Haft growled. The question was rhetorical, he knew full well what the Jokapcul were doing with the women. "That's more they have to answer for. Let's go."

Archer and Hunter were ready to go when they reached them; they reported they had seen men and older boys herded into the enclosure north of the town's ruins. The Light Horsemen had made good use of the time they'd spent holding the horses—nine geese and a dozen ducks, all dressed, were hanging over the withers of the horses in front of the saddles. The sun had set by the time they got back to the valley.

CHAPTER
TWENTY-TWO

A dozen or so additional people had made their way to the valley—or been found and led in—while Haft and the Zobrans were on their reconnaissance. There had been joyful reunions between husbands and wives, worried parents and terrified children who'd thought they lost loved ones forever. Most people were glad at the return of the patrol, and not merely because the men had made it back unharmed—the twenty-one fowl were enough to make stock for stew, though few actually got any meat in their evening's meal.

As soon as they turned the bird carcasses over to the cooks, Haft and the Zobrans met with Spinner, Fletcher, and Silent. Doli sat so close behind Spinner that her shoulder leaned into him. She refused to budge even when he told her to leave because it was a confidential meeting.

"Where's Alyline?" Haft asked. The Golden Girl was nowhere to be seen. Haft suspected she thought his plan was good, but decided against helping and was unwilling to tell him about it. *Curious, it's uncharacteristic for her to be afraid to face someone—especially me.*

Conditions in the valley were very primitive. They didn't even have paper or parchment to draw a map on; Haft had to draw lines on the ground with his knife and use sticks and stones as landmarks. They sat on logs and studied Haft's map by torchlight. The Zobrans added details that he missed, and Birdwhistle corrected a distance.

"My longbow has greater range than your crossbow," the former poacher said. "I have greater need to judge distance accurately."

Haft glowered at him, but his glower wasn't serious.

Four sticks were the pen where the women were kept overnight south of the burnt-out town; four more showed the similar fenced cage for the men in its north. A fist-size pebble served for the odd new construction in the center of the clearing. Small pebbles represented a group of wagons, probably theirs, that were parked between that construction and the ashes of Eikby. A twig marked where horses were kept on tether lines between the construction and the tents on the east side, and another marked the tether lines below the cluster of tents to Eikby's southeast. Hashmarks in the dirt showed the low tents that didn't look like they could hold more than two or three men. In the center of each cluster of tent rows was a circle of tents high enough for a man to stand in, and inside that circle was an even bigger tent. None of the men on the reconnaissance had seen anything that might be a kitchen; they figured meals were cooked over the fires scattered throughout the tent areas.

Except for the east road, they hadn't seen where sentries were placed.

"We don't have to worry about night sentries," Spinner said. "What we need to concern ourselves with is the time the Jokapcul take the prisoners out of the pens, and when they start sending out their patrols. This raid has to begin while all the Jokapcul are in camp and the prisoners are still locked up.

"Damn!" He realized they didn't have Haft's diversion. "It can't begin then. Without a diversion, we have to wait until the patrols are out. By then, the prisoners will be scattered and harder to rescue. And then, we may not be able to rescue all the people."

"Why won't there be a diversion?" Alyline's voice cut in.

They all spun to the sound of her voice. Even Doli's breath caught—at the edge of the glow cast by their torches, the Golden Girl stood in all her splendor.

From the top of her head to the soles of her feet, she was gold. Her hair was the color of flowing honey. Her eyes sparked amber. Her skin was burnished sunshine. The short vest that left her shoulders and arms bare and didn't fully close between her breasts looked like cloth of gold, as did the narrow sash that girdled low on her hips. Her pantaloons were likewise gold and flowed so gently they appeared made of sheerest fabric, though they were opaque and blocked view of her legs. The diadem that circled her head was of sparkling gold chains interwoven with gold coins. Gold bands circled her upper arms, gold bangles dangled on her wrists, gold rings adorned her fingers, gold hoops were suspended from the lobes of her ears. Gold coins hung from the hem of her vest and spanned the girdle of her pantaloons. The golden hilt of her dagger protruded from the golden sheath that angled across her belly on its own golden belt.

Alyline stood with one hip cocked. She slowly, sinuously raised one hand above her head and brought its lesser fingers together. The tiny cymbals on those fingers came together in a tinkling clash.

Alyline smiled wryly and asked in a husky voice, "You wanted a distraction for the Jokapcul? By your reaction, I'd say they will be distracted."

Silent was the first to recover. "By the gods, I would willingly die to see you dance."

"You can die, but you cannot see me dance." She looked at Spinner and Haft.

Spinner turned away. Haft just shrugged.

She stepped into the circle. "Move over," she said, bumping Haft's shoulder with her hip. He scooted over. She studied the makeshift map intently and quickly grasped its major elements. "Different pens for men and women?" she asked. When Haft confirmed that, she asked, "The women's pen is the one closer to the soldiers' tents, almost between them?" When Haft said it was, she said, "Where do you want me to do it?"

"Come in here shortly after dawn." Spinner pointed to where the west road entered the cleared land. "You'll be facing the sun, so you should be visible at quite a distance. Walk toward the camp until you're sure they see you. Then turn around and return to the forest—but walk slowly enough that some of them can follow you on foot. The Bloody Axes will escort you to the road, they'll wait out of sight for you to re-join them, then they'll bring you back here."

She nodded. "What will you be doing?"

"We'll take out this guard post just before dawn." He pointed at the guard post on the east road. "As soon as the soldiers are distracted, four of us with the Lalla Mkouma will go to the pens and free the captives. We'll bring them back along the east road, and then circle north of Eikby back to here."

"What about women who are in the soldiers' tents when you free the others?"

Spinner looked at her; he hadn't thought of any of the women who would be kept in the soldiers' tents overnight.

"If you don't free them as well, it will be harder on them than it already is."

"There will be thirty of us," Haft said. "We'll have the demon spitters, and Xundoe has more phoenix eggs. Don't worry, we'll get them."

"Thirty of you," she repeated. Haft nodded. "And how many of them are there?"

Haft looked thoughtful for a moment, then answered, "Three hundred. Maybe a few more."

"Thirty against more than three hundred. You are fools." For a long moment she looked into a place only she could see, then her eyes searched his face for a moment, then she put her hand on his knee and softly said, "And so am I. Thank you."

Spinner looked at her hand on Haft's knee and tasted ashes in his mouth. Since that first night when he learned she was a slave and resolved to free her, she hadn't touched him with anything but anger and had refused to allow him to touch her.

Haft warily looked at the hand on his knee; Alyline had never been anything other than hostile to him. What mayhem did she have in mind now?

Sensing what was going on, Fletcher tried to bring everyone's attention back to the planning. "The men with the Lalla Mkouma should just send the prisoners to the forest instead of leading them. As soon as they get the prisoners moving, they should go to the tents and search for women who might be in them."

Then they met with the soldiers who were going on the raid and gave them their orders. Xundoe dispensed demon spitters to those who would carry them. Haft's demon looked unhappy about having to work with someone else, but grumbled, *"Arr'righ,"* when Haft asked him to help the soldier. Then they tried to sleep, they had to be on the move hours before dawn. Sleep came hard for most of them.

Dawn touched the treetops, waking the highest perched birds soon after Spinner, Haft, and four longbowmen reached their position near the east road guard post. Silent and five swordsmen were on line behind them. Just enough light filtered down for them to make out the shadowy lumps that were the sentries. Two of them were sitting on the log, one faced the road into the forest, the other watched toward their camp, probably on lookout for their sergeant. The other four were on the ground, sleeping.

Each of the six charged with taking out the guard post knew where he was in the line. Each counted Jokapcul from left to right and found his target—on the right, Spinner had the rightmost Jokapcul as his target, Haft second from the left had the second leftmost as his. Too close to the guard post to talk, Spinner reached to his left and tapped the man there. He in turn tapped the man on his left, who in turn tapped the next. When the tap reached the last man, he tapped back, raised his bow, nocked an arrow, and took aim at his target. When the tap got back to Spinner, he aimed his crossbow at the rightmost Jokapcul and said in a low voice, "Now!"

Two bolts and four arrows sprang to their targets then Silent and the swordsmen rushed between the bowmen to make sure the guards were dead.

As soon as the guards were confirmed dead, Spinner and Haft quickly positioned their men and assigned each an area to watch and verified they knew all of the signals they might use that morning. Xundoe gave the Lalla Mkouma to Haft, Silent, Birdwhistle, and Hunter. Then they waited. By then, the dawn sun was shining on the tents and a drum was beating to wake the Jokapcul soldiers.

*   *   *

Alyline stood behind a tree where the west road emptied into the cleared land. A few paces away four Bloody Axes and the two remaining Blood Swords stood next to their horses, one of them held hers as well as his own. She waited for the sun's first rays to reach the road near her feet. She listened to the waking birds in the treetops sing their morning welcome to the rising sun, watched the surface of the road turn from blue-black, to dark bluish gray, to gray, to the brown of its dirt. The sound of a distant drum drifted to her. When the sun was strong enough, she took a deep breath and stepped onto the road.

She walked erect and brisk as far as the ruined gate in the broken fence, then slowed to a sinuous walk. She ignored the stench rising from the carcasses of the horses killed in the battle the night before last, didn't look to her sides to see the dark stains on the ground where Jokapcul blood had flowed. Instead, she kept her eyes on the camp, watching for the first Jokapcul to spot her. It wasn't long before a newly risen soldier, walking from his tent to the latrine, noticed the golden glint and turned to it. His abrupt change of posture told her he had seen her. Others saw him looking, looked where he did, and froze as though mesmerized. In moments nearly every soldier in the camp was staring at her. They began to crowd forward for a better view.

The Golden Girl stopped and stood in the middle of the road, swaying her hips from side to side. She sinuously raised one hand skyward and turned her torso to the side and back again. Her arm lowered and the other snaked above her head. But in her swaying she did not move her feet, she did not dance.

One Jokapcul took a few steps forward. Others followed suit. In moments a mass of soldiers was walking rapidly west, toward this apparition. The Golden Girl turned languorously about and resumed her sinuous walk but back toward the fence. The Jokapcul followed. She didn't walk so slowly they could easily catch up with her, nor did she walk fast enough to entice them to run. She looked behind and saw the more adventurous ones were gaining—but was relieved that most of the soldiers stood where they were and just watched.

The fence looked miles away, the forest beyond it seemed lost beyond the horizon. Yet she resisted the temptation to run. Perspiration beaded on her forehead. Behind her, raised voices called to her. She couldn't make out the words but she knew what they were saying: *Stop, beautiful one! I will show you what a real man can do, my beauty! Be mine, my heart, and we will both live in paradise!* Those and other things that she had heard countless times from the men who paid the dear price for a night with her at The Burnt Man Inn. Nights she had given unwillingly, for the slavemaster who pocketed the price would have punished her most severely had she not given what he was paid for. She wanted to scream in terror and fly blindly from the men following her; when Spinner and Haft freed her she resolved no man would ever again touch her without her leave and desire. Now many men were following and—she looked back coquettishly—closing rapidly. If they caught her they would touch her as they willed, with no consideration of whether or not she gave them leave. They would touch her—and more—as many as could at once, and the others would jostle for their turns.

She could hear the footsteps of the men behind her. Sweat began to flow down her back and between her breasts. The fence and the forest seemed farther away than before.

She maintained her pace.

Distant hoofbeats came to her ears. She tossed her hair and looked back again. The nearest Jokapcul were close enough that the closest among them could see her smile, so she smiled at them. Farther away, just leaving the camp, she saw horsemen galloping her way. She faced front again, her breath so fast and shallow she was growing faint. She forced herself to breathe slowly and deeply. Horse carcasses and bloodstained dirt to her sides—the fence must be closer than it looked. She focused her vision on the missing gate and took a very deep breath. Men cheered when her shoulders lifted and her back arched.

Then she was through the gate and the forest no longer

seemed impossibly distant. Behind her, the footsteps speeded up. Angry cries sounded as the hoofbeats caught up with the walking men and the riders attempted to force their way through.

She looked back and smiled again, and the smile wasn't forced. She smiled because the Jokapcul were struggling among themselves, trying to be the first through the gate. Others, farther from the gate, were scrambling over the fence, falling in their haste; many gushed blood when they tore their flesh on the barbs, and some screamed in agony when the imps rushed out of their houses to feast on them.

Then she was past the first tree. The tree she'd stood behind waiting for dawn was only paces away. Hoofbeats sounded behind her, hoofbeats echoed within the trees. Men shouted in anger. She heard the clash of weapons as she reached her tree and stepped around it.

Dawn flooded across the cleared land and illuminated the charred remains of Eikby, the pens where the prisoners were kept, the tents of the Jokapcul. Too much was in the way, they couldn't see beyond to the far fence where the Golden Girl was beginning her walk toward the camp. The thirty crouching men waited tensely. Spinner walked behind the line, steadying the men, making sure no one would shoot prematurely and give them away. The increasing daylight revealed tall poles towering above the highest tents in the center of the masses of tents. Heads rested on the tops of the poles. The insistent drum roused sleeping soldiers from their tents, they began walking toward the latrines, then stopped in waves from a center the watching men couldn't see. In moments, nearly all of the Jokapcul were stopped, staring to the west. Some began edging forward, slowly began walking, picked up their pace.

"Now," Spinner said in a voice just loud enough to carry to the group.

Haft and Silent rose to their feet, a Zobran next to each. The four spoke to the Lalla Mkouma perched on their shoulders and vanished from view.

Silent and Hunter went north of Eikby's ruins, to the men's pen.

Haft and Birdwhistle headed south to the women's. Two guards stood outside the enclosure's gate, looking west. They exchanged words, and one left his post to see what the other soldiers found so fascinating. He turned back, shouted something, and ran to join the soldiers looking west.

Haft sprinted forward and swung his axe in a vicious overhand arc. The Jokapcul collapsed heavily, sliding off the axe blade. A few women who happened to be looking in the direction gasped and stepped back. Haft swung his axe at the lock on the gate, and shattered it. The broken gate slammed open. More women and children looked up at the sound, women trembled at the sight of the guard lying before the open gate; children tried to hide in their mothers' skirts.

When a disembodied voice near the fence said in Zobran, "Come quickly! Run to the forest," a woman screamed.

Haft swore at himself when he heard the scream and rubbed the leg of his Lalla Mkouma. "Rub her leg," he said to the Zobran. "Let them see you."

Birdwhistle made a startled noise; he'd forgotten. He popped into view, startling several women and children, who stared at the tiny women perched on the shoulders of Haft and Birdwhistle.

Haft saw a woman from the company and ran to her. She recognized him and, crying out in a relief, flung herself into his arms. Other women from the company also recognized him and Birdwhistle. They began shouting in their excitement. Haft signaled for everyone to be quiet. They calmed down and he said, "Spinner and some soldiers are in the trees. Gather everyone and run to them. Is anyone in the soldiers' tents?"

One woman said, "Yes." She rattled off the names of women she didn't see, then finished with, "I think there may be more in the tents." Others chimed in with names of missing women.

"All of you, run for the trees. You'll find Spinner and safety there. Don't worry, we'll get the others out of the tents." He turned away and ran back to Birdwhistle then they vanished as the women streamed toward the trees. One of the men in the forest stood up and advanced into the clear so the women could see him. His wife and child saw and sprinted toward him. The others, encouraged, ran after them.

When Spinner and Birdwhistle reached the tents east of the women's pen, Jokapcul officers and sergeants were shouting and shoving among the soldiers who were watching their companions trail after the Golden Girl. Two officers and a sergeant were chivvying three squads to the horses and making them saddle mounts. The invisible men ran quickly along the lines of tents, each checking a different line, looking in one tent after another. Most were unoccupied, but when they found a woman they made themselves visible and sent her on her way to safety. By the time Haft reached the last tent, the three mounted squads were on their way to catch the soldiers following the Golden Girl. He found a woman huddled in a corner and made himself visible.

"Come, I'm here to rescue you," he said in his best Zobran.

The woman whimpered and moved away from him.

"Really, come with me. You're safe now."

She covered her head with her arms and whimpered again.

Haft crawled into the tent and took her by the arm. "Come with me."

"No, please, not again." Her voice was thick with weariness and fear.

He pulled firmly but gently and drew her toward the tent's entrance. When she was in the light the first thing he saw was she was naked, he grimaced at the bruises that covered her body and swelled her face. The second thing he saw was who she was.

"Maid Marigold! It's me, Haft. Where is your dress?"

"Ooo! Zheez hurd!" the Lalla Mkouma gasped when she saw Maid Marigold's condition.

"Please, no. I hurt!" Maid Marigold tried to pull away.

"Maid Marigold, look at me." He took her face in his hand and turned it to his. "Open your eyes, look at me. It's Haft."

She whimpered again, but squinted between her bruised,

swollen eyelids. Her gaze wavered for a moment before her eyes focused on him.

"Haft?" she gasped. "Is it really you?"

"It's me, truly. I'm here to rescue you."

She flung her arms around his neck, almost dislodging the Lalla Mkouma, and held on like a drowning woman to a floating board.

"Ey! Naw poozhin'!"

Maid Marigold noticed the miniature woman on Haft's shoulder and jerked back. "What's that?" her voice shook.

"It's all right, that's a Lalla Mkouma. She's good."

The Lalla Mkouma preened.

Maid Marigold gave the Lalla Mkouma a suspicious look, but decided if Haft said it was all right it must be. She collapsed into his arms. "Oh, Haft," she burbled into his shoulder, "I couldn't allow myself to believe you'd come for me. But you did, you really did!"

"Where's your dress? We have to cover you before we go out." He heard shouts of surprise and anger, and men running to obey barked commands—the Jokapcul must have discovered their prisoners were gone. "Please, now. Rush!"

"Over, over . . ." She waved vaguely toward the corner where she'd huddled.

"Gittum!" The Lalla Mkouma hopped off his shoulder, scampered to the corner of the tent, and quickly returned with a dress. The woman flinched at the little demon's contact with her bruises. *"Liffum ahmz,"* she said as she pulled the dress over Maid Marigold's head.

Haft had to take hold of the woman's arms and pry them from around his neck. Between them, he and the Lalla Mkouma pulled the badly ripped dress over her head and shoulders.

Outside, shouting and barked commands grew louder. Hoofbeats thundered. *Hoofbeats?* Haft didn't have time to wonder about that.

"Can you make us both invisible?" he asked the Lalla Mkouma.

"Naw zwetz. Old'er kloze."

Haft backed out of the tent and wrapped his arms around Maid Marigold. The Lalla Mkouma hopped from the woman's shoulders to his and began spinning. He lifted Maid Marigold in his arms. Her feet and ankles showed outside the demon's circle of invisibility, but there was no remedy for that. He sprinted to the forest and didn't look back.

CHAPTER
TWENTY-THREE

The Golden Girl heard hoofbeats behind her and echoing in the trees, men were shouting in surprise and anger—and the unexpected clash of weapons. She stepped around the tree she'd hidden behind waiting for dawn and froze at the tableau before her. The four Bloody Axes and two Blood Swords stood facing eight horsemen armed with swords—bandits! They'd forgotten about the bandits!

Startled by the sudden appearance of the Golden Girl, the bandits gaped at her for an instant, all the time the Skraglanders needed to break the stalemate. They dropped the reins of their horses and charged, bellowing war cries. Their axes and swords swung up and chopped down and six bandits fell immediately. The other two lasted only a few seconds longer.

"Come, lady," Sergeant Phard said in badly broken Zobran when the last of the bandits was down, "we must go." He led her to her horse and put her on it while the others mounted and kept watch around them. There were still hoofbeats and clashing weapons in the trees, but most of the fury sounded like it was in the open ground between the forest and the fence.

As Phard was leaping onto his horse, a dozen horsemen crashed through the trees at them.

"Traitors!" shouted one of the bandits when he spotted the Blood Swords. "Kill them all!" He led a charge at them.

"You!" one of the Blood Swords yelled back. "You are the traitor!" He heeled his mount forward.

The other five Skraglanders were already in motion, smashing into the bandits and breaking their charge. Three of the bandits crashed to the ground in the first contact and didn't rise again. One Bloody Axe went down when two bandits swung their swords at him and he was only able to deflect one blow before the other blade struck home.

The Bloody Axe swung his sword right and left, sent bandits reeling away as he closed on their leader. The other bandits paired off, two of them on each of the other Skraglanders.

"You!" the Blood Sword roared.

"I will kill you!" the bandit leader roared back. The two collided and sword crashed against sword.

The Golden Girl calculated the odds and didn't like the result. A few yards away, two bandits and the other Blood Sword circled each other in melee, the bandits gaining the upper hand. She shook off her fear and heeled her horse into the fray. Her stallion shouldered one bandit horse hard in its hindquarters; struggling to keep his balance and regain control of his mount, the bandit didn't even see her when she opened his throat with a backhanded slash. He dropped his sword and the reins, clutched at his throat in a vain attempt to slow the gushing blood. His horse, abruptly freed, leaped at the other bandit's horse and both stumbled. The Blood Sword finished his remaining foe.

"Thank you, lady," he shouted as he looked for someone else to fight.

"You disobeyed!" the bandit leader shouted. "You deserter!" He swung his sword and the Blood Sword effortlessly blocked it.

"You joined the bandits!" He swung at the bandit leader's side, the bandit leaned out of reach and his horse screamed as the sword's point nicked its neck.

The Blood Sword released by the Golden Girl's help raced to the aid of a Bloody Axe and slammed his blade into the back of a bandit about to strike a killing blow. A second later that Bloody Axe's remaining foe was down and the two went to the aide of the others.

"Die!" the bandit leader shrieked as he thrust his sword at his opponent's belly.

Deflecting that strike with a thrust of his own, he shouted,

"Die yourself, Captain!" and the Blood Sword stabbed deeply into the bandit leader's chest. He fell backward off his horse, thudded to the ground, and lay still, his eyes staring blankly at the sky.

The Blood Sword spun around in time to see the last of the dozen bandits fall. After the initial clash, no more Bloody Axes had fallen, though several were bleeding.

"It's Captain Dumant!" the other Blood Sword exclaimed when he looked at the fallen bandit leader.

"It was," the soldier who killed him said.

"Put him on his horse," Sergeant Phard pointed at his lone dead man, "and let's get the lady back to safety."

As they sped off, they heard the thunder of demon spitters behind them.

"What happened? What are the Jokapcul doing?" Spinner asked anxiously when Haft appeared in front of him. He didn't even glance at the woman in Haft's arms. "I think I heard demon spitters."

"I don't know, I was busy rescuing Maid Marigold and didn't take time to look. Are you sure you heard demon spitters?"

Spinner strained to look beyond the ruins and tents to the far side of the open land. "Maybe not," he said, but he was afraid the Jokapcul had caught Alyline, her Skraglander guards had gone to her rescue, and all were lost. Then Haft's first words got through to him and he looked at the woman who now stood clinging to Haft. He barely recognized her bruised face.

"Maid Marigold?"

She nodded, the movement exposing a breast. She took one hand from Haft just long enough to tuck the flap back into place.

Spinner, remembering that night in the inn, looked quickly around and saw Maid Primrose struggling through the crowd of prisoners to come to his side. He turned red.

"We should go," Silent said from next to him. "Before the Jokaps come back and find everyone gone."

"Go. Yes, we need to go. Silent, get the people moving. Haft, send scouts out to the front, I'll set a rear guard." His face's bright color lessened when he saw the steppe giant intercept Maid Primrose and herd her back to the other freed people.

"Right," Haft said dryly. He'd also seen Maid Primrose and noticed Spinner's blush. He headed toward the former prisoners, straight to Maid Primrose. He had to peel Maid Marigold off himself and push her to her friend.

"Stay with Maid Primrose," he said. "I have to go ahead and make sure our trail is safe."

"Don't leave me!" Maid Marigold wailed, reaching for him.

"You're safe now, don't worry. Take care of her," he said to Maid Primrose, who gathered Maid Marigold into her arms and tried to sooth away her tears while looking longingly at Spinner.

Haft took Birdwhistle and Hunter ahead to scout the trail. The three of them were invisible before they got out of sight in the trees.

Farther back, Xundoe speculatively eyed the Jokapcul tents. "You and you," he said to the two nearest soldiers, Muves and another Skragland Guard, "come with me." He sprinted into the open.

"Xundoe, come back!" Spinner shouted. The mage ignored him.

Xundoe was panting heavily by the time they reached the tents. He inadvertently looked at the poles that towered above the largest tents, jerked his gaze away from the heads mounted on them. With a shake, he brought himself back to what he was doing to look around and plan his next steps. Thirty yards to his right front, just beyond the more northern group of tents, a tight knot of Jokapcul officers watched the battle between their troops and the unexpected bandits. His eyes widened when he saw the mayor's chain of office hanging around the neck of one of them. He forced himself to look up at the heads again, was the mayor's among them? Yes, the head of the mayor of Eikby stared blindly toward the women's enclosure.

Xundoe looked around. He didn't see any Jokapcul other than the officers in the camp; they had all gone to join in the battle to the west, even the magicians were gone. Two fires burned among the tents to his right; two more fires burned in the formation of tents to his left. He shrugged off his pack and reached into it for a phoenix egg while he told the two Skraglanders what he wanted them to do. They nodded and soft-footed into the clusters of tents, Muves to the right, the other man to the left. Xundoe waited until they reached the nearest fires, then padded quickly forward. When he closed the distance to twenty yards he stopped and, even though there were no tree branches to deflect his throw, he remembered to plant his feet before he twisted the top of the Phoenix egg. He threw it at the feet of the Jokapcul officers and turned and ran before it hit.

The egg landed between two of the officers and cracked open. The phoenix rose up and unfolded its wings, turning all the officers into brief torches before the phoenix began to flap its newly opened wings. Its wings set flame to several nearby tents before it lifted its body from the ground and spiraled into the sky.

As soon as Xundoe threw the phoenix egg, the two Skraglanders each grabbed a brand from a fire and ran along a row of tents, setting them ablaze. While they were doing that, Xundoe ran into the nearer of the two largest tents and immediately found treasure. Not anything so mundane as gold and jewels, but a magic chest! He flipped it open, saw it was full, and hefted it—it was almost too heavy for him to lift. Awkwardly, he lugged it out. One of the soldiers ran up to him.

"Fire this tent, then take this chest to one of the wagons," he ordered.

The soldier gave the chest a suspicious look, but did as he was told.

Muves arrived just in time for Xundoe to take him along to the other large tent. It also held a magic chest, though it wasn't as full as the first one. He sent Muves to the wagon with the chest while he ran to get horses. The route to the horse lines took him close to the hospital pavilion. A shout turned his head toward it and he saw Eikby's healing magician looking at him.

"Come with me!" he shouted. The healing magician glanced around quickly at the wounded Jokapcul he'd been tending, but needed no further encouragement. He gathered his healing demons and ran behind Xundoe.

On their way back to the wagon, Xundoe looked west. If any of the Jokapcul fighting over there to the west had noticed their camp was ablaze, they were too busy fighting to react to it.

The four men quickly hitched the horses to the wagon and climbed aboard. Only then did Xundoe remember there was no way to get the wagon to the narrow valley they were using as a base. He decided that it was important just to get the magic chests away from the Jokapcul. They'd do what they'd have to do to transport them after abandoning the wagon. He lashed the reins and sent the reluctant horses between the burning tents to gallop along the ash-covered road through Eikby's ruins. They sped straight along the east road.

"Where are we going?" the healing magician asked, holding tightly to the side of the bouncing wagon.

"Away from here," Xundoe shouted back. "I don't know."

"Watch for a track to the left, I'll show you a place to hide the wagon until you know where to go."

A half mile farther the little-used track led to the left as the healing magician had said. Xundoe slowed down to follow it. The track ended at an unoccupied cabin set in a small clearing at the foot of the mountains.

They unharnessed and hobbled the horses and hid the wagon behind the cabin. Xundoe quickly redistributed the contents of the spell chests. He stuffed as much as he could into his pack and gave some to the healing magician to carry. Then he he closed the chests and called to the soldiers, who lugged them as he led the little group westward along the foot of the mountains.

Alyline and her Skraglander escort got back to the valley first.

"What happened!" Doli demanded when she saw the blood on the Skraglanders.

"Nightbird!" Fletcher called out as soon as he saw them. "We have injuries!" He looked closely at Alyline and the men and realized that not all the blood on them could be their own. He signaled Sergeant Phard forward and turned to Alyline. "Tell me what happened," he said when the Bloody Axe leader joined them.

Alyline stood slightly stooped, with her arms wrapped around her. "It worked," she said with a slight tremor in her voice.

Fletcher looked about and saw Zweepee on her way, carrying a cloak. He signaled her to come faster. She broke into a trot.

"Many of the Jokapcul f-followed me. The rest stood and wa-watched." She nodded thanks when Zweepee arrived and wrapped the cloak around her.

"Come, dear, come over here and sit." Zweepee took Alyline by the shoulders, guided her to a fallen tree, and sat her in front of a fire.

"W-When I got back to my escorts there were b-bandits."

Phard picked up the story and told about the eight bandits who had surprised them. "And before we could get out of there, more came, led by Captain Dumant. Remember him, the Blood Sword officer who wanted to assume command after we rescued his squad from the bandit attack?" He spat into the fire. "He must have come upon the bandits when they were still confused by our raid, then organized them for this attack." He grinned. "He wasn't expecting to find the Jokapcul in Eikby, I wager." He briefly outlined that fight. There wasn't much to tell about the hasty trip back to the valley.

"What of Spinner and Haft?" Fletcher asked.

"We couldn't see that far, but they must have been successful. I think all the Jokapcul still in the camp came out when the bandits attacked."

When they were north and west of Eikby, Haft told the Zobrans to continue. He dropped out of the van and went to the edge of the forest to see what he could. When he rubbed her thigh, the Lalla Mkouma turned off her magic. He didn't know that Xundoe had gone back into the Jokapcul camp and hadn't seen the fire start among the tents, so he wondered what happened that most of them were burned. To the east of the cleared land he saw some fighting still going on, but the fighting seemed to be the end of a battle rather than the beginning or middle. He couldn't see who the Jokapcul were fighting, only that there were more than the six Bloody Axes and Blood Swords who formed the Golden Girl's escort. He waited while the column of people passed by. Spinner was still with the rear guard.

"Have you seen Xundoe?" Spinner asked.

"No. The last time I saw him he was with you."

Spinner shook his head. "He took two Skraglander Guards and ran back into Eikby. He refused to come back when I called him."

"That explains it," Haft said.

"Explains what?"

Haft pointed at the burned tents.

Spinner looked at the tents and nodded. "I thought I heard a phoenix egg crack open."

"Xundoe's getting brave."

Spinner nodded again. "He must be trailing us. We should wait for him to catch up."

"No. He knows where the valley is, he can make it back on his own. And if he's got two Skraglanders with him, they'll be all right."

Spinner looked west, to where the battle was almost over. "You're right. We shouldn't split up any more than we already are. Do you have any idea who the Jokapcul were fighting over there?"

Haft shook his head. "Not unless the bandits got themselves organized a lot faster than we expected them to. Whoever it was, it looks like they took quite a toll before the Jokapcul finished them off."

That looked to be true, there were nowhere near the number of Jokapcul visible as there had been when the drumbeat roused them from their tents.

"Unless more of them are in the forest, chasing down survivors."

"Unless."

"Let's go."

"Good idea."

The trip back to the valley took longer than the night movement had, and Silent dropped out along the way to keep an eye on the Jokapcul.

The rescued people of Eikby were staggering with exhaustion by the time they reached the valley, but regained their energy when they saw who was there to greet them. The camp rang with cries of joy as families and lovers were reunited. There was an undercurrent of sobs when other husbands, wives, children, and parents weren't among the freed people. Few of those who came to Eikby with Spinner and Haft rejoiced; most members of the company were in the camp when the Jokapcul attacked and those still missing were killed there or during the flight after the first battle.

Maids Marigold and Primrose had no families to look for when they reached the valley camp. Maid Marigold was the only one of her people spared by the Jokapcul, because she was young and pretty, and they had uses for all the young, pretty women. Maid Primrose had no family. She had been traveling with them two years earlier when bandits attacked their caravan just miles outside Eikby. Only three of the nearly fifty people in the caravan managed to reach the town, and neither of the other two were from her family.

So when Maids Marigold and Primrose reached the valley they immediately began looking for Spinner and Haft. As did Alyline and Doli.

The Marines arrived with the rear guard. The people they'd just freed began crowding around them, enthusiastically giving thanks for their rescue. Spinner and Haft didn't stop to accept the crowd's adulation. They thanked the people for their appreciation and tried to press on. They needed to find Alyline and Sergeant Phard and find out what happened with the diversion.

Maids Marigold and Primrose reached their heroes just before Alyline and Doli did and threw themselves on their saviors.

Haft was looking quite pleased with himself when Alyline stepped in front of him. "Just the person we're looking for!" he exclaimed. "As you can see," he waved his right arm at the crowd, "our part of it went well, and yours must have also. What happened?"

Alyline looked at him expressionlessly. She shifted her gaze to Maid Marigold, took in the bruises on her face and arms, and the torn bodice that was again threatening to expose her breast, and back to Haft's grinning face. If he hadn't been so pleased with himself, he would have recognized Alyline's expressionlessness as a clear sign of danger and begun planning his escape. But he was, so he didn't.

"I've seen you. You're one of the leaders. I'm Maid Marigold." She let go of Haft's arm and held out her left hand to Alyline. She read Alyline's lack of expression better than Haft did.

Alyline ignored the hand. "You better pin that up, you're about to expose yourself."

"Oh!" Maid Marigold drew her hand back and tried to tuck the drooping flap in more securely.

"I won't ask if you did that, Haft," Alyline said coldly. "I don't think you did." She slowly shook her head. She spun on her heel and walked stiffly away.

Confused, Haft stared at her receding back.

Maid Marigold watched her curiously. "You're one of the leaders," she said nervously. "She's one of the leaders." She looked at him plaintively. "Are you lovers?"

"Lovers?" The word was almost a croak. "Her? Me? Lovers? Absolutely not!" He blinked several times and shuddered.

She leaned closer to him.

A few yards away, Doli, racing to throw herself into Spinner's arms, skidded to a stop and gasped, staring wide-eyed and openmouthed at that, that—that *woman* with her arms wrapped around Spinner's neck, smothering him with the kisses he never allowed *her* to smother him with! Even worse, he seemed to be enjoying it as his body was twisting against hers and his hands gripping her arms!

Slowly, fists clenched tightly at her sides, she drew herself to rigid erectness. With great effort, she got her breath under control glaring at them grimly for a moment longer before emitting a banshee scream and springing forward to wrench that, that—*tavern* wench off the man who was rightly hers!

Maid Primrose cried out when a hand roughly grabbed her shoulder, yanked her from Spinner, and almost threw her to the ground. She staggered then regained her balance. Her eyes darted about in terror, expecting to see Jokapcul charging through the camp. Instead of Jokapcul, she was confronted by a screaming woman.

"You get your hands off him, he's mine!" Doli stalked forward. "I don't know who you think you are," she snarled, "but you stay away from him. He's spoken for."

Surprised and flustered, Spinner took a moment to collect himself. "Doli—" His voice cracked and he tried again. "Doli! What are you doing? We just rescued her from the Jokapcul."

She spun on him. "She's the one you spent that night with in the inn, isn't she?"

"Ah—"

"Don't deny it, I can see it in your eyes."

"But, Doli, you know I—"

"Don't you 'but' me, Spinner. You not only cheated on me, you cheated on that Alyline, too!"

"Spinner," Maid Primrose recovered enough to speak, "is this woman your lover? Were you unfaithful with me?"

"No! No, nothing like that." He held his hands up defensively. "She's not my lover, she's *never* been my lover!"

"That's not from lack of opportunity!" Doli spat.

Maid Primrose grabbed Doli's shoulder. "You're not his lover," she said angrily, "yet you attack me for kissing him after he rescued me?"

Doli covered her face with her hands and bawled. "He doesn't want me," she wailed. "He only wants her!" She took her hands from her face and turned around, pointing. She kept turning, but didn't see Alyline anywhere. "That Golden Girl, she's the only one he wants, and she won't have him!"

Maid Primrose turned on Spinner. "You pine for someone else, and you took *me* when you couldn't have her?" She stormed right up to him. "Am I just some convenient vessel you relieve yourself with when you can't get what you want?"

"But that's not what happened."

The two women turned to each other.

"He betrayed you and this other woman?"

"He used you?"

"The nerve of him!"

"That beast!"

Doli suddenly noticed Maid Primrose's bruises. "Oh, you've been hurt! Come with me, let me take care of that."

The two walked off together, arm in arm like old friends.

All around people were staring at Spinner and Haft.

Xundoe and his party came in with the healing magician a couple of hours later, sweaty and weary from a long trek with heavy burdens. So far as they knew, the Jokapcul had made no attempt to follow them.

It was after sundown when Silent returned.

CHAPTER
TWENTY-FOUR

Just a week earlier Eikby had had a population of more than two thousand people. Including those the raid had freed, barely a thousand people had found refuge in the valley—and more than a hundred of them were from the company. Some of the townspeople were known to have fled east before the Jokapcul arrived and it was certain that some who fled north deliberately bypassed the valley to head for Princedon Gulf on their own. There were likely other terrified people still wandering in the forest west and north of the valley. But all of those combined were only a fraction of the missing thousand. The people just brought in confirmed that most of the missing had been killed. They also told what they had been constructing.

"It was an elaborate pyre," Plotniko, the master carpenter, explained to the leaders of the company. "The Jokapcul commander told me through an interpreter that the pyre was modeled after the principal castle of their king. King wasn't the word he used, it was a title I'd never heard before, but it meant king. It was a great honor, he said, for conquered dead to be cremated in a replica of the king's castle." He shook his head. "They slaughtered us. How could anything after that be thought of as an 'honor'?

"I saw the bodies lying about, those that hadn't been burned in the houses and buildings when the Jokapcul torched the town. Swordsmen and archers stood outside the burning buildings to drive people back inside when they tried to escape the flames. Still, hundreds of people were killed in the open. I don't know how they decided which of us they would kill and which they would keep alive to do the work they required. The way they chose seemed completely random. I was with Master Builder Stupnikow, hiding in a stone storage shed when they found us. They dragged us out and threw us at the feet of an officer. Their leader said something. I looked up and saw him point at Stupnikow. Two of the soldiers plunged their swords into his back. Then the officer spoke again and pointed at me. I was certain they were going to kill me then. But they didn't. Instead, two of them grabbed my arms and yanked me to my feet. They dragged me to a growing knot of people inside a circle of mounted lancers. Many people screamed and cried; we thought they were going to murder us for sport. Instead, they kept us to work the fields, gather bodies—and to build that pyre."

He looked at them with haunted eyes. "Somehow they found out I was the master carpenter. They gave me plans and put me in charge of building the pyre. It didn't take long to realize the pyre I was charged with building was far bigger than was needed for the dead we were gathering. It was big enough for all of the dead—and for all of the living. I only hoped they planned to kill us first and not simply herd us into that place before they lit it.

"I knew there was only the ghost of a hope that someone would come to drive the Jokapcul away and rescue us, but I never gave up on that ghost. So I made sure the work went slowly. Maybe it was too slow; they killed workers every day to frighten the rest of us into working faster.

"Then someone attacked two nights ago and they suffered severe losses. Was that you?" He smiled wanly when Spinner said it had been. "Some of them started killing us, but their officers made them stop. They needed us to build a hospital pavilion and carry their wounded to it. It was the first time since they first attacked that we'd seen them care for their own wounded. No one told us why. But the attack, *your* attack, told me we were going to be rescued. I didn't expect the rescue to come so soon, though, and for that I and all the others who survived thank you."

There was more Plotniko told them, but they already knew what happened to the women.

"I will make them suffer for that," Haft muttered at the telling. He stroked Maid Marigold's hand where it rested on his shoulder, she settled more closely against his back.

As horrible as was the number of dead and the telling of their dying, the living still had to be cared for. There wasn't enough food in the valley to feed the thousand people, nor was it possible to feed them for longer than the shortest time by hunting and foraging in the nearby forest. They couldn't stay in the valley, they had to move and soon. But as short as food was, everything else was in even shorter supply. Their options were limited.

They could stay where they were and fend as best they could until starvation and deprivation overcame most of them—or the Jokapcul found and killed them, whichever came first.

They could strike out to the northwest and hope to find succor at the bandit base. That wasn't a good option either. They had no reason to believe the remaining bandits—if any had survived that battle with the Jokapcul—would welcome them with anything other than violence and death. Besides, the bandit village was too close to what had been Eikby; the Jokapcul would find and destroy it soon enough.

They could go north as one group. But the way would be slow and painful, many would be lost along the way—and the Jokapcul would inevitably find and kill the survivors.

They could break into small groups and head north. Any individual group would stand a better chance of making its way to the gulf intact than would the whole, but any group also stood a good chance of being lost to starvation, bandits, or Jokapcul patrols.

The one option nobody discussed was returning to Eikby. Not at first.

They met again when Silent came back. If the steppe no-mad noticed that Doli wasn't hovering near Spinner, he gave no sign, but he did cock an eyebrow when he saw Maid

Marigold clinging to Haft. He got down to the business of telling them what he found in his observation of the Jokapcul camp after the raid.

"They seem thoroughly disorganized," he said to the others gathered around the fire. "I didn't see any officers and only one sergeant."

"If they don't have any officers left," Spinner said, "it's no wonder they're disorganized. They're trained to do nothing without orders from an officer."

"Right." Silent nodded, that was a well-known oddity of the Jokapcul army. Even sergeants did little more than relay officers' orders. "They haven't even collected the bodies of their dead from the west forest. I counted sixty of them and more than a hundred dead bandits in the forest fringe to the west." He looked at Alyline. "What happened there?"

She told him quickly rather than repeat the detailed debriefing she and Sergeant Phard had already given the others.

"You say most of the Jokapcul who followed you were unarmed?"

"No more than belt knives, most of them. I don't know about the horsemen, but they were probably well armed."

Silent whistled appreciatively. "They certainly are fierce warriors, if they began mostly unarmed and still killed so many."

"The Blood Swords accounted for nearly a score of the bandits," Spinner reminded him.

Silent looked at him for a moment. "Then they still killed better than one to one," he said with the respect of one good fighting man for another.

He resumed his narrative. "I didn't see any movement in the hospital pavilion. Either their wounded are already recovered, or they stopped attending to them now that the healing magician is no longer there. I suspect they weren't taking care of them and I'll tell you why: I saw some of the Jokapcul fighting among themselves. If they're fighting among themselves, I doubt they are caring for their wounded. The dead I counted at the forest fringe? Not all of them were killed in the battle, several of them looked liked they lived for some time

after being wounded. I think many of their injured could have
been saved had anyone bandaged their wounds; instead they
bled to death.

"Not all of the fighting I saw in the camp was with hands
and weapons, many of them contented themselves with yelling at each other. I couldn't get close enough to hear what
they were yelling about, though." He snorted. "Not that I can
understand their gibberish anyway. Some of them were digging through the ashes of the tents, but it didn't look like they
found much that was usable." He nodded to Xundoe. "It's
good that you thought to burn their tents, that increased their
disorientation."

Xundoe smiled broadly; he had never gotten much praise
when he was in the Zobran army.

"They've lost half the force they arrived here with," Spinner said after a moment's thought. "And all their officers and
nearly all of their sergeants."

"That's right," Silent said with a wolflike smile.

"No leadership, disorganized, fighting among themselves,"
Haft mused. He looked up sharply. "We can take them. We
can wipe them out!"

"Not so fast," Xundoe interjected. "What about magicians?
You haven't said anything about magicians. We know they had
at least two with them. Just because I took away two magic
chests doesn't mean they can't still do us serious harm."

Silent shook his head. "I saw nobody who looked like a
magician. And *no one* held anything that looked like a demon
weapon. I don't think they have any, and if they do, they're
probably too disorganized to use them effectively."

"Fletcher, how many men do we have?" Haft asked.

"There are the thirty who went with you on the raid and the
forty who stayed here. We haven't finished sorting out the
people you freed, but there are at least a half dozen more
Eikby Guards and a couple of our own men among them."

"What about the men who aren't soldiers?"

Fletcher scratched his jaw in thought. "We haven't finished
counting them. Probably two or three hundred."

"Do any of them have any training? Can they fight?"

Fletcher shook his head. "I don't think any of them have training, but I'm sure most of the men who lost their families will be willing to fight."

Haft closed in on himself to think about it. Then he shook himself out of it and asked, "Silent, how many Jokapcul do you think are still there?"

"More than two hundred."

With a shake of his head, Spinner interrupted, "It's no good. We have maybe eighty soldiers and veterans. I don't like the odds, they outnumber us by too much, unless we use the untrained men. But that's no good; untrained men going up against Jokapcul will only get killed. We can't attack."

"We've got demon weapons," Haft said eagerly. "They don't. We can reduce the odds right away and hit them while they're confused."

Xundoe jumped in. "I haven't finished cataloging the contents of those two magic chests yet, but already I've found more phoenix eggs. I think Haft is right."

Alyline spoke for the first time. "Remember what only eight of you did against them with demon weapons two nights ago? Only a few of you went into Eikby this morning. . . ."

"Seven of us actually went in," Xundoe said proudly. He really did deserve that promotion he never got, and now it was too late—there was no more Zobran army to give him one.

She nodded at him. "Only seven of you went into Eikby with demon weapons this morning and wreaked great damage—and you killed all of their remaining officers. I say if we hit the Jokapcul fast and hard with demon weapons, then Haft leads a charge into them, we will completely defeat them."

Haft swallowed at the hard way she looked at him when she suggested he lead the charge. She *could* be thinking he was the best man to lead it—or she could be thinking the man who led the charge would get killed. He didn't know what he had done, only that her former dislike for him seemed to have turned to a white-hot anger.

"I think Haft and Alyline are right, Spinner," Fletcher said.

"But—"

"We can do it!" Xundoe said gleefully.

"They're right," Silent said.

Spinner sighed. "If we attack we'll lose more people. And we'll have to leave here immediately after because the Jokapcul will send more troops as soon as they learn about the defeat."

"The Jokapcul are going to send more troops and we have to leave anyway," Alyline said. "But if we defeat this force severely enough, those who come after us will come less eagerly."

Spinner sighed again; he knew they were right. "Dawn tomorrow," he said.

They began making plans.

Shortly after midnight, one hundred men, all but twenty of the soldiers—who remained behind to guard the camp—plus the veterans, and several hunters and former poachers, began moving from the valley to Eikby. When they were directly north of the fowl ponds they split. Under the command of Haft, twenty archers, the Bloody Axes, and the few survivors of the Eikby Guardsmen, left the forest to assume positions on the banks of the southmost ponds. Haft and three of the others were armed with demon spitters. Spinner took the bulk of the small force around to the east of Eikby's burnt-out ruins. They stopped well short of the guard post on the east road.

Haft paired his men, archer and blade, and set them behind the coops and trees clustered on the south side of the ponds. When they were in place he let them sleep in shifts, one man awake watching while his partner slept. That positioning, as slow and silent as it was, didn't eat up all of the time remaining before dawn, and he had nothing to do but wait once he took his own position.

"Sleep, Sir Haft," Sergeant Phard told him. "You will need all your strength when dawn comes."

But Haft was too tense and too eager for the dawn's attack to sleep; it was all he could do to keep from fidgeting. He would have occupied himself by checking his men's positions, but they were too close to where he believed many of the Jokapcul slept for him to risk moving about. Everything was quiet save for the hoots and *squee*s of night flyers and the buzzing of insects.

When the larger group reached its area of operation, Spinner grouped his men more closely than Haft had placed his and let two men out of three sleep while he took the Skragland Borderer named Kovasch and continued forward to see if the guard post was manned. It was, and the Jokapcul manning it were far more alert than those of the night before. He made out four sentries sitting up, but couldn't tell how many were lying down, either awake or asleep. Spinner wondered if an officer had survived and Silent simply hadn't seen him. If not, someone else must have managed to take command. He left Kovasch in place to watch the guard post and returned to the rest of his men. There, he briefly conferred with Xundoe and Silent. The mage and the giant each took a Lalla Mkouma and vanished.

"Ooh, oo biggun!" Silent's Lalla Mkouma burbled as she perched on his shoulder—she giggled when he tickled her under the chin with a fingertip as big as her head.

Xundoe slipped his right hand through the whirlwind that flowed around him and the wind that swirled around Silent and reached up to the level of his shoulder to take hold of the back of the giant's belt. As quietly as his name, Silent walked out of the forest into the clear. Xundoe kept pace to his left rear. Together, they moved into the Jokapcul camp and trod softly among the sleeping bodies scattered here and there with no apparent concern for units or discipline.

The mage wasn't very happy that he hadn't had time to catalog all the contents of the chests he'd brought back from the Jokapcul camp. He'd had to use too much of the short time available to instruct the men with Haft on the use of the demon spitters. He'd argued that Haft give the instruction, but the Marine insisted he didn't know enough—which, coming from the normally supremely self-confident sea soldier, surprised Xundoe. The chests might have held demons he'd find useful in these wee hours of the night. The handful of phoenix eggs he'd secreted about his person were wonderfully usable, of course, but unlike most demons, a phoenix egg could be used only once and no matter how many of them the chests might hold, the supply was limited. He couldn't help thinking that the chests might hold a tome that would tell him other, perhaps better, ways of using the demons he already had. He'd *love* to get his hands on one of those tomes Lord Lackland had conjured that told the Jokapcul magicians how to use demons that had never before been used in warfare. Of course, he'd heard that the tomes were printed in some language not even the scholars at the University of the Great Rift could decipher with certainty. Still, no matter how few people had actually seen them, the illustrations in the tomes were legendary for their exquisite detail. Why, he—

Silent reached through the twin whirlwinds and touched Xundoe to signal that they were at the southernmost corner of the pyre. Nobody was nearby.

Xundoe wrenched his thoughts away from the chests, and flinched from the stench of decay that came from the structure. How could he have gotten so close to it without noticing the smell? He breathed through his mouth to keep his gorge from rising as he poked a hand inside a recess in his robe and withdrew a dowel and a cone. He propped a cone next to the corner of the structure and held it in place with the dowel. A phoenix egg came out of another recess of his robe. He gingerly placed it in the inverted cone. Breathlessly, he withdrew his hands, ready to close them on it again if it showed any sign of falling, but it stood steady. He signaled Silent to go to the pyre's next corner before he gave the top of the phoenix egg a half twist and drew softly away. The egg kept its balance. He did the same at the next corner, then they headed north and he planted eggs at each of the north corners of the pyre. He was certain the Jokapcul would trip all of them and release the four phoenixes if they counterattacked Haft's group to the north. If not, then he'd have to find a way of releasing the phoenixes when the battle was over. There was no possibility he'd try to retrieve any uncracked eggs—he doubted they could be safely handled after their tops were given a half turn. He looked north, but could barely distinguish the coops and larger trees from the dark bar of forest beyond them.

They returned to the east forest for the hodekin.

The rest of the night was quiet. Only a few times during the night did the watching soldiers discern the shadow of a Jokapcul making way from his sleeping position to the latrines and back. No sentries made rounds within the Jokapcul camp. The dome of the sky slowly grew lighter.

North of Eikby's ruins, Haft made sure all his men were awake. He and the other three men with demon spitters made their stealthy way closer to the sleeping enemy, where they took position and listened for the first dawn welcomings of the treetop birds.

East of the burnt-out town, Spinner led a squad of archers and a squad of swordsmen through the darkness to where Kovasch still watched. It was a good place from which they could attack the guard post as soon as it was light enough to see.

The first ray of sunlight hit the treetops and an avian cacophony sang to it.

CHAPTER
TWENTY-FIVE

A Jokapcul at the guard post may have heard an unintended noise, or might have caught a vagrant scent that didn't belong or he may have simply looked at random. Whatever happened, a sentry saw a too-regular shadow thirty yards away and shouted a warning.

Spinner reacted instantly with a shout of, *"Now!"*

But the eight Jokapcul moved just as quickly and only two of the ten arrows hit their targets. One sentry dropped with an arrow in his chest, another paused to break off the shaft of an arrow that stuck in his shoulder. The ten swordsmen charged, yelling war cries, swords held ready to slash. Spinner dropped his crossbow in favor of his quarterstaff and joined the rush. The archers got off another volley but they'd had to try to avoid hitting their own men and all their arrows went off target. They dropped their bows and took up swords to join the melee.

Screaming, the two groups came together. Four Jokapcul were knocked off their feet by the rush of the larger Skraglanders, but only two of them bled from wounds, and only one of those two stayed down; the other bounded back to his feet. A Jokapcul ducked under a sword swing and thrust forward and up with his lance. His Skraglander opponent staggered, clutching the shaft of the lance buried in his upper abdomen, wrenching it out of the hands of his killer as he toppled to his side. The Jokapcul scooped up the Skraglander's sword and leaped to the aid of a sentry being pressed hard by another attacker.

Spinner found himself sparring with a lancer who was almost as good with his lance as Spinner was with his quarterstaff—the lancer didn't have to be as good to hold his own, the sharp blade his lance was tipped with saw to that. They thrust and jabbed and parried and slammed the shafts of their weapons together. Spinner was bigger and stronger and able to knock away the Jokapcul's strikes, but the enemy sentry was more agile and danced out of the way of the strikes and swings of Spinner's quarterstaff. After several moments of fencing the lancer feinted, easily dodged a strike at his throat, and turned his parry into a thrust. The point of his lance ripped along Spinner's side as the Frangerian barely evaded the stab. He continued his sideways movement and turned it into a spin that slammed the butt of his staff into the side of the Jokapcul's head and flipped him over and to the ground, dazed. Spinner put his full strength into a swing into the temple of his downed opponent.

All about him, sword clashed against sword, clanged against lance head. For all the bravery and strength of the Skraglanders, individually the Jokapcul were fiercer fighters. By the time the archers reached the melee, four of the Skraglanders were down and only two Jokapcul were out of the fight. The enemy was gaining the upper hand, but the reinforcements turned the tide for the moment.

The Jokapcul had spread all around Eikby as well as their campsite to sleep, five were waking nearby when the guard shouted his warning. Their shouts roused several others who followed them as they raced to the aid of their fellows. Farther away, on the fringes of Eikby and in the campsite, other early rising Jokapcul heard the shouts, picked up weapons, and began running east, shouting the alarm as they went.

Silent heard and saw and realized the plan of attack was already unraveled. It was time for Plan B, but they didn't have a Plan B. He bellowed orders. The archers began shooting at the Jokapcul racing to the guard post, and the rest of the soldiers followed him in a mad race to join Spinner and the others before the reinforcing Jokapcul reached the guard post.

North of Eikby, Haft heard the first faint shouts from the east and knew something had gone wrong—but what? He couldn't tell at that distance. He strained to look into the Jokapcul camp. The sky above was already a brilliant dawn blue, but the long shadow of the forest kept the light on the ground dim. At first he saw nothing but the same spiky shadows he'd been watching since he'd moved his men into position a few hours earlier. Then he made out what appeared to be random movement, which quickly resolved in the growing light into forms moving rapidly to the east. Whatever had gone wrong, Spinner and his group were about to be attacked by what might be overwhelming numbers. He couldn't wait for the signal for his part of the attack to begin.

"Demon spitters!" he shouted. *"Fire now!"*

The demon in Haft's weapon popped its door open. *"Wazzu whanns?"* it demanded.

"Do you see that group of men?"

The demon looked along Haft's pointing arm. *"Dry mee,"* it said confidently and *snick*ed its door shut.

Haft aimed the tube at a knot of a dozen men more than a hundred yards away. He pressed the signaling lever and the demon spat just as the Jokapcul began to run east. He had aimed at the middle of the group and might have killed or injured all of them, but they moved far enough by the time the demon's ejects got there that only seven were knocked down by the blast. The others spun about, saw what happened to their companions, and ran for cover.

To Haft's sides, three other demons spat and downrange three more eruptions gouted dirt, flesh, and blood. All of the Jokapcul were awake now. Some, startled from sleep, groped for weapons and leaped to their feet. Others scrambled for cover. Unintelligible shouts and cries came from the direction of the camp.

More light flooded the cleared land as the sun inched above the trees. Not as many men were running east as had been, which was good, but he didn't see any coming his way, either, which wasn't. He looked for another target, but no one was standing and he couldn't tell which of the indistinguishable splotches on the ground were Jokapcul and which were debris. He stood to get a better angle. In the camp, someone saw him and let out a yell. Individual Jokapcul jumped to their feet and sped toward him. He looked for several running close to each other and sighted his demon spitter on a quartet. He signaled, the demon spat, and the four tumbled through the air and crashed to the ground. They didn't rise again.

Silent's roar reverberated through the trees and it startled the Jokapcul who were fighting for their lives at the guard post. They looked around and the sight of the giant barreling at them terrified them. They broke and ran. Twenty yards away they passed the first of the Jokapcul racing to their aid. That soldier skidded to a stop and peered indecisively into the dimness under the trees. He turned his head to look at the fleeing sentries and never saw the arrow that took him in the heart. He grunted softly and fell onto his haunches where he teetered for a few seconds before toppling over.

Another twenty yards out, the fleeing Jokapcul collided with others coming to their aid. They shouted at one another as they tried to sort themselves out. Even with no officers to tell them what to do, they were still willing to fight and managed to get themselves on a line to charge back at the men in the trees. Just as one of them shouted for the charge to begin, the first demon spitter struck in the camp behind them. Some ran to battle, others held and looked back to see what the threat behind them was.

Spinner took advantage of the respite to get his troops set in two lines, archers behind swords, axes, and pikes. He ordered a volley of arrows shot at Jokapcul who milled about less than fifty yards away and watched as four of them fell with wounds. A second volley launched just as half of the Jokapcul began their charge and the sound of demon spitter eruptions came from the other side of the ruins. Two more Jokapcul fell to the arrows. The archers had time for one more volley, then Spinner ordered them to pick targets and fire independently.

The first shrieking, sword-swinging Jokapcul reached the line of blades. Two swords and a pike took him down before his sword could connect. The next two were several yards apart when they reached the line, and were also cut down before they could cause an injury. Each of the first seven to arrive was summarily cut down by multiple blades—without officers to order them, the Jokapcul picked their own targets and lines of approach, they failed to attack in concert, and soldier after soldier died one by one, each bleeding from multiple wounds—and none of them lay a blade on the men they attacked.

Until enough of them arrived at the same time. Then the battle was engaged in earnest.

Spinner stood in the middle of the line. The Frangerian held his quarterstaff with both hands at its midpoint and began twirling it round and round. The spinning staff deflected a thrusting lance head and broke the lance's staff. Spinner shifted his grip and an end of the quarterstaff shot out and slammed against the head of the lancer, knocking him to the ground with blood and gore oozing from his shattered skull.

To Spinner's left, Silent twisted side to side, thrusting and slicing with his mighty sword at the Jokapcul who swerved and dodged away from him, preferring to attack the lesser men on his flanks. One learned the lesser man on one side of the giant wasn't lesser when the end of Spinner's quarterstaff shot out and took him in the face, sending shattered bone into his brain.

Some yards away a screaming Jokapcul twisted between two others who were heavily engaged with the two swordsmen in front of them. He lashed out to his right with his sword and his blade slashed through the neck of a Prince's Sword— the first of his squad to die. He pivoted left to strike another Prince's Sword, but arrows from two of the bowmen still behind the front line sunk into his chest and side, and he fell backward, tripping the Jokapcul swordsman who's opponent he'd just slain. Another Jokapcul bounded through the hole in the defensive line and raced, screaming, at the bowmen. Three arrows took him down, but he was close enough when he fell that his outflung sword gutted the archer directly to his front.

The archers tried to shoot over the heads of the men in

front of them, tried to shoot between them at the Jokapcul
struggling to cut down swordsmen, lancers, axemen and break
through. But it was difficult to shoot without injuring their
own men. Most of them lay down their bows and drew swords
to join the front line.

Xundoe stood close behind the line between Spinner and
Silent. He pointed his small demon spitter at Jokapcul after
Jokapcul. Each time, the demon in it spit with the sound of a
bough cracking, and most times the demon spat an enemy
soldier fell. Soon there was a gap in the Jokapcul line as they
swerved away from the deadly center to attack the ends of
the defensive line. The mage tucked his demon spitter in a recess of his cloak and withdrew a phoenix egg. He stepped
forward between Spinner and Silent and looked to his sides.
A thick mass of Jokapcul was beginning to push the line to
his left backward. He twisted the top of the phoenix egg and
threw it behind them. The egg cracked when it hit the ground
and the fiery bird arose from it with screeches and unfolding of its flaming wings. Flaming Jokapcul, torched by the
phoenix, slammed forward into the backs of others, burning
them and knocking them to the ground. The defenders saw
what was happening at the rear of the men attacking them and
pushed forward. The Jokapcul broke and scattered, leaving
behind more than half their number incinerated or broken and
bleeding.

A hundred yards away a demon spitter thundered and
Jokapcul and defenders on the right of the line tumbled when
the spit struck. Xundoe saw the Jokapcul with the demon
spitter and drew his small spitter to fight back, even though he
knew the range was too great. He shrieked out a terrified
warning when he saw three more Jokapcul with demon spitters join the first.

Individuals and small groups of Jokapcul grabbed their
weapons and began sprinting toward the fowl ponds north of
Eikby's ruins. A few took up bows and shot arrows, but none
hit targets—the archers didn't know where their enemy was.

"Archers!" Haft yelled. "Pick targets!" He knew volley fire

would at best be marginally effective against the scattered Jokapcul rush. Arrows began flying from behind coops and trees. A few of them found their marks, but for every Jokapcul who fell, three more joined the rush. The Jokapcul archers knew where the enemy was now and shot at the places they saw arrows coming from. But the range was too great and their arrows that didn't go wide fell short.

"Demon spitters, fire at groups!" Haft obeyed his own command and sighted in on a half dozen sword-swinging Jokapcul. His demon spitter thundered, and five of the enemy solders he aimed at went down; the other staggered on with a hand clamped against his side.

The other demon spitters thundered and three more groups of Jokapcul flew apart, streaming blood. A lone invader ran past a corner of the elaborate pyre and the thudding of his feet too near a dowel dislodged it to drop the phoenix egg it held propped up in its cone. The phoenix egg fell and cracked open, releasing its fiery charge. The Jokapcul flashed briefly bright, dead before he was aware he'd killed himself. In the flapping of its burning wings, the phoenix ignited that corner of the pyre. Other Jokapcul gave it wide enough berth to be safe from its growing flames. Running wide of the pyre made the Jokapcul bunch more then they had been and the next shots from the four demon spitters tore apart more of them than the first shots had. The Jokapcul archers were momentarily distracted by the sight of the rearing phoenix. When they resumed shooting, most sent their arrows toward the demon spitters, but again most arrows dropped short and the rest went wide.

A charging Jokapcul suddenly fell forward as though something had grabbed his running foot and held it fast to the ground. He screamed and rolled onto his back, clutching his ankle, broken when his foot plunged into an unnoticed hole dug by Xundoe's hodekin. Several more Jokapcul fell to the simple foot traps before the rest realized the danger and slowed their rush to watch for the small holes in the ground. Their slower speed made them easier targets for the archers and more of them fell with arrows protruding from their necks, shoulders, torsos, and thighs. They also clumped more as those farther back caught up with the leaders. The demon spitters found more targets and tore holes in the growing mass of Jokapcul.

Haft hadn't gone forward during the early hours to see exactly where Xundoe had the hodekin dig, but he knew where it was supposed to make its holes, and he'd heard some of the digging in the dark, so he was aware of about how close the Jokapcul were to the near end of the mined area as he continued to work the demon spitter.

Without warning, one spit after a feeding, his demon popped its door open and clambered out. *"Thass id,"* it piped and crawled out. Its mouth worked as though it was dry. *"Naw mo."*

Haft was confused as he pulled another pellet from the food canister and offered it to the demon that climbed up his shoulder to lay on top of his head. "Food?" he asked it.

"Naw vood," the demon said. *"Drie. Naw mo zpitz."*

It took him a moment to understand the demon's words, but when he did he remembered the demon that had stopped spitting during an early stage of the attack by the Jokapcul mixed troop. The demon that had climbed onto the head of the swordsman who used it and refused to reenter its tube. The demon had used all its saliva and couldn't continue to spit!

Haft saw no point in worrying about a weapon that no longer worked. He picked up his crossbow, made sure it had a bolt ready, and fired at a Jokapcul who was at the edge of the holed area.

At the edge of the holed area! He looked quickly side to side as he reloaded and saw a few Jokapcul break onto unmined ground. He fired, then plucked the demon from the top of his head, careful of how he set it down next to the tube—he wanted it to still be with the weapon when he came back to it. He bounded to his feet gripping his axe.

"Blades, charge!" he shouted. The Bloody Axes and few Eikby Guards broke from hiding, bellowing war cries, and charged to meet the Jokapcul. Designated bowmen lay down their bows in favor of swords and joined the race. They crashed into the leaderless Jokapcul. The Jokapcul archers couldn't

fire at them for fear of hitting their own men, Haft's archers continued to pick off the Jokapcul feeling their way through the mined area.

The first Jokapcul through were each met by two or three men and cut down, only one of them managed to gut an Eikby Guardsman before a Bloody Axe decapitated him. More came through—and died for their trouble. But they managed to take down two more Eikby Guards and a Bloody Axe. Behind them, a soldier concentrating too hard on where he put his right foot was careless about where his left foot went and stepped into a hole. He went far enough off balance that he fell heavily—close enough to the forward corner of the pyre to trip the phoenix egg perched there. He died quickly when the enormous bird popped out of its cracked egg and unfurled its flaming wings. Nearby Jokapcul saw and panicked, they spun around and began running away.

"Into the trees!" Xundoe shouted.

Spinner saw the demon spitters facing them and echoed the mage's cry. Silent saw and bellowed it out. Almost all of the defenders broke and ran into the trees behind them. A half dozen were engaged with Jokapcul and died along with their opponents when the demon spitters thundered. Spinner and Xundoe ran together among the fighters, making sure all were behind trees thick enough to give them some protection from the Jokapculs' demon weapons. One was behind a tree with hidden rot. That tree collapsed on him when a demon spitter shot hit it. Another picked the wrong moment to look around the side of his tree and was speared by three large splinters from a smaller tree that was struck and shattered by another shot; he bled to death before anyone could come to his aid.

The thunder of the demon spitters stopped, and the edge of the forest became filled with the sounds of shrieking Jokapcul searching for the hiding fighters.

"Vanish!" Xundoe rasped to Spinner, as he thrust his pack at him. He commanded his own Lalla Mkouma to turn him invisible.

"Wazzoo way'um vo!" she said as she spread and spun her robe. The mage blinked out of sight.

Spinner blinked at the place where Xundoe vanished, then realized how he could use the Lalla Mkouma. The pack jiggled in his hands.

"Hunter!" he shouted. "Where are you?"

"Over here," the Zobran Border Warder answered from behind a tree not far away.

Spinner bolted to him and dropped to his knees behind the tree. "Here." He opened the pack and stuck his hands inside. Two giggling Lalla Mkouma clambered up his arms to perch on his shoulders, hugging his neck, pecking tiny kisses on the points of his jaw.

"Now, now," Spinner chided. "Only one of you. This is Hunter. You know Hunter? He's a good guy."

"Unnah gud'ghie!" one of the Lalla chimed. She took the hint and scampered from Spinner's shoulder to Hunter's.

The Border Warder looked askance at the demon, but didn't resist as she clambered onto him.

"Let's vanish and go hunting."

Hunter's face lit up when he realized what Spinner wanted to do. "How do I get her to do it?" he asked.

"Has anybody seen Silent?" Spinner shouted as he and Hunter vanished.

Clashes of blade against blade rang throughout the small section of forest, cries of fury and blood lust, agony and death, reverberated among the trees.

"Bows!" Haft shouted when the Jokapcul in the minefield began running. He dashed back to his demon spitter and huffed out a sigh of relief when he saw the demon was still there, curled up sleeping.

"Are you ready to go again?" he asked hopefully as he gave the demon a gentle shake.

"Naw. Doo Dry'ed." the demon piped without opening its eyes. *"Goam aay, lemmum zeeb."* It curled more tightly and rested its head on its folded hands in an unmistakable manner.

Haft sighed again, but wasted no time in picking up his crossbow. He loaded a bolt into it as he ran forward. The archers who had stayed behind when the Bloody Axes and guards ran to fight blade to blade followed in a wide line. Several of the Skraglanders dashed back to pick up bows, and returned to rain arrows on the backs of the retreating Jokapcul.

Flames were spreading rapidly on the pyre, whipped through the ventilation channels built into it. Burning wood shifted on the southeast corner of the structure, dislodging the phoenix egg balanced there. The fiery bird cawed out of its shell and unfurled its wings, sparking new flames on the pyre, and incinerating the three Jokapcul in the van of a group assembling there to race around its far side and envelop their attackers from the side. The rest of the soldiers in that group screamed and fell back, their fighting spirit broken.

Jokapcul swordsmen and lancers ran from the minefield, their only thought escape from the arrows raining onto them from behind. The Jokapcul archers now had clear targets to shoot at, and their arrows began to strike home. Four of his men were down before Haft called a withdrawal. They pulled back to cover and resumed shooting into the Jokapcul camp. The last of the phoenix eggs on the pyre was dislodged, releasing its bird. The fully engulfed pyre shot flames a hundred feet into the air.

Invisible inside their Lalla Mkoumas' whirlwinds, Spinner and Hunter ran among the attacking Jokapcul, cutting them down from behind, from the side, and from the front. Most of the soldiers they attacked saw no sign of the death blow being dealt them, those who did caught only a quick glimpse of the end of a quarterstaff or a sword blade before it struck its fatal blow—not having to parry or defend in any other way, Spinner and Hunter were able to make almost every strike count.

Xundoe saw the trail of bodies left by the invisible men. He looked elsewhere for congregating Jokapcul, saw a group, and lobbed a phoenix egg at them.

A hundred yards out of the forest Silent, who still had his Lalla Mkouma, fell invisibly on the men with the demon spitters. He gathered the weapons from their bodies and ran back into the forest. He stopped halfway there and watched the phoenix emerge from its egg, unfurl its wings, and torch several Jokapcul, setting a small forest fire in the process. The Jokapcul broke and began running back to their camp. Silent lay down the demon spitters and drew his sword. He stood waiting, an invisible bladed barrier to the fleeing enemy. When those who ran to the sides of the road got past him, those who ran on the road were piled dead in front of him.

The Jokapcul who had attacked east met those who had attacked to the north. They screamed their tales of horror and terror at one another, then began a mad rush to the southern forest.

The final battle for Eikby was over.

CHAPTER
TWENTY-SIX

Haft stood looking where the last Jokapcul had fled into the forest south of Eikby. His axe dangled from his hand alongside his leg; a drop of blood grew on the lower point of its half-moon blade, fattened, fell to the ground by his foot.

"We beat them," he said in a flat voice, almost as though he didn't believe it himself. "How many troops did we take on? And we beat them. They are gone and we are left holding the ground." He turned to Spinner. "We won."

Spinner nodded absently, he was looking at the bodies that covered the battlefield, at the people who roamed over it, separating the bodies of their own from the Jokapcul dead. They would take the time to bury their own, the Jokapcul corpses would be cared for by the carrion eaters who were already congregating and beginning to gorge themselves.

"At what cost?" he asked in just as flat a voice.

"A lower price than the Jokapcul paid."

"But we only have a small number of men. They seem to have countless numbers."

Haft's shoulders rose in a shrug.

"We still won this time."

"This time," Spinner agreed. "But they'll be back in a few days, and there will be more of them when they come again." He looked at Haft. "We surprised them this time. You know that, don't you? They didn't expect us to have demon weapons and to strike at them the way we did."

Haft nodded. "Surprise and daring—and a few good men. That's how we beat them." He looked at the bodies, at the members of the company and the townspeople carrying their dead to stack at the side of the communal grave that was being dug in the field west of Eikby's ashes.

"In a few days they'll be back," Spinner repeated. "And *they* will occupy this ground. Then they'll hunt for us. They'll be ready the next time. We won't surprise them when they catch us again." He nodded at the people going about their grim business. "There are too many of us, too many civilians. We won't be able to move fast enough to stay ahead of them."

Haft flipped his axe up so he gripped it close behind its head, with its haft parallel to the ground—the spike that backed its blade lay almost against his forearm. He glared at the southern forest.

"So we'll find another way to surprise them. We have to, you know. There are too many of them and too few of us."

Spinner nodded, he knew that. But he didn't believe they could find an effective way for their small numbers to surprise Jokapcul who expected to be surprised.

"We have fewer fighters now than we did a few hours ago."

A flinch twitched the corner of Haft's mouth.

"We have two or three hundred more men," he said. "We'll have to train them to be soldiers, that's all."

"Two or three hundred Marines wouldn't be enough."

Haft shrugged. "Wasn't it you who said a week or two ago, 'We don't need Marines, we just need soldiers'?"

Spinner chuckled wryly. "That was when we thought we were only facing bandits."

"And our half-trained soldiers beat the bandits. Think of the Jokapcul as better bandits. Soldiers can beat better bandits. But the Jokapcul have to catch us first." He saw Alyline and Zweepee not far off, supervising gleaning the Jokapcul camp for anything usable and filling the wagons.

"Alyline, Zweepee!" he called. "How much longer? We have to get moving soon."

Alyline ignored him.

"We'll be done by the time the grave is filled," Zweepee called back.

Part of Haft was glad the Jokapcul had burned so many people alive, that meant there were fewer bodies for them to collect and bury. He couldn't suppress the shudder that thought caused.

At last their dead were collected and covered in the communal grave. They had food and supplies and enough wagons to carry them in, even if most of the food and supplies were unfamiliar booty from the Jokapcul camp.

"Which way do we go now?" Fletcher asked.

Spinner sighed. "North. We shouldn't have turned back when we were in the Eastern Waste."

"Most of us would have died if we had continued in the Waste," Silent said.

Spinner stood in his stirrups and looked back at what had been Eikby. "Someone said they came here for us. Might the town have survived if we hadn't come here?"

Haft spat. "The Jokapcul were on the peninsula, they would have gotten here soon anyway. You've seen what they do. Some of our people were from towns and villages that stood in their path and you've heard from them what they did. If we hadn't been here, any people the Jokapcul left alive would be slaves. At least some of them are still alive and free."

"If you call being a refugee being free," Alyline said.

Spinner lifted his arm, and brought it forward. The long column began moving in fits and jerks as wagons, riders, and walkers began the trek north by west, around the foot of the mountains, headed toward Princedon Gulf. Soldiers, former soldiers, and other armed men rode ahead and to the sides of the column. The strongest force of soldiers brought up the rear to defend against Jokapcul or bandits who might come upon them from behind.

Spinner had no idea where they were going. Neither did Haft. All they knew was that they had to find an open port and shipping across the sea to Frangeria. All anyone else knew about their destination was, wherever the two Frangerian Marines went, so would they.

The Dark Prince sat erect on a midnight black stallion. A black cloak flowed down his back from his shoulders, a stygian waterfall that pooled and spread across his horse's hindquarters. The black of his shirt blended with the cloak, the black of his trousers merged with the black of his saddle, which was barely discernible against his horse's hide. His black-gloved hands looked like ravens perched on the pommel of his saddle. His eyes were coals in his face as he glared about the blackened ruins of Eikby.

Under the close supervision of Jokapcul soldiers, slaves, former citizens of what had been the independent city state of Penston, moved through the ruins gathering and stacking the dead on loose-woven wooden platforms for cremation. Children too small to gather bodies ran among them, chasing away the carrion eaters. Other slaves from Penston moved from one side of the cleared land to the other, gleaning everything that could be found on the ground.

"They are of no consequence," the Dark Prince said to the Kamazai Commanding. "You said the bandit band led by the two Frangerian Marines was of no consequence."

The Kamazai Commanding shifted uncomfortably on his saddle. A mixed troop and four troops of light cavalry had come to Eikby. They were more than enough to destroy the town and the bandit band that rested there. The town was destroyed, but all that remained of the five troops—*six hundred officers and fighters*—who had come to Eikby was a handful of broken, dispirited soldiers. Those surviving had told his interrogators the bandits had destroyed *them* and freed the people they had kept as slaves. How could that have happened?

Never before, not once since this army had first landed on the west coast of Nunimar to conquer the kingdoms of Matilda and Rampole, had any Jokapcul force larger than one troop been defeated—and then only when fallen upon by a much larger force. Yet there at Eikby, a force the size of a large troop had utterly destroyed five of his troops. It simply wasn't possible!

The Kamazai Commanding had no response to give Lord Lackland.

The Dark Prince turned his coal eyes on the Kamazai

Commanding. "The main army," he said in a chillingly calm voice, "will continue to follow the coast of the Princedon Peninsula until all the Princedons are mine. The bandits and the townspeople went north. You will send a powerful kamazai with a strong force to find and follow the path of the bandits. When they find them they will kill them. When the main army reaches the head of Princedon Gulf, it will meet them, and they will have the heads of the bandits mounted on posts to greet them. Do you understand?"

"Yes, Lord . . ." The Kamazai Commanding cleared his throat. "Yes, Dark Prince. I understand."

"It is good that you understand," the Dark Prince said with heat. "Because if that does not happen, I will serve the High Shoton both that kamazai's head and yours on silver salvers." He flicked his stallion's reins, the horse turned about and began trotting south, back toward Penston and continued conquest.

*Check out the first book in this thrilling
new series by David Sherman*

ONSLAUGHT

DEMONTECH
Book I

**It's a different war and another universe,
but the Marines are bigger, badder,
and better than ever!**

The Dark Prince's power to summon demons has
made his forces second to none. Not content to
merely seize his father's throne, the renegade
royal dreams of world conquest—and with his
army and his black arts, there is little to stop him.
So unexpected is the invasion of New Bally that
out of hundreds in the city, only two escape capture. Haft and Spinner will need all their courage
and cunning to retrieve their weapons from their
enemy-held ship and escape into the forest
beyond—where they hope to regroup and drive
back the invaders. Luckily, Haft and Spinner are
no ordinary men. They are Marines. . . .

**Published by Del Rey Books.
Available wherever books are sold.**

**The hugely popular Starfist saga
featuring Marines at war in outer space
is military science fiction written
by real combat vets:
David Sherman and Dan Cragg.**

*Read all the explosive novels,
each one packed with hell-torn action
and blazing adventure.*

Starfist I: First to Flight

Starfist II: School of Fire

Starfist III: Steel Gauntlet

Starfist IV: Blood Contact

Starfist V: Technokill

Starfist VI: Hangfire

Starfist VII: Kingdom's Swords

Starfist VIII: Kingdom's Fury

Published by Del Rey Books.
Available wherever books are sold.